THE GOOD SON

Novels by Craig Nova

TURKEY HASH
THE GEEK
INCANDESCENCE
THE GOOD SON
THE CONRESSMAN'S DAUGHTER
TORNADO ALLEY

THE GOOD SON
CRAIG NOVA

Delta/Seymour Lawrence

A DELTA/SEYMOUR LAWRENCE BOOK
Published by
Dell Publishing
a division of
Bantam Doubleday Dell Publishing Group, Inc.
666 Fifth Avenue
New York, New York 10103

ISBN: 0-385-29717-3

Reprinted by arrangement with Delacorte Press/Seymour Lawrence

Printed in the United States of America

Published simultaneously in Canada

May 1989

10 9 8 7 6 5 4 3 2 1

BG

To Abbey

Acknowledgment

I would like to express my gratitude for the generosity and foresightedness of a woman I was never able to meet, J.S.B.

C.N.

Note

For lack of a better word, there are in this book a number of short "naturalist" chapters. While these sections are the attempt of one character to explain the events of her life, they are also intended to be as accurate as possible. Most of the information for these chapters comes from the author's observation, but he is thoroughly in the debt of naturalist writers. In particular, he would like to acknowledge the work of the following: R. L. Atkins, Neltje Blanchan, Enid Blyton, Donald J. Borror, C. Frank Brockman, John Bull, William Henry Burt, Stephen V. Chelminski, Boughton Cobb, Isabelle Conant, Roger Conant, T. A. Coward, Vitus B. Droscher, Thomas H. Everett, John Farrand, Jr., Art Flick, Merrill C. Gilfillan, Richard Philip Grossenheider, W. J. Holland, Leland O. Howard, Robert M. McCurdy, Margaret McKenny, Donald H. Menzel, Olaus J. Murie, Roger Tory Peterson, George A. Petrides, Clifford H. Pope, Richard H. Pough, Julia E. Rogers, Leonard Lee Rue III, Ernest Thompson Seton, George W. D. Symonds, Clarence M. Weed, Richard E. White.

C.N.

Note

This book is a work of fiction, and the characters in it are not drawn from any person, living or dead.

C.N.

BOOK I

Chip Mackinnon
North Africa. 1942.

My father is a coarse, charming man, a lawyer, and a good one, and when I was flying over the desert and the German pursuit pilot began pouring round after round into my plane (a P–40), I was thinking of how I learned to drive, and how it affected my father. The desert sky was beautiful, the bleached color you sometimes see in blue glass that has rolled up on the beach. There were pillars of smoke here and there and some fires, too, which were made pale by the sun. If I had been shooting down the German, I imagine I would have been just as zealous. I wonder what kind of car he learned to drive, a Mercedes or Dusenberg perhaps: I learned to drive a Buick.

My father's chauffeur was named Wade, and although it took a while, we became friends and went to the movies together. I liked Wade for a number of reasons, not the least of which was a sense of mystery about him. When I was young I was impressed by the knowledge that Wade had been in prison (in Wyoming), but when I got a little older I realized it wasn't the prison that made him mysterious so much as an un-named, but finally discovered regret. He understood regret. After we became friends we started going to the movie theater in a small town near where my father owns a piece of land on the Delaware River (a piece of which land and a house built for my dead brother I now own). The theater was not very large and the seats were shaggy with stuffing and sometimes Wade and I would be the only people there, staring at that screen which had a hole in the upper right hand part. The hole looked like a bat.

Wade was thirty-five when he started to work for my father, and he was a tall, thin man, with a long nose and chin, pale, tea-colored eyes. He favored a dark green sweater worn over an undershirt when he wasn't working. At other times he wore the blue trousers and jacket my father required of him. On weekends, when I was home from school, Wade drove my father and me to that land on the Delaware. Wade was a little nervous, but this was not unusual, considering the man for whom he had to work.

I like to think of the land as it is in the fall, when the leaves are gone and you can see the woods, the fieldstone that projects from the ground like the prows of speedboats, the greenish park-statue color of the lichen. We drove along the Delaware for a while and then turned where the Mongaup River passed under the highway. The ground was scaled with leaves of red and brown. We climbed a road that went through the trees and finally stopped in front of a two story clapboard house that had shutters which were painted black. There was a front porch and an elm tree before it and my father used to like to sit on the front porch and drink a mint julep. There's a new road on the land now, one that's a little straighter and doesn't wash out so easily. My father made it himself with a bulldozer he bought as army surplus. The machine was a bargain and it was still painted green. There are both cow and sheep barns, although there is no silo. The cow barn has been made into a garage with an apartment (where Wade stayed) and another out-building has been fixed too so that the housekeeper and her husband had their privacy.

I learned to drive in 1936 and the car was a Buick, a new one.

It was black and had comfortable seats covered with a fuzzy material. The Buick had a three-speed transmission with the gearshift on the floor. The starter was on the floor, too. The paint was waxed and kept pretty much spotless, and the car had whitewall tires. Usually, when my father and I got into the backseat, after having come from the apartment in New York (in which there was an imitation Mexican garden, complete with terra-cotta tiles), my father said, "Wade, now we'll begin the process of drinking and driving, slowly along." He made Wade stop at every bar on the road, where my father drank quickly and alone. About halfway to the farm he started smoking cigars (actually you could call them "seegars" because that's what they smelled like, and he wouldn't have the windows open, either). My father enjoyed the odor. I didn't, though, and just like clockwork, about three quarters of the way to the farm, I'd get sick. These trips were usually made at night, on Friday, and my father and I sat together in the backseat. My father bore a striking resemblance to W. C. Fields, although I don't think my father was as funny. In any case, in the spring before I learned to drive, I can remember sitting in the backseat beside my father, watching his bean-bag nose, his profile against the passing lights of other cars. I began to squirm. The backseat was filled with smoke. "Wade," said my father, flicking an ash onto the floor, "Wade, stop the car. The boy's going to puke."

Wade stopped the Buick. Usually, I was able to get out of the backseat myself, but there were times when I was already gagging, and then my father opened the door, held the cigar in one hand, and helped me into the gutter or drainage ditch at the side of the road. My father enjoyed his cigar while I vomited. One night, just before I decided to learn how to drive, I was kneeling in the drainage ditch and I looked up and saw the Buick against the passing lights, saw its monstrous, high, silky shape, and the open back door, out of which came the bluish smoke of the cigar. My father didn't look at me, and Wade didn't either. Wade was a polite man. On this particular night, when I could see that phantom of the Buick, when I could taste the bile and acid while I was kneeling in the ditch (I think it was filled with some daisies and Queen Anne's lace: there was some gentle, lingering odor there), my father said, "You done?" I shook my head and heaved again, and then I climbed into the back of the car, the skunky odor there. My father must have paid a fortune for those cigars, too: he said they were made by blind men in Cuba, and I guess this was true, because the men who made them didn't always know what they were putting inside. I sat next to my father and he reached over and closed the door.

"Stop at the next bar, Wade," he said, his voice thumping like a drum, even though he wasn't that big, really. "I need a drink."

I can still name, in order, those roadhouses and taverns and saloons where my father stopped to drink. Wade and I sat in the Buick.

"How's school?" said Wade.

"Good," I said, still tasting the sour vomit.

"That's good," said Wade. "Education is what you need."

"Yes," I said.

A few years before, when Wade began to work for my father, our conversations stopped here, but after a month or so, Wade said, "Do you mind if I ask you a question?" and I said, "No," and he said, "What the hell was the Battle of Hastings?" I gave him my schoolboy's knowledge, and he nodded with a sincere reverence. There were words and phrases, events, things that he heard in conversation or saw in the paper, and he didn't know where to go to find out about them, and he had been ashamed to ask anyone his own age. So after we went through the Battle of Hastings in the parking lot, we moved onto other subjects, although I'm sure I failed him on many occasions, since I really didn't have much to say about the Manichaean Heresy, the Papacy at Avignon, the Boxer Rebellion (it is a small triumph, however, that Wade understands that the Boxer Rebellion had nothing to do with Madison Square Garden). I did give a fair account of quadratic equations, geology, Mount Everest, and Middle English (of which I recited a few lines, "The Wife of Bath"). After I had given it, Wade said, "Chip, you wouldn't put me on, would you? You wouldn't pull Wade's leg, now? Because that doesn't sound like English at all. That sounds like the talk of, you know, someone who's taken leave of his senses." "No," I said, "I'm not fooling you. Maybe it's my accent." Georgraphy was our great triumph, and we played a game with it. I'd say "America," which ends in "A," and then Wade would have to say "Alaska," and then I'd have to say "Amsterdam," and then he'd have to say "Manchuria." Wade loved this game, and we'd play it when we sat in the parking lots while my father filled his gut with bourbon.

It was after we first played this game that Wade suggested we go to the movies in a small town near the farm. He had lost, being caught by St. Croix, not knowing of the existence of X Rock, Antarctica; Xenia, Ohio; or the Xie River; but he was not ashamed, and I was fairly sure he was in the market for a *National Geographic Atlas*, if only for the index. He suggested we go the next night, and we did, with me still in the backseat of the Buick and Wade driving. After we had seen our first movie, I sat up front, and we weren't so awkward anymore. We saw many movies. Wade sat next to me in the dark, with a box of stale popcorn and a bottle of cheap liquor in a paper bag, his eyes set on the screen. He couldn't stand missing a minute, not one frame, although if the picture were very bad, he didn't mind if I went to the lobby and read the day-old paper that was there. The seats in the theater were usually ankle-deep in trash, popcorn boxes, and candy bar wrappers, and Wade smoked his cigarettes in the middle of the movie, or continuously when he wasn't eating the popcorn or sipping from the bottle in the bag. He started a fire one night, and the manager had to put it out with a fire extinguisher that made a whitish foam. Wade apologized for starting the fire, but then stepped over the row of seats in front of us with his long legs, sat down, and continued to watch. The manager wanted to throw him out, but then he saw me, and knew that my father had a new chauffeur, and thought the better of it. My father made quite substantial political contributions and everyone wanted to run for the town's only salaried (and otherwise lucrative) job, that of superintendent of roads.

Wade and I went to the movies whenever we could, and we saw some terrible ones, which troubled me, if only because they didn't trouble Wade. It was not a matter of entertainment for Wade, or so it seemed. During the particularly bad ones I no longer went to the lobby and looked at the old paper, but instead watched Wade, his eyes set on the screen, his papered bottle rising and falling, his hands lighting the cigarettes and dropping the still burning matches. In those days I favored pirate films, with lots of swinging from ropes. One night there was a historical epic. In it there was a scene in a Middle Eastern harem, which had twenty-five or so women dressed in spangled tops and sultan's trousers (tight at the ankle). Wade's eyes were wide and unblinking but he stopped the bottle halfway to his lips and dropped the box of popcorn. He stared at a small, dark, attractive woman who was lounging before some man with a headdress. She looked quite appealing. Then the scene changed and Wade went back to sipping the bottle, although he didn't pick up the popcorn. After the film was over, and we were back in the car, Wade said, "Chip, that was a good film." I didn't say anything, and I forgot about the dark woman with the small lips. She turned up again, though, in a western, and Wade watched her carefully. After she left the screen, Wade took a hard pull from the bottle. He looked at me, and saw my curious expression, but we didn't speak about it. Now I never went to read the papers and could not have been dragged from the theater, since I was also looking for the "extra," that dark, taut woman with the small lips and who had above one eye a slight distortion that might have been caused by a scar. It gave her face that slight asymmetry, the touch of the freakish, which makes a woman beautiful rather than pretty. I was looking for her if only to discover the reason she had such an effect on Wade. The closest we ever came to speaking about the woman was the one time I said, "Look. It says here a cast of thousands. That looks good, doesn't it?" Wade said "Yes" and went to the liquor store to buy a bottle in a sack.

On the night I decided to learn to drive, Wade and I sat for a while in the parking lot of a roadhouse and then Wade turned in his seat and said "Morocco?" (which isn't too far from where the German pursuit pilot came up on my tail and began putting round after round into my P-40) and I said "Orinoco" and he said "Oregon" and then my father came out of the bar, his mood not much improved by the bourbon.

We continued until we came to my father's favorite part of the road, a piece about two miles long: it was cut into a cliff above the Delaware. The road wasn't much to speak of. Straight up on one side, straight down on the other, and it was crooked, filled with sharp turns, because the cliff wasn't smooth. There were a couple of guardrails, old ones made of planks that wouldn't stop a man on a bicycle, at the places where the road turned toward the precipice and the river below. One of these guardrails looked like a broken clotheshorse: a drunken policeman had gone through it while chasing a speeder.

When we came to this section of road Wade began to twist in his seat and finally my father said, "Wade, stop the car. I'll take it through the turns. You get in the back with the boy."

Wade stopped the Buick. You could see the beginning of the cliff ahead, the receding and twisting road much farther on: it was as though the first turn were a sound, a shout, and the other turns echoes of the first. Wade got out of the car and peered down at the river, which could be seen well from where he stood, although his perspective was more like one you'd have if you were looking at the river from an airplane. You could see the silken and roily water through the mist that was just above the surface. Wade stared at it, and got into the backseat.

"Are you going to puke anymore?" my father said. "Because if you are, you better do it now. We're not stopping until we're on the other side. I don't want a mess in the car."

Wade had his hands clasped together and he was squeezing them between his knees. He was trembling hard.

"No," I said, "I'm through. I won't make a mess."

"Well," said my father, "thank God for small favors."

My father put the Buick into gear, turned on the high beams, and began. The gas pedal was down to the floor.

"Chip," said Wade, "we're going to die."

There was a section of road before the first turn, a piece about three hundred yards long, and it was straight. My father called it the "chute." The Buick began rocking a little from side to side as my father slapped the gearshift lever from first to second and from second to third.

My father grunted as we went into the first turn. It wasn't so bad, because it turned inward, toward the cliff, rather than toward the river. It was the river turns that got to Wade and me, too, and those were of course the turns my father lived for. I was glad it was night, because you could see cars coming in the other direction. I saw my father's round head, his shoulders, and his arms gripping the wheel in black silhouette against the lighted and moving landscape (or against the moving wall of fieldstone when we turned away from the river and the lighted air when we turned toward it). The Buick went through the first turn without skidding. My father had the seat adjusted so that he was able to straighten his arms from his shoulder to the wheel, and this is the way he drove through the turns, only taking his right hand from the wheel when he had to shift. By the time we were in the third turn the Buick had begun to drift, and Wade rocked back and forth, still holding his hands between his knees.

"You've got to straighten out the curves, Wade," said my father. He meant by this that he didn't go around each turn while staying on his side of the road, but by following a route that went from one side of the road to another: it made for less turning, and he could go faster that way. Wade groaned. This advice about "straightening the curves" changed to "straightening the bends" after my father had gone to England. Anyway, after giving us the theory, he remained silent, being intent on the car, the way it drifted from side to side, the alternating visions of sheer granite and foggy air. The Buick smelled of cigars and liquor and Wade's dread. My father was silent with one exception, which was when Wade began to mumble (prayers or quiet entreaties in which my father's name was occasionally audible).

"I didn't ask for your advice," said my father.

He continued driving. I imagined the car crashing through the guardrail and flying (like an airplane without wings) over the river. Then my father would say, while still struggling with the wheel and shifting down as the engine raced, "Son of a bitch. We're going Democratic." On this particular night my father didn't get to give his political impressions while in a Buick which was on its way into the Delaware, because he went through the last turn with the car almost out of control, and then slowed down, pulled over, and put on the hand brake. He sighed, flicked some cigar ashes onto his pants, and said, "Wade, you can take it from here."

Wade opened his eyes and looked around and saw me, with my eyes so wide open I felt them getting dry.

"Chip," said Wade, "I should quit this job."

My father turned and looked over the seat and spoke with the cigar in his mouth. He sounded as if he were under water or beneath a pillow.

"Wade," he said with half a smile (the other half being taken up with the cigar). "You been in the slams, Wade. And you're too honest to lie about it, aren't you?"

"Yes," said Wade, stiffening a little, but still shaking. "Yes, I was incarcerated."

"Times are hard, Wade," said my father.

He was a customs lawyer and the Depression hadn't done so

much to him as it had to others. My father was drinking a mint julep and thinking about fishing trips when his colleagues and acquaintances were throwing themselves out of windows and sucking at exhaust pipes or filling their skulls with bird shot: this improved my father's disposition, but in a way that could only be appreciated by himself. Wade had been locked up for stealing, in Cheyenne, Wyoming, ten miles of the telephone company's wire, which he then tried to fence through a plumber, who was smart enough to see that the phone company's reward was less than the price of the wire, but more than could be had for it on the market, especially since there was only one customer, and that was the phone company.

"Yes," said Wade, with a certain resignation and knowledge, too, of how hard times can be: as hard as the stone out of which penitentiaries are made. He had, for a moment, the wide-eyed expression I usually saw on his face at the movies.

My father got into the backseat, and Wade stalled the engine (in his nervousness and fatigue) before getting the Buick back on the road.

"I'm going to have a mint julep," said my father, "just as soon as we get to the house."

I was tired of this section of the road. In the middle of the previous winter, after I'd been sick in a culvert that was filled with new snow, and after my father had stopped at more than his usual number of bars (or at least had more than his usual amount of bourbon, because the number of bars couldn't be increased), we came to the turns.

"Wade," said my father, "stop the car. I'll drive."

It was still snowing and the road hadn't been plowed. The flakes were large wet clumps rather than separate pieces: they looked like soapy foam.

"Mr. Mackinnon," said Wade. "I know you like to drive this piece, but I think tonight it isn't such a good idea."

My father got out of the car and stood in the snow.

"I'll drive, Wade," he said.

My father was slowly describing a large circle with his head. He was slapping at the snowflakes, too, mistaking them, I guess, for moths.

"Get in the back with the boy," said my father.

He opened the door, but Wade climbed out on the other side and then got into the back with me.

"I just need a little cold air on my face," said my father as he climbed in behind the wheel and rolled down the window.

"We've just been lucky, that's all," said Wade.

"Father," I said, "I don't think this is such a good idea."

"I'll ask for your opinion when I want it," said my father.

The Buick took off. The headlights played on the snow, and it looked as though all of the flakes, the white bits, were coming from one place and that we were headed straight for it. The Buick hit the stone wall on the right-hand side of the road, just before we came to the spot where my father usually said, "Wade, you can take it from here." The car seemed light for a moment, and my father's arms moved back and forth at the wheel which no longer offered any resistance. "Son of a bitch," said my father as we slid from one side of the road to the other, swinging from guardrail to bluestone (which was cracked by springs that ran even in winter so it was covered with large, sloppy carrots of ice) and Wade kept saying, "This is it. Chip, this is it after all." I felt dizzy and strangely constricted and without coordination (quite similar, actually, to the way one feels when the airfoil and control surfaces and cables of one's airplane have been stitched by a 20 mm cannon, especially if one is convinced the shells from the cannon have proximity fuses) as the car moved one way and then the other and finally into the drainage ditch next to the bluestone wall: it was like a crash landing in the Arctic. The icicles and snow went into the air and you heard the ice crack and squeak as the car went through the crystalline stalactites and into the wall itself. There was the unmistakable sound of the bumper and the fender grinding against stone. The car continued scraping along the wall, knocking the frozen, carrotlike icicles into the air, some of which fell in the road, and some of which landed on the car. The rear end of the Buick began to swing away from the wall (and toward the river) when the front end hit a piece of bluestone squarely. Wade said, "Goddamn you, Mackinnon."

"Don't be a fool," said my father. "If you're going to be familiar, call me Pop."

The Buick came to a stop. A beautiful cloud of steam, silky and wet, rose from the radiator. There were bits of snow falling in the light from the one headlamp that wasn't broken. The windshield was cracked and in the center there was a glassy spider web. The steam looked like billows of a white parachute. When I thought of the silky dampness (while I was over the desert) it reminded me of the time I first touched a woman's satin evening gown on which champagne had been spilled. My father ground the starter and the engine turned over without catching until the battery went dead.

My father got out of the Buick and stood in the snow, while looking at the front end in the dim light of one headlamp. The snow fell on his bald head. He opened the hood and stared at the dark interior, in which you could hear the hissing sound of snow-flakes as they landed on the overheated engine.

"Son of a bitch," he said, now standing in the dim, yellowish light again. "You can't get much more Democratic than that."

He looked in the window at us as though we were the contents of a package given to him by his worst enemy. It was my first automobile crash and although I was a little sick, I had enjoyed the smashing of the fender and the breaking of glass. My arm was sore, but I don't remember how it got that way, and my knees were watery.

"Some crash, huh, Wade?" said my father. He slapped the roof of the Buick and put his head back and laughed.

"I've been fired for less," said Wade.

"Ha!" said my father. He hit the roof of the Buick and laughed some more. Wade started to chuckle.

"Chip," he said. "At least I won't have to drive your father around for a week or so. Not until they fix the car. That may not seem like much, but to a man in my position it's a great deal."

I rolled down the window.

"You don't look hurt," said my father, whose head was now covered with snow. "I guess you aren't."

"No," said Wade, "I don't think we're hurt."

"Chip?" said my father.

"No," I said.

"How are we going to get to the farm?" said Wade.

"We're going to walk it," said my father.

Wade looked at his street shoes. My father wore galoshes, since he wanted to be comfortable when he walked from the Buick to the bars. I was wearing street shoes like Wade's. We had coats, and we put them on, and then took our suitcases from the trunk. My father switched off the ignition and shoved a knob on the dashboard. The snowflakes seemed to go out.

We started in single file, my father in front and me in the rear. We carried our suitcases as we walked in the snow. There was about six inches of it, anyway. All you could hear was the *quash, quash, quash* of our feet and the distant rush of the Delaware. It was cold, and the snow was sticking.

"My feet are snug," said my father, "how about yours?"

Wade sighed.

We walked down to the Mongaup and over the bridge there. The water looked dark and slick against the snow on the bank and on the stones and bits of driftwood, the junk washed up in the spring flood. My teeth were chattering so much it sounded like someone shaking dice in a leather cup. Wade groaned. We started up the road to the farm, which is about two miles from the Mongaup.

We kept climbing and finally we could see the lights of the house. There's a road that comes through a pine grove and then passes through a gate and turns and goes up to the house and barn. We went to the porch and my father opened the door and stood in the hall, letting the snow melt from his shoulders and suitcase and head onto the floor. It was made of planks and they were pegged. The housekeeper, who always wore white dresses (as though she were a nurse, and which probably revealed her attitude toward the family) came from the back of the house and saw my father standing there like something abandoned in a storm. Wade and I stood slightly behind him, and each of us carried a suitcase. All of the suitcases were covered with melting snow. The housekeeper waited until she saw the first drops from our clothes, from my street shoes and Wade's and from my father's galoshes, and then she went upstairs.

In a moment my mother appeared in her dark skirt, which came all the way down to her ankles. She wore a white blouse and had on a dark sweater, too. Her prematurely gray hair was worn in a bun. Before the war she was not pretty, but she was not old. Her skin was smooth and her hair was thick. Her voice was deep and it had a reassuring breathiness and timbre, which I usually noticed in movie stars or women who are beautiful enough to be indifferent. She had a large nose and high, full cheeks.

"It's good to be home," said my father as he dropped his suitcase in its puddle and put his cigar into the corner of his mouth. The cigar wasn't lit and the housekeeper stared at the puddle.

"What happened?" said my mother. Her tone was not gentle, but it was not angry, either: she always seemed to be asking for the facts of the matter, or for the presence of necessity. I could almost hear her say, Is this the way things are done? Is it? And is it necessary?

"What happened?" she said, after my father had been standing there for a moment with the cigar in the corner of his mouth. His cheeks were full, as they usually were when he was thinking.

"Nothing," he said. "Wade had an accident. Wasn't bad."

Wade had turned out the door and was bending over his small bag (which usually contained a toothbrush, comb, a change of underwear, a shirt, three or four extra pairs of socks, and some magazines filled with dirty pictures) when he heard my father. He came back inside, shaking his head, not so much in denial as in disbelief. He brought the bag with the extra socks and the dirty pictures with him and held it in front of his knees with both hands.

"Mr. Mackinnon . . ." said Wade.

"I'm not firing you for it. . . ." said my father.

My mother glanced outside and saw that the snow was still falling. The storm looked like the white petals of apple blossoms in springtime: the white bits fell gently onto the porch.

"It's a hard storm," said my mother, "that explains it . . . Wade."

"Yes," said my father, looking at me. I was quiet. It was our first secret. Wade still held the bag and stuttered when he tried to speak.

"No, Mis-mis-mis-Mac-mac-mac . . ." he said.

"Mackinnon," said my father. "At least you didn't panic. I guess that's worth something. A good thing in a man. I appreciate it, Wade, and I'm giving you a raise. Five dollars a week."

My mother was suspicious, but there was on her face that question: What happened? and Why? Is there something here I do not understand? and What can I do about that?

Wade turned to my mother and said, "Mrs. Mackinnon, I . . ."

"All right!" said my father. He looked like a black barrel and his voice sounded like it came from the bottom of one. "Ten dollars."

All the snow had melted and we were wet. My mother watched us carefully.

"Ten dollars is a lot of money, Wade," said my father, "especially for a man with history. . . ."

The water ran down my neck. Wade stared before him, at nothing, as he stood under the light in the hall.

"Take it," I said.

Wade turned his sad, tea-colored eyes on me, on my father's full face with the cigar in the corner of his mouth, on my mother's inquisitive expression, and said, "All right. Ten dollars," and then took his bag with the socks and the dirty photographs and walked through the snow to his apartment over that cow barn which had been turned into a garage.

"You don't look hurt," said my mother.

"I'm not," said my father, "neither is Chip. Good highland stock." He touched himself on the chest. "Although Chip's is probably a little diluted . . ."

"You dragged him through the snow in those shoes?" said my mother.

"He walked it himself," said my father as he slowly went into his study, which was off the hall before the door. It was a room my mother called the "parlor." There was a fireplace in it and the fire had been set. My father took off his coat and sat in a chair next to the fender and said, "Some things can't be helped."

I walked outside and up the stairs over the garage where Wade had his apartment. There was a light on. I tapped on the doorframe.

"Come in," said Wade.

He was crouched before the stove, putting paper and kindling inside and pieces of white oak on top of them. I stood in my wet coat.

"Close the door," said Wade. "There's a draft."

He opened the damper and lit the fire. The kindling popped and then the oak caught: it sounded like someone breaking twigs in the stove, or those party favors you pull to make a noise. Wade had his pale eyes set on the stove as he sat before it and waited for it to warm up the room.

"Why didn't you say something?" said Wade.

"He would have fired you," I said.

"Yes," said Wade. "He would have at that. He would have fired me."

The stove began to warm up and Wade touched the top of it quickly with his finger, wetting it first, the way you do to see if an iron is hot.

"You got a raise," I said.

"Yes," said Wade, looking now not so angry at my father as at the plumber who sold him down the river in Wyoming for the reward money. He seemed to be thinking of coils of copper wire.

So, when I first felt the bullets ripping into the P-40, I could see Wade's face in the springtime after my father had driven the Buick through the turns above the Delaware. I noticed that night, standing with Wade under the light in front of the garage where the Buick was, that Wade's hair had some gray in it. He had a sharp, curved nose, pouches under his eyes and in his cheeks: the pouches were trembling. I was thinking about his face and its resemblance to Stan Laurel's when an oil line in the P-40 was shot through: the smoke was as black as a bat.

"You know," said Wade, "he really shouldn't do that."

"No," I said.

"We're all going to go in the soup for his shit," said Wade.

"Yes," I said.

"It makes me mad," said Wade. "I don't have to tell you it scares me."

"Look," I said, "teach me to drive."

"You?" said Wade.

"Me," I said, "then we'll fix my father."

"And Chip," said Wade, "how are you going to let your father know you can drive?"

"I'll think of a way," I said.

"Yes, certainly, you're his son," said Wade, "but listen, Chip, do you suppose I have to be in the car when the . . . demonstration is made?"

"Probably," I said. "Yes."

"I'd rather be someplace else," said Wade.

I turned back to the house.

"All right," said Wade, "but you better learn and learn well. One false move and we're done. Is that clear?"

"Yes," I said. "Thanks."

On the early spring evening when I decided to learn to drive and had made arrangements for lessons, I walked from the garage to the house and across the porch. My father was sitting in the living room, in front of the fire.

"What's wrong with you?" he said.

"Nothing," I said.

"Then go to bed," he said.

Wade and I began a half month later, on my Easter break. I was sixteen. Wade drove my father and me up for the first weekend and then my father took the train back. The Buick had been fixed and it was as black and silky as before. When I went into the cool garage I could sense that industrial presence, as though the steel mills and smoke stacks and buildings with hundreds of small windows, the foundries and manufacturers of drill presses all had a beautiful dream and this machine, the sleek Buick, was it. I climbed the stairs to Wade's apartment after he had driven my father to the station.

"Come on," I said.

"Let's wait," said Wade.

"You put him on the train, didn't you?" I said.

"Yes," said Wade.

"Well, let's go," I said.

"Maybe he stopped and got a taxi," said Wade, "maybe he forgot something. Let's wait."

So we sat in his apartment, looking out the windows of the garage. Wade smoked cigarettes and flicked the ashes in his hand and then emptied them into the stove.

"You know why I got locked up?" said Wade.

"For stealing telephone wire," I said. "You told me yourself."

"Yeah," said Wade. "But I didn't tell you why I stole the wire."

Wade had a sister, who was tall and good-looking (he said), although her hair was turning gray by the time she was twenty-five. She had eyes of a strange color. ("Almost purple, Chip," said Wade, "and they were beautiful to see.") Her name was Sherry and she wasn't very smart. When Wade was in Cheyenne, his sister got pregnant, and the father was out of town within a half hour of being told of Sherry's condition. Sherry had the child, and when she went into labor she had a midwife come to the shack she shared with Wade. The child was born dead and it was a monster, having two heads. The midwife took it away. There was a carnival in town, and a few days later, when Sherry was up, although feeling stricken and like a fool ("which she was," said Wade), she borrowed the price of admission from Wade and went to the carnival. She saw her baby in a display of monstrosities. The baby was in a jar filled with formaldehyde. Sherry told Wade about it and Wade went to see the manager of the carnival, who wouldn't part with the baby, which he had bought from the midwife. Or he wouldn't part with the baby for less than five hundred dollars. "It really packs them in," the manager said to Wade. "He was probably damn right," said Wade. "It was strange to look at." Wade looked for the midwife, but couldn't find her, and then stole the wire and got sent up for it. Wade only did a year and a half and when he got out he took his sister and they went to Oregon, where the carnival was, and one night they broke into the wagon which held the baby and they stole it. They buried the baby in the Cascades among some spruce trees.

"He's not coming back," said Wade, flicking his cigarette into the cup of his hand. "Let's teach you to drive."

"Sure," I said.

We went down into the darkened, damp garage.

"Wade?" I said.

"Yes, Chip?" said Wade.

"Did you bury the baby in the bottle?" I said.

"No," said Wade. "We put it in a pillow case. Sherry cried to beat the band."

There were patches of snow in the woods and a little ice on the road. Wade drove and I sat in the front seat on the passenger side until we came to a back road that wasn't used by anyone, except poachers and people who were lost. When Wade stopped the car he looked in the rearview mirror, over his shoulder, and on each side of the Buick, as though he expected my father to come crashing out of the still-dormant woods and say, "Wade, I want you to explain, in your own words, what the hell you're doing."

"All right," said Wade, "get behind the wheel."

He climbed out and I slid over. We moved up the seat so I could reach the pedals, although I was growing fast and really didn't need the seat moved up that much. Wade was six feet, anyway. I sat with my hands on the wheel.

"Do you know how an internal combustion engine works?" said Wade.

"Jesus Christ," I said.

"All right," said Wade. "I just wanted to make sure."

He showed me how to work the clutch and change the gears, to put on the brake: it didn't take much explaining since almost any American boy understands machinery the way an American Indian child understands animals: more in the eyes and fingertips than in the brain. I took it easy, at least in the beginning, driving along, trying to change the gears so smoothly you couldn't tell it was being done.

"That's good," said Wade, "that's all right."

We continued, after the thaw, whenever we got a chance.

One afternoon, a Sunday in the middle of genuine spring (when the oak was flowering with reddish clusters and the maples were blooming, too, but their flowers had seedpods that looked like green wing nuts), Wade and I were on a deserted stretch of macadam. It was a crowned road that ran straight for a while before making a hard turn to the left. I felt the list of the Buick because the crown was high.

"How do you control a skid?" I said.

"You're going too fast!" said Wade.

I gave the Buick a little more gas.

"You're going too fast!" said Wade.

"I thought you were going to teach me," I said. "Well?"

We continued along the straight part of the road gaining speed: the Buick had a sloppy quality in the way it was being driven, something of the aspect of a woman who is walking quickly and showing that she needs a girdle.

"All right," said Wade. "Stop the car."

I stopped the car and slid over as Wade got out and walked in front of the Buick and I saw his elongated reflection in the lacquered hood.

"I'm going to show you this and then you'll practice it by yourself," said Wade. "Is that clear? I don't want to be in the car."

He put the seat back.

"What's wrong, Wade?" I said.

"Nothing," he said.

He looked at me once with his pale, reddish eyes, and then turned the Buick around and drove back up the straight part of the macadam. He drove precisely and steadily, almost unnoticeably: it seemed Wade had never been in an accident and never driven (or would have been shocked to find out that people did drive) faster than forty miles an hour. He stopped and turned the car around. We faced the straightaway, the long piece of paved country road. The understory and the bittersweet and blueberries were beginning to grow, but it was still too early for the mountain laurel to bloom.

"I had it tuned," said Wade.

He said this like, I got a lawyer and put him on retainer because I knew you'd end up like this.

"Good," I said.

"Yes," said Wade as he put the accelerator to the floor.

The trees on both sides of the crowned piece of macadam rose and jumped toward the rear of the Buick as Wade went through the gears. The tops of the trees, not filled with leaves yet and having that splattered ink shape against the sky, touched the shiny hood of the Buick, were smeared there, and then slid away. I smiled, because the speed of the car gave me that buzzing sense of wonder, the odd sense of being stunned, that I felt the first time a woman smiled at me over a glass of champagne (I remember the glass had a hollow stem and the bubbles seem to rise to her lips). The Buick went straight down the piece of macadam and there seemed to be something consciously steady in its path, or something more intricate than just having a driver who kept the car moving in a straight line: there was the illusion of a certain safety, or peace, or sanctuary in the road, and that the man who was driving had found it, and that he would not lose it, although it could be lost if the car were moving along a path that was just a tenth of an inch away from the one it was on. The turn went to the left. Directly in front of us were woods, the gray pillars. When Wade approached the turn he didn't brake. He double-clutched and shifted down and I could feel a gyroscopic tug, the turning of the driveshaft, engine, and transmission, which tug or pull kept the car moving in that same sense of sanctuary as the Buick went through the turn in something that approached a straight line, one that ran from the right side of the road to the highest point of the turn and then back to the right side again, where we faced another straight and crowned piece of macadam. Once, in the middle of the turn the Buick had begun to drift: the rear end broke from the line on which Wade was driving and he touched the wheel a little, just turned slightly into the skid and the car came back into that sanctified line. When we faced the next stretch of macadam we were in second gear and Wade shifted into third as the engine whined itself into that Frankenstein pitch, the point where you begin to believe machines live. Wade kept his foot on the floor. We must have been going close to eighty when we were a hundred yards out of the turn.

"That'll come in handy," I said.

"Yes," said Wade.

He slowed down and pulled over. He looked as though he expected all the trees to turn into dragons, that every crack in the road would become a lizard. He lit a cigarette and slid over to the passenger side. I got behind the wheel, turned the car around, and started back toward the farm. Wade smoked Camels and I remember seeing the desert and pyramids on the package.

"Yes," said Wade after a minute, "I suppose that will come in handy."

He shrugged and looked down at his feet. I was too young then to understand regret but when, in the P–40, in the stench of burning oil and in the sound of the wings opening into metal flowers, I saw Wade's shoulders and the expression on his face as he stared at his feet in the Buick, I was glad, as the horizon began its lazy turn and as I could distinguish the cactus below, that I hadn't said anything to Wade.

At the time we sat quietly in the car and then Wade said, "What do you say, Chip, to a matinee?" and we drove down to the railroad town where the movie theater was and sat on the seats which were as shaggy as an unshorn ram. We watched the flickering images, the screen's frosted grain. It was a jungle movie and Wade was bored by the animals.

Now when we practiced, Wade drove to a place where there was a straightaway and a turn and got out of the car to sit on a stump in the woods, as far back as he could get while still being able to watch me and the Buick as I drove down the straight part of the road and went through the turn. Sometimes I could feel that sense of sanctuary, that sureness, and other times it eluded me. On these occasions Wade said, "You're oversteering," or "You're shifting down too soon," or "You've got to be more delicate at the wheel. Never, never, jerk it," after which comment or comments he'd go back to his stump and beckon and I'd go through the turn again. As the summer became hotter we looked for other places, sections of road that were both deserted and filled with tight turns. I practiced there, too, while Wade sat in the woods, far enough from the road so that if I had been a poor student and left the road in the Buick at a high rate of speed, Wade would be able to attend to the smoking wreck.

"I'll just get out of harm's way," said Wade with a shrug and a glance at his wing tip shoes, before tramping into the undergrowth.

"You have a talent for it," said Wade.

He said this, I guess, because he thought it was a small miracle (or a large one for that matter) that we had managed to get through most of the summer (practicing sometimes five days a week) without putting anything more than a small scratch on the Buick, and this was done by Wade, when he was turning around on one of those country roads. And I suppose I did have a talent for it. It was one of the things that got me into the air over the desert with a Messerschmitt behind me.

In September, when the sky turned that gas-flame blue, Wade said to me, "Chip, I can't teach you anything more. That's all."

I nodded.

"Okay," I said.

"You'll be going back to school, soon," said Wade, "won't you, Chip?"

"Yes," I said.

"I was wondering, Chip," said Wade, "if you could tell me what *de jure* means?"

"According to law," I said.

We were driving back to the farm, along the Delaware, past the place where there was an eel trap: the water was low and you could see the V shape of the trap just beneath the surface. The V had the same shape as a flight of geese. We drove for a while without saying anything.

"There aren't going to be any more driving lessons," said Wade.

"I know," I said.

"Shit," said Wade. He glanced at the Delaware. Its surface looked pressure-flaked by the wind.

We came up to the farm and Wade parked the car in the garage. He got out of the Buick on his side and climbed the stairs to his apartment and left me in the cool darkness of the garage, in the odor of the Buick. When I decided to jump from the P–40 and had begun to work the canopy back and when the horizon had already turned up to ninety degrees and I was working my way through the smoke (it was like standing just behind the smokestack of a train), I was also glad I hadn't thanked Wade.

I went back to school, and life became more regular again, classes and studies, the smell of chalk, ink, and new clothes. Weekends were spent at the apartment with the imitation Mexican garden or at the farm. I missed the Buick lessons, and those evenings in late June and early July when I went to the Mongaup River and fished for trout, watched the delicate and small dragons that were mayflies.

In early November, on a Friday evening, my father said, "Come on, you pissant, we're going up to the farm."

I took a small bag and we went downstairs, where Wade had the Buick waiting. We got into the backseat, and my father said, "Wade, now we'll begin the process of drinking and driving, slowly along." Wade seemed a little hunched up, uncomfortable, pushed against the wheel. As soon as we got through the tunnel and across the New Jersey marshlands, my father said, "Wade, I'm thirsty. You better stop at the first place you come to." We drove through the deadfish smell of New Jersey and came to a bar. Actually, it was just someone's living room with a beer sign in the window but that suited my father. Especially when he was a little on the jumpy side. Wade and I, of course, stayed in the parking lot.

"How's school?" said Wade.

"Fine," I said.

"That's good," said Wade, "education's the thing."

He still seemed to be hunched a little at the wheel. I waited for a while, but Wade didn't ask about Madame Curie, or Cromwell, or the Reign of Terror, or the Wars of the Roses. We just sat in the parking lot.

"Argentina," I said.

"You're too old," said Wade.

"What?" I said.

"You're too old for that stuff now," said Wade, as he sat behind the wheel, hunched and cramped and oddly braced.

"What about the questions?" I said.

"Too old," said Wade.

"Oh," I said.

We sat in the parking lot and watched the beer sign in the living room window. It was fall and there weren't any insects to look at and you could still smell New Jersey.

"I'd be embarrassed," said Wade.

"Come on, Wade," I said.

"Too old," said Wade.

"What about the movies?" I said. "I can't be too old for them, can I?"

Wade sat for a long time before he turned and looked at me and said, "No. You're not too old for them. I guess you can still come along. But, Chip, you'll have to ride in the back." And we kept going to the movies, too, both of us sitting in the dark and waiting for that woman to appear on the torn screen, although we didn't see her very often.

My father came out of the bar with that look of angry satisfaction he usually had after a couple of snorts. Wade still sat in that cramped position.

"Wade," said my father, "scratch that place off the list. They're doing something to the hooch. Something I wouldn't recommend."

Wade humped up a little more and started the engine.

"Guess I'll have a cigar," said my father with a smiling glance at me, "maybe that will improve the quality of the rotgut."

My father smoked one cigar and then another. We stopped at a couple more roadhouses and Wade and I sat in the car without saying a word. The last roadhouse had as a marquee or awning a large plaster of Paris steer, beneath which you had to walk to get in or out of the restaurant. I looked out the window of the Buick and saw my father admiring with his shoe (a kick at a hoof, a little kick at the hock) one of the hind legs of the steer. I suppose he was almost satisfied with the amount of bourbon he had been able to drink in one place.

We drove for a while and my father smoked and went on about how he'd like to run a few head of cattle because then he could collect the manure in a garbage can and bring it to that last restaurant and climb up on the plaster of Paris steer so that when someone whose looks my father didn't like came out of the roadhouse my father would be able to dump a pile of manure on him. My father laughed about this. A little later I began to squirm. Just like clockwork.

"Wade," said my father, "stop the car. This so-called son of mine is going to puke."

Wade stopped the Buick and my father opened the door. I kneeled in a culvert and heaved my guts out. It was cold and I could see the light mist in the air from my breathing.

"You done?" said my father.

"Just about," I said.

"Well, hurry up," he said, "I didn't drive sixty miles to spend the night watching a pissant heave his guts in a ditch."

It was fall now and I kneeled in leaves, could hear their cold rustling when I moved. It seemed to me I'd made a stop in this particular ditch before. My father flicked some ashes out of the open door of the Buick.

"Don't tell me you can't even puke right," he said.

He really had had a couple.

"I'm done," I said, "I'm through."

My father didn't notice the change in tone, but Wade did. I could see his pale, hound's eyes in the rearview mirror. They followed me as I came in through the door and slid back on the seat. I wiped my face with my handkerchief and sat in the cigar-scented air.

"Well, Wade," said my father, "the boy's done. Can't you see that. Get a move on."

"Yes, sir," said Wade, still sitting straight up, braced in his seat.

The night was cool, although not cold enough to freeze water yet. The cool days usually made my head feel clear, and I'd like to walk in the woods and hear the geese honk at night. I tasted the sour, acidic vomit, and sat in the Buick. Whenever a car passed in the opposite direction (and it had to be the opposite direction: if someone passed *us*, Wade would have been taken up on a warrant), Wade looked into the backseat, into my eyes, and he seemed to be asking, Well? Well? What did we spend the whole summer doing? What was that for? What are you going to do with it? But at the same time he seemed to be thinking (alternately with the questions), I hope the boy doesn't do anything. I couldn't stand it. I shouldn't have taught him anything. I get sick just thinking about the boy doing something.

Whenever my father decided it was time to take the wheel he made a gesture with his arm: it looked as though he were saying, After you, you first. His right arm was held graciously away from his body. He usually sat on the left side of the car, so he came close to slapping me with the back of his hand when he was about to take the wheel. We came to my father's favorite stretch of road, that part where it was straight up on one side, straight down on the other and filled with turns. When we approached the "chute," my father began to make that gesture, After you, after you.

"Stop the car, Wade," I said, consciously lowering my voice a shade deeper than it normally is (and a shade deeper than my father's normally is, too): this was easy because my voice was changing and I could make it go as high or low as I liked.

"Stop the car, Wade. I'll take it from here."

Wade stopped the car. My father sat there with his arm still extended in such a manner that could be blessing, salute, or just half-cocked. He gave me one of those glances that are supposed to say, I hereby order that you be taken to the State Correctional

Facility at Ossining and there to be electrocuted until you are dead: it's time you took a hot squat, you little pissant. I didn't hesitate. I got out and walked in front of the Buick, passed the headlights and Wade, too, as he walked in the other direction, and all I can say about him is that he didn't look overjoyed, although there was something in his Stan Laurel terror which seemed to imply complete ignorance of anything that had taken place in the preceding months.

"I don't know anything about this, Mr. Mackinnon," said Wade, and you could tell the lie was sweet, although he was saying it because he was getting ready to die. He wasn't sure he'd get a chance to deny it on the other side of the turns, and I don't think it would have given him much pleasure to say it while we were nosing into the Delaware. And I understood, too, why Wade had been sitting in that cramped, braced position: he'd already moved the seat forward.

"Chip, you little bastard," said my father, "how are you going to get through there? You've been puking half the way up here. And, anyway, you can't even drive."

I flipped on the high beams.

"That's right," said my father, "those are the lights. Now get the hell . . . "

I put the Buick into first gear, released the hand brake, put the accelerator to the floor, and let out the clutch. I could see in Wade's face an expression compounded of dread, fear, and delight. He was watching my father as the Buick's tires burned, as I kept the accelerator on the floor and went through the gears. We went up the straightaway, approached the first turn, and we were going fast: Wade had had the Buick tuned and the carburetor adjusted. I'd be willing to bet he'd found out the exact altitude of (and the percentage of water in the air on) these particular turns and had the carburetor adjusted accordingly. The Buick was running well. The weather was perfect, too. It had rained a day or so before, but nothing had frozen, so the road was without a grain of sand on it and I could feel the rough macadam, the clean and comfortingly abrasive surface. I was in third as we approached the first turn. There was a little mist coming off the Delaware, which was five hundred feet or more below. The bluestone looked like a curtain, a straight drop, on the right side of the road. I had an instant to look in the mirror and I saw that Wade's sweet revenge had become that terror which just makes you want to turn your head: he looked more like Stan Laurel than even I had thought possible. My father was holding onto the strap that hung from the side of the car and he was alternately giving Wade suspicious looks and me the Sing Sing glare. This last softened a little when we approached the first turn.

"Chip, Chip," said my father, "now just wait, Chip . . . just wait a minute."

I shifted down, double-clutching and punching the engine on the way, and felt the Buick rise into the gyroscopic sense of sanctuary, the straight line that went from the bottom of one turn to the top of another. Wade nodded in the rearview mirror, although he seemed a little grim about it. I shifted up again and headed into another turn, one of those where the lights swung over the empty space above the Delaware.

"Some people think all you have to do is straighten out the bends, Wade," I said, "but that's just not true, because you've got to use the gearbox, Wade, you've got to keep the rpms up."

We still stayed in the sanctified line, although there were times when I could feel it slipping away and then I looked into the mirror and Wade nodded or shook his head (still a little grimly, it seemed to me) meaning, Don't jerk the wheel, slow down. I was scared when I could feel it slipping away, because I thought I might not be able to get it back and this would give my father a chance to air his political beliefs in the midst of breaking wood, a racing engine, and Wade's last long shriek of terror. There weren't any other cars on the road. I didn't brake once. I saw in the mirror my father, who was hanging onto the strap and filling his cheeks with air until they looked like big tomatoes. I kept the accelerator on the floor, shifting up and down, swinging toward the guardrails and then back to the sheer walls. We skidded once and I touched the steering wheel as gently as a loving, private caress and the Buick came back into line. Wade nodded and smiled through the dread. Then the old man gave Wade a mean look, but Wade just kept staring ahead, watching the oncoming, lighted, and moving landscape and air. We must have been doing eighty when we came to the other side.

"Chip, my boy," said my father, "Chip, Chip . . . "

I shifted down and put my foot against the brake pedal. On the right side of the road, on the side away from the Delaware, there was a flat, sandy place where people parked their cars sometimes. It was now empty. Beyond it there was more bluestone wall, rising straight from the sandy parking spot. I hit the brakes and turned the wheel. My father and Wade were pressed into the springs of the nap-covered seat as the rear end of the Buick swung around. They stared, without saying a word, at the landscape which had stopped being split into two moving planes by the car and was now one collection of moving streaks, all of which went in the same direction.

Wade had not told me about sand. As the Buick spun I sat behind the wheel and felt that the grip of the tires was gone. The car was light, its motion now slick rather than rolling. Later, in El Paso, where I learned to fly, I felt again that terror. I was on a runway in a machine made of aluminum and steel which was about to become ethereal and buffeted, bumped by wind. The Buick went directly across the sand and hit the wall. We first struck the bluestone on the passenger side and I saw the right, front window crack and heard the thump as both fenders buckled. A headlamp broke and bits of it came across the hood: it looked like someone had broken a champagne glass over the grill and the Buick ornament. The dust swept over the car, but the engine was still running, so I put it in gear, pulled away from the wall, and stopped.

"Sand," I said. "Sand. Lousy sand."

My father still held onto the strap that was attached to the inside of a window post. Wade couldn't get out of the Buick. The door on his side was crushed shut, so he was trapped.

"Why didn't you teach him about sand, too?" said my father as he turned his face on Wade.

"I thought he was going to stay on the damn road," said Wade. "At least I hoped he would."

"So it was you," said my father, "wasn't it?"

We sat in the Buick and listened to the engine run. My father lit a cigar.

"Let's get out and look," he said.

We got out. Most of the side was crushed, and the fenders were pushed against the tires. Wade and I were able to pull them back with our hands and a stick my father found at the side of the road. He smoked his cigar and watched. Then the tires were free and we all sat down, each looking in a different direction. We didn't want to look at one another for a while. I smelled the smoke of cigar, but that's not why I didn't feel well. After a while my father said, "What's wrong with 'bends?' "

"What's wrong with 'turns?' " I said, sitting on the bumper of the Buick.

"I thought 'bends' had a little more tone to it," said my father.

Wade was sitting at the other end of the Buick, holding his hands, shaking his head and swearing a little: every now and then I heard my name in the angry mumble. After a while, though, we heard his feet moving in the sandy soil.

"He drove the turns all right, though," said Wade.

"Yes," said my father, "I guess that's true. Chip, you drive the rest of the way. Wade, you get in back with me."

I drove up the hill to the farm, passed the trees, the bright leaves, the maples being the brightest, a color that looked like the orange a horseshoe is before a blacksmith begins to hammer it. We listened as a tire rubbed against a smashed fender. I stopped the car at the house and Wade got out and took the wheel.

"It didn't work out the way we saw it, did it, Chip?" he said.

"No," I said and walked to the porch.

The light was on and my father and I saw one another clearly. My father's color was still a little high, but he was beginning to settle down to his natural, bourbon red. We stood opposite one another. Every now and then my father made that I'm-going-to-take-the-wheel gesture with his hand and looked at me and grunted. He'd drop it, or scratch his ear, or search his coat for something in an aimless, patting fashion, but he'd go on staring at me: his eyes had a peculiar quality, as though he were looking at me through a knothole. He lifted his arm again, and sighed, and knocked me across the porch. He hit me with the back of his hand, but he had made it into a fist, so the knuckles came down on the cheekbone. I could tell, even as I was flying through the air and in the crash as I made a heap against the house, that my face was going to look sick for a while. My eyes smarted, but I wasn't crying yet. He hadn't said anything, and there hadn't been any sound aside from the muffled slap (like the sound of windfall fruit) and the thump I made as I hit the house. I picked myself up and tried to laugh. He hit me again. It wasn't like the first time. There is a difference between the way a man hits another man and the way a man will strike a child: my father made the difference quite clear when he knocked me down the second time.

"I'll bet you think you're pretty smart," he said.

"Not now," I said.

"I don't want you scaring me," he said. "I don't want any surprises."

He picked me up and gave me a good shaking.

"No more," he said. "Do you hear me? No more."

One of my eyes was closing. I felt this pain once again, later, when I hit the sand in the desert after standing in the smoky wind, after letting go of the hot grip and falling. I saw the creased umbrella, the white silk overhead. The Messerschmitt passed by.

As I rolled on the hot sandy dirt, as my face scraped across it, I thought of my father, the porch, the Buick.

"You hear me?" he said.

"Yes," I said, but I only meant I heard him: that's all I agreed to.

"Good," he said.

He opened the door for me and we went into the living room. There was a fire in the fireplace and I sat on the fender.

"You going to puke again?" said my father.

"No," I said.

"Well," he said, "don't do it in the fire."

My father made two mint juleps and handed one to me. He made them with crushed ice and a lot of mint. We sat opposite one another and drank our juleps. Mine was good. I touched my cheek, which felt strangely stuffed.

"Anything broken?" said my father.

"No," I said.

He looked disappointed and sounded so in his grunted acknowledgment.

"Nothing that I can feel anyway," I said.

"It's not important," he said, with a shrug, as though excusing me from some obligation. "Drink up."

My mother came into the room in her long black dress and her black shoes. She had been upstairs in her study and I'm sure she had seen the side of the Buick when we had pulled up to the house. Her expression was one of curiosity and of longing.

"I want to know what happened," she said.

My father sat in his leather armchair and looked at his drink.

"I decided to drive those turns above the Delaware and I hit a wall. Wasn't bad. No one hurt, except Chip. He's got a little mark on his cheek. I want you to know that it was something I did and that I was in charge. That's all."

My mother stared at us for a while, still with that questioning expression on her face.

"Chip," she said, "is that what happened? I want you to explain."

"No one expected the sand," I said.

"Sand?" said my mother.

"That's where the car hit the wall," I said.

"There was no need for a sense of tragedy," said my father, still staring at me. His color was more normal now.

"All right," said my mother. "Are you two ready to eat?"

"No," said my father. "I don't think we are. You want another drink, Chip?"

"Yes," I said.

"Don't get him drunk," said my mother, as she stood at the door with that puzzled look on her face. Then she went into the dining room to wait.

"It doesn't matter," said my father, giving me another drink. "You're old enough now, you little pissant, to drink as much as you want. Aren't you?"

My eye was swollen shut when we sat down to dinner. We ate a meal of roast pork with apple cider and cream gravy, mashed potatoes, brussels sprouts, and we shared a bottle of white wine. I ate carrot cake. My father drank brandy. While we ate my mother watched us with her smooth face and her hair in a tight bun. She wasn't very old then, probably thirty-six. Her eyes were dark, and her fingers were long, and she had that puzzled expression, which sometimes became one of anger, as though someone were keeping some special knowledge from her.

"I guess you'll be all right, Chip," she said.

"Sure he will," said my father, "we're not going to have any more trouble, are we?"

I started to laugh and the old man fired up.

"No," I said, "no." But all I meant was, No, don't hit me again. Not tonight. You'll have plenty of other chances.

When I was in prison camp there were seven of us in our sleeping porch or shack. We were woken up each morning by Ansell

Augustus, a pilot from Texas who was crazy to be a disc jockey when he got home. He'd wake up at five o'clock in the morning and start brushing his hair. The shack wasn't large. That endlessly repeated sound was maddening. The Red Cross had told Ansell Augustus that he'd soon be receiving the first installment of a correspondence course for disc jockeys, and he could hardly wait for it to arrive. ("Then we'll have some fun," said Ansell Augustus, "when I'm announcing to you boys.") Sometimes when he woke up I'd take down a letter I'd received from Wade. It was written in a sloppy, large scrawl which reminded me of a child's drawing of a rabbit. "I hope you are all right," it said, "but I thought you'd like to know that your father doesn't drive those turns above the Delaware the way he used to. He says he's given it up for the duration, which I hope for your sake isn't long. Regards. Wade. P. S. I miss you at the movies. That girl we looked for was my wife. I married her when I was twenty-five and she was fifteen and she left on a Greyhound a year later. A carnival barker paid her way. I loved her, so that's why I wanted her to go."

Mrs. Mackinnon's Book of Animals, Reptiles, Plants, Trees, Birds, Bugs, and Flowers.

Mayflies are beautiful, delicate, and benign: they live not much more than a day and I think that it is this shortness of life mixed with beauty that fascinates me. I am not a pretty woman. My favorite mayfly is one that appears in late June and early July. Usually, it is found near water, streams especially. My favorite, *Potomanthus diaphanus,* is white from its tail to its eyes. I am an arbitrary woman, so such questions as which appeared first, egg or adult, don't bother me. Mayflies begin as aquatic creatures, and they live on the bottom of streams, beneath stones there, or in silt. At this stage they are called nymphs and they look like a bug or insect. *Potomanthus diaphanus,* or cream variant (as my husband calls it: he likes to fish for trout), in its nymphal stage is brown or dark brown. It has six legs, three on each side, a kind of carapace over its thorax, a segmented tail (that looks something like a lobster's), and at the end of a tail, three small, featherlike appendages. I don't think the nymphs are attractive, because they are graceless, and they move with the earthbound insect's (barely audible, but nevertheless distinctly) squeaking joints. They do not seem to have pride, either. In late June and early July, in the evenings or late afternoons, the nymphs begin to move, to squirm and climb out of the silt or from under the stones at the bottom of the stream: they either swim to the surface or to a rock at the surface of the water, and there they break their cases, the earthbound insect's skin. The case splits up and down, just like a zippered suit, not crossways, like medieval armor. The creature which emerges from the armor is the fly, the cream variant. Many of the mayflies are taken by trout at this point. When it leaves the case its wings are folded, but the fly has pouches under its wings that are filled with fluid, and this fluid is pumped by the fly into the wings: they become extended, and, in a few moments, dry. You can see the veins in the wings through which this fluid runs: the wings are glassine and the veins look like those sharp spines you see sometimes in a piece of ice, those dandelion-like puffs in a cube. When its wings are dry it flies from the stream to the nearest tree. This is the first few hours of the cream variant's life. It is beautiful now. It has four wings, two large ones and two small ones, the small ones being located at the bottom of the larger wings. Its body is gently segmented, pure white. It has a tail, comprised of three long threads that extend from the end of the last segment of its body. It has four almost unnoticeable feet. You can see the cream variant easily when it flies: it's as white as linen and it flies smoothly and slowly over the stream and against the early summer foliage. Its tail is delicate, so capable of being injured easily. If there is any breeze over the stream, the cream variants ride it, and you can see them floating on the moving air. At this time the flies are ready to mate, and they do so in the air, the male taking the female from below as they hover over the stream (or if they are lucky, riding the breeze). They separate and the female returns to the stream where she dips her eggs into the water. When the metamorphosis from nymph to fly takes place, the jaws are lost, so even if the female escapes the trout she will end up the remainder of her time, like the male, starving. Even if there were something for them to eat, the flies would not be able to do so. I find this a pity, but I also find that it makes me more appreciative of them, that it enhances their delicacy. The eggs, of course, hatch and become nymphs, which feed on aquatic life (small, almost microscopic freshwater shrimp, for instance) and take their places under stones or in silt, waiting for that time, when the temperature of water or air is right (usually in June and July) for them to begin to make their way to the surface. There are hundreds of species of mayflies, and they hatch at different times of the spring and summer, but none, I think, is as lovely as *Potomanthus diaphanus*, although almost all are as delicate, and I love to be near a stream in the summer when there is a breeze so I can watch the flies (with their hair-fine tails and blur of wings), some bright, others gray, floating above the lazy, sluggish water.

There are times, however, when the mayflies move away from the stream, and, in the evening, after mating, they mistake a macadam road for water, and they try to lay their eggs there. Many times I have picked a cream variant, or other mayflies, off our Buick. Occasionally I will have a lovely dream, in which I rise from the brook and find myself with a body that is as white as porcelain, and wings that are as clear as cellophane: I can see the stream (which is the same color as the sky) and on both sides of me there are green walls, broken here and there by small creeks that run into the main stream. There are flowers, too, the pinkish and white petals of mountain laurel, or the white petals of rhododendron. I just float on the breeze, which is as pleasant as sweet breath, and watch the water and the foliage as I drift by. There is no sound aside from the smooth hiss of joints as I work my wings. It makes me feel wonderful when I wake up, but, even though in the dream I do not end up smashed on the Buick's windscreen, in real life I end up riding in the backseat.

Chip Mackinnon

North Africa. The Desert.

1942.

"Before the war I could get the London *Times* Sunday edition," said Anahid, "and do the crossword puzzle. But now all is disruption."

We were walking in the desert, across soil which was brownish and rocky and on which there grew tough shrubs, low bushes with branches as hard as the wire used to make coat hangers. From the air the slight variations in the desert had been blended into a monotonous terrain, but on the ground you could see a bit of mica, the stubborn growth, plants that had roots enough to cover the space taken up by a basketball court. The side of my face was swelling and I stopped for a moment to touch a greenish brown and spiny shrub: it had four or five yellow flowers, none of which was larger than the buttons on my uniform.

"I'm afraid we haven't the time to admire such things," said Anahid. He was carrying my parachute in a large washerwoman's hump. "There are Germans around, and I'm not sure you'd like to speak to them just now."

Anahid said "speak" in a disagreeable way. He wore a khaki shirt, shorts, Arab headgear (a piece of white cotton which was held to a cap by two black bands), and a pilot's wristwatch. There was a pair of aviator's glasses in his breast pocket. He also carried a walking stick. His legs, hands, and arms were thin and hairless.

"The flowers are beautiful," said Anahid, "they bloom once every fifty years or so. It's a sign that they're dying. Sad, and beautiful, wouldn't you say, Captain? You know, I don't think you've told me your name."

"Mackinnon," I said.

Anahid stopped, pushed the hump of silk onto his shoulder, and took my hand. He pumped it up and down as though he expected water to come out of my mouth.

"Pleased to make your acquaintance," he said.

Anahid went back to fingering the silk.

"It is of excellent quality," he said, "excellent. The market is a little on the buyer's side, but still, it's better than leaving it in the desert for the Germans to find."

"We could have buried it," I said.

"Bury silk?" said Anahid with a look of horror. "Oh, no, Captain Mackinnon. No. Wasted beauty is an injury to Allah."

The sun was almost down, although the ground was still hot. A snake was moving with a sideways motion between the stones, over the brownish dirt: without the movement it would have been invisible. The snake looked as though it were covered with the dirt on which it crawled. Anahid stopped, held the parachute in his left hand, stretched out the snake with his walking stick. He put the walking stick in his left hand along with the parachute and picked up the snake. It hung in a straight line.

"Nasty creature," said Anahid.

Its belly was white, but the back really did look like the desert soil.

"Mackinnon . . . Mackinnon?" said Anahid. "A Scot?"

"A few generations removed," I said.

"Ah?" said Anahid. "The Mayflower, perhaps?"

"There weren't any Scots on the Mayflower," I said.

In the distance you could still see the fires, the burning planes, although the diving drone, the distant whine and bump had stopped. There were a few stars out in a sky which was the same color as that on a package of Camels. A breeze had come up, too, and I smelled the faint odor of burning rubber and aviation fuel.

Anahid looked at me and at the snake, and then threw the snake away.

"I've learned something today. Education is grand, don't you think? It's a good thing I found you before the Germans."

Anahid's fingers gently rubbed the silk of the parachute.

"You understand, Captain Mackinnon," he said. "There will be certain unavoidable expenses."

Anahid's eyes were a dark caramel color and they were as articulate as a used-car salesman's: shrewd squint, dilated innocence.

"If you get in touch with the Americans . . . " I said.

"Captain Mackinnon," said Anahid with sympathetic bewilderment, "do you see any Americans?"

"No," I said, looking now at his aviator's watch.

"The esthetic is of course one of function," said Anahid, holding up his wrist. "Don't you think?"

"Look," I said, "I've got thirty bucks. How about that?"

"It is a beginning," said Anahid.

Anahid put out his hand and I pushed the thirty dollars into it. He looked at my wallet (a going-away present from my father) and at my wristwatch, which was identical to the one he was wearing.

Then it got much darker, and the sky had that purple squid color. The stars were so thick now that they seemed dusty, more like talcum powder on a piano top. I could just make out the circular, uneven horizon.

"You are a well-spoken young man," said Anahid.

The side of my face was swelling and the pain shot into my neck and eyes: it hurt to talk.

"Did you attend a college?" said Anahid.

"Yes," I said.

"Ah," said Anahid. "Which one?"

"Yale," I said.

We walked through the scrubby growth for a little.

"I have a great surprise for you," said Anahid. All I could see of him now was the moving, milky glow of the silk.

"I don't want any surprises," I said, making a gesture toward the desert, the horizon, "given the circumstances."

"Ah, Captain," said Anahid, "a surprise is a wonderful thing. Is it true that a man who attends Yale washes his hands after urinating, while a man who attends Harvard washes his before?"

I kicked a bush in the dark, and I could see that it had small yellow flowers on it.

"I always love the desert at this hour," said Anahid. "So peaceful."

I was carrying a .45 automatic, a heavy pistol: Anahid heard me work a shell into the chamber.

"Captain, dear Captain," said Anahid, who had stopped, turned, and put his hand on my forearm. "You have been rescued. You have nothing to fear."

I heard myself grunt (and I noticed it was exactly the same noise my father made when he was told that the car wouldn't start or that a decision in court had gone against him). I put the pistol away.

"That's better," said Anahid, "much better. Without me you will be quite alone. Allah says the desert requires a friend."

"He must be right," I said.

"He always is," said Anahid. His voice was a little muffled because of the silk and because he was getting further away from me. We were on a thin path, something like a deer run, a path that Anahid knew well, but which left me momentarily confused. In the distance I could see one whitewashed building with a dark roof. Later, I found out that the roof was thatched. The walls of the building were the same luminescent color as the silk.

"It costs money to attend these schools," said Anahid.

I tried to catch up with him.

"Yes," I said. "I suppose it does."

"Are you well off?" said Anahid.

He stopped and faced me.

"I don't think you could call me poor," I said. "No. Not exactly."

"Ah, Captain," said Anahid, "modesty is lovely. But between friends, just between ourselves, because after all there is no one else to hear, do you have, say, a trust?"

"No," I said.

"Hmm," said Anahid, "I've heard that some American pilots do."

He turned again and I began following the silk until we reached the house with the white walls and the thatched roof. It had one door, no windows. As far as I could tell the house was surrounded only by the flat, scrubby land.

"You know, of course," said Anahid, "the Germans control this part of the desert? I think they are getting tired, and gasoline has become a problem. You shouldn't have long to wait."

The inside of the house had the musty odor of a mildewed bale of hay. Anahid lit a lantern (army issue), and I saw that there were bits and pieces of German and American uniforms around, a couple of rifles in the corner, a case of canned rations. There was another door which led to a back room, at the rear of which there was a piece of wood on the floor. The wood was really a hatch, and it was hinged on one side and locked on the other. Anahid quickly opened it and gestured for me to climb in. There was a hole beyond, about five feet deep, twelve feet long and a couple feet wide. He gave me a can of Spam, some biscuits, and a little water.

"Sometimes, although quite rarely, snakes and scorpions get in there, so if I were you I'd watch where I put my hands," said Anahid.

He gave me a little shove and I jumped in. It was warm in the hole, and I smelled the soil, the dusty air. Anahid still had the hatch open a little. I put down the Spam, biscuits, and water, and tried to get comfortable, but I kicked something. It groaned. By the light of the lantern I saw a blanket over a body. I heard it groan again.

"I told you I haven't got any more money," a voice said from the edge of the blanket, "you've taken my clothes. I haven't got it, I say. You'll have to wait."

Anahid squatted by the hatch. I gave the figure under the blanket a little, exploratory push.

"Get your filthy feet off me," the voice said. "Leave a poor devil alone."

"Sorry," I said.

I began turning the key of the Spam. You could hear the gentle, slipping squeak in the dark: it was quiet while I was opening the can and the sound reminded me of filament sliding from a spider's body.

"Say," said the voice, "is that Spam?"

"Biscuits and water, too," I said.

"How about me?" the voice yelled at Anahid. "I get hungry, too, you know."

Anahid silently closed and locked the hatch. The man in the hole with me made a pitiable sigh.

"Do you want some of mine?" I said.

"Yes," said the man. He smacked his lips. "Biscuits and Spam."

His fingers reached mine in the dark, and I could feel their thinness, the long nails, the webbed bones of his palms. The hole smelled: someplace there was an open slop bucket. The man ate with surprising relish and after he had a little water he began to perk up. I noticed that he took the lion's share of the Spam and biscuit.

"He doesn't look it," said the man in the blanket. I could see now that he was dressed in something like a jockstrap and that he had the blanket over his shoulders. "But Anahid is one hard nigger."

I finished the Spam and biscuit, saved a little of the water.

"He found me in the desert," I said, as though my presence needed explanation.

"Me, too."

"You want a cigarette?" I said.

"A cigarette?" the man said.

"A Camel," I said.

"Yes," said the man, "I'd like a Camel."

I took out two cigarettes. The man inhaled deeply as I lit one for him. He opened his eyes and looked at me as I lit mine.

"Say," said the voice. "Don't I know you?"

"Maybe," I said, putting out the match. I was still hungry, and I remembered a bit of advice my father was fond of giving to me: "Never let a hungry man cut up the pie."

"Sure," said the man in the jockstrap. "Davenport College, Yale, Class of '40?"

"Yes," I said.

"Chip Mackinnon," the man said, "it's Bobby North."

He put the cigarette in his mouth and grabbed my hand with both of his. It was like being held by a few sticks of kindling.

"Well, well," I said. "I heard you were shot down."

"And damn lucky to be alive, too," said North, "considering what I've been through recently."

"Looks like you've lost weight," I said.

"You don't know the half of it," he said.

When he pulled on his cigarette I could see that his hair was long and that he had a beard: a castaway in the desert. He slurred a little because some of his teeth had fallen out.

"Well, here we are," said North with cheerful idiocy. He looked around and groaned miserably. I heard a muffled, sandy thump, then the sound of North slapping his thighs and legs. I felt the slight breeze made by the movement of his arm.

"Look out," said North, "the little beggars are on the move."

He began beating the sandy soil while holding the cigarette between his lips.

"The scorpions are beastly," said North.

I heard another slap.

"Not a moment's peace in months," said North, slurring now

quite openly. "Do you think that little monster catches them and lets them loose in here?"

"I wouldn't be surprised," I said.

Both North and I were leaning against the sandy wall. North stopped fidgeting, pulled his blanket around his shoulders, finished his cigarette. I put mine out and felt North's finger's searching for the butt.

"Say," said North, "did Anahid ask you any questions?"

"He wanted to know if my ancestors were on the Mayflower, and the difference between schools."

"Ancestors is more what I'm after," said North. "You know, did he ask if you had a trust?"

"Yes," I said.

"Damn if he isn't a swift little snake," said North. It seemed to me that there was a touch of admiration in North's voice. "Swift."

In the dark North made a striking, cobralike motion.

"What did you tell him?" he said.

"That I didn't," I said.

"A big mistake, chum," said North.

"Why's that?" I said.

North slapped in the dark again. I lighted the butt of a Camel for him.

"They don't seem to go for you," said North, "but just wait until you haven't got any clothes on."

"Well?" I said, knocking the hard, segmented shell of a scorpion off my knee.

"I told Anahid that I did have a trust and he's getting in touch with my bankers. It's the only thing that stands between me and the Krauts," said North.

We sat in the dark, smelling the open slop bucket.

"The worst of it is that I haven't got one," said North, "but then I don't think it's going to be easy to get in touch with my bankers."

"What about me?" I said.

"I wouldn't want to think about it," said North.

"Well," I said, taking out the .45, "there's going to be one less Arab around to enjoy the desert air while I'm getting mine."

I felt North's dry and light fingers on my hands, on the automatic.

"No, you don't," said North, "then where would we be? The Krauts would have us in no time at all."

By morning both of us were thirsty. It was dusty in the hole and being in it was like living in a vacuum cleaner bag. The scorpions didn't improve and the slop bucket became stronger with the heat. North slipped into a semicoma, a kind of suspended animation which made it possible for him to live on next to nothing. He came out of it, though, the first time a scorpion stung me. This happened just before Anahid opened the hatch. I'd say it was afternoon of the day after the first night I spent in the hole.

"Ha," said North. "What do you think of that, Mackinnon?" when he heard the serious slap, the yelp of surprise.

"It's a nuisance," I said.

"Ha," said North, "tell me about it in a couple of days."

Anahid opened the hatch just a touch.

"Captain Mackinnon," he said, "are you thirsty?"

"Yes," I said.

"You can have some water," said Anahid, "but you must give me your pistol."

"Just listen to the little snake," said North.

I handed the pistol over, or began to.

"Butt first," said Anahid.

"Smooth," said North.

I gave up the pistol and Anahid gave us biscuits, Spam, and water.

"Your bankers," said Anahid to North, "seem very lackadaisical. Not a word in more than two months."

Anahid closed the hatch again and we were left in the darkness: after a while your eyes got used to it and everything had a strangely purple cast. North's features were as dark as eggplant skin. The days passed. I gave up my wristwatch. Spam and water. On one occasion Anahid was gone for two days and North explained that Anahid was probably searching the desert for survivors.

"Damn hot, isn't it?" said North.

I grunted.

"You know," said North, "what I really think about when I've had a little Spam is women. Fingernails, eyes, hairlines, escutcheons, skin, nipples, laughter . . . "

"Escutcheons?" I said.

"The shape of the pubic hair," said North.

"I know what you mean," I said.

As the days passed and empty Spam tins piled up. Anahid became impatient, and a little surly: less water, less food.

"The fact of the matter is," said North, "I don't think Anahid believes me anymore. About the trust, I mean."

He said this with the edge of betrayal in his voice.

"I've got a drawing account," I said, "there's got to be five thousand in it, anyway."

"Say," said North out of the dust and the blackness, "that's something. You better let Anahid know, and don't waste any time."

We sat in the dust. North slapped at the scorpions. In the middle of the night, he said, "Do you remember filthy Susan?"

"No," I said.

"Too bad," said North.

In the morning the hatch was opened: looking at it gave you the feeling someone had just taken your picture with a camera that used a flashbulb. In the bright foggy aura I saw Anahid's squatting figure.

"Good morning, gentlemen," said Anahid.

"What's with our rations?" said North. "Wouldn't you say they're a little thin these days?"

Anahid shrugged. I noticed that he had a piece of stationery in his hand.

"Say," said North with plain desperation in his voice, "do you know that Mackinnon and I were friends at school and that he has a drawing account that's probably got at least five thousand in it?"

"I knew you and Captain Mackinnon were classmates," said Anahid. He fanned himself for a little while with the piece of paper. It was cream colored and had an embossed letterhead of some kind on it.

"Well," said North, "if I were you I wouldn't waste any time. I'd get a counter check and have Mackinnon sign it. You'd do that, wouldn't you, Mackinnon?"

"Yes," I said.

"Mr. North," said Anahid, "do you have any idea how hard it is to get a letter from here to New York? And to get an answer?"

"I wouldn't imagine it's a snap," North said.

North and I squinted at Anahid.

"I heard from your bankers today," said Anahid with a weary sigh, "they say you don't have a trust. As a matter of fact, the only account you have is for checking, and that one is overdrawn seven hundred fourteen dollars and thirty-four cents. Your bankers would like your present address."

"They're welcome to visit me any time," said North. He slapped at the soil and made a bleak sort of cackle.

"Yes," said Anahid, "thank you for telling me about Captain Mackinnon. No, Mr. North, I'm afraid I can't believe you anymore."

"Wait a minute," said North.

Anahid had already closed and locked the hatch. We sat in the dry darkness.

"The jig's up," said North. "It's the Krauts for us. But, take it all around, it couldn't be too much worse than this."

"I suppose not," I said.

I had saved one Camel and we shared it. The short rations had made North even thinner than before and I was amazed at how light his fingers had become. I took the last part of the Camel.

"You understand about being overdrawn," said North.

"Of course," I said.

"I got a little wild before coming overseas," said North. "Was that the last cigarette?"

"Yes."

"Damn," said North.

We sat against the sandy wall for a couple of hours. Talking just made us thirstier, but once North said, "Filthy Susan."

In the late afternoon we heard the sound of German voices in the house. Through the hatch I could hear the sounds of bickering, although I couldn't hear the terms. It sounded as though Anahid's German was excellent. The hatch was opened and North and I crawled out into the harsh flashbulb light. We were taken outside where there were German soldiers who had their rifles pointed at us. I saw a German officer give Anahid some money. My German is passable and it was clear that the officer was abusing Anahid for allowing North to fall into his condition. I hadn't been able to get a good look at him inside, but now I was amazed to see the stooped figure under the blanket, blinking his eyes and rubbing the scorpion stings on his arms and legs: the stings were red and raised about an inch and they were the size of dinner plates. His ribs looked like some native instrument. North was a little confused so he was smiling at the soldiers who had their rifles pointed at him. The officer spoke a little more to Anahid and then Anahid gave him an Arabic saying which, translated (by Anahid) from Arabic into German, means (roughly), "The empty stomach is closer to Allah."

They made me lean against the officer's car and I was searched. North was too filthy to touch and he was obviously unarmed (and if he had any poison on him it's clear he would have taken it a long time before). After a little while North's head began to clear. The officer gave us a little water, and then we were put in the backseat of his car. North sat on the far side and I sat in the middle. The officer was on my left, and he was obviously trying not to smell North.

"The miserable cur sold us down the river," said North.

Anahid stood in front of the whitewashed walls of his house and watched as we drove off. He was wearing two wristwatches.

"You should have let me shoot him," I said.

North sighed.

"Speak German," said the officer. He looked tired. "Or please be quiet."

"We were talking about being sold," I said.

We drove slowly across the desert landscape, the scrubby bushes, the brownish soil, past flowers which were yellow. In the distance Anahid could still be seen, squatting in the shade in front of his house.

"The filthy dog," said North bitterly. He was looking over his shoulder.

"Your friend seems upset," said the officer.

"I guess so," I said. "How much did he get for us?"

"We negotiated separate deals," said the officer. "You were more expensive, being in better condition. And fresher, too."

"I see," I said. "But how much for me?"

"Dollars?" said the German.

He was watching the scrubby horizon, although every now and then he glanced at North with a sort of bewilderment, as though he expected not to find him there.

"That would be best," I said.

"Black market exchange?"

"Yes," I said.

The officer did a little figuring on the tips of his fingers and said, "Sixteen fifty."

I sat in the bumping car and watched the pale sky, the repetitive landscape. North pulled on his blanket and squinted. I took the dark glasses from my pocket and slipped them on North's face: it gave him a certain rakish lunatic quality.

"Can I ask you a question?" I said to the German.

"Yes," he said a little wearily.

"What kind of car did you learn to drive?"

The officer smiled fondly, as though thinking of a sweetheart, and said, "My father liked Italian cars. It was a Ducati. And you?"

... *Ein Ducati. Und Sie?*

"A Buick," I said.

"Yes," said the German, "I've heard they are good cars."

Ja, Ich habe gehoren, das diesen Wagen gut sind.

North rubbed his scorpion welts. Years later, after the war, he jumped out of the twelfth floor of the Yale Club. I have my suspicions about what was going through his mind on the way down to Vanderbilt Place: the white sunlight, the heat of the desert, money changing hands.

Mrs. Mackinnon's Book of Animals, Reptiles, Plants, Trees, Birds, Bugs, and Flowers.

The wild turkeys on this land are alert, quick, and they live their lives according to a rigid schedule. They are large birds, sleek, appearing almost oiled or greased in some way: the sunlight gleams on their feathers the way light will be smeared across a phonograph record. The birds have a burnished copper color in their tails, and a darkish color to their backs and necks. The hens have whitish heads and the gobblers have either a reddish head (if they're young) or wattles (if they're old). The feathers in the tails or wings of the bird are marked with alternating and undulant bands of white and copper. An adult bird averages between thirteen and twenty pounds, and a twenty-pound gobbler is a very large bird. They are loyal and precise and that is why I am drawn to them (aside from the fact that they are beautiful: when they are feeding and their necks are down and they are moving in the grass the birds are as sleek as drops of black oil). They do not fly often, but when they do the sound of their wings as they take off is startling, windy, violent, as though they were doing themselves some injury. They have a wingspan of over four feet and when they fly they stick their necks out. Their keen sight

can be noticed any day, or almost any day, if you are familiar
with a flock. In the morning, as soon as the grass has dried a little
(turkeys as a rule don't like moisture too much), the birds leave
their roost, which could be in any number of places, in the top of
a windfall, dead oak, or in the branches of a spruce or hemlock
or some other softwood, depending upon the time of year. If
there are chicks the roost will be close to the ground. The birds
come away from their roost in strict formation, a gobbler in front
and a gobbler at the rear, with the hens, young gobblers, and
chicks in the middle, feeding at their leisure, while the older
gobblers keep watch. The birds like to feed in grassy places
where they can find insects, wild grains, or they will go into the
woods to find berries (raspberries are a favorite). If you are very
quiet and still and the flock comes close to you and you want to
see how acute the bird's sight is, just flick your finger. Their ears
are sharp, too: sometimes I think they can hear me blink. Once
I saw the flock feeding in a pasture, a hay field, and I climbed a
stone wall to get a better look at them. The large wings of a
gobbler were moving, striking at something, and I thought a
weasel or a raccoon had gotten one of the chicks. The gobblers
turned and saw me, and two of them, the forward guard and
rear guard took off and came after me. I got down from the wall,
but they continued, even though I meant no harm, not the least.
I ran a ways, and the birds turned back. They were precise: because that day I was wearing a blue dress, and whenever the
flock saw me in that dress, they would scatter. I burned it: I
couldn't stand seeing the chicks and hens run at the sight of me.
I sat in the parlor with a fire going and kept poking at the dress
until it was gone: I didn't mean any harm, certainly no harm by
my appearance. The gobblers that came after me were in charge
of the band, and they held this position not by caprice, but by a
careful process of elimination. In early spring the gobblers and
hens mate. There is a ritual, a dance, that the birds go through.
A gobbler displays, makes a fan of his tail and puffs out his chest

when he is in the neighborhood of a hen: she will respond by making a sound that is between a squeak and a cluck and it is vibrant, too, as though a banjo string had been plucked inside a cedar box (actually hunters use a cedar box and a bone to make the noise), and the gobbler will approach her, still displaying, rocking back and forth, looking proud and foolish and serious. The hens are drawn by it, though. They mate and the hen makes a nest (sometimes in the top of a tree that is on the ground or in tall grass, but, in any case, on the ground), lays eggs, incubates them, and, by the end of May you can see the flock moving with a bunch of chicks. They are small and brownish, and they move quickly. When the males of the brood of any hen grow up a little they begin to fight among themselves (they do this by grabbing one another's throats, or by hitting one another with their wings, or by fighting the way chicken cocks do, with talons), and the one gobbler who defeats his brothers then becomes the leader of them, and they in turn (and now in a group), go after other groups, until one gobbler is in command, each vanquished group becoming allied with the victor. I understand that in very large flocks in the south and southwest there will emerge only one gobbler, and only he will be allowed to mate with hens. On this land there is a hierarchy, but it isn't so thoroughly established. I think that two, or perhaps three gobblers will share joint command and that they are continually vying with one another. They are willful birds, too, being able to survive long periods in winter by simply staying on the roost. When an old gobbler realizes that he is no longer viable, when the early springtime ritual is beginning to become the domain of the younger birds, he will become solitary: he will not eat, or feed with, or sleep with the flock. We have a gravel pit on this land and the middle of it is sandy: I have seen a solitary bird taking his dust bath there, lying on his back and flapping his wings, seemingly indifferent to anything aside from the warm sand and sun. In summer or winter you can almost set your watch by the exactness of the time when the birds leave their roost and begin to look for food and by the time they return (unless there is a storm or deep snow): when I don't see them for a day or two all I can say is that I feel an empty pang, as though I had been excluded from something I wanted to join.

Pop Mackinnon
New York. The Deal. 1949.

I had two sons, both pilots. Chip came back from the war. John is dead.

I had been raising a few sheep on my land and I needed a ram to cover the ewes, so I took my new man to the auction. He knows animals. His name is Darius Stadt and his head is full of metal. He killed one of my boys, I guess, since he was in the war, too, only on the German side. We call him Derek (Persian emperors are a little too much for my blood) and he says he was on the Russian front when a mortar blew him out of the conflict. He only has one eye. During the hunting season (and most of the other times, too) I work Derek hard, making him drive the deer through the woods to those of us who have taken stands. Derek knows animals. I used to have another man, but I got rid of him and his wife, who was our housekeeper: her white dresses and nurse's shoes made me nervous. Derek has a wife and she cooks for us now. I'm putting on weight.

"How much should I pay for that ram?" I said, at the auction.

They have an auctioneer there, a gimp-minded man who wears a cowboy hat and who has a rawhide whip, but this outfit doesn't fool me at all. I understand money, having made enough of it for my sons and wife. She is a trim woman with a sharp mind and a love of books. My wife is always looking for rules, which I break, leaving her with the unending search for explanations. She spends a lot of time in the woods. She likes to spend money, though, the same as everybody else.

"Thirty-five dollars," said Derek. "That's a fair price."

I got him for thirty. It felt good, because thirty-five was a fair price. The cowboy didn't fool anybody, not even the marks, and that takes some effort. Derek loaded the ram into the back of the truck and he got some help from one of the hands at the auction. The ram didn't like the loading and he charged the man who was helping and I can tell you that man got out of the way fast. Derek started to smile the way he does when someone has been taken down a notch: he likes that, and his smiles seem kind, as though he were a sweet man, one with his mundane but nevertheless dear memories a little out of focus. Considering the amount of metal in his head, I imagine his memories are a little out of focus, but I sincerely doubt their sweetness.

This was in the fall and we drove the truck from the auction to my land. The leaves had already turned and dropped, leaving the rootlike crowns of the trees against the sky. The lichen, which is green in the middle and a little white around the edges, could be seen easily in the woods, on the trunks of trees, and on stones. We took the road that starts where the Mongaup runs into the Delaware: I built the road myself with a bulldozer I bought as army surplus after the war and Derek walked along next to me while I was on the machine. He couldn't stand to look at it, since the bulldozer was still painted green. The road is better now, and I put in a few culverts so it doesn't wash out the way it used to. I like that fall sky, the height of it, and the haughtiness, too.

"Are you ready for hunting, Derek?" I said. "Are you ready to drive deer?"

Derek looked at the woods, the dead leaves, that gray color of bark, and then turned his head so he could hear the ram butting in the back of the truck. When he turned I could see his one eye, the side of his face that was porcine and squinting with injury.

"That's a good ram," said Derek.

All business, you see?

In the spring the ewes had lambs and Derek came out of the barn, time and again holding a newborn, bloody and yellow, the umbilical cord looking like a wet shoelace. He just looked at me and held up the lambs, not smiling, not holding them in any gentle way, but just wanting to show me that his estimation of the ram had been correct.

I nodded.

"He's a good one," said Derek, still holding up a newborn. "But you got to watch him. He's dangerous."

Derek's wife, Charlotte, walked through the ram's pen a little later that spring. Actually it's more than a pen, something like a small pasture, on the other side of which there are a number of drums for trash. This pasture is in front of the barn where the ewes and lambs were. When the drums are full Derek hauls them to the dump. Charlotte had an old fry pan with her and she wanted to throw it out. So she had it with her when she started directly for the trash cans, rather than going around the fence, which anyone who was less stubborn would have done. Charlotte probably went in there, too, to look at the lambs and ewes. She likes her mashed potatoes with a pound or more of butter and it shows. She keeps getting bigger and bigger each year but Derek doesn't seem to mind. Perhaps because he can only see half of her at one time.

Charlotte walked into the pasture and the ram turned and hit her hard. She went up against the wire which was strung along a number of posts that were as thick as telephone poles. The wire was taut (having been stretched by a tractor when it was stapled to the posts) and you could see it vibrate as Charlotte bounced, and you could hear it hum, too, a distant, banjo twang. I don't know which surprised her more, the ram or the barbs on the wire. She was trying to use the fry pan as a shield so it looked like there was a lady boxer (one who was not in very good training) with a fry pan and she was on the ropes all right: the ram whacked her again and Charlotte let out a shriek. I was on the front porch, enjoying a mint julep.

I like to make them with shaved ice and fresh mint (I have some planted along the side of the house so I don't have to go far for it) and good bourbon. After it's made you should let the glass sit on the porch (or any place where it is hot) for a few minutes and when it's all frosted up, it's ready to drink.

Chip pulled up in front of the porch in his Buick convertible: it had been my present to him after the war to take with him to finish law school. When my boys were younger I sent them to Yale, because I wanted all the nonsense knocked out of them. A passing appreciation of books and so on, but no more. I wanted my sons to have sensible ideas. When John (my dead son) went to New Haven I gave him a string of polo ponies, just to be certain the cure would take, that the nonsense wouldn't do any damage. You can't expect a man who plays polo to do too much in the way of silliness. Green fields and leather boots (made in England) will knock the living piss out of Hegel, Kant, Spinoza, and the rest of the blah-blahs. I wanted my boys smart, but I didn't want them thinking too much. Chip played, too. Afterward, of course, I wanted them to follow me in my own profession, which is the law, because law is the thing, the most sensible of all, because it works like a boa constrictor, the best of all snakes. My favorite. A boa doesn't actually squeeze anything. The snake just wraps itself around a man or a lamb or some unfortunate creature and waits for whatever it's wrapped around to exhale: the boa then takes up the slack. It's a procedure, and the law is nothing else if it's not a procedure. You can trust a snake, especially a nice Harvard one, so that's why, after the war (after having all the nonsense knocked out of him in New Haven) I sent Chip to law school in Cambridge. John only had time to have the nonsense (and a lot more) knocked out of him, so he didn't get any further.

Chip arrived for a break (it was his last year) in that Buick with the red paint and the chrome and the white fold-down top just as Charlotte was being whacked up against the fence. He slowed down by the porch and then saw Charlotte and speeded up again and drove down to the pasture. That red Buick looked nice against the grass. The mint julep was fine, too. Chip jumped out of the Buick and slammed the door: he looked like a gentleman, since he was dressed in a white suit and brown shoes. His tie was of a soothing color. The ram whacked Charlotte again and she went up against the wire. I could hear her shriek. Chip put his hand on one of those posts and jumped into the pasture where the ram was starting and stopping, giving Charlotte what for. *Whack*, shriek. *Whack*, shriek. The wire hummed. Chip walked in that shit in his brown shoes and white suit and the ram turned on him.

"Give me the frying pan," he said.

Charlotte looked a little dazed and reluctant to let go of it, so Chip had to remove it from Charlotte's tightly clenched fist. From a distance it looked like Chip was taking a large black lollipop away from her. I sipped the julep.

The ram had spun on the earth when he turned toward Chip, and there were slick double cuts in the mud. Chip was now holding the fry pan and Charlotte was standing next to the fence: it seemed to me that she was relieved. The ram lunged and you could see his hooves kick away from his body. It made him mad to slip in the mud, and he lunged some more and picked up speed. The fry pan was a big ugly thing that never cooked right anyway (it made pancakes that were burned in one place and barely brown in another). Chip glanced up at me, just as the ram really began to charge: it's one of the reasons I love my son. I sipped the mint julep. It was just right now. The glass was covered with moisture. When Chip looked at me I knew what he was thinking. I had another sip. Chip was thinking (if I know a son of mine, and I'm pretty sure I do), How hard should I hit this ram? My allowance will be docked if I hit it too hard, if I kill it, and how come that old bastard of a father of mine isn't down here in the shit with me? How hard should I hit it? Charlotte was standing on one leg, and she was rubbing her thigh where the ram had hit her: it was a strangely graceful gesture (before the spuds got her she must have been something). The ram charged and Chip swung the fry pan and I could hear the clear metallic ring (somewhat like the sound a blacksmith makes when striking a hot piece of iron) even though I was fifty yards away. The ram went down. Charlotte took the fry pan from Chip and started toward the trash cans, limping some, but at least she was moving under her own power. The ram was in a heap, and I could see his black face, the white fuzz on his body (clipped short: the sheep had already been shorn). Chip stared at the felled ram with the expression of a man who has opened the financial pages of the newspaper to see how some stock he owns (but which he suspects to be shaky) is doing. Chip gave the ram a little prodding with his toe. The ram twitched. Chip gave it a little more prodding with his filthy shoes (but even in the shit you could see they were of good quality) and the ram stood up. It was a little wobbly and there were manure marks on its fleece where Chip had prodded it. The ram didn't seem interested in butting anything. Chip pushed it a little more, gave it a gentle swat to make it run. The ram seemed dazed, but all right. Chip walked from the pasture to the porch. He wiped his shoes on the grass before walking onto the gray floor where my chair was sitting. I don't allow any manure on my porch.

"He's all right," said Chip.

"Are you sure?" I said.

"He's walking, isn't he?" said Chip.

"I didn't get him to walk," I said.

I was smiling now.

"I didn't hit him where you bought him," said Chip.

You see, he hit the ram hard but not too hard: he saved being docked (which may have been more than the price I paid at the auction: I don't mind turning a profit wherever I can). Chip stood on the porch and didn't even look at the shit on the cuffs of his white trousers. I'm a little rough myself, but I'm a lawyer in the old style. I would have at least looked at my cuffs. Chip made himself a mint julep and sat down next to me.

It was late in the afternoon and we sat and watched the sun set behind the orchard. It isn't a large one, perhaps fifty trees. It was spring and the air had that little bit of moisture in it, that tangy sense of growth. Just when the colors turned blue-black, when things seemed as though they were being absorbed by the sky, we saw deer in the orchard. There was still a little light, and you could still sense the dome of the sky. The deer twitched their tails and looked up when I rattled the ice in my glass. The turkeys were moving in a flock and there were some chicks with them. Chip watched them, and at this moment, when the turkeys and deer were in the orchard my wife came to join us.

She had a glass of something and she sat on the rail of the porch and stared at the birds, at their sleek movements. The spring turkey season was about to open.

"Glad to have you home, Chip," she said, still not taking her eyes off the birds.

"We've already been at it," I said.

"Of course," she said, watching the birds as they moved out of the orchard and into the woods. The birds seemed to soothe her, but she spoke with a low voice, as though she were afraid that her clothes weren't right, or that she wasn't behaving. Usually, in the evenings, when she came out she'd just tell me, in the bass voice of hers, to be quiet, please. Then she'd watch the birds or deer, the way the foliage moved, or that last bit of dusk, the strange, haunting blue that comes just before dark. She had that faintly stricken, lonely expression which just confused me. She enjoyed watching small birds, too, titmice and chickadees in the fall, nuthatches in winter, cardinals, flycatchers, and orioles in the spring. Sometimes she came fishing with me and sat and watched the stream. This was an amazement, but sometimes afterward there was the feeling of a tacit truce: we were gentle for a while. Or she would be angrier than ever. Now she looked into the orchard and watched until there was nothing to see, then gave Chip a squeeze on the arm and went into the house. She would have sat with us a little longer if the fireflies had been out.

Charlotte came by.

"Hello, Chip," she said, but I could tell she was mad. She had her hands made into fists and she still wasn't walking with what you could call ease of motion.

"Hello, Charlotte," said Chip. "I'm glad to see you, but I'm sorry about the ram."

"What were you doing in there?" I said.

"Looking at the ewes," she said.

"How were they?" I said.

"You'll have to ask somebody else," said Charlotte. She was hot as a radiator. "I'm going to be all over bruises for a month."

All over? Well, I almost asked her to take a look, because that would be a good quarter acre of blue and yellow skin. She stood and glared at me for a moment and then walked to the barn, the apartment at one end she shared with Derek.

"One of these days she's going to hit me," I said.

Chip rattled the ice in his glass.

"Why didn't you go down there and help her?" he said.

"I saw you coming up the road in that Buick. You drive fast enough," I said.

If I had any sense I would have hit him again, the way I did the night he took the wheel and went through the turns above the Delaware, but I was blind. I pride myself on knowing what men are up to: the law explains that pretty well, since it is really an old collection of rules concerning man's desires, his scheming, his everlasting attempt to sell his brother (or just about anyone he can get his hands on) down the river. The law doesn't explain enough about women, and it certainly doesn't give you what it does about men, that delineated center, the place in the heart or mind or fears which you only need mention to a man to make him flinch.

I watched Chip for signs, but I didn't see any. It was spring and the previous September we struck what might be called a deal. We began to come to terms out by Chip's Buick. It was one of those hard September mornings when it seems as though every edge is more visible than usual, sharper. Chip brought his bags from the house and put them into the red Buick that had the wicker seats and the cream-colored top. It was as plain as a nickel that Chip thought it was silly to go back to school (prison camp has its way with nonsense, too) and that he was going more to make me happy than anything else. I went out to the car with him so we could talk.

"You'll be back in November," I said. I was standing next to the Buick and there was a cool breeze and bright sunshine. The Buick was red, no doubt about that. I picked it out myself. "For the hunt, won't you? I want that. It'll be the first one after the war."

"Yes," said Chip. "Sure."

I gave him a checkbook, a large one with three checks on a page: it felt solid and was an easy way to keep things straight. I told him what he could spend a month.

"You're getting older, Chip," I said. I was working up to it kind of slowly, you know, just to see how things stood between us. My hands were still on the checkbook, so we stood there, next to the Buick, in the September air: we felt its cool, silky quality.

"I mean you can have a good time," I said, "you understand? I've got nothing against a good time. Especially since you got locked up. But then there's getting serious, too."

Maybe it was the time Chip had spent at the farm (after he'd got out of the camp, more than a year before, he'd been living pretty much alone up here), maybe it was the weather, the fall joy. In any case, Chip looked at me and said, "Serious?" with an expression I should have recognized, because it wasn't much different I imagine from the one I had on my ugly face when I asked Charlotte how the ewes were after she'd taken a good whacking by the ram.

"Don't make me mad," I said. "You know what I'm talking about."

"I guess I do," said Chip. Still had that smile, or whatever the hell it is: on me, when I see it in the mirror, it looks as though I'd just eaten something good.

I tapped the checkbook with my finger.

"I understand perfectly," said Chip, "I understand better than you know."

He was still smiling, and it looked as though he was feeling good. It might appear that I believe you can buy almost anything, and I guess that's why Chip was smiling at me. I certainly believe it when I'm feeling a little exposed, or awkward. But goddamn it, he knew perfectly well what I wanted.

"Well?" I said.

"What you gave me isn't much of an allowance to go courting on," he said.

"I thought it was," I said.

"No," he said. "It's enough to have a good time. But it's not enough to go courting."

I made a noise: I guess you could call it a snort. I rubbed my face too, ran my fingers over that doorknob nose of mine because I knew it was turning red, just like my baggy cheeks. I have a bourbon face: there's nothing that can be done about it. Chip leaned against the red fender of the Buick and I could see myself reflected there, and it seemed that my face disappeared in the color of the car. There was a hawk hunting over the orchard and the field below the barn: its wings were spread, braced against the thermals. Chip was looking at my eyes: they're the brownish color, I suppose, of my leather briefcase, which has been polished by years of being dragged across courtroom tables and desks with glass tops.

"What do you mean?" I said. "Speak plainly."

"You want a refined woman," said Chip. I could see he was unable to stop himself. He knew he was ragging me. "You want poise, don't you?"

"Oh," I said. "You don't think it's enough for them?"

"No," said Chip.

He was making me think that there was something like a big auction, or maybe a department store where these things could be purchased: you know, models would come out (the way they do in a fashion show), and you could say, There, that's the gesture, that's the voice, that's the movement of eyes, or hands, the little twist in the walk, those are the clothes, yes, that's the woman who's been around money long enough to be able to deny having anything to do with it.

"All right," I said. "A hundred a month."

"For each?" he said.

He wasn't smiling anymore at all. I must have snorted again or made some noise that passed as an answer.

"You know," said Chip, "I met an Arab in the desert. His name..."

"I don't care about any goddamned Arabs," I said. I was fixed (speaking frankly has its disadvantages, too), exposed in my desires, which were as precise as a diamond cutter.

"That's two hundred more a month," I said.

"And what about family?" said Chip.

I guess my eyes were shiny as newly polished shoes.

"And beauty?" he said.

"Is that extra?" I said.

"Same rate," said Chip.

"All right," I said, looking at him with something that probably verged on madhouse suspicion, "all right. That's four hundred a month more. I'll see to it."

I began fishing in my pocket: I had a number of envelopes there and I was searching for the right one. My stationery might be a little heavy. Chip calls it Windsor, but I like people to see a letter when it comes from me. My envelopes are a little larger than most. I searched in my pocket and found the right one. I was mad enough to insist that he shake hands with me on it, but I thought the envelope, the note in it would be better. That it would teach him he wasn't anything but a little pissant. Still.

"You thought you were fooling me," I said, after I had cooled down a little. "You thought you were just playing me along, didn't you?"

"No," said Chip, although he began to laugh a little.

"Sure you do," I said, "I know how you think. You're my son. That counts for something."

He started the engine of the Buick. You could see he felt a little bad about baiting me. Over the field, just at the edge where the stand of softwood is, the hawk quivered in the air and disappeared.

"Aren't you ashamed?" I said with a kind of hound dog sadness, a droopy-eyed and injured look. It would be enough to break your heart.

"Yes," he said.

He put the Buick into gear.

"Well," I said, "don't feel too badly about it. You got your extra four hundred a month."

"I guess so," said Chip.

"Sure you did," I said, "a deal's a deal. But just so you won't feel too bad you can take this and read it."

Just wait until you do, too, I thought. Just wait. I offered him the note in one of my envelopes which, while not quite as large as the paddle part of an oar, are nevertheless large. Chip has blue eyes and a good, strong nose (the way mine looked before the sauce did something to it), clear skin (tanned now, too, because of the time he had spent in the sun: it just made his eyes seem bluer and his teeth whiter), although some of his hair fell out in prison camp. He gave me one of those looks, you know, that he gives me from time to time that are supposed to make me feel as though I escaped from some passing opera company. Anyway, I gave him the note on the stationery which is probably as heavy as that used by the Queen of England and said good-bye.

His mother came down to the car just after I left and I could hear her pleasing, deep voice as she asked him to write and to be careful. She gave him a kiss and then stood and watched as the car drove away (with that letter, or note, just ticking like a little bomb). The car went across a bridge (that runs over a pond where there are trout) and turned and went into the grove of pine. My wife sat at the edge of the pond and looked at some midges that were hatching. Occasionally a trout rose. She sat there for some time, glancing up the road and then peering into the green water, watching that perfect arc a trout makes as it turns.

As soon as the car was out of sight I took a walk out to the dump (which is behind an apple orchard that needs but isn't getting any attention), enjoyed the fall air, the acrid smell of dead leaves, and threw the other envelopes I had into the satisfyingly large pile of empty champagne and bourbon bottles, old tins of caviar, and cans of preserves from Canada. Those preserves from Canada were the best: they were filled with strawberries as big as your thumb and they were sweet, too. Anyway, I threw those other envelopes into the dump and then walked back to the woods, saying to myself, Well, even though it's a little early, I think you deserve a mint julep.

I made myself one and sat out on the front porch. I knew that note was on the passenger side of the Buick, as though I had decided to come along for the ride and had reserved a seat for myself. Chip probably tried to ignore it for a while, probably drove down the farm road to the Mongaup and then turned onto the highway that runs along the Delaware. There's a place halfway through those turns where you can stop and look down at the river: Chip wouldn't have been able to get much farther than that before his curiosity got the best of him. He'd pull in there and probably step out of the car so he could look at the Delaware. The Pennsylvania shore is covered with a mixture of soft and hard woods, so there are long green streaks on the hillside, in the timber which is the color of fall deer. In the river, which is low, there are shoals of smooth rocks and there isn't much white water either. From Chip's place you could see a wide section of the Delaware, which is placid. So he stood out there (I'm pretty sure) with that stationery in his hand, being sorely tempted to throw the note into the river without bothering to read it. But I'm sure this only lasted for a minute. No, he stood there, probably remembering the sound we heard last night as a flight of geese passed over the farm. You could hear their honking and could see their disproportionately small wings working in an untiring cadence. Their heads were stuck out, too. Then he'd open the envelope, pull out the note and read. By the end he'd be laughing (from the smart), holding his stomach and laughing until the tears came. *Then,* I'll wager, he threw the note and the envelope into the river, first making them into a large and satisfying ball. And he must have been thinking, That bastard. That dirty son of a bitch I've got for a father. Oh, what a bastard. He'd get back in the Buick and drive along, thinking, Maybe I'll stop at the first place I come to and have a drink, if only to the old reptile's health. That will teach you, he'd think, that will teach you to go around feeling sorry for the old fucker.

"Here's something to show you," the note read, "you little pissant. I had planned on giving you five hundred more a month than the basic stipend for living (if that's what you want to call what you do) expenses, which was generous, and don't you forget it. But I knew if you did it yourself you wouldn't push the extra money over four hundred. So, you see, you little pissant, I saved myself a hundred a month just by letting you think you were making a fool out of your father. See you at hunting season."

So I was feeling pretty good, enjoying my mint julep, and contemplating my son's discomfort when the telephone rang. I could hear Charlotte answering it, and I waited for her to come and get me or to get my wife. She didn't do either, but she did come out on the porch and start to walk down the steps.

"Who is it?" I said.

"It's for Wade," she said.

"Who is it?" I said.

If Chip had read my note in the middle of those turns above the Delaware, then this was the time he'd be in a bar to drink my everlasting health (and damnation, too).

"It's for Wade," said Charlotte, as she walked toward the garage where Wade was in his apartment.

At the time I thought it was strange, but it didn't bother me. The fact of the matter was that Wade never received a phone call, at least none to my knowledge. I don't think he had anyone to call him, aside from an idiot sister (who gave birth to a monster). Anyway, Wade came up from the garage in his shirt sleeves, walking with his thin, loping, bent-shouldered gait, keeping his long face toward the ground as though he were trying to find something (like a postage stamp, I guess) that he'd lost. He was hurrying a little, too, because he was excited. He nodded to me and went up the steps and into the house, where I could hear the buzz mumble, buzz mumble of his short talk. I don't like to admit it, but my hearing isn't as sharp as it used to be, so that's all I could hear, being, of course, naturally curious. Wade came out on the porch and nodded and went back out to his apartment.

We were going back to the city that evening, so after a while I got up to pack my bag and to put some papers in my leather briefcase. It's one that was made in England. And as I was in my study downstairs, shoving my sheets of foolscap into the manila folders I used, I looked up and saw the gun case on the wall: through the glass you can see three Mannlichers (iron sights, 6.5 mm: one is mine, one is Chip's, and the other belonged to John), and two shotguns, both L. C. Smiths, one a 16, the other a 12 gauge. This last is the thing for hunting turkeys, one barrel having a full choke, the other being straight open. This allows you two kinds of shots, distance and short-range. The shotgun was light, too, and I swung it up on my shoulder and click, just like that, I knew something was wrong. It's a sloshy, neutral pop (sloshy, in my case, I guess, because of thirty-five years of hooch), or it's like hearing in the woods a telltale or unnatural sound: you just stop. I did, with the L. C. Smith pointed right over the fireplace. I stood there for a moment and then put the gun away. There was something wrong with that telephone call.

Of course, by the time I put the gun away and got out to the dump the letters I had thrown there were gone. It was afternoon now and warm and I smelled the coffee grounds and empty sardine tins and rotting potatoes. The flies were buzzing over the trash in their jumpy, mindless arcs. I stood there with an expression on my face like that of a man who's just realized the poison he'd tried for so long to avoid (and with considerable success, too) was in the dessert (baked Alaska, say) he'd just eaten with such relish and heartfelt enjoyment: worse yet he has to stare, as that hideous sickness rises and spreads throughout his body, at the miserable dogs who'd slipped it to him.

When I was back in my study, sitting in front of my open briefcase and with my papers spread out before me, I heard the rustle of my wife's dark skirts. She put her face (with its round cheeks, high forehead, and full lips) into the room and waited. Her eyes are a nice color: the dark, gray-blue of the fieldstone, the slate from which the walls on this land are made.

"What's wrong," said my wife. "Is it money?"

"Money," I said, "has never been my problem."

She didn't look convinced, but at least she left me alone. The fact of the matter was that I really didn't know exactly what figure Chip would settle upon so I had prepared for any number between two and seven (believing, in which belief I was correct, that we would deal in hundreds, one jump at a time). Of course the last one, the one for seven, read, "This is just to show you something, you little pissant. I was planning on giving you eight hundred a month more, but I knew if I let you do it, you'd only work it up to seven. So I saved myself a hundred bucks a month just by letting you think you could get smart with your father. See you at hunting season."

I must admit that writing this last one caused me some grief, because seven hundred more a month was a hell of a lot of money. You see, I had arranged the envelopes in my pocket by number, or in sequence, so when we hit upon four I just counted up to it (the lower numbers being closer to my side), took it out and gave it to Chip. That was easy. The only bright thought was that although the envelopes were gone from the dump it didn't necessarily follow that Chip already had them.

I went outside and stood in the cool September air. It cleared my head. I stood in front of the garage, which is a white clapboard building with a pitched roof. Wade's apartment was under the cathedral ceiling.

"Wade," I said.

He opened his window and leaned out the sill: he looked like a horse sticking its head out of a stall door. Wade was in a shirt and you could see his suspenders.

"Yes, Mr. Mackinnon?" he said. Not happy looking either. Jumpy. But pleased, too.

"Wade," I said, "did you go out to the dump today?"

"No, sir," he said.

"Are you sure about that?" I said.

"Yes, sir," he said.

"And you didn't pick up any envelopes, I suppose?" I said, just to hear him lie.

"Envelopes?" he said.

"Yes," I said. "Mine."

"No, sir," he said.

I went back into the house and finished with my packing. Then I took out a sheet of my stationery and wrote a note and sealed it up. It was getting late, four o'clock anyway, but it was still warm. I walked up through the orchard (I was able to smell the apple trees) and then went up to the dump and threw the note where the others had been. It looked a little too clean so I rubbed it down in the slops of the dump, the juices of watermelon rind and rain-brewed coffee. Just enough. The flies were still there, but their buzzing didn't sound so bad as before.

"Wade," I said, standing in front of the garage again, "Wade!"

"Yes, sir," he said, still in his shirt sleeves and suspenders and still looking both jumpy but pleased.

"Wade," I said, "I was just out at the dump. I'm sorry about accusing you of taking my envelopes." This lighted up my nose, I guess, but that's all. "The wind must have blown them away, or some of them, because there's still a couple out there."

He stared down at me with his grieving face, but I knew he was as suspicious as a horny Baptist preacher. Wade hadn't worked for me for all those years without learning something. I thought I had told my tale reasonably well, and it looked to me that the tall fish would take a little nibble.

"We'll be going back to the city in about an hour," I said.

"Fine, Mr. Mackinnon," said Wade.

I walked back to the house, but I knew that even though Wade wasn't hanging out the window he was still watching me. In the woods I could hear the pop-pop-popping of the tractor: Derek was pulling logs out for firewood. I like to burn white oak, although birch makes the nicest ashes.

I'd usually spend part of a Sunday afternoon in a bath: it does wonders for my disposition. Diogenes is my favorite man: he sat in a tub and cultivated rudeness. I went upstairs and began to draw the water, but I wasn't in it when Wade came out of the garage and up to the house. I could hear him ask my wife where I was and she said I was in the bath. But I wasn't. I was in my bedroom and I was looking out the window as Wade began loping his way up the road to the dump, and he was still moving with that bent-shouldered, long-legged gait which made him seem forever cheated of some insignificant thing. I got into the tub and soaked. The water was so hot it itched. I sat there for a while and felt relieved, because the last note would go along (through the mail, I guessed) to Chip.

When I was dressed and my wife and I were ready to go, standing down behind the front door and waiting for Wade (who was late, having spent a considerable amount of time looking for the "couple" of envelopes but only in fact finding the one), my wife looked at me and said, "What have you gotten away with? What?"

I busied myself with my briefcase, searched through the sheets of foolscap.

"Was it gangsters?" she said in her diagonostic voice. There's a game we play at breakfast. I'll have the paper, and I'll read an obituary (omitting the cause of death) and then my wife will try to guess it. Pneumonia? she'd say. Exposure? Bullet wound? Anyway, that's the tone she used when she said, Gangsters? Being a customs lawyer and also being in practice during Prohibition my wife naturally assumed I represented hoodlums (I did not). This suspicion on the part of my wife was enhanced when she discovered a still on my land. The men who ran it were arrested, on my say-so, not because I was opposed to the still and not because they didn't ask if they could put the still up (which they didn't), but because the still was killing all the trout in my stream. I explained this to my wife, and she was glad about the fish no longer being destroyed, sorry about the men, but still suspicious as hell of me.

"No," I said, "it wasn't gangsters."

Wade stopped the Buick in front of the house. He took our bags and we got into the backseat. Wade got in the front.

"Are you all set, Wade?" I said, just to hear his voice, to see whether or not he had found that letter: he had. And he was worried too about not finding any more than just that one.

"Yes," said Wade, looking straight ahead and gripping the wheel, "I'm all ready."

"That's fine," I said. "Let's go."

I didn't hear anything from Chip until he came back for the hunt. I was in my study, enjoying the fire and a drink and reading a gossip magazine (it is a small weakness, and the fact of the matter is that I enjoy them, advertisements in the back especially, you know, for trusses and to improve bustlines). I was reading a piece about William Bendix. Chip stopped the car in front of the house and came in: this was a sure sign he was mad, because I'd told him a hundred times to park his car someplace else. It was a while before opening day, so the guests hadn't arrived. Chip came in and stood by the fire.

He dropped the envelopes on the table next to me, on top of my fan magazine (which I didn't have time to hide). Of course, he'd got the extra note, too. It was open, and I could read my own sharp hand.

"Well, you little pissant," it said, "if you've got this one you've probably got the others, too, and if that's the case you've got more sense than I gave you credit for. You'll make a good lawyer if nothing else. But whatever the price was (or will be: we'll settle this at hunting season), you know what I want and you know you'll do it. Don't get all exercised about this: a little skirmishing is good for a man of my age. And just in case you're feeling vain about it, remember you're the one who got shot down. See you at hunting season."

"Roll the log," I said, "it feels a little cold."

Chip turned the log: it was a piece of white oak resting on a good bed of coals. I could feel the heat as soon as he turned it.

"Maybe I should have burned them," I said, pointing to the letters on the table.

"Why didn't you?" he said.

"Because I wanted to see if you were smart enough to find them if I just threw them in the dump. It was the figures, wasn't it?"

"Yes," said Chip. "No one could have known that closely."

"Wade got them for you," I said, just as gently as I could, "didn't he?"

"What about the seven hundred a month?" said Chip.

"What?" I said.

I could hear an engine outside: I realized Chip hadn't shut off the motor of his Buick or turned off the lights, either. I could see them on a tree just outside the window.

"You were ready to pay that much and I want it," said Chip.

"I'm already paying you four," I said.

"You were ready to pay seven," said Chip.

"I'm paying you plenty," I said, "and where is she! Where is she!"

"You pay me the rest," said Chip.

I realized the whole house could hear us, that our voices were as insistent as a sawmill.

"You pay me the rest and I'll bring her," said Chip.

"When?" I said. "I'm paying you now."

"You give me the rest," said Chip.

"When? When will you bring her?" I said.

"In the spring," said Chip, "you just fix it up about the whole seven hundred."

"I'll do that," I said.

My wife stood in the door, her face flat with anger, her fieldstone eyes moving back and forth.

"What's wrong here?" she said.

"Nothing," said Chip.

He picked up the envelopes and threw them into the fire.

"I forgot to turn off my Buick," he said.

We stayed there for a while and listened to the close but definitely sad sound of the idling car. My wife stared at me with her hard, questioning glance. It wouldn't have done her any good to ask outright, to say, What are you two doing? I don't think we could have explained. The inquisitive glance was bad enough. I felt uncomfortable.

"I think I was beaten by my own son," I said. "Is that enough?"

"No," she said, "no. Not by a tenth, by a hundredth . . ."

"All right," I said and turned up empty hands.

My wife waited and cradled against her breast a large book of moths with color plates. I didn't say anything and then my wife carried that ten-pound book upstairs to read in her study.

I always thought we'd come to some compromise, or that at the least I wouldn't end up paying the whole seven hundred a month more. This made me feel like a fool, and I was mad about it, although I was glad Chip had burned the letters. I was mad about it all winter and even into the spring, and was still brooding about it a little even when the ram was whacking Charlotte up against the fence. Of course it wasn't the money: it was the control. So I was relieved, when Chip sat next to me on the porch, in his white trousers with the shit-stained cuffs, and said, "I'm bringing her next weekend."

"That's good," I said, feeling better with each passing second, "that's fine."

It's too bad that there weren't any fireflies that night because I would have liked my wife to spend some time with me, in the dark, watching and maybe talking a little. But in the morning my wife and I were up early. I had a breakfast of sausage and eggs, pancakes, orange juice, and milk. Bowl of strawberries and cream. My wife and I played our game, but this morning she read and I guessed. I got the three she tried on me: apoplexy, brain tumor, and one automobile accident.

Mrs. Mackinnon's Book of Animals, Reptiles, Plants, Trees, Birds, Bugs, and Flowers.

When fireflies blink their lights, they are signaling to one another, telling others that they want to mate, that they ache to do so. Usually, the fireflies on this land don't appear until late June or early July, and usually they appear on those evenings when it is muggy and you sit outside and are quite still to avoid feeling the effects of the heat and moisture. The fly itself (when it is seen during the day) could be confused with almost any undistinguished insect: its wings are a grayish, dull color. It has four legs, and feelers, and it is hard to see (or notice) at the end of the fly's body three yellowish rings, each one a little smaller than the last. The flies are ordinary, but at night they become something quite different. It is their ability to change, to become something other than what they usually appear to be, that makes me care for them. At night you can see them blinking, signaling, looking at times like the bits of white light struck from the starter a welder uses to ignite an acetylene torch. Or like the sparks that come from a piece of softwood (spruce, say) that has been thrown into the fire. They make no noise when their lights are blinking. It seems to me that the lights come in clusters, and that they appear most often under trees at the side of a field. The rate of their blinking is important, too, because it is the way one member of the species identifies himself to another. One species blinks every two and a half seconds, and another every three, or so. There are hundreds of species, so each fly must be accurate in its judging of the amount of time between blinks and the duration of the blink as well. Most flies move along a field or orchard, but because the different species blink at different rates, the shape or the pattern of their flights appear in different forms. The flies don't move in a direct line, but in an undulating, bobbing manner. There is one fly that makes a little arc in the orchard, and that is the one I like the best. The arc is the shape of the end of your fingernail. And you can see these arcs spread out, all at about the same height. Usually, the female is close to the ground, and it is the male who is higher up, and who makes the bright, moving patterns. The female will notice that there is a flashing at the right cadence and for the right amount of time, and she will signal in return (in much the same way that a turkey hen will make a cluck to which a distant gobbler will respond). So she is identifying herself, making herself appear enticing: I can feel it, or see it. It is as though I called out to someone, but my words were seen rather than heard, and they looked like chandeliers, light struck diamonds, gold. I can see myself in that bright and exciting shroud, can feel the buzzing (almost carnival-like) lights, the humming brilliant ache. I like to sit on the porch and watch them or stand on a back road near a hay field where the flies will be blinking. They are identifying themselves and in this I can feel their loneliness, too.

Mrs. Katherine Mackinnon
The Meeting. 1950.

The woman's name was Carolyn Cooke. Chip brought her in the spring. They came up the road in the red Buick and I saw it like a silk streamer as it went through the pine grove and across the pond's bridge. There were wild flowers, cow vetch, jack-in-the-pulpits, Queen Anne's lace, and cornflowers everywhere. I watched the car from my study and closed my book (Fabre's *Insects*) and was standing behind my husband's chair when the car stopped in front of the porch.

She was wearing a white dress with small flowers on it. The skirt had pleats and they moved when she walked. Her figure was fertile-looking, but not full. She had greenish eyes, dark hair, a wonderful carriage, and beautiful hands. Chip opened the Buick door for her and she walked up the steps. There was something a little taut in her movements, a powerful restraint, and I was charmed by it, and noticed it in the way she sat or climbed stairs, in the manner she held a glass. I was watching closely, thinking, Why is that? Why? She climbed the steps and stood before Pop, and then, because of something in her eyes, or a bit of her smile that trembled, I knew she was afraid.

And what was that agreement? I thought. What are they doing with this woman? I came onto the porch and felt myself reaching out for her, taking her hand, wanting to comfort her, but since I was excluded from the arrangement, I was only able to say "It's nice to see you" and to take her hand. My hand was dry and warm and hers was a little damp.

"My son drives like a maniac, doesn't he?" said Pop.

"He drives well," said Carolyn. Pop hadn't stood up. "I think he probably wanted to see you and Mrs. Mackinnon."

"Sit down and have a drink," said my husband.

Charlotte brought out two more wicker chairs, and Wade went out to the Buick to get the luggage, which he brought in at the side of the house.

"Perhaps Carolyn would like to wash or relax," said Chip.

"There's time for that later," said Pop, "the chairs and the tray are already here."

"Yes," said Carolyn, "let's have a drink."

We sat down and Pop gave Carolyn a drink. Bourbon, neat. Pop drank his bourbon at a hundred proof. There were three fingers in the glass he had given Carolyn, and as I looked at her I thought, Has she ever tasted hard liquor before, has she? Pop stared at her. Chip sat down and crossed his legs. Carolyn took a drink and pretended it didn't matter at all.

"Is that too strong?" said Chip.

"No," said Carolyn, gasping a little in spite of herself.

"You see?" said Pop, "she likes it. A woman after my own heart."

The deer came into the orchard and began grazing there. The deer never arrived slowly. I just looked up and they were there, as though by legerdemain.

"Chip's spending a goddamn fortune," said my husband. "What can we do about it?"

"Chip's been generous," said Carolyn. "And then things are frightfully expensive in Boston."

"Of course he's generous," said Pop, "it's my money . . . but then maybe you're right about things being expensive. Just the other day I had to get a pump . . ."

A turkey came into the orchard, too, stopping and starting, looking for insects in the grass. While it moved and searched I was trying to see if what I thought was correct: that Carolyn had managed to stick up for both of them, to make everything seem all right. Things were expensive. Chip was generous.

"It's lovely here," she said.

"Of course, it is," said Pop. "I wouldn't let my son take you someplace ugly."

Pop put on his tan hound's smile.

"What's your father do?" he said.

Carolyn laughed, blushed, and looked at Chip. He sat in his chair, toying with his glass, compelled by that damn agreement. I wanted to ask him, wanted him to explain.

"Why nothing at all," she said. "He's an ambassador. I think I'll have another of those delicious drinks," and gave her glass to my husband, who took it in such a way as to let his hand touch the perfectly shaped nails of Carolyn's fingers.

"To where?" said my husband.

"I think that's enough," I said. "Don't you?"

"No," said my husband, watching Chip. "There isn't any danger of a son raising his hand against his father, is there? Carolyn?"

She stared into the orchard.

"You can trust your son," said Chip. "But if I were you I'd make some pleasant conversation."

"What's wrong with this?" said Pop.

Chip made his wicker chair squeak.

"Why, nothing at all," said Carolyn. "Don't you worry for a minute."

Carolyn took her drink from my husband's hand, touched his fingers with hers, and gave him a little pat and a squeeze over his pained joints, where age made itself sharply noticeable: her cool, damp fingers soothed him. My husband opened his eyes and stared at her.

"Did that upset you?" said Carolyn.

I admired her. Right then. You see, but I wanted to ask, are you ashamed?

"No," said my husband.

"I didn't think it would," she said, with a smile now. "You wanted to know where my father is an ambassador?"

"Yes," said Pop, settling back into his chair, and being a little more careful, touching his fingers. "That's what I wanted to know. Chip doesn't give any information anymore. Tight-lipped."

"Paraguay," said Carolyn, "and I meant that about doing nothing. He dresses up and drinks champagne and tells a lot of lies and doesn't make any money at all."

"Hmm," said my husband. "You tell him I make plenty."

Pop sat back and sighed with satisfaction. Carolyn laughed lightly.

"You have no idea how glad he'll be to hear that," she said.

"You tell him," said my husband, "with my compliments." He slapped the arm of his chair and said, "I knew Carolyn and I talk the same language. I saw it when she walked up the steps."

"That's good," said Chip, squeezing his glass. "Fine."

"Of course," said Carolyn, looking into Chip's eyes, trying to catch them, but Chip had turned to the orchard. The turkeys hadn't gone, and the deer were still moving, ticking their tails every few minutes.

Charlotte brought in some canapés, cucumber sandwiches, and puff pastry with warm cheese inside.

"But," said my husband, "maybe he doesn't have to make any money? Maybe he has an income administered by trustees at, say, Morgan Guaranty, who have your interests at heart, too?"

"Maybe," said Carolyn.

"That's enough," said Chip.

My husband drew back and splashed a little of his drink.

"Goddamn it," he said, "you kept me waiting all winter. What did you expect?"

"It's all right," said Carolyn, putting her hand on Chip's, squeezing it and shaking her head a little, as though saying, Please, please, please. Chip waited with her hand on his and said, "All right, make a little pleasant conversation."

Charlotte brought some small pigs in a blanket and put out some caviar and small crackers and onion and chopped hard-boiled egg whites and yolks.

"Would you like one of these?" she said to Carolyn.

"You've got to understand," said my husband, "I've got nothing against champagne or caviar or cigars. Charlotte," he said, "go into my study and get a box of cigars that doesn't have a broken seal." When she brought them, my husband said, after pushing the large box into Carolyn's hands, "For your father with my compliments. I don't want him to think I'd give him stale cigars. You tell him these were made by blind men in Cuba."

Chip leaned against the railing, sipped his drink, and watched the deer.

"Now, Chip," said my husband, "is that nice enough?"

"It's better," said Chip.

"My son doesn't compliment me very often," said my husband. "I have to settle for things like that."

Carolyn smiled and said, "Why, Chip speaks of you often."

My husband laughed and said, "Oh, yeah. Oh, yeah. I'll bet he does," and then went back to laughing in his drink for a minute before looking up and fixing on Carolyn again, and saying, "What does he say?"

"Can't you guess?" said Carolyn.

"If I put my mind to it, I imagine I could," said my husband, not laughing now, "but it wouldn't do the bourbon any good to turn it into those kinds of thoughts. But I'll tell you this, that no matter what he said, it didn't really prepare you for, with all due modesty, the full impact of me, in the flesh and with three dimensions?"

"No," said Carolyn.

"Ha!" said my husband. "Say, what's the chance of getting invited to one of those swell parties where everyone wears white tie and gets announced and drinks champagne?"

"You were doing all right," said Chip.

"I still am," said my husband.

"I could get you invited," said Carolyn, "but then you'd have to go to Paraguay."

"Why, I've got nothing against traveling," said my husband. "Wouldn't you like to take a little trip to visit your father? Or to enjoy the climate and change of scenery in Paraguay?"

"No," said Carolyn. "I see my father in Boston. Or Washington."

Chip made himself another drink and I passed the tray. Chip looked rigid, and handsome, too, in his light suit and dark tie, and with his angry complexion and eyes. We sat for a moment without anyone saying a word, watching the deer and the turkeys. It was getting dark.

"Mr. Mackinnon," said Carolyn, after she'd finished her second drink, "may I ask you a question?"

"Of course," said my husband.

"Do you have a turkey call?" said Carolyn.

"Why, of course, I do," said my husband with his smiling suspicion, "right inside on top of my gun case."

"Do you have a slate call?" said Carolyn.

"Of course, I've got a slate call," said my husband, "and a cedar box and a membrane too."

"I like the slate call," said Carolyn. "Do you mind if I call a bird?"

"Chip," said my husband, "will you go into my study and get the call? Bring the sandpaper for the peg."

Chip went inside, and while he was gone my husband just stared at Carolyn, not being anything but rude. Chip came back and put the call into Carolyn's hands. She opened it and took the sandpaper from around the peg, and roughed it up. She held the slate part in the long fingers of her left hand and the part with the peg in her right hand. When she rubbed the peg against the slate (in a circular motion) it made nine short noises, nine *squeaks*. Her fingers were tapered and the nails were shaped and had a little clear polish on them. The birds had approached the end of the orchard, and the front guard, the first gobbler, and most of the hens, who were in the middle, had already stepped into the woods (on their way to the roost), but the rear guard, that last gobbler who was still in the orchard, stopped, and suddenly, too. My husband watched him, as did the rest of us. Carolyn waited, her long, perfect fingers still holding the call. The gobbler turned his head one way and then another, watched the hens in front as they moved further into the woods, and after he had started toward them Carolyn's fingers made those sounds (which I had listened to for years: a hen's call in spring), *squeak, squeak, squeak*. The gobbler stopped again. My husband leaned forward in his chair. The first time the gobbler had heard the noise he'd been a little intrigued, being half-convinced that some old gobbler had lost what it takes to keep his hens in line, but now he was convinced there was a spare hen around, and a young and sweet-sounding one at that. Of course he began to strut, putting his head up, and taking a look around, trying to find the young hen, the gobbler obviously believing that the hen was intrigued by him. My husband brought himself more out of his chair and stared at the gobbler, and put his hand over his mouth and nose. The gobbler turned and left the rear unattended, and stepped toward the last apple tree in the orchard. There wasn't much light (things were taking on the beginning of that blue cast), but I saw Carolyn's eyes clearly, the expression in them which seemed to be both sharp and gentle at the same time, which is to say she looked at people to see what their weakness was, although she didn't really hold it against them. My husband stared at her fingers and then at the bird. When the gobbler was convinced he'd been having a dream on the eve of the mating season and began to turn back to the edge of the woods (feeling, I should imagine, ashamed for being led away from the rear of the flock), Carolyn worked that call again, making nine squeaks, a little closer together this time.

My husband opened his eyes and blew up his cheeks. The gobbler stopped at the edge of the woods and broke into a full peacock display.

"Well, I'll be damned," said my husband.

Carolyn capped the call and left the bird out there by the woods.

"I'll take that," said my husband, putting out his hand for the call, just to get his aching knuckles touched, but Carolyn dropped the slate-topped cylinder into his hand without even brushing against his fingers. So my husband held the call and we watched as the gobbler finally gave up, dropped his tail, and, after taking one look back into the orchard, walked toward the woods with a crestfallen gait, seeming to be, as he disappeared from the orchard, the picture of forlorn hopes. My husband tugged at his lip.

"I'll be damned," he said.

"My father and brothers hunt them," said Carolyn. "Sometimes I'll call one from a blind."

"Why, of course, you do," said my husband. "We'll have your brothers and father over to hunt."

"They'd love it," said Carolyn.

"That's just fine," said my husband. "We'll have them next fall to hunt deer."

Charlotte came onto the porch and told us that dinner was served. We went in. It was a little cool in the dining room so my husband lit the fire, and we ate, listening to the occasional pop of the seasoned oak, beneath which there was some dry, gray birch. The chill left the room quickly. We ate brook trout, a saddle of venison, broccoli, roast potatoes, drank decent wines, had a light chocolate desert. Carolyn carried herself, and moved her hands and shoulders, and smiled in such a way that made me feel that all of us were a little more real than usual, and she had the aura, too, that nothing bad or terrible could ever happen to her, that such things had been excluded from that rare and beautiful world in which she lived. Of course this was an illusion.

After dinner and while we were having our coffee, Carolyn and

I talked about books, and she knew her natural history, from Aristotle to Lorenz, and even some tracts written by Northwestern trappers. I enjoyed myself, although I had questions.

"Now, look here," said my husband, glancing at me and then back to Carolyn, "I don't want you to get the idea that around here we just talk about bugs and plants. There's lots to do. So I want you to come and visit this summer."

"I'd love to," said Carolyn.

"Well, that's just fine," said Pop. "There's lots to do. There's a brook on my land and we'll go down there and drink champagne in July. It's a nice cool way to spend an afternoon."

It is, too: there have been many times when my husband and I took a basket to the stream in the middle of summer, and I have seen through the bubbles in a glass of champagne a hawk, a deer in its red coat, and the sluggish movement of a copperhead.

"It sounds wonderful," said Carolyn. "But I'm going away for most of the summer."

"Where?" said my husband. "I thought we understood one another?"

"Genoa, Florence," said Carolyn, and then having in her voice the quality I suspect one sees in a bit of black garter, added, "We do."

"What do you want to go there for?" said my husband.

"It's lovely," said Carolyn. "Don't you think so?"

"Some people probably like it," said my husband.

He went on drinking his brandy, although he must have remembered the venison, which was mild, but in which you tasted the land, the blueberries, the grass, a lick of stone. Carolyn and I spoke of southern France.

"Well, hell," said my husband, "I guess you aren't going to run off with some greaseball, are you. You know, one of those wops with one suit who's working his way across the Atlantic."

"Mr. Mackinnon—" said Carolyn.

"Call me Pop," he said.

"Pop, then," said Carolyn. "Do you mean an *Italian*?"

"Whatever," said my husband.

Carolyn shook her head, smiled toward her lap, and then looked directly into Pop's eyes and said, "No, Pop, I don't think I'll run off with a *greaseball*."

"That's good," said my husband. "Enjoy the scenery and the food."

Carolyn started to laugh and couldn't stop, so Chip brought her a glass of water.

"I must have had too much wine," said Carolyn.

"Yes," I said, "that happens quite a bit around here."

Chip was still silent, and he looked like a stranger to me. I wanted to take his hand, wanted to ask him . . . but there wasn't time.

"So you think that's funny?" said Pop.

"No," said Carolyn.

"Would you mind if I told you a bad story?" said Pop, after he'd finished another brandy.

"I would," said Chip. "I'd mind plenty."

"When I want your opinion, I'll ask for it," said Pop.

"Go on," said Carolyn.

Pop spoke for a while: it was a joke about a painting of Custer's last stand, and the punch line was, "Holy Cow, look at all those fucking Indians." Pop bent over and laughed. Carolyn sat there for a moment and smiled. Chip had to hit Pop on the back.

"I guess I'll have to apologize for my husband," I said and took Carolyn upstairs, although we heard him, through his difficult breathing, say, as we went upstairs, "like hell you will." Carolyn seemed a little pale as we came to the second landing and as we went into her bedroom. It was an extra room and had a double bed. Her suitcase was on a stand at the bottom.

"Would you like a little air?" I said. "The view is lovely."

I opened the window, and she walked next to me, still looking pale, and now not having that smile with which she had charmed my husband into treating her like a member of the household, which is to say she had charmed him to the point of getting herself insulted.

"I think I've got a little headache," she said and sat down next to the window.

"I'll get you some aspirin," I said and left her there, staring into the darkness of the orchard. I walked down the hall and the stairs, too, hoping that both Chip and my husband heard the dry, leafy wake I made, the rustling outraged gait, but they didn't. After I got the aspirin I stood outside the dining room door.

"I like her," said my husband, who was still sitting down. Chip was on the other side of the table.

"I thought you would," said Chip.

"That's right," said my husband.

The table had been cleared and in the candlelight the grain of the polished wood was visible: the grain had the shape of metal filings that are spread on a piece of paper with a bar magnet underneath. The table had been made from planks cut consecutively from the same saw log. The grain curved toward two poles.

"When are you going to be married?" said my husband.

"I haven't asked her," said Chip.

"When are you going to ask her?" said my husband.

"What makes you think she'll say yes," said Chip, "after that joke?"

"What was wrong with it?" said my husband, although his voice was weakening a little.

"Why don't you take it easy?" said Chip. "Why don't you?"

"I'll take it however I goddamn well please," said my husband. "And I don't need you suggesting otherwise."

"Is that right?" said Chip, stopping now and facing his father. "Do you mean to tell me that she's going to sit still for your locker-room stories?"

"It was funny," said my husband.

"Well, that's what you think," said Chip, now standing absolutely still, "but let me tell you that when she gets out of here on

Sunday the chances of her coming back are slim. First she'll probably write a letter to a friend which will read something like, 'Dear Allison, I can't tell you what a thing has happened to me . . . I mean you really wouldn't believe this beastly place I went to where they ate raccoons and other things . . . Chip's father must be a little touched . . . I was waiting for him to have a fit all through dinner.' "

"All right," said my husband, "all right."

"Word gets around, too," said Chip.

"All right," said my husband, putting down his brandy and holding his head between his hands. "Maybe I shouldn't have told that story. Not so soon anyway. But will you ask her? Will you? I mean tonight."

"Yes," said Chip.

"That's something anyway," said my husband, looking up from under his brows again and not pleasantly, either.

I went upstairs and found Carolyn still next to the window. There was a glass in her bathroom and I brought her some water in it and took two aspirin out of the bottle I was carrying which was big enough to make a terrarium. Carolyn took the pills (which were about the same color as those stars beyond the window) and said "Thank you."

I stood next to her and both of us looked out the window. I saw Polaris. I took her hand, without thinking, without anything aside from the need to touch it. I felt and was able to see twenty-five year's difference in texture and color: her hands were pale and smooth, and mine were a little brown and rough.

"I don't feel very well," said Carolyn. "It must have been the wine."

"Perhaps," I said.

Carolyn let me see her tired face and said, "It's not that I mind so much really. Not really, I suppose. But I'm so ashamed and so tired. And it's not that I don't care for Chip, either, because I do very much. But sometimes I'd rather have my dress looked up or my diary read."

I squeezed her fingers a little and then put them down.

"I understand," I said.

"Is that true?" said Carolyn, still looking out the window.

"Of course," I said, "I understand more than you know. Why don't you get some sleep? We'll take a walk tomorrow. There's a lot of blueberries this year. We can pick some if you like."

Carolyn touched my dry fingers for a moment and then said "Good night."

I heard the rustle of my skirt as I walked to the door, but Carolyn stopped me there and said "Thank you."

I was about to say, Don't worry about a thing, my dear, aspirin is something this house is full of, but I knew what she really meant, so I just said "Good night."

In the hall I passed Chip, who went straight into Carolyn's bedroom, carrying a glass of brandy, and not even making the pretense of going into his own room. I went downstairs and sat on the bottom step and listened to my husband who was moving around, from his study to the dining room, crashing into things in the dark, and moaning, occasionally breaking a glass and saying, "Son of a bitch. Son of a bitch."

After he'd stopped walking back and forth and had stopped swearing, I stepped into his study.

"Who's that?" he said.

"Me," I said.

"Goddamn it," he said, "what am I going to do?"

"Wait," I said, picking up one of his aching hands and rubbing the fingers of it, but he was too jumpy for that.

I went into my study and turned on the light with the green shade and picked up my book. I sat there for a while, smelling the cigar smoke that lingered in the upstairs. The book had some large plates, and I looked at the legs and feelers of *Ephemerella* nymphs. They were ugly, but seemed necessary, armored. After a while I heard the front door open and I went down.

Chip was standing on the porch, in the dark, smoking a cigar and drinking a glass of brandy. There were no fireflies out and the orchard was dark. He didn't turn when I stepped outside, but he knew I was there. I came out a little farther so I could see his face. His expression was set and hard.

I wanted to ask . . . wanted to begin . . .

He said something I did not hear, or only partially heard, and it sounded like, "I don't think I have ever failed anyone," but I wasn't sure.

I thought of those times years ago when Chip was thirteen or fourteen and I took him walking along Fifth Avenue, where we went shopping. He watched those women there, from South America, Europe, or Texas, dressed in silk and *crêpe de chine*, their long legs swinging down the avenue, their eyes cool and haughty and beautiful. He stared after them, although not so much as to be rude. In those days, I put my hand on his shoulder and said, "What a warm day! Would you like to stop for a drink?" And he said, "No, I'd like to walk on the avenue a little more." Now I was afraid to touch him, but the expression of longing was still there or more there than ever.

After a while, when he had finished his brandy, and after we had stood in the dim light of the porch, I said, "Do you remember those walks we used to take on Fifth Avenue?"

"Yes," said Chip.

We stared into the orchard.

"Are you all right?" I said.

"Of course," said Chip. "I'm fine. Just fine."

Mrs. Mackinnon's Book of Animals, Reptiles, Plants, Trees, Birds, Bugs, and Flowers.

On our land we have white-tailed deer, and their gaits and stances, all of their movements seem delicate and taut. They are survivors, and they have withstood wolves, cougars, and people like my husband, and worse, and yet they always seem doomed, although I know they aren't. Their alertness is piercing, because once (after having used the prescient senses of hearing, sight, and smell) they have decided there is no danger they go back to feeding, or playing, or pursuing one another: it is at that moment when they can be brought down. Their sense of hearing and smell are the most keen, and eyesight after that. They are very sensitive to movement, but not to color. A deer sees in gray, black, and white.When they run, they flash up their tails so that the white part shows, and any other deer will see that white, the movement of it and take fright. Deer also have a wonderful sense of touch, and I think that they can feel, in the hard soil of November, the approach of men. It moves me that they are so unaware of themselves, of their coloring and beauty, especially unaware of it because they live in that forest and the fields where everything is black, gray or white. Deer seem to have four coats, or fashions, the first being a lightish brown in the spring, a pale buff color which is the same as hay fields that haven't started to grow after the winter. In the summer deer have a red fox color, and they stand out in the frenzied green of the undergrowth and ferns, and in the fall, when the days begin to grow shorter the deer have a gray wolf color, similar to shagbark hickory (which blends in perfectly with the woods after the leaves are gone: if a deer is still it is almost impossible to see). In the middle of winter, the deer have a black, dull gray cast to their coats, and just looking at it makes me think of cold stone and frozen earth overhead. There is a brittleness the deer have in their eyes at this time, an expression that I admire because it is complicated but still graceful and somehow very definite: there is in this glance something of an accusation, but at the same time a terrible acceptance.

In the early summer, the males of species begin to grow horns, and antlers develop quite quickly, and in a way that's different from the growth of almost any flesh I know of. The horns are not nourished from the inside out, but the reverse: there is a skin that is filled with veins and arteries, and this expands and feeds the horns as they grow, and when they are done, when they have reached their maximum size this skin will die, and the buck will find a tree (not too large a one, either) and begin to polish the horns, to make them a whitish color and to give them that smooth texture. I have never touched a buck's horn in velvet, but I have heard that the blood in the tissue makes the horns seem warm. When the horns are polished, and after the first cold snap in November, a buck's neck begins to swell as the animal goes into rut. They are careless (or uncaring, not sloppy, but intense and preoccupied) and this makes them doomed, but unyielding and grand. They search out, fight over, pursue the does, which come into season a little later, giving the bucks the time to establish, among themselves, the right to go courting. During this time the bucks no longer keep their ordinary routine: they look for and follow does if they aren't engaged in fighting, in demanding territory. Many hunters and people who spend time in the woods think that the size of the antlers is solely dependent on the robustness of the animal, and, although robustness is important, diet is even more so: there are deposits of calcium and other trace elements on this land, and bucks here have been known to grow quite large and beautiful antlers. When I see the bucks, arrogant and indifferent, when their horns have been polished, I am amused and proud, and a little sad: it is usually when a buck is following a doe that he is killed by a hunter. The does come into season, and enjoy the bucks, and then, in early springtime they will seek a felled tree top, or a covered patch, a dry swamp, and give birth, labor taking about an hour. They will have twins when there is a lot of food, triplets when conditions are even better, and only one fawn when there hasn't been much to eat the previous fall. It is remarkable that the fawns have no odor that is detectable to other animals, not even hounds. When they are a little older they give off scent from a gland between the hooves of the hind feet. In the spring and early summer you can see the fawns in the orchard or in the fields, browsing now in the same manner as their mothers, twitching their tails just before they look up. The fawns lose their spotted coat in the fall and look like small versions of their mother, with whom they winter for the first year, and then are forced to fend for themselves, to take part in the life of the deer, the males growing horns and beginning the struggle for land and females, the young does coming into season, feeling the itch and the desire, the excitement. Once, when I was driving in our Buick, I saw a pregnant doe jump from one side of the road to the other. It was late in the spring and the doe seemed to have been past her term, because she had already begun to turn that fox-red color, and when she jumped she made a perfect arc, swollen in the middle, her hind feet and forefeet together (her head down), the shape of her path the same as the blade of a scyth. She looked like a muscle: white tendons tapering into and enlarging at the muscle itself, which in turn tapers into another tendon. I can still see the arc, the perfect jump in the lights of the Buick. It is a curve I have seen in many animals, birds, and fish.

The bucks, when their necks are swollen, when their horns are clean, make me feel the danger and the definiteness of desire and need: it is as though I can feel the woods, the land more fully when the bucks are definite and not so much unwary as concerned about things more important than danger. They are proud and head-strong, the color of timber, dismissing of anything that is not fe-male: I am glad to see the desire, its demands, and I can only say that I am both relieved and ashamed when I go to the front of the house in the middle of November and look out the window or stand on the front porch and see the bucks hanging from the elm in front of the house. Their eyes are always open, seeming blue and deep when the light hits them. I am very quiet and careful when I watch them during the year, and I delight in them, al-though I feel that they are never far away from that doomed arc you see in a deer hanging at the end of a rope. The venison on this land is mild and delicious, and my husband and I like it warm and served with roast potatoes and a bottle of red wine.

Pop Mackinnon
The Ram. 1950.

I had to wait until morning. The hooch had made me nervous, too, so I spent most of the night crawling in my old skin and watching the color of the sky through the window.

Derek woke me.

I thought the tapping at the door was Chip, and I said "Come in" even though I was in my pajamas and had what's left of my hair smeared around my head. I needed a shave, too. I sat with my bare feet on the floor and looked at Derek, who stood outside my bedroom with his green knitted cap with its knitted visor in one hand and his squinted face appearing all the more damaged because of the formality of the wall behind him.

"You won't believe it," said Derek.

He moved that hat around and opened his one eye wide. There was a little smear of blue in the other.

For a moment I thought: Maybe they've run off in the middle of the night and called to say they'd eloped.

"What wouldn't I believe?" I said, still smearing my monk's hair around the sides of my head.

"The ram's gone," said Derek.

He moved the cap from one hand to the other and generally looked as though some of those pieces of metal in his head were vibrating a little. I guess I seemed a little disappointed (and maybe mad that I hadn't insisted the night before that Chip in fact elope), because Derek turned the good side of his face away.

"I don't know how he got out," said Derek. "I dunno. I dunno."

"Son of a bitch," I said.

"I dunno. I dunno," said Derek.

I sat there for a moment, staring at my ugly feet, and then Derek went out in the hall. In five minutes I came out, and Derek was still there. When we got down by the pen it was just after dawn, and most everything was blue, but in the west you could see the tops of the trees turning that red-gold color (like some women have in their hair) as the sun rose over the ridge on the other side of the Delaware. There was a little smoke from the stove in Derek's apartment (the room and bath, actually), and I smelled its haunting odor, that strange incenselike miasma in the spring air.

"How the hell did he get out?" I said.

"I dunno," said Derek. "He was a good one."

The cold made the wounds in Derek's face a little red, his squint more pronounced.

"Does that hurt you now?" I said.

Derek put his hand to his face, the stretched injuries.

"I dunno," said Derek.

We began going around the pasture, the small one, trying to find the spot where the ram had managed to get out.

"I dunno," said Derek, still touching the side of his face, "I don't feel hardly nothing at all."

Derek pointed to a break in the fence. It was a good, new fence, made with barbed wire that was still its silver-gray color and the wire was stretched from one metal standard to another.

I held the end of the wire and Derek said, "I dunno. I dunno," but I was thinking of Carolyn's fingers. Derek took his cap off and put it back on and then kicked the fence. I heard it buzz like a fly.

I felt like kicking it, too, but we fanned out through the woods, moving downhill, toward the Delaware. The mountain laurel was in bloom and so were the shadbushes. The undergrowth was so thick you couldn't see very far, not until you got down to the bottom of the hill. I didn't see Derek, but I heard his steady tromping and thrashing around, and I knew that he was walking with one arm raised over the side of his face that had the good eye.

There's a ridge that crosses my land from the farm all the way to the Delaware, and I knew we were on it, because when we came to a clearing or a stand of pole timber, we saw the swale that runs next to it. The swale was wide and deep and, of course, as long as the ridge. I was walking, thinking, Well, have I spent enough time making noise in the bushes to go back and get my breakfast (sausage, Irish oatmeal with raisins, scrambled eggs, cinnamon toast, raspberries and cream), when Derek stopped in the brush and whistled, beckoned with his arm, then pointed.

"Son of a bitch," I said.

Derek came a little closer and we both looked down the ridge and saw, in the understory, the brush, that ram. It was standing in front of a shadbush, and staring over his shoulder at us.

"We can chase him," said Derek, pulling down his cap in a strangely military fashion, "but that's not so good, I think."

The ram stood there. Below, through the timber, the Delaware was as blue as the morning light.

"Not unless we want to run him into the river," I said.

Derek screwed his cap around on his head and tilted his good eye toward the ram.

"We got to go down," said Derek, "you know. Below him."

He made a fork with two fingers.

"You on one side, me on the other side," he said. "Then we run him back to the farm."

We walked down and I was thinking about Derek, his gestures, when we talked about running this ram. It was almost as though he'd been saying, There's a couple of Russians down there. You take that flank, I'll take the other. We'll kill them bastards. Maybe that's when he got blown out of the conflict, after making such plans, maybe that's where he learned to say "I dunno. I dunno." Both of us walked in a swale and that ram stood there, still looking over his shoulder, not exactly arrogant, but not what anyone could call appreciative, either. He had a black muzzle, face, and his fleece was white, recently shorn. Derek was to my left, moving through the brush: we gave the ram a wide berth, but something in my gait, or in Derek's, spooked him a little, and he started trotting (slowly) downhill.

I went to my right, through the understory which was at least chest high (every now and then I'd go through a small, deep swale where it was wet and swampy). I was watching where I was putting my feet, too, because there are rattlesnakes (timber and Eastern massasagua) on this land. They came in with the canal, built a hundred years ago and abandoned for sixty. There was a piece of fieldstone sticking out of the ground which I didn't see and I tripped over it like a man who just doesn't notice a step. I sat there for a moment, breathing hard, smelling the mulchy odor of humus. No bones broken. I stood up and started after that ram, on a wider course, this time.

Derek didn't look as though he'd had an easier time than I did when we met, almost at the river, but below the ram. We saw his condescending black face as the animal now stood above us, peering through the brush. Derek was scratched on his forehead, and he was blinking his eye.

"We want to be closer together, this time," I said.

The ram turned uphill. We kept following him but after a hundred yards I could feel it. I heard Derek and saw him every now and then, fighting the brush. The ram turned its black face and watched us. We started up the hill, Derek and I closer together now. Sometimes the ram broke to my right and I'd move over, at the same elevation, or climbing a little as I made the traverse. I made a barking sound, a *"Woof, woof, woof!"*

The sun had risen a little more, and the golden-red color was slowly moving down hill, toward the ram, and us. I was breathing hard now, and so was Derek. I heard the click of the ram's hooves over stone, the cantering slate-striking gait.

I went down again, although this time I didn't even remember hitting the ground, the hard stones there. I came up with a piece of dead wood in my hand, a limb from the top of a rock oak. It made a club. Derek was speaking German, now.

"Mr. Mackinnon! Mr. Mackinnon!" said Derek.

We came a little closer together, both of us breathing hard. Derek had a scrape on his cheek and was bleeding from it. I looked down at my pants, a kind of brown khaki, and saw the spots of my own blood. I touched my face and looked at my fingers, but I could tell it wasn't anything but some scratches. Derek and I touched each other's face, trying to show some concern or at least acknowledgment.

Derek pointed uphill and we both began. I could feel that dry mouth, the thirst that doesn't seem as though it could be quenched. Derek was walking along, trotting every now and then when he had the energy, and since we were pretty close together he was walking through the brush without protecting that eye.

"Put your hand up," I said.

We came out of the woods and into the first field, the border of which is held by a stone wall, large pieces of bluestone and fieldstone piled one on top of another as carefully as those stones found in the ruins of South American jungles. The ram went right over the wall and kept on going. Derek and I had a little harder time of it, each of us getting one leg over and then falling the rest of the way, in the same manner as a child taking a spill from a pony: rolling sideways. Derek was holding his side, having developed a stitch. I was holding mine, and we stumbled after that ram, both of us bent at the waist, bleeding a little, roughed up by not more than thirty minutes in the woods.

We were still going uphill, and I saw (from under my brows) the barns that ran uphill, long narrow ones for livestock. Since they went uphill they were built like steps, three in number. They had shingle roofs and the siding was painted green and the trim was white. Beyond the barn I saw the house, that tall elm tree in front of my porch.

The ram saw the familiar, homey territory and shied away from it, began to move to the right, which wasn't so bad because the ponds were between the ram's pen and the woods further to the right, on the other side of the road. To get to the woods the ram would have to go all the way up to the bridge and cross, or to keep on going straight, through the orchard and then into the woods on the other side. There was a funnel, or narrowing of space, since the pen, barn, and houses weren't that far from the ponds, and I was convinced that someone at the house or garage (maybe even Wade: God knows he spends enough time with his horse neck stuck out of the window of his room over the garage), would see us and the ram and have the sense to come out and help. I was still making that sound, *"Woof, woof, woof,"* whenever I could, which wasn't that often. Derek had that rank expression of grimness, one he probably had in the snow when he was saying, All right. We'll kill them bastard Russians.

The ram passed the house and Chip stepped onto the porch. He was dressed in a white shirt, slacks, and a jacket that was the same color as the fieldstone (some kind of tweed). He looked at the ram and then at Derek and me, and as he jumped over the railing of the porch, as he started for the ram he heard me yell and wave that piece of limb wood, that now-diminished club.

"Chip!" I screamed. "Chip! You wait. Don't you move!"

The ram stopped, too, as Chip hit the ground beyond the porch. Chip walked into the field a little ways and Derek and I stopped next to him. I gestured with the piece of limb wood.

"Well?" I said.

I had to stoop for a moment to rest my knobby big hands on my knees. Just to catch my breath.

Chip put out his arm, touched me on my back.

"I don't need your help," I said. "Just wait a minute. Don't chase that goddamned animal."

Chip stood there, with his hands in his pockets. He glanced at me and Derek, the club I had in my hand (now across my knee), the drops of blood. I was still breathing hard, and that made it difficult or impossible to speak. Once Chip made a gesture, or a movement toward the ram, and I had to stop him by taking his coat sleeve and giving it a tug.

"Well?" I said, still laboring. "What did she say?"

Derek looked at me and Chip and dropped the arm with which he had been protecting his eye. He bent at the waist and put his arms on his knees, too.

"She has to go home," said Chip.

"What do you mean?" I said, unconsciously taking the club from my knee.

"She has to go home," said Chip. "For the sake of appearances. To think about it."

"And she's going to think about it all summer long?" I said.

"What?" said Chip.

"Is she going to make us wait while she goes to Florence?"

"No," said Chip.

"Well?" I said.

"She has to go home just for appearances. She'll marry me."

"That's good," I said. "That's fine."

The ram cantered right along, through the orchard and into the plantation of white oak. Derek and I puffed and heaved.

"What about . . ." said Derek.

"Doesn't matter," I said. "we'll get him later. Chip's getting married."

"Charlotte says she's an honest woman," said Derek.

What the hell does that have to do with it, I thought. Honest women are a dime a dozen. Derek fixed his wide, blue eye on Chip and nodded, and then went back to breathing. We walked a little ways together. Wade had his horse neck stuck out of the garage and as we went under his window he said, "Congratulations, Chip."

"Thanks, Wade," said Chip.

We walked a little farther. I felt like leaning a little on Chip, but I keep my hands to myself.

"What about that ram?" said Derek. "He was a good one."

"We'll get him later," I said.

I got into a tub that was so hot it felt like I was making soup out of myself. That's good, I thought, that's it. I'll take a big towel and rub myself down. I sat there in the tub, the hot water, trying to soothe my joints. I thought everything was going to be fine.

I heard Chip in the hall.

"Chip," I screamed. "You come in here."

My tub is built high off the floor, on a little platform. It keeps the drafts off me in the winter and with the added height I can look out the window, too.

"I want to give you a little something," I said. "Just a little something to show my appreciation."

Chip came in and stood at the foot of the tub, next to the porcelain knobs.

"It's not necessary," said Chip.

"I'm offering you a present," I said. "I have a gift."

Chip looked out the window, shook his head.

"Do you like this land?" I said.

Chip turned his eyes on me again.

"Yes," said Chip. "Yes . . . I've . . . always . . ."

"All right," I said, "it's a piece of property. Don't task my generosity. Now will you take my gift, so things will have been done as they should be?"

"Yes," said Chip, glancing once out the windows. "Yes."

"That's good," I said. "Do you suppose you can run a little more hot water into this tub?"

Chip worked the knobs and let in so much hot water I started to squirm, and at the moment I began to protest, he shut the faucet off. After a little the heat felt good. I sat in the tub and soaped my chest and arms, and my old legs with their knees that point a little bit the wrong way. I was turning pink in the water and thinking, I know what I'll give that boy as a reward. I've got just the thing.

I'll take him down and give him the house I built for his brother, John, who was killed in the war. Forty acres, too. The house and land are in the middle of sixteen hundred acres I own, so, as I sat in the tub, generally feeling that things were as rosy as the pinkish color my skin was turning because of the hot water, I thought, If anything goes wrong, at least I'll have the little pissant surrounded.

I wasn't even bothered, really, that the ram got away.

Mrs. Mackinnon's Book of Animals, Reptiles, Plants, Trees, Birds, Bugs, and Flowers.

We have a field that is enclosed by a stone wall, and beyond the wall there is a line of trees, maples, oaks, some ailing birch, and a little pine. Just beyond these trees a number of birds roost, mostly grouse, but a small flock of turkeys, too, and in winter, in January, when there was a foot or more of snow on the ground, I have carefully approached this field, and seen a red fox going from tree to tree, from maple to pine, looking for a bird that had frozen on the roost. To see a fox run is a joy, since they have a prancing bounce, a high-tailed jump, which seems just the opposite of their condition, a variety of imprisonment, or confinement, if only for the fur on their backs. They are efficient and they seem to have the ability to learn as well, not to mention having a sense of smell which verges on the magical. The foxes on this land are not large, and as nearly as I can make out, we only have the red variety. They are about eighteen inches at the shoulder, a reddish yellow on their backs and sides, white or grayish on their throats and stomach, and they have a small white tip at the end of their tails. When they are adult they have a smilingly curious and bitter expression, sharp eyes, a suspicious movement of the head. They are efficient not only in the way they hunt (taking frozen birds in winter and moving from hay field to grain field in summer, which is to say, from mice to grouse and pheasant), but in the way they treat their success. If a fox has more than enough rabbit, or mice, he will store the surplus, usually by digging a hole. They are efficient, too, in the way they establish a den. There is one I know of, in a hollow. The den is on the side of a hill, in claylike soil. There is a flat place before it and the door is shaped like the silhouette of a light bulb. The den was at one time a woodchuck's burrow, and the foxes moved in when it was unoccupied. The doorway has its distinct shape because the fox will run with its feet underneath his body, while a woodchuck has feet that are positioned more like a rabbit's and will make an entrance that has the shape of a small mound. The den is located in the ideal place: it is elevated a little, so the fox can look around. I guess it is the discipline of its needs that makes the animal seem imprisoned, or without luxury (which, for example, is about all a woodchuck seems to have), although there is one exception to this, and that is in the summer, when the raspberries are ripe. The foxes like raspberries and I have seen a vixen with her pups enjoying the juicy bundles. Foxes do not hibernate, and theirs is a winter courtship. In late January I have heard the vixen's seasoned cry, a high bark, which, in the cold air, in the snow, seems to come from a strict yearning, but I imagine vixen and dog fox giving comfort to one another, warmth, and drawn, intense pleasure. The vixen will have her pups in about fifty days, and the dog fox will remain monogamous, at least for the season. The vixen gives birth to her pups in the den, and the dog fox brings her food when she is confined. The pups are born blind, but are soon able to see, and by the summer they will be taught to hunt, to kill mice or birds, and to enjoy the raspberries. The pups will disperse in the late fall and will be able to mate themselves the following January. Foxes are creatures of regular habits, working the land in a routine: trappers know this and they take advantage of it by trying to establish the fox's routine and then placing traps along the usual route. There are many signs, urine posts, scat, rabbit hair at a den, the den itself, tracks. Foxes have as their defense an ability to learn and that almost clairvoyant sense of smell. A trapper must boil his traps and any tool that he will use in putting out a set, and he must wear gloves when he touches his tools or his trap. A trap must be waxed, too, because the fox can smell the rust on untreated metal. A fox's sense of smell is so keen that it can tell, by sniffing the urine of another fox, what the second fox had been eating, and if it had been something interesting, will follow that same fox to see where it had been hunting. If a fox smells blood on a trap, or rust, or the scent of human beings, or dogs, or gasoline, it will, in many cases (if it has had a chance to learn) dig the trap up and turn it over. My husband does his best to keep the poachers, the trappers off our land, but every now and then I will find a set. So the foxes here are not only imprisoned by their needs, those winters spent without hibernation, and by the efficiency required to fulfill those needs, but by steel as well. When I think of foxes, it is usually with the memory of one running or trotting, looking over its shoulder at me with that bitter, haunting expression which seems to come from knowledge, although I think of them as well eating raspberries, or running for the joy of it, and of foxes giving themselves a little bath in sand or dry dirt. Sometimes, during the winter, after my husband and I have ridden to New York City in our Buick, I will see a beautiful woman wearing a cape or a short coat made of fox, and I will be able to hear for a moment that strident, confined call of a vixen in winter, when she is able to call, to make her desires noticed, and I can feel, too, in that same instant, the pain of the woman's beauty, and it will seem right, for a while, that she should be dressed in the skin of such a confined, imprisoned creature.

Chip Mackinnon

Homecoming. 1946.

In the prison camp there were eight of us in a hut. When you looked outside you saw acres of tree stumps on the other side of the barbed wire. We cooked over a small stove, waited for the Red Cross boxes, and amused ourselves. Ansell Augustus, the pilot from Texas, received his correspondence course to be a disc jockey and soon he was on the camp's P.A. system, playing Frank Sinatra records. We also had to watch for what were called ferrets: these were Germans who climbed under the huts and listened to what was being said. One morning, when I was up at the usual hour, listening to Ansell Augustus brush his hair, I looked over the side of my bed and saw a finger poke through a knothole in the floor. Of course everyone in the hut was awake, and all of us noticed the ferret's finger at the same time, even Ansell, who continued to brush his hair. As I sat there, looking at that finger probe around, and as Ansell slowly made his way to the knife he had hidden in the wall near the stove, I was thinking about the time my father caught a poacher on his land. It was at hunting season, and I must have been sixteen. We watched that moving finger, which was just trying to feel what was there: only a ferret could be stupid enough to stick a finger in a hole just because he had found one.

"Come on, you little pissant," said my father, "I'll bet there are poachers in Trout Cabin. Take your rifle."

I took from the case in the farmhouse a Mannlicher-Shoenauer my father had given to me. It had set triggers (this means it had two triggers, the first to set, or make quite delicate, the other) and was compact, light, and accurate, not to mention (as my father had) expensive. There were a number of my father's friends (which is to say, lawyers and business associates) who had come to hunt, but my father decided that just the two of us should look into the shot we had heard coming from Trout Cabin. I put the Mannlicher, which had a sling, over my shoulder, and walked behind my father, who was already half-filled with bourbon and anticipation of having someone at his mercy.

On my father's land there is a gorge, which at its deepest is over five hundred feet, and through which there runs a stream. There are a number of falls over bluestone or fieldstone ledges, and a couple of deep pools where there are brook trout. When my father said Trout Cabin he meant the stream, the gorge, and the land on either side of it. The ledges of bluestone and slate are stepped, and this makes the water fall in a series of white arcs (or arc in arc, silk water topped by fluff).

"Goddamned poachers," said my father, turning that satchel of a face toward me and squinting a little. "And by the way, stop pissing around with my razor. If you need one, which I doubt, I'll buy you one. Are you blushing?"

"No," I said, fingering the cool leather strap of the rifle.

"That's good. You know those goddamned poachers will shoot bears, too. Not to mention the deer. And you know what they do with a deer? They grind the thing up and mix it with pork for hamburgers. Hamburgers, for Christ's sake. Does that sound good to you?"

"No," I said.

He was still squinting at me.

"If there's any deer shot it will be by my leave. Will you shoot one?"

"I like venison," I said.

"That's good," said my father, "and brandy, and cigars made in Cuba."

"I don't like cigars," I said.

"You will," said my father, "but don't get the idea you own the place. You're just as much a stranger here as anyone else. I'm watching you."

He opened up one eye and made it large: it looked as though he were staring at me through a fishbowl.

"You don't own a thing," said my father.

"That's right," I said.

"Then how come you're driving my Buick when I'm not around?" he said.

"I wanted to go someplace," I said.

My father sighed and blew up the satchels of his face, and said, "Do you know why I had boys?"

"No," I said, looking away from him. The frost had started in earnest and the ferns had turned the color of gingerbread.

"They're easier on me than dogs. Every time I had a dog that I'd just got broken in right, it would die on my hands."

I was watching the sky, which was a faded blue, more like a shirt of that color which had been washed a hundred times. I smelled the faint mossy odor in the mist that rose from Trout Cabin.

"At least that was the theory," said my father, "although you seem to be proving me wrong."

"I'm not going to die," I said, watching him against that gray landscape.

"I didn't mean the dying part," he said, "and don't be too sure on that score, either."

"I can't promise about the Buick."

"Well, I can promise you that if I catch you, there isn't going to be any need for promises."

He turned in those leaves, seemed to cheer up at the prospect of a trespasser, and said, "Come on. Goddamned poachers."

The poacher had made a mistake, and that's why we caught him. He was young, about my age, and he was wearing a cloth, corduroy cap, a red coat (which was wet), and a pair of pants with holes in them. He had a black, thin beard, pale skin, and dark eyes. He was blowing on his hands and his teeth were chattering. At his feet, next to the stream, was a spike buck. The poacher's mistake had been the way he approached the land, or at least the way he had approached this spike buck. There is a large piece of land on the far side of Trout Cabin, covered with white oak and jack pine, and no one goes there very often. The boy knew this, and he came onto the land from the far side and that meant he was facing Trout Cabin, the gorge, when he saw the deer: when he shot, the buck fell into the bottom of the stream. So that meant he had to climb down after it (this isn't easy, especially if you're carrying a rifle) and drag it out of the water (which isn't warm anytime, and certainly not warm in November). The boy's pants were wet, too, and he had been wearing a pair of cotton work gloves for warmth, and they were damp, as well. The boy had been carrying a 30/30, lever action, pitted and rusted. When we came over the ridge and stared down at the boy he stopped blowing on his hands, took a knife from his pocket, and started gutting the deer.

"Let him finish," said my father.

The water in Trout Cabin was noisy, and the boy went about his work, not hearing us and not looking up. He worked quickly.

"Chip," said my father, "what are you going to do about this?"

"I thought it was your land," I said.

"That's right," said my father. "What are you going to do about it?"

I looked down at the boy in the wet red jacket, the old cap and torn pants. He was pulling the gray and reddish paunch out of the deer.

"Is that rifle loaded?" said my father.

He pointed to the Mannlicher.

"Yes," I said.

"Have you got a round chambered?" he said.

"No," I said.

"Well," he said, "chamber a round."

I did so and put on the safety, and my father looked at me with his bourbon nose and hangdog face and said, "You take care of this," said my father. "Look at the kid's rifle. Some kind of cheap shit thing."

We walked down into the gorge, my father staying behind me, whispering in my ear occasionally, making sure I understood him. I saw the water above the boy, arced, slick, looking in the places between the falls like a large piece of silk that was spread over a floor. The rhododendron were still green, and there were some tall spruce growing near the brook.

The boy looked up. He stared at us for a while, and then took his rifle, that pitted and rusted 30/30, and hid it in some brush that was growing at the side of the stream. He did this quickly and not well, so we could still see most of it. The boy went back to staring at us, his eyes following us as we worked our way down the bank. He couldn't stop shivering, though, and I saw his teeth chattering.

"Can I help you?" I said.

There was a lot of splashy tumbling from the stream, and the boy was on the other side so it was hard for him to hear, but my father was standing right next to me.

"Chip," he said, "what in hell is wrong with you? You want to *help* him?"

"What?" said the boy, still staring directly at me. He was cold, but he kept staring right through the chattering.

"You can leave the deer right there," I said.

"That's better," said my father.

"You're Mackinnon, aren't you?" said the boy.

"What the hell are you doing in here?" I said.

The boy looked at the deer and then up and said, "It's like this.

By the way, my name's Moore. I'm from up river, and I was invited over to hunt at Stuart's. This isn't Stuart's?"

Stuart's was the piece of land that bordered my father's.

"Don't let him friendly you up," said my father.

"Stuart's is a quarter of a mile away," I said.

"Is that right?" said the boy.

The deer was lying at his feet, its head thrown back, its gray fur wet and steaming a little, too, as the heat left the animal's body. The steam from the deer and the paunch mixed with the slight mist that came from Trout Cabin. Moore picked up his knife and wiped it on his trousers.

"Then I guess this is your deer," said Moore. He spit near its head. Moore picked up his rifle, too, and knocked some of the leaves off its stock and barrel. He took off his gloves and wrung them out and then put them in his pocket.

"Then I guess it's all a mistake," said Moore, still staring. "Wasn't much of a buck, anyway."

"Bark, Chip," said my father, "what the hell's wrong with you?"

"You knew where you were," I said.

"Is that right?" said Moore, his face now drawn into a smile which showed his teeth and made his pocked skin stretch.

"Don't let him be so goddamned friendly," said my father.

Moore held his rifle and smiled, and said, "I don't think you'll have me arrested, not over this mistake. Let's call it a difference of opinion. So I think I'll just walk down the stream here."

"Son of a bitch," said my father.

Moore looked at the still-warm buck, and then turned, began to walk down to the Delaware.

"Wait a minute," said my father.

Moore turned again, still shivering, carrying that rifle, and wearing his wet cap. Beyond him there was the leaf-covered contour of the gorge.

"What kind of cheap shit rifle is that?" said my father.

Moore looked down at the 30/30, which was cradled in his arm, and his lower lip began to tremble. He stood just a little way from the dead deer, the fur now darker than its usual gray timber color, and when he looked up, he wasn't smiling at all, not even in that showman's parody of it. His face was drawn and he seemed surprised. So he looked at the rifle I carried and at my father and said, "I think I better be getting along."

"And stay the hell out," said my father.

I watched as Moore went along Trout Cabin, his head down now, obviously just wanting to get to the county road at the Delaware as quickly as possible. I could almost hear his voice over the noise of the stream, and see his lips moving in his pale face as he said, I've got no land, you old son of a bitch. And that was my brother's rifle and he left it out in the rain when he got drunk and there wasn't much bluing to begin with.

"We should have had the sheriff," said my father. "He's probably got brothers, and soon we'll have every piece of scum up here shooting deer off my land."

The last bit of Moore's red coat disappeared as he pushed into the woods below us. My father gave me his satchel face, his courtroom mahogany eyes.

"Well, Chip," he said, "what did you learn?"

"If you want to arrest someone," I said, "don't let him pick up a rifle first."

"Ha!" said my father, "my little scorpion, that's right. And do you know why you didn't think of that right away?"

"No," I said, although I had my suspicions.

"Because you don't own a goddamned thing," said my father. "Now get this buck taken care of. When you get up to the house I'll let you have a drink."

My father filled his jowls with air, gave me that large smile of angry satisfaction, and then started to climb over the bluestone ridges, up the side of Trout Cabin, being careful about where he put his fingers (Trout Cabin was filled with copperheads) even though there had already been a good frost.

There is a small button on the Mannlicher, next to the port: I pushed it and the bright, almost Christmas-like cartridges (bright brass and copper) filled my hand. I put them into my pocket and crossed the stream. The buck was still cooling, steaming some. Its horns weren't more than three inches, rippled like a stalagmite, and they had the color of nicotine stains. I took the rope from the pouch of my jacket, and put it under the deer's chest, feeling the hole where the bullet went in and where it came out, too. I made one loop around the rib cage and one around the neck. The entrails steamed a little and the mist from them still mixed, or folded into the mist from Trout Cabin. I could feel with my hand the heat as it lifted away from the deer's body. It was always dark in Trout Cabin, at the bottom anyway: you'd have to be down there at noon in early summer to get any light on you. There was a jungled, damp as mushrooms, quality about the air and soil. As a matter of fact, there were mushrooms there in the spring and fall, and some even in the snow: red and yellow ones, some pale as parchment, all having that old rubber quality, a spongy ease of crumbling. So there wasn't much light, and what there was had that dawn or dusk quality, a smoky, veiled aspect, the colors all being a shade darker than usual: bark the color of ground coffee, water that was deep-sea green, vines and creepers that looked black as telephone cable. I put the Mannlicher over my left shoulder and the rope over the other and began to pull the deer down to the Delaware, hearing, as I went, the deer's legs drag in the leaves, and feeling the loose, floppy movement of it when we went over a stone or around a stump. As you went down to the Delaware, as Trout Cabin flattened out, there were some large trees, easily a hundred feet or more high, mostly spruce, and they must have been twelve feet around. There was moss on the ground, which was quite green in the misty, veiled light. I dragged the dead animal under those trees, over the ground, and walking that way, working with the buck didn't make me feel any less a stranger. I stopped when I was almost at the mouth of the stream and saw the Delaware. It was wind-scaled and shiny, indifferent. When I dragged the buck out by the road and left it in some dead ferns, I noticed that because of the rope it had a packaged quality, the aspect of something that was going to be mailed.

There is a highway which runs along the Delaware, and I walked out to it, looked at the river, which seemed wide there. There was a cool breeze and weak sunlight. Moore was standing on the same side of the road, about a hundred feet from the mouth of Trout Cabin. There was that blue mist rising from the river, and through it I saw that red and wet jacket, the old trousers, and the cap. He was still carrying that 30/30. It was probably four in the afternoon, not so late as to be dusk, but the shadows were long, and not distinct, because of the blue mist. Moore seemed to be pacing back and forth, but in fact was slowly working his way in my direction. The afternoon light made his pale skin, that foxfire complexion, seem buzzing, or indistinct, as though his face were made of moving moth wings. I stared at him for a moment as he paced back and forth like some odd sentry, never going back to the point where he began and always coming a little farther than where he last stopped. Occasionally he took a pint from his back pocket and had a small drink, and then went back to his pacing in the mist, blue light and long shadows.

I left the buck at the side of the road and began to walk back to the farm to get a pickup that was usually parked in the barn. Moore stopped, looked at the river, and took a long drink from his pint.

The farm was deserted when I got there, since everyone was out on a drive, which is to say, three or four men had taken stands, and the others were walking through the woods, pushing deer to those who were waiting.

My brother had come to hunt as well, and he was in the woods with Pop and the others. John and I were sharing a room and I looked into it. On the nightstand next to John's bed, or on his side of it anyway, were ten or twelve scraps of paper that the housekeeper had written messages on and left for him. John accepted every invitation he received, no matter from whom or for what, and decided, as late as possible, where he was going to spend a weekend, or dance, or dine. He didn't bother telling those he was going to stand up: his absence was the evidence they had of it. There were also in the room two hams which he had won from the housekeeper at cribbage and a pile of pornographic magazines he had won from Wade in a small two-handed poker game. My brother had learned to be a snob at Groton, but now he was at Yale, although the card-playing continued. Now he spent his weekends in Syracuse, Schenectady, or Hartford, and carried a .38 in a fancy shoulder holster. In the closet in a green metal box that came from a business supply house there was six thousand dollars. Recently, John had been trying to get my father into high-stakes card games, although he hadn't been successful. My father was afraid of John, not because of the cards, but because John might cut him, might turn up his nose at one of my father's *gaffes*. I taught John to use the .38. When he bought it, before going to New Haven (and in anticipation of those poker games in those middle-sized industrial towns of New York and Connecticut), he brought it up here and said, "Do you know how to shoot a pistol?" "In theory," I said. "Well," he said with a smile, "you better give me the theory." We went to the gravel pit and shot the thing until its barrel was too hot to touch, waited, and went at it again. John never could handle it, but he said, "It makes a nice ache under the arm. And no one else knows I can't shoot it."

I stood in the room which was filled with our collective debris: two copies of Herodotus (we were going to argue with Pop about the size of Xerxes' army), stained trousers, red shirts, dirty long underwear. I left a note for John which read, "Received from John Mackinnon, two hams and five pornographic magazines. Chip Mackinnon," and then took the hams back to the pantry, and the magazines back to Wade. Wade stood at his door, took the magazines, and threw them onto the bed which was behind him.

"Thanks," he said. "What about a movie? Maybe tonight?"

"If I can get away," I said.

"Good," said Wade. He waited for a minute and then gestured to the magazines on the bed. "She could show up there, too."

"Who?" I said. "You mean the girl, the woman we look for in the movies?"

"Yes," said Wade.

He sat down on his bed and pushed the magazines onto the floor.

"Let's see if we can make that movie tonight," I said. "When everyone's getting drunk."

Wade watched as I went downstairs and into the garage. I opened the door and took the truck, a '32 Chevrolet, to pick up the deer the poacher had shot.

The truck was black, rusted along the bottom of the door and fenders, and it sounded like a tractor because it didn't have a muffler, but even though there was so much play in the wheel you could hardly tell where you were going, you sat high up and watched the landscape bounce around you. The truck ran well, as though running had become a habit, and once started, there was no stopping it. The truck didn't have any windows, and the air was cold. I drove along the Delaware and stopped next to the mouth of Trout Cabin.

Moore was still there, now not much more than thirty feet away, but he was making it clear that he was standing on the shoulder of the road, on public property. He was still shivering and staring at me, not with a smile, or anything like one. When I went back into the brush to pick up that buck, he came closer, although not actually off the road. The waiting hadn't warmed him up: his lips were the color of a bad bruise, and his skin was pale. Every now and then he glanced at the pitted rifle and then at me. He ran his finger over the rusted spots on the barrel and the scratches in the stock. The deer was where I had left it, and seemed undisturbed, still looking trussed, packaged. When I bent over to pick up the rope and haul the deer to the truck I smelled on the buck's dark coat the distinct stench of urine. The rope was wet, too. I had left it dry.

Moore was standing by the truck.

"Up there," he said, pointing into the woods, "I said it was just a misunderstanding, but I knew where I was."

The pint bottle had about a third left in it: peach or apricot brandy. It was the color of polished brass. Moore had another sip, and it seemed to help him, since he'd stopped shivering. He put the pint away and worked the lever of the 30/30, and I saw a shell rise from the magazine to the chamber. The hammer was back.

"Somebody pissed on your buck," he said.

"Why don't you get out of here," I said.

"This ain't yours," he said, gesturing to the shoulder of the road. "I can stay here all day."

"All right," I said, "stay."

The sky over Moore's shoulder was the color of wood smoke. No one was on the road, or at least on the long section that I was able to see. I started to walk back to the deer, but Moore said, "Wait a minute."

He moved the rifle back and forth across my stomach, pointed it at my face: I could feel for a moment the distant sky, the nausea, and the shattered bones, the sense of my head having lost its shape.

"So you think it's cheap shit," said Moore.

He moved the barrel so that it swung over my stomach, genitals, knees.

"Go away," I said. "You haven't got business here."

"Sure I do," said Moore, with a little of that smile coming into his grim face, lifting that pocked skin. "We're getting to be acquainted and friendly. This way, when we meet in the woods again, we'll understand one another a little better."

"I think we understand each other," I said.

Moore drank some more of that liquor, and it made him gag a little.

"No," said Moore, "we ain't friends yet. The next time you find me in the woods, you just give me a wide berth. Or if you say anything or stop by, it'll just be to kiss my ass and tell me how sweet it is."

Beyond Moore there was the wall of the gorge of Trout Cabin, a high wall of fieldstone, gray and hard, the color of that dead buck's eye. I heard the idiot's babble made by the brook. Moore was waiting, and I glanced at the barrel of his rifle, and between the pits and the rusted spots there was some writing, names engraved with an electric needle which had been ordered through the mail.

"Now is that more friendly?" he said.

"Whatever you say," I said.

Moore smiled and said, "And you were calling it cheap shit."

He waved the rifle around some more, and I felt the bore as it swung from my head to my knees, crossing stomach and chest: it was an odd sense of emptiness, similar to what you'd feel if you were standing next to an open (but unused) casket.

From where I stood I saw a mile or so of the road as it followed the river in those long bends, and at the farthest point there was a truck, a flatbed. It was coming toward us.

"You don't want any trouble, do you?" said Moore.

"No," I said.

That truck was moving slowly, and I could almost hear the sound it made, or thought I could.

"But you did before, when you first smelled it, didn't you?" said Moore.

"Yes," I said. "Someone's coming."

"Let them come," said Moore, taking another sip from his pint. His face was beginning to lighten, too, away from that moth-wing color. "Are you going to go to one of those schools? You know, that one like the lock. That Yale."

"Probably," I said.

"Do you have a sport?" said Moore.

"I row," I said.

"What?" said Moore.

"A scull," I said.

"What's that?" said Moore.

"A boat," I said.

We stood in that smoky, bluish light, felt the cool breeze. Moore shivered. The river was that same smoky color, too, and a couple of ducks were flying down it, just skimming the surface, quacking, working small wings. Wood ducks. I saw their orangish bills.

"Well," said Moore, "now that we're friendly, and you understand about the woods, and how they're going to be from now on, and I know about your rowing a boat, and your deer's been freshened, why don't we shake hands? Like friends, you know."

He smiled and moved the rifle from his right hand to his left. The pint was in his back pocket. He was awkward with his left hand, and the barrel waved around, the muzzle passing my face and chest and then back again. The hammer was still back. Moore put out his hand, which was stained with the buck's blood.

"There," he said.

Up the river, in that bluish smoke that seemed to be absorbing landscape, trees, everything but the Delaware, which now had the appearance of tarnished silver, the truck coasted and backfired, once, and then regularly, Bam, Bam, Bam: it sounded like distant antiaircraft fire.

I took Moore's damp hand and shook it. He held on, and looked at me and smiled, while still moving that rifle with the cocked hammer. I saw the names engraved on the barrel, "Billy,""Cathy," "Joe," "Ann," "Mike," and some shapes, too, hearts, diamonds, spades. The truck seemed to have speeded up a little and wasn't more than a hundred yards away. I pulled from Moore, but he squeezed a little.

"What's wrong?" he said. "Too good to shake a friend's hand?"

"No," I said.

We shook hands for a moment longer, and then Moore let go.

"Don't you feel better?" said Moore.

"Get out of here," I said.

Moore smiled. I started to walk around the truck and to the deer. Moore didn't stop me, although he still had the rifle pointed at my head. When I was next to the cab, Moore looked inside and said, "What kind of gun is that? Why's it got them funny triggers?"

"They're set," I said.

"Why's it got two?" said Moore. "And that funny-looking stock?"

"I'll show you," I said.

Moore pushed that muzzle at me and said, "That's all right."

The truck that had been coming along the river road pulled onto the shoulder above Trout Cabin. It was blue, and had a flatbed, and a piece of plywood behind the cab with a hole in it so you could see through the rearview mirror.

"I don't know whether to shoot you or burn down your house," said Moore.

He looked over his shoulder for a moment and glanced at the truck, the blue one with the flatbed. A man who was about thirty was driving, and he must have been Moore's brother: the features were the same, only the driver's were just older and a little thinner. There were a couple of other men on the bed both also wearing red, torn coats and caps. They carried rifles, too. On the right hand side of the cab there sat an older man, around fifty, although it was difficult to be sure about it: he had short hair, a wide face with features that were asymmetrical, so he could alternately appear as charming as a southern politician and as mean as a lead pipe kept under the seat. He was wearing a blue coat with a brown collar and a blanket lining. The older man stepped out of the cab, and when he did so he walked with a penguin's gait, leaning on one leg and then the other, keeping each one straight, as though he had no knees. He was bareheaded, and his hair was the same color as the mist that came from Trout Cabin.

Moore looked at the man and then back at me. His face was just taut now.

As the older man walked from the truck I saw that at one time someone had tried to murder him, and hadn't made a very neat job of it, either: there were four or five scars on the side of his neck, each one a white welt (the color of white satin), and the scars looked like they could have only been made by a dull knife (maybe a kitchen tool, a paring knife, which would mean that the scars were a woman's work) or a saw blade, but certainly not by anything that had been made for the job. The scars were white because they were old, but they still seemed mean, and they were worn with thorough indifference: there was something in the color that suggested timelessness and the brightness of lightning seen against a gray sky. There was also something in the man's features, in the color of his lips and teeth, his eyebrows and hair, which had the same aspect as the whiteness of the scars. When the man stood next to Moore and looked at him, his eyes were filled with the expression of wild and cruel disbelief: it almost seemed as though his eyes were scarred themselves.

"Gene," he said gently, "what's the matter?"

Moore looked stricken, as though his features were made of cloth and had been held together by a fist and the fist had just let go: his face was blank with terror.

"This boy's been giving me trouble," said Moore.

The man went into the brush a bit and stared at the deer and came back.

"Who's that?" I said to Moore.

"My father," he said.

"That's right," said the man. "Gene's my boy. As are those boys on the truck. Now what's the trouble?"

"He was pushing me out of here," said Gene.

When the man had been speaking of his sons, his expression had been bland, but now his eyes were edged again with that disbelief and cruelty. He stood next to Moore, and said, "You shot that deer?"

"Yes," said Moore.

"You mean to tell me that you shot a deer on his land and now you're menacing him with a gun?" said Moore's father.

Moore looked at me. The man at the wheel of the truck and those who had been riding on the bed turned their heads very slightly in Moore's direction, but none got off the bed and the driver didn't open the door.

"Well," said Moore's father, "Gene, if you're going to shoot him, you better tell me. Joe can dig the hole."

"No," said Moore, putting the rifle down a little, moving the muzzle from my face.

"No?" said his father. "You mean you aren't going to shoot him?"

Moore reached for his pint and tried to have a sip, but his father took it (with hands that had that same whitish quality) and put it in his own back pocket. His father took the rifle, too, and he did so with a damaged gentleness, which lingered as he worked the lever and ejected all the shells that had been in the tube: each one, new and having the aspect of nautical clocks and barometers (that bright brass and copper), turned once and fell to the ground. The earth there was gray dust. There were four of them and they lay next to Moore's father's boots, which were new and cheap.

"Pick them up," said Moore's father.

Moore kneeled in his wet, yellowish trousers and his wet coat and began picking them up, first rubbing a shell until it shone before putting it into his pocket and reaching for another, never looking up. His hands were almost the same color as the dust, the fingers and thumbs chapped by the cold. The shells seemed bright and they took a shine. Moore picked up one and then another and the next, kneeling so that he was in front of his father and sideways: his ear and the side of his head were exposed. Moore rubbed the last shell and looked at it, seeing, I suppose, the elongated reflection of his father, those ironlike pants with the red lines in them, the red shirt and blue jacket with the brown collar. Moore put the last cartridge in his pocket with the others and I heard the faint click as the last hit those already there. His father didn't move and Moore waited for just a second, his hands spread out on that gray earth.

Moore's father closed the action of the rifle, let down the hammer, and stood next to his son, looking at him with a sad, disbelieving, and hurt expression. Moore started to get up. His father raised the rifle and brought it down with one quick motion. The stock hit Moore on the ear and on his head above it. Moore didn't scream or yelp, but covered his ear and the side of his head as he fell onto his side. He lay there for a minute, trying to rock back and forth, even though he was on his side, but he couldn't move much in that gray dust. His brothers still didn't budge from the truck, although all of them watched him. After a minute Moore sat up, and was then able to rock back and forth.

"Don't you ever point a rifle at a man unless you intend to use it," said Moore's father. "Do you understand me?"

Moore's father raised the stock of the 30/30, and Moore tried to squirm away from those new and cheap boots, and tried, too, to acknowledge what he had been told, but he got confused, and sometimes he nodded and the rest of the time he shook his head, so that more than anything else he made a halting circular motion. After a while he stopped and held the side of his ear. He made some small noise.

"What's that, Gene?" said his father.

"I heard you," said Moore.

"Well, that's good," said Moore's father. "I'm glad."

As Moore tried to get away from those boots I heard the clink of the cartridges in his pocket. Moore tried to stand, but he began to tip over before he could get his legs together.

"Joe," said Moore's father to one of the men who were silently watching and smoking cigarettes. "Get Gene to the truck. He seems to be ailing."

Moore looked up at me once, but he didn't really see me: the high stones behind me, the cool air, the dirt, those evergreens and the oaks which were forked and bare, his father's new boots, his father and brothers, and I had become part of that hot ear, dizziness, and nausea. Joe was the one who had been driving, and he and one other walked from the truck and picked Moore up. When he was on the bed of the truck, his legs stretched out before him and his back and head propped up on the piece of plywood behind the cab, Moore's father said to me, "You're Mackinnon, aren't you?"

"Yes, sir," I said.

"Sir?" said Moore's father. He opened his eyes and showed me that white-edged and hard wonder. "Sir? Boy, you don't have to say that to anyone. You own the land. Is that clear?"

"Yes," I said, feeling the cool breeze, the distance and indifference of the trees behind me, and seeing, too, that whitish mist rise from the surface of the Delaware.

"Good," said Moore's father, "then everything's as it should be."

Moore's father looked toward the buck and then at the rifle which he now carried in his hands: he wasn't the kind to have an accident. The action was open and the chamber was empty.

"Mackinnon," he said, "I'm sorry for your trouble."

He gave me one more funny look, which changed for a moment into that glare edged with white scar tissue, and then smiled and said, "I can tell you're that old rattlesnake's son. You stood up here just fine. You tell Pop Mackinnon that Mr. Moore sends his compliments along with that buck, hear?" He nodded at me and went back to the truck, walking with that stiff-legged, penguin's gait. When he was sitting on the right-hand side of the cab he gave a signal, and Joe started the engine and pulled onto the road. The truck wasn't really blue, but it had been, so now it was the color of the sky on a day when the sun will almost, but not quite, come out. Moore held his head when the truck started, but his brothers just stared at the river or at nothing. Moore's father waved and reached over to toot the horn. I watched as they drove away, the truck becoming smaller and smaller and more the same color as that white mist from the river until it was indistinguishable from it.

I went back to the brush and dragged the buck out and onto the bed of the Chevrolet. After the tailgate was up I went back to the cab and just sat down on the running board, putting my head against the door and pushing hard. There were some cigarettes in my pocket and I lighted one, thinking of my father, who said, "If you want to smoke, make it a cigar, and take it after dinner. Drink brandy with it. Tastes good that way."

There were some ducks skimming the water and I watched them. I wanted to stretch out in the woods someplace and sleep for a little, or maybe in the cab of the truck, but I didn't have the time. I sat on the running board.

John came out of the woods and walked to the truck. He was almost six feet, had dark hair and blue eyes, our mother's clear, smooth skin.

"Stand up," he said. "Chip, that won't do. You understand?"

"Yes," I said.

I stood up.

John raised an eyebrow when he saw my pale face: it was that gesture, the slight, that my father was afraid of.

"I'll drive," said John.

The ducks kept moving along, just skimming the surface of the river, but always keeping a course that was absolutely in the middle, even in the broad turns.

"There are rules," said John.

I was sitting next to him in the front. When he drove he did it with a definite style, one that was affected: it seemed as though he were demonstrating out of a training manual exactly how the thing should be done. As he drove he talked to me about my collars. He had found some shirts in the farmhouse and he thought the collars were too wide. I listened to him, and pushed my head against the metal cab of the truck, and said, "Pull over. I'll ride in the back with the deer."

"What's wrong?" he said.

"Nothing," I said. "I need some fresh air."

He raised his eyebrow again when I climbed out.

So John drove and I sat in the bed of the truck, trying to stay out of the wind and watching the buck, too, as we drove along the river and then up the farm road. There were lots of trees along the dirt road, and in the springtime and summer they formed a complete canopy, but now the trees were bare and had that shattered look. The buck's eye was open, and as we went along, under the trees the eye was alternately dark as fieldstone (or the deer's own fur) and blue and luminous (when a little of what was left of the light came through the trees), the eye almost winking, it seemed, but having something that was far more articulate than just a wink, a quality that was contradictory: knowledgeable and dead. I watched it blinking on and off (like some muted neon sign) and looked up when it stopped, being surprised to find that we were at the farm, under the tree in front of the house where the bucks were hung.

"Well, you little pissant," said my father, "you can have a drink. Just as soon as you do one thing for me."

"What's that?" I said, as we were hauling that buck out and stringing him up. Standing around us were some of my father's clients and other lawyers who had come to hunt. They wore vests and plus fours and one had on a tie.

"Some of my colleagues don't believe me when I tell them you can hit that piece of metal at a hundred yards."

My father pointed to a stone wall that was on the other side of the pond. The distance was a little over a hundred yards and against it there was an old frying pan. Sometimes my father made a man he didn't like shoot at it and hit it three times out of four before letting that man into the woods to hunt.

"Will you do it?" said my father.

I went into the cab of the truck and took the Mannlicher, pushed the shells into the wheeled magazine. The lawyers and guests stood behind me, holding their drinks and smoking cigars. The light was going fast, and I had a little trouble with the rear sight because of it. I looked around for a moment and noticed that my father had gone into the house. He was in the study with John and through the window I saw them having a drink, my father nodding (about something they were discussing) Yes, yes, yes. I held on that piece of metal and made it ring, and worked the bolt and made it ring, right through that now-blue dusk.

"Well, Mackinnon," said a man in plus fours when we had gone inside, "Chip can shoot."

"What?" said my father, "Oh. That. Yes. Get him a drink, would you?"

I sat on the front porch and drank my out-of-season mint julep and watched the trees in the orchard and beyond disappear. There were no fireflies and no turkeys, either, and the only deer around were hanging from the tree right next to the porch. I heard the voices inside, laughter, and I saw that yellowish and warm light from the house.

Usually John had left by the second day of the hunt, but this year he stayed until the end. On the Saturday night before we were going back to school, and after I had come back from the movies with Wade, John and I sat in our room, even though the others had been cleaned and we could have gone back to our usual arrangement. John stretched out on his bed and looked at his copy of Herodotus. The house was quiet.

"Don't stare at people," John said. "It distracts them."

"Oh," I said.

It occurred to me that John had an accent, one that was both clipped and languid. I thought about being at the Delaware, about the ducks just skimming the water.

"Have you ever had someone point a gun at you?" I said.

"No," said John. "It's not one of the things I look forward to, either."

"What's wrong with my shirts?" I said.

"I told you," he said. "The collars are too broad."

I listened to his voice, that accent, the certainty there. Then I went out into the hall and downstairs. There was a light on in my father's study and I opened the gun case and took out an L. C. Smith 12 gauge. The room had the comfortable smell of leather and cigars. I sat down in one of the chairs and opened the breech of the shotgun and saw that the bore was smooth, shiny, recently cleaned. There was the odor of Hoppes gun oil in the room. I carried the L. C. Smith upstairs. John was lying on the bed and I put the muzzle against his temple, just hard enough for him to know what it was.

"What does it feel like?" I said.

"Nothing at all," said John. "You know better than this." He raised an eyebrow, but he didn't move away: it was this gesture he had perfected. Superior, aloof, and with the weight that correctness can carry. "We were taught about guns early on. You know the rules, don't you?"

I shook my head and thought, Smug and certain, too.

"What does it feel like?" I said.

"Nothing," said John, "since you won't pull the trigger. It's not done."

We were aware of the silence of the house, of its size, the long halls upstairs, and the rooms off it that were only filled with furniture. John turned his eyes toward me, but to do so he had to look along the barrels, which needed to be blued and had the color of tobacco. I'm sure John smelled the odor of Hoppes oil. The shotgun had double triggers, and each one had a smooth surface, and each was spring loaded, restrained. The firing pin slipped forward, toward the chamber, and it made a small click which echoed down the barrel. John pulled away.

"Sleep tight, John," I said, as I took the shotgun downstairs and put it away. I was almost sick in the fireplace, and then I came upstairs again. John was still reading, looking as though he hadn't missed a line, but the world was no longer such a pretty place for him. There are times I think that the explosion which hit his plane over the tire factory in Germany began with that click we both heard in the barrels of that L. C. Smith shotgun. Formality was not the same for me, either: afterward, when I dressed for dinner, when I put on starched linen or black tie, I felt in the white cloth, in the fabric of evening clothes a hollow, ringing ache. In the morning, John was gone by the time I woke, and he left a note that read, "Received from Chip Mackinnon, one healthy shock. John Mackinnon."

During the next year we didn't see each other. Although, when John's winnings in those games in Hartford and Schenectady and New Haven rose beyond a certain point he made a package of dirty bills and sent them to me, usually with a note that said, "Keep this." After I'd received one of these, and when I was at the farm, I took a can from the dump (Canadian preserves, coffee, or Iranian caviar), wrapped the money in wax paper, put it inside, and dipped the can in paraffin. I went into the woods with a compass, picked a tree or a rock for a heading, and buried the coffee or preserve or caviar tin. I made a map the first time I did this, and improved it each time another one of those packages showed up. The first one had a thousand dollars in it, and the others (five in all) seemed to have about the same weight. I put the map in a can, too, and left it on a rafter at the top of the cow barn that had been turned into a garage. The bats roosted next to the can. When I was burying the money, or receiving the packages I wasn't curious, although after I realized that John had said, "Keep this," rather than "Keep this for me," I knew that he was preparing for my troubles rather than his, or that he had forgiven me for something I hadn't yet done. The last bundle had a note which read, "You haven't met her but you already miss her? Isn't that right? Keep this." I buried that bundle, marked the map, and put it in the can next to the bats. I had plenty of time to think about the last note later, after I had met her and was driving around the country with her in that Buick with the wicker seats, the girl beside me and her luggage piled behind us. She didn't have much luggage. One small suitcase and a box tied together with string. "It's an Oklahoma Gladstone," she said, when I picked it up and put it in the car.

So, when I saw the ferret's finger push through the knot in the floorboard of the prison camp hutch, I was thinking about the light in Trout Cabin, the poacher there, the water that fell over the fieldstone steps like a piece of green silk, the expression on my brother's face when he heard the click in the barrels of that L. C. Smith shotgun, and the coffee can (with the map inside) on the beam hung with bats. Ansell Augustus read from the announcer's manual, practiced diction for a hair oil ("You don't want to be a flyaway . . . ") as he stepped across the room and took the knife from its hiding place above the stove.

We all turned on our sides. The ferret's finger was searching, still poking around. The knife had been ground from a piece of iron plate and it was heavy, certainly heavy enough for Ansell as he lifted it up and brought it down, cutting the finger neatly off at the first knuckle from the hand. The rest of the finger disappeared, was pulled back into the space beneath the hutch. There wasn't much blood. All of us listened for a noise, a shout or a groan or a yell, but there wasn't anything aside from the scurrying sound as the ferret worked his way from under the hutch, and began walking toward one of the guard towers, moving in that first grainy light of dawn, one hand holding the other, still not making any sound, as though trying to say to those on whom he had been spying, I'm not here, I'm not here. When Ansell saw that the ferret was walking away from the hutch he stood for a moment with the heavy knife in one hand and the brush in the other and began to tell us about how Raven Malone (a skater) smoked Camels and found them enjoyable, and then, when the ferret was about a hundred yards away, Ansell took the end of the knife and flicked the finger into the hole out of which it had come. He put the knife back in the slot behind the stove and went back to brushing his hair. I listened to that repetitive noise (it sounded like an old man breathing) and looked into that atmosphere which had the aspect of film that was underexposed and only half-developed. In the distance I saw the ferret walking, still holding his hand, but not

making a sound, obviously too embarrassed to admit that there
was anything wrong: for a while he walked back and forth in front
of the wire, one hand in the other, silently shaking his head and
hopping up and down.

The ferret lost his finger the week before the guards disappeared. One morning we noticed that the gate was open. I stood
before the space beyond it, and was able to feel the absence of
wire. It made a strange ache, but I stood there, not stepping out.
Everyone was thin, and the rations had been light recently, and
more than anything else the sense of clarity that came from being
so hungry was an illusion. I wanted to step out, but I sat down in
the dust and squeezed my head. After a while I denied that oddly
nauseating ache caused by the empty space beyond and turned
back to the camp. Others did not wait and were shot on the road.
In a few days, a jeep pulled up, and in it was an officer I knew, a
man who had been in my brother's class at New Haven and from
whom my brother had won three thousand dollars. My brother
had also taken the officer's girl friend. I sat in the dust before the
gate as the officer approached, and then I stood and made my
manners while the officer recognized me, looked sour, and walked
into the center of the camp.

I was flown to New Jersey on a hospital plane in which there
weren't very many sick men, and I was lucky, too, to find a taxi
to drive me the thirty miles to Manhattan. The springs were gone
and the seats were worn out. I was wearing a pair of khaki trousers
which were clean but not pressed, a green jacket without insignia,
and a shirt which was too big. I was wearing a tie and a cap. We
drove up Park Avenue and the taxi stopped in front of the apartment building which had (on the floors where my father and
mother lived) the imitation Mexican garden complete with a sky-
light that was nothing more than some blue glass with light bulbs
behind it. Halfway up the walls of the garden there were two
layers of terra-cotta tile and above them a painting of blue sky with
a couple of white clouds and a bird with some red and yellow

plumage. In a tub there was a small orange tree which every year or so would have oranges a little bigger than marbles. My father liked to sit there in the late afternoon and drink a Carta Blanca or a Dos Equis.

It was early evening when I rang the bell, after having taken off my cap and tucked it under my arm. There was no one to answer the door, so my father did it himself, being, I suppose, a little angry that a neighbor was going to bother him (thinking this, of course, because the doorman hadn't announced anyone). He was wearing a blue suit and a white shirt, a dark red tie and dark brown shoes. He looked older and a little sour.

"Son of a bitch," he said, "what happened to your hair?"

"It fell out," I said.

"Well," he said, "it doesn't matter. I'll buy you some more."

My father took one of my hands in both of his, which were thick, and had large fingers. He pumped my hand up and down and squeezed hard. His face seemed to collapse a little, or to fold into its creases. He closed his eyes and blew up his cheeks and made a flat, dimpled chin. There wasn't much moisture in the folds around his eyes, but he was crying. He said something with his chin still puckered, but I wasn't able to hear, so I bent closer to him and said, "Father? What did you say?"

"I can't say that it improves your appearance," he said.

"No," I said. "I suppose not."

"You know John's dead?" he said.

"Yes," I said.

"That's good," said my father. "He got shot down over a tire factory."

"I didn't know that," I said.

My father nodded, and gave me a hug, and then led me into the living room where he asked with that puckered chin if I wanted a drink, which I did want, and then he put his head against my chest and said, "Goddamned tire factory."

"Pop, Pop," I said.

"You're not old enough to call me that," he said.

He went to a bar which was on a mahogany chest and began to make the drinks, occasionally rubbing his bald head and looking at me. It wasn't that I was bald so much as the hair I had was a lot flatter than it used to be.

"Goddamn," said my father, "I better get your mother," but she was already there, standing in the doorway of that living room with the striped wall paper and the white woodwork. It wasn't that she jumped up and down, but she couldn't quite be still, as she held my arms and pushed her head against me, almost whimpering, but not quite being able to do so.

"Why didn't you call me?" she said to my father. "Why didn't you?"

"I was confused," said my father, making that puckered chin again.

"Are you all right?" said my mother, "Is there anything that can be done? Is there anything you need?"

We stood close to one another and stared. I shook my head. My father gave me a drink, and I told them about making liquor from Red Cross raisins and sugar. They stared. I walked through the living room and dining room and into the kitchen. My father was behind me and he said, "If there's anything you don't see, don't stand on ceremony. I'm not a man who likes to go without so I stocked up with cigars and brandy and a bunch of goddamned canned junk and Hershey bars." His chin was pitted and flat again. "I can't show you the cases right now."

My father went into the imitation Mexican garden and sat under the blue glass. I looked in at him and then went up the staircase at the end of the hall. The stairs were more like something you'd find in a lighthouse, made of metal, and all coming off one post. There was a railing, too, and the stairs were painted white. I climbed them and came into a corridor which had gray walls and carpet, and a white ceiling, not to mention that faintly musty smell of home. There were some prints on the walls, large renderings of flowers (from some scientific presentation), a map of the land on the Delaware. In my room there was one single bed, a desk, a chair, an Amish bureau with a doily on the top and some photographs, too, one of me with a trout and the other of me with a dead buck. There was a small red book which had names and addresses of friends and girl friends. The handwriting didn't seem correct and the book smelled a little musty. At the end of the room there were casement windows, and they ran from floor to ceiling, had curtains before them and a small iron balcony on the other side. The room seemed to be filled with air that had been trapped in the previous winter, so I opened the window, and pulled back the curtain, and then sat on the bed, sipping my drink, listening to the voices of the people on the avenue (who were taking a stroll in the warm spring evening).

There was the sound of traffic, too, the muted beep of a horn, and that almost silky quality left behind by those long, black, and muffled automobiles. After a while I opened my closet and found my clothes, tweed jackets (the color of fieldstone and the color of barley), evening clothes, dark suits, a brown suit with a vest I used to wear at lunch with a green tie, shoes, more shoes than I remembered having: wing tips, French toes, dark oxfords, brogues, and some shiny, simple black shoes to go with evening clothes. And suspenders, too, more suspenders than I thought possible ("Braces," said my father). At the back of the closet I found a bag of golf clubs. The heads of the clubs were covered with socks that had numbers on them. I stood there, under the hanging clothes, fingering the strap of the leather bag, and finally I dropped it and walked to the window, through which I saw the darkened apartment across the avenue. Years before, when I had been looking into the windows across the street for a glimpse of a woman, a rolled stocking on a smooth leg, a loose garter, exposed throat, or nude, pubescent girls having a pillow fight, I saw a film projected on the now-darkened wall opposite me: it was a piece of pornography in which everyone wore a pair of glasses and a mustache so they all looked like Groucho Marx.

My father opened the door to the room and dragged a wooden case behind him. He had carried it upstairs and was blowing hard and his face was red. The box looked like an ammunition case, and the top had two hinges on one side and a snap lock on the other. My father had been in the kitchen, moving things from one box to another. Now he opened the one he had pulled into the room and put on my bed fistfuls of candy bars, a bottle of brandy, packages of cigarettes, tins of sardines and ham. The brandy in the bottle was very old, clear and clean and as bright as a Christmas ball.

"Go on," said my father.

I looked at the things spread on the counterpane.

"Anything you want. Pick. Pick."

I took a package of cigarettes.

"You need more than that," said my father, "what about some sardines? Or a ham."

He was crying again. I took a ham and put it in my closet, underneath the clothes and next to the shoes. When I was kneeling under the musty clothes, I heard someone come into the room, and when I stood up, I saw Wade.

He was wearing his blue trousers and jacket and he was carrying a blue cap. His hair was gray above the ears now and his eyes were still the color of strong tea. He squeezed his cap when he came into the room. My father started putting the candy bars and sardines back into the box, arranging them carefully, while Wade stood between us and squeezed his cap until his hands trembled. When I reached to touch him he shook his head. I saw his eyes though, and the expression in them, that keen regret I had first seen after we went to the movies together.

"How have you been Wade?" I said.

"Just fine, Chip," he said.

"What have you been doing?" I said.

"The usual," said Wade, "and, of course, I've been going to the movies. Maybe we'll go to one soon. During the war there were two good ones. I can't tell you how good they were."

Wade stared at the wall when he said this and my father continued his careful arrangement of the sardines and packages of cigarettes. My mother came up, too, and stood in the doorway for a moment. I sat down on a chair and my mother looked at us and then told me that she had found a new fox's den.

And on that morning after I had proposed to Carolyn and had been for all practical considerations accepted, and after my father had chased that ram through the woods (without ever catching him), after my father had sat in his tub on that platform and promised me a reward, we took a walk. We began at the farm and walked until we came to another dirt road which wasn't used that much and was really just two ruts in stone. We turned on that one, which went down into the woods.

"Get that air into your lungs," said my father, but the way he made balloons of his jowls made him look as though the air wasn't much farther than his cheeks. He did carry his paunch a little higher, and he tried to stick his chest out, between the lapels of his jacket. "That air probably has vitamins in it or something. I bought this place because of the air."

My father was wearing his panama hat, too, with the broad blue band. My mother said it made him look like a tropical pimp, but my father just smiled and said he knew what was what.

"Are you breathing, Chip?" said my father.

"Yes," I said.

"I mean deeply, boy," he said, "are you getting the full benefit of this air?"

"Yes, sir," I said.

"That's better," said my father, when he saw me expanding my chest and working my diaphragm. Both of us went along the road, downhill, swinging our arms and making the noise of a couple of billows that were worked hard. The road went straight for a while, then turned, and went straight again: on one side there were fields with stone walls and on the other side there were the woods, stands of pine mixed with chestnut, red and white oak. The fields had grown up again, too, filled with spruce, and you could see the half-rotting birch which had been overtopped and killed by the softwoods. The road turned a little more and then dropped straight down, crossed a small dike (through which a spring ran, even in September) and stopped in front of a stone house.

The house had walls that were three feet thick, and it was two stories, or at least a story and a half: there was a loft under the cathedral ceiling, and that made four rooms, a kitchen and a bedroom downstairs, an open space above them (under the ceiling) and a large, high-ceilinged living room before a fireplace, which was almost big enough to stand in and could take logs that were six feet long. The loft was made from beams that were six inches square, and the first beam went across the shoulders of the chimney, which was made from the same stone as the house. The insides of the cathedral ceiling, and the floor of the loft, and the walls of the bedroom were made from cedar planks. The house was in a long swale, protected, and in front of it there was a red maple. Before the war there had only been four walls, each about three feet high, and, of course, no roof, since the house had burned down in 1900. During the war, my father had finished the walls, put on the roof, and had the inside taken care of, too.

My father stood with his back to the house and stared at the woods, or the sky. He was still breathing hard.

"I always liked the smell of cedar," said my father. "And I want you to remember that during the war I picked up every one of those goddamned stones myself. I built it for John and now I can't stand to look at it. So it's yours. Here's the key."

He pushed the key into my hand, still keeping his back to the house.

"There's forty acres to go with it, too," said my father, pulling on the brim of his panama hat. "I'll have it surveyed and recorded next week. Do you want to go inside and take a look?"

"No," I said.

"That's fine," said my father. "Let's walk up that road. Let's breathe some of that air."

I put the key in my pocket.

"You get that stove going in winter," said my father, "and it's warm. You understand."

My father kicked a stone.

"It's a damn good reward," said my father. "No matter where it came from or what it was meant for."

"Yes," I said.

"That's good. It's settled."

We went up the road in earnest, each of us taking a stony rut, my father's cheeks filled with air, his hat pulled down over his ears. He kicked the stones as he went.

Mrs. Mackinnon's Book of Animals, Reptiles, Plants, Trees, Birds, Bugs, and Flowers.

On this land there are copperheads, a variety of pit viper, and if you are in the woods or near a stone wall or ledge and smell the distinctive odor of newly cut cucumbers, the chances of seeing a copperhead are good. The odor comes from the snake's skin. It is easy to step on one because they seem dull and sluggish, but in fact are not: they are stocky snakes with short tails, and because of this they don't move as fast as other snakes (racers, for instance), so when they hunt they pick a spot and wait. Their eyesight is fairly good at short distances, but they detect their next meal in other, more keen ways. Their sense of smell is very pronounced, and when you see a snake slipping its tongue in and out it is sampling the air's odor. Copperheads also have a very refined sense of heat. They are called pit vipers because they have a small indentation on each side of the head between the nostril and the eye, and this is the site of an organ which can detect changes in temperature at a distance of a yard of less than one fifth of one degree. It is quite easy for them to notice warm-blooded animals. So when they are waiting, looking, sentient (in a way that is as alien as a shark), it is easy to step on one, since it is the way they hunt and the way they protect themselves. It is a brown and yellowish snake with a copperish head and markings of brown that have an undulant shape, something like those long rippled balloons you see at fairs. When a rodent comes near, the snake strikes, waits for the animal to die, and then follows by scent to the place where the meal is. The venom kills in a number of ways: first by destroying the flesh it contacts (actually the venom digests the flesh of the rat or chipmunk or fieldmouse or arm into which it has been injected) and by affecting the nervous system as well. It also lowers the body's resistance to infection. The immediate symptoms in humans of a bite are rich bleeding from the wound, pain, and swelling. I am aware of the snakes when I am in the woods, and they make the land seem more intense, or not to be taken for granted, and this requires concentration, which, in itself, is an escape and a variety of pleasure. In the spring the snakes mate immediately after leaving the den. In early April I can sense the snake's definite desire. The male begins to look for a partner as soon as he has become active, after forcing off the sluggishness of hibernation, after awakening. The mating itself takes place slowly, with the snakes wrapped together, the lower parts of their bodies pushed together, joined. There are times when they coil and uncoil and seem to roll one over the other, and times when it looks violent and intense. The female gives birth to live snakes in the middle of summer, and the labor takes a few hours. The young snakes are born in separate membranes and some have been seen actually striking (and killing) when they were still emerging from the birth sack. They are born hungry and they begin to feed on whatever they can, earthworms, insects, bird eggs. During gestation, the females congregate. The snakes gather together, too, in winter to hibernate. One snake follows another to a good site by the odor left in the snakes' track. Snakes in the summertime will avoid the direct light of the sun (because it's so hot) and will rest or hunt in splotchy, shady places, but in the fall and spring, when the sunlight is cooler, the snakes will take their ease or look for food in a place without shade, usually on a slope with southern exposure. It is also true that most dens have this same exposure. Twenty-five or thirty or more snakes may occupy the same den during the winter, coiled together, conserving moisture. Above ground the den is insulated by snow, by the air that is trapped in its crystalline pattern. The snakes emerge again in the early spring, desirous, impatient, looking for the recognition of the mate. Copperheads move by establishing places on the ground where the body can take hold and then running the entire length of itself through these holds: their movement is similar to that made by pulling a rope after having weaved it through three or four stones on the ground. The entire snake passes over the same piece of ground, even though the path they take is not straight. So I concentrate when I am walking along stone walls or in the splotchy places in the spring, and I am glad for the absorption of it, of the definition of the woods. I can sense the copperheads, just as cool or as warm as the air, waiting, intent. I try to understand or to imagine the texture of rocks against their stomachs, and while I know something of desire, the copperheads make me feel thrown back on myself, aware of my bonds with other people, and because this awareness almost always comes when I am alone, it makes me long for human voices, a gentle touch, a joke. It is this, more than anything else, that makes me dislike the snakes: they make me feel so lonely and so much in need. So I concentrate when I walk, enjoying the intensity of the woods, but I watch where I put my feet and hands. I look for the brown and yellow blotched coils and attempt to detect the odor of freshly cut cucumber.

BOOK II

BOOK II

Annie Cooper
Southern Ohio. 1950.

It doesn't bother me when I have the sensation of evil just beneath the surface of things in this town, as though the place were a movie set and there was something bad behind the bank, the welder's, the stationer's and luncheonette, the box factory and the factory where women sew, the Penney's and the gas station, but I am troubled by the knowledge, which presents itself time and again, suddenly and always without warning, that what ended as evil began as love and, for lack of a better word, passion. Twenty-three hundred souls live here. It says so on the sign just outside of town. The people here loved my sister, Jean, and I did, too. Considering the way things turned out, however, it would be damn difficult to prove it.

We lived out of town in a farmhouse, although we didn't have the land to go with it, not the whole four hundred acres, just ten or so, enough to have a garden and a field with a windbreak. My mother liked white, so the clapboards were the color of bleached linen sheets, and the kitchen was white, too, as were the muslin curtains there, the bedrooms upstairs, and the front parlor. On a bright day it made your eyes ache to stare at the house from the field. It is true that Jean's color was lovely and clear and it was nice to look at her against a white background.

I remember last spring when Jean was twenty and I was twenty-one, and I came into that kitchen, which was large and had a white enameled stove. There were black lines on the floor, where we stood when our mother told us to, or between which we walked back and forth, our gait and manner of movement being closely scrutinized. The standing and walking did wonders, in a way, since the girls in the family had the best posture, the most elegant carriage you have ever seen. My mother danced and was well-read and spoke French she taught herself, and she could have gone away, too, to one of those Eastern colleges, but she didn't, and this went to her head. My mother decided we should not frown or laugh, because we'd crease our skin or wrinkle it. That was the theory. We all became good poker players, and I must admit that Jean had lovely skin (although I'm not sure her laughter being strictly private helped that much).

Jean was standing with her toes just touching one of the black lines (which were made with black tape) and in that perfect posture with her hands clasped together in front. Jean stared out the window beyond my mother's head, at the early spring sky, which was filled with clouds. You could smell that there'd be some snow, even though it was after the first of April. My mother had before her some drawings which were done in Jean's hand. Jean was graceful with pen and ink, and, I think, a little talented.

"Did you do these?" said my mother.

"Yes," said Jean, still looking out the window, not flinching one bit. I could see a little of the drawings as my mother turned them over in their folder: a man's torso, and his arms, muscled and nice, his waist, legs, genitals. Defined chests, arms. Bland faces.

"Why?" said my mother.

Jean looked at that sky, not moving, not flinching, now just being silent. The pages turned in my mother's hand. From what I could see, the drawings weren't just sterile renderings of the human body, not the kind of thing you'd see in a manual of first aid: there was something in the lines, the definition of features, muscles, the stances of men that had been produced by Jean's longing, her serious (but not melancholy) desires.

"Did you have a model?" said my mother.

"No," said Jean, "aside from magazines and the encyclopedia."

"Have you been sleeping with someone from this town?" said my mother, watching closely.

"Of course not," said Jean. This was not said with satisfaction or pride.

"I won't have that," said my mother.

Jean stood at the line with her hands at her sides, still as a photograph. I watched her quiet stance, a slight tick in her face.

"I'll show these to your father," said my mother, still lingering over some of those at the bottom of the pile which I couldn't see very well, but seemed to contain images over which some ache and care had been exercised.

"Oh," said Jean. "No. I don't want that."

"He'll be home soon," said my mother. "Why don't you go upstairs?"

"Come on," I said.

"Are Annie and I still going to the movies?" said Jean.

"I don't know," said my mother.

"Let's go upstairs," I said, "and get ready anyway."

So we climbed the stairs and got into our robes and then went into the bathroom. On Friday nights we had to double up on the baths, because the hot water heater wouldn't do for four baths close together. Our bathroom was upstairs and it had imitation tile, those big white sheets that have dark lines and grooves which divide them into small squares. The porcelain of the tub was scrubbed so clean it was as smooth as silk. We had white towels, large ones, with a heavy nap. I never minded taking the water after Jean. It smelled good and clean and made me feel I had a secret. I sat on the seat and let water into the tub, watched as the bathroom filled with steam, the clouds slowly turning into one another like cigarette smoke. Jean wrapped herself in a towel, just from her arms to the top of her thighs, and looked out the window, beyond which it had finally begun to snow, the first flakes seemed produced by legerdemain. Jean dropped the towel and stepped into the tub, making her ankle and foot stiff and a little pointed when she did so. Her legs were long and slender. She stood in the water and said, "Ouch. That's too hot," but then waited for her skin to get used to it rather than turning on the cold, standing on one leg a little more than another (making a dip with her hips) and turning to look out the window at the snow: there was a wind now and the snow came in lines like white and shaggy string. Jean stood there without the towel, waiting for the water to cool. There was a little perspiration on her lip and at the sides of her nose, which was long and slender and perfect. I put a bar of Ivory soap in the brass rack that hung over the tub.

It was mostly flat land beyond the window, but the dark and leafless trees in the yard and along the road were becoming etched by the snow. The faintly swollen but mostly flat plane of Jean's stomach met the two white planes of her thighs, making a Y shape (like the corner and ceiling of a room with white walls) as she began to ease herself into the hot water. "Ah," she said, closing her eyes, "ah." The hot steam rose from the surface of the water: you could see it curling there, the sleigh-runner curves. Jean put her head back and exposed her long neck. It felt good, but she wasn't able to say it. Her fingers were long, too, and they were at the edge of the tub, gripping it. I had a magazine with pictures of women in skirts and dresses (which magazines my mother ordered from Paris, a place she had never been), clothes made from silk or satin or wool (from England), and underwear from France, too. Smooth, clinging things with delicate and fine lace.

"It's too late for snow," said Jean, still with her head back and gripping the sides of the tub: she couldn't say it (would not have been allowed to say it), but I know that she wanted to open the window and let a few of the snowflakes come into the bathroom and land on her skin so she could sit in the hot water and feel the sharp points as the flakes touched her neck, throat and lips, a nipple. I looked up from the magazine and stared at her, now lying with her head still back and obviously feeling the heat of the water, but no longer gripping the sides of the tub: she pushed her short hair up so that it hung a little bit over the edge of the tub. Her hair was the color of silver that's tarnished just a bit. Usually, when she was done I'd give her a towel with a heavy nap, help wrap her in it and dry her just a little, sensing her skin as she pushed against the towel, and I'd feel, too, the fluid movement of her breast as I held the towel so that she could take it herself.

"Did you draw those pictures?" I said, watching her face.

"Yes," she said, moving her head slowly from side to side against the hard and white porcelain.

"Why?" I said.

Jean lifted an arm and made a gesture in the curling mist from the tub (it was cold in the bathroom), one that was part defining something (unspeakable or unexplainable) in the air and part caress.

"I wanted to," said Jean, still with her eyes closed and dropping her hand so that it touched her knee.

"Did you?" I said. "Have a . . . model?"

Jean gripped the lip of the tub and pushed her head back against the porcelain. "No," said Jean.

She frowned for a moment but then pushed her hand against her forehead (as she had been told to do) and put her head back so she could look out the window, at those lines of snow which were swung across the glass (like a curtain made of strings), and then ran the soap under her arm and down her sides and across her long legs. The razor was in a silver holder and I gave it to her. She watched carefully as she dragged it along her legs, stopping to wet the razor every now and then before going back to them, although she really didn't need to use it at all because there was only a little down on her legs which was about as smooth as shaved skin. She rubbed one finger along her calf, looking to see if there were any spot she might have missed. Years before when the light down began to grow I said, "Look." And ran my hand along it and it was just velvet.

Jean put more water into the tub and held a blank expression on her face although I could see the cords in her neck become taut. I know she wanted to say, "That's good. That's so good. It's hot and I can feel it." But instead she pushed into the tub more and brought up her legs a little. The trees outside the window now looked only half as thick as they were before, since they were half covered with snow, absorbed by the landscape beyond.

"Do you want me to wash your back?" I said.

"No," said Jean, "thanks," and took the brush by its long handle and soaped it and worked it hard on her back, sitting up a little to do it, making the muscles in her stomach contract into that fine, tight, segmented pattern. Her breasts were small, and they moved a little as she scrubbed her back. I sat still as Jean slid under the water and said, "That feels good. Really wonderful. Ummm." Jean had small, delicate and very pink nipples, the same color as her lips.

"Do you think mother will show those drawings to father?" I said.

"I hope not," said Jean, although we both knew he'd be embarrassed when confronted with them, but proud that his girls were already so definite.

"What would you like?" I said.

Jean fully stretched out in the tub, which meant her legs were raised and the ankles hung over the end, because her legs were long. Her arms were over her head, against the porcelain, and her hands were caressing or holding her hair (which was really the color of birch ash). I saw the flat part of her underarms, the plane there which diminished and turned into the plane of the slender muscle which ran under her breasts. The skin was slick. There was the taut plane of her stomach. A slight swelling around the navel.

"Ah," said Jean, with her eyes closed. "I'd like to be someplace. On a wide and warm beach with no one around. No one. Aside from whom I wanted. I could lick the salt. . . ." She shook her head and frowned, and then pressed the frown away. I saw she was able to stop the beginning of tears which filled the bottom lids of her eyes, moisture that was the same color as the water that came out of the tub's dated and swollen fixtures. She just stopped them, without a tremble or a twitch. "Or maybe just a hotel room in Chicago where I could close the door and have a stranger." I showed her some hats from the magazine, but she didn't like them very much. We examined the underwear, looking so smooth, and catching the light, as though it were polished silver.

"I wonder what it's like to wear that?" I said.

Jean brought her hand along under her thigh and then began to bring it across her stomach but stopped and put her hand on the side of the tub.

"It's just smooth and comfortable. And it makes you feel special and no one knows it," said Jean. When she smiled just the corners of her full lips turned up.

It was late for snow, and we were getting so much of it, but I didn't mind sitting there, watching her. I showed Jean another picture of a woman who was dressed in a brassiere and briefs, which were a brown silk color. I saw a little of the faintly creased texture of Jean's lips, the slight indentation which was in the center: it made them seem a little pursed. Behind Jean there were the white walls and the imitation tile, the white curtains, the snow blowing in strings by the window, so when she opened her eyes to look at the photograph it was startling: it seemed for a moment that blue ink had been dropped on white linen or paper. "Yes," she said, "those are lovely, too." Lovely, she said, lovely, putting her lips together as though she were tasting the word: you could tell she wanted to say, Lovely, you could walk around with those under your clothes and look at a man and feel a little tightened, drawn. She put a little more water in the tub and said, "Ah. Ah," and stood up. I pushed the towel against her as she turned away from the window. The water ran down her stomach and legs, reflected for one moment the light over the medicine chest, smeared it into long silver shapes.

I took off my brown terry robe and got into the water. There's nothing wrong with my figure, but there's not much right with it, as though Jean took all there was and didn't leave anything over, or as though I left what should have been mine, and Jean brought it with her.

She wrapped herself in a towel and sat on the seat, the dimples showing in her shoulders. She crossed her legs and wrapped her hair into another towel and made a turban before picking up the magazine from where I dropped it. She saw my hurt, frightened face.

"I don't think anything will happen," she said with a kind smile. "We'll still be able to see the movies."

"It's not the movies I'm thinking about," I said.

"I know," she said. "I don't want father to see them, either." She sat for a moment with the magazine, and said, after having laughed so hard she really looked as though she'd been crying, "He'll just *die*. I mean that. They'll have to come with an ambulance."

We both laughed.

"No," I said, "I wasn't thinking of father, either."

She thumbed through the magazine, and said, "Don't worry. I'm not supposed to marry anyone from this town." She looked at a woman in a raincoat. Wet hair. Jean said that she wasn't supposed to marry with definite regret.

"But then you can't go away, can you?" I said. Because people were born and then lived, worked, and died here, usually at the sewing factory or gas station, welders, stationer's, cosmetic plant, hardware, or grocers. "Can you?" I said, half pleading (because I didn't want her to go, either).

Jean frowned and pushed her hand against her forehead and said, "Wait until Dad sees those drawings. He's going to die."

Jean offered to scrub my back and I let her, feeling the hard bristles which somehow felt wonderful and cleansing. I turned once and saw Jean's blue eyes set on the lines of snow beyond the window. When she was done she put down the brush and smiled and touched my hair. She dropped the towel and stared at herself in the mirror which was on the door behind me, not with any vanity, but more with surprise at her own taut loveliness.

"You can't go away? Can you? Can you?" I said.

Jean held that same face we were supposed to use to keep from making wrinkles and gathered her things and went to dress, leaving me in the steam and the scented air.

It was still snowing when we got downstairs, dressed now and ready to go. My father was sitting at the table opposite my mother, a drink before him and the paper open to the baseball. My father was a tall man with his hair perfectly parted and combed to one side, and he was wearing a white shirt with a bow tie and his jacket was hung behind his chair so we could see his red suspenders which were his pride. My mother didn't like them. My father was then in his early forties, and he sold Buicks and sometimes we had money and then there were times when people either didn't want or couldn't afford Buicks and those times were just hard, but they never stopped my father from going to the smallest showroom in the world (one car) and sitting at his desk on his oak chair, passing the time of day with anyone who would stop and listen to his stories about the girls he had sparked twenty-one (and then twenty-two and then twenty-three and then more) years ago, always with his coat hung over the back of his chair so the visitor or prospective buyer could see that blue bow tie and his red suspenders (which he went to Chicago twice a year just to buy). He drove the demonstrators each year himself and gave to us any old piece of junk he couldn't sell, you know, when someone was trading up to a Buick. We had a Ford we were going to drive in the snow, a red '38 with seats that were as lumpy as down pillows left out in the rain. Our father had a matched set of silver brushes, too, in which he took a lot of pride, and which he used every morning and afternoon.

Jean had on a green dress and a white sweater, and some clunky boots because we were going to go out in the snow. My mother looked at those boots and shook her head, and then poured herself a drink, so our parents sat opposite one another, each drinking quietly, my mother with her library book and my father over his paper. My mother was fair, too, and had fine bones like Jean, but she didn't resemble Jean much even though their features were similar, and it wasn't just age, either (although my mother was burned out now, the color of an old filament in a bulb). Jean had a different style and carriage and gait, which came from that aching restraint, from the wildness which needed to be formed and was formed into something beautiful. My mother was just bitter.

My mother wasn't jealous but she was certainly glad she had found those drawings. She just couldn't resist Jean. Sometimes when she'd had a number of glasses of Jim Beam and was positively giddy she'd walk back and forth between those black lines herself, showing us that we had to be graceful even when cockeyed drunk, and at these times she'd say, "You know, Jean seems to be a little different than my other children" (stop here, turn, moving perfectly and not slurring, either), "and some people have had the nerve to say that I jumped the fence" (stop, black lines, turn) "but they don't know a thing. If you want to know about jumping the fence why all you have to do" (black lines, perfect turn) "is to ask that man sitting right there in his white shirt and red" (stop, black lines, turn: Jean and I got drunk one afternoon and tried it ourselves) "bow tie and he'll tell you everything you want to know," (stop, black lines, turn) "especially when you asked him what he does driving those young women around in the demonstrator convertible" (turn, black lines, not a glance in his direction, where he sat at the table with the paper, fingering his bow tie) "while he's supposed to be earning an honest living on spring afternoons," (stop, black lines) "you ask him, I say, what they do in that Buick together, those women from out of town, from Sandusky or Toledo." My mother stopped and looked at him and he just kept turning the pages, saying, "See Buick's stock's up. Cars must be moving." Once, after an evening of walking and speech-making, Jean took my father aside on the floor of his show-room (which held one new and shiny Buick) and asked him what he was doing in a convertible with a young woman, and my father looked at her and said, "Jean, she was young and smooth and sweet-smelling and we had a good time and it was wonderful." He said this with tears in his eyes. Jean came home and said to me, "I understand him now. I understand him perfectly."

So they sat there, opposite one another when we came into the kitchen. The manila folder with the drawings was under my mother's hand. Jean looked at my father and then through the window over the sink where you could see those lines of windblown snow. I can remember the white icebox, the chrome handle on it, the fixture over the white sink, the light sharp in each bright bit of metal. Jean looked at our mother, but our mother didn't do any-thing at all, so then Jean went to where my father had his face over the paper. When Jean stood next to his chair he put his arm around her waist and pulled her a little and said, "How's my girl? How's my beautiful lady?" He hugged her a little and left his hand on her hip for just a minute. Just a minute. Then it slipped down to the table and picked up his drink. My mother watched. Jean pushed her lower stomach against his shoulder, just because she wanted to touch him, to show she understood he was tired (and that's all). My mother sipped her drink. "I'm all right, Dad," said Jean. "I'm just fine. How are the Sox doing? And the Tigers? What are the Tigers doing?"

"It's too early to tell," said my father, "but I don't expect much from Detroit."

My mother put her hand on the manila file which held Jean's drawings and moved them a little.

Jean moved back from my father, and he looked up, one hand pulling a little on his suspenders, the other holding his glass.

"What's my beauty going to do tonight?" he said, looking at her and smiling. He hadn't even said hello to me.

"What do we always do on Friday night?" said Jean, watching my mother's white hand on the manila envelope. You wouldn't think there was anything in that folder aside from some clippings from the newspaper if you were going to judge by Jean's voice, which was as cool as a pipe in winter. Those black lines did wonders.

"Hello, Annie," he said, seeing me. "Why I guess you go to the movies."

"That's where we'll go," I said. "Thanks for noticing me."

He laughed and I went over and took a kiss, although I wanted to give him a kick.

My mother moved the envelope back and forth on the white tablecloth. Jean smiled at my father, and then looked once around the kitchen, lingering on the chrome, the silver in its box, which was lined with red velvet, a silver teapot which sat on the counter, all bright and silken in the light.

My mother held the envelope, and said, "You'll be careful tonight?"

"Certainly," said Jean.

"I've driven in more snow than this," I said. "It isn't much."

"I wasn't thinking about the snow," said my mother.

"What about Cleveland?" said Jean, looking over my father's shoulder.

"They never do much," said my father, "until late in the season. Listen to your mother."

"Can you be trusted?" said my mother. "You'd never get involved with a boy from this town, would you?"

"No," I said.

"Jean?" she said, still holding the drawings. "Do I have to come with you?"

"No," said Jean, looking at my mother with that cool, distant expression in her eyes, still standing next to my father who was born in this town and who had spent his life in it, and wasn't ashamed about it unless he was at home sometimes and my mother and Jean and I spoke French, not one word of which was understood by him. He just kept quiet and read the baseball and waited for springtime and a new demonstrator and the back roads with those women from Sandusky or Toledo.

My father looked up from the baseball and said, "Listen to your mother."

"I could have gone to Vassar," said my mother, "and you can, too."

"When?" said Jean.

"When I can trust you," said my mother. "Now why don't you get in that car and go to the movies with your sister. And don't bother me for a while."

My mother put the drawings aside, in a magazine she had read and which was obviously going into the trash.

"Thanks," said Jean.

"I don't need any thanks," said my mother. "I just want trust."

I saw all the bright spots in the kitchen, all those places where the light was reflected and constricted, my father bent over the table, the dark lines of print on his paper.

"Why don't you come with us," said Jean to my mother, walking across the kitchen and taking my mother's hand. "Why don't you? We'll have a good time."

"I'm too old," said my mother, "to go to the movies."

"You're not too old," said Jean, drawing close to my mother and giving her a kiss. "I don't think so."

"No," said my mother, "I don't want to go into town."

She shook her head and put her hand on the magazine that now held the drawings. Jean gave her another hug, which my mother didn't return, and then put on her coat.

"I don't think it's going to snow that much," I said.

"No," said my mother, staring straight at my father's bowed head, his hand that held the drink.

" 'Bye," I said, at the door, waiting for Jean.

"Have a good time," said my father, looking up and smiling that old smile that must have had every woman in town interested in taking a ride with him (and long before the new demonstrators, too).

The snow was stinging our faces a little bit, and there was more of it on the ground than I thought. Jean went around and got in on the passenger side, and I slid behind the wheel. The snow was so light that I could get it off the windshield just by turning on the wipers. The puffs of it slid away. The Ford started without any trouble, and we went out the drive and onto the road, where there was snow all around us, like some plague of albino insects. Jean's coat had a rabbit-fur collar which had been dyed and she held it up to her face. The land was flat, better in snow, although the springtime was good too. The worst was dry and cold winter, with no snow, when everyone's topsoil turned into black, dry rain.

Jean stared at the whitened flat land, and said, "What's at the movies?" but I know she was thinking, That was close.

"Western," I said.

"Oh," said Jean, still staring straight ahead. She held that dyed fur against her throat, her long fingers set off by it.

The road ahead of us had only been driven by my father, so there were two marks in the snow on my left, going in the other direction. There was a tree at the side of the road and it made the sky look like a black bowl that was cracked.

We came into town with the snow blowing against the windshield: the town isn't dead, just nicely laid out. It's all pushed up along one street, as though there was a parade and everyone was afraid of getting left too far back. As you go down the street there are on one side a gas station, the pharmacy, the luncheonette, the park where there's the war memorial with cannon, then another store which is empty, then the movie theater with its small marquee and handmade but still moveable letters. On the other side of the street there is a hardware store, a church with its pointed tower and gray stone, the telephone company's office, the library, the B.P.O.E. with two big elks outside, an insurance office (where the oldest woman in the world works: she's got a bun of white hair the size of a spool of thread, one black dress, one tooth, and she keeps the books in longhand, sitting on her stool behind the wooden rail with the swinging door, always humming, just beneath her breath), and Fire Department, which is of no account: your house burns down and they come to watch, since that's all there is to do, but they make a hell of a noise on the way, so I guess they're not completely worthless.

I parked in front of the theater. The street runs downhill a little after that, so we wouldn't have any trouble getting started. Jean looked up and said, "Alan Ladd. It's not a western after all."

"No," I said. "It's an African."

"Better scenery," said Jean, getting out into the snow and slamming the door.

We were a little early, so we stood around in the overheated, damp lobby, saying hello. Matthew Hales was there, a young man two years older than Jean, tall, good looking in a dark-blue-eyed and tanned-skin way. He wore blue denim trousers and a special jacket he had ordered through the mail. It didn't fit right because his shoulders are broad. He had white teeth and a cowboy haircut, all whitewalls on the side. He was talking to some friends, who stopped what they were doing and watched us as we walked in. They all tipped their hats or said hello. Jean smiled and we sat down on the moldy, circular couch in the middle of the room. Matthew was not what anyone in his right mind would call smart, but if perseverance or ongoing hard work is a substitute for brains, then the man was a genius. He was violent occasionally, which at least shows he had a heart and that sometimes he knew more than he could understand.

When the movie began he sat behind us and after the credits he said quietly to Jean, "I own half the farm now since my brother was killed during the war and my father's not going to live forever."

"Don't talk about your father and his dying," said Jean. "It's like wishing him dead."

"I'm sorry," said Matthew. "It's not like that exactly. . . . Look, come outside after the movie."

"I can't," said Jean.

"Why not?" said Matthew.

Jean shook her head.

Matthew sat behind us while the movie went on: some men in funny sun hats got eaten by small fish after the men had fallen in a river. After a while, in a cave, some other men found a chest of diamonds, and it looked like it was filled with ice cubes. They made a nice rattle when they were picked up. The picture ended and we went outside.

"All right," said Jean, "for a minute. Let's get in the car."

I waited in the snow. Jean sat on the driver's side and Matthew on the other. I looked in every now and then. Later I found out what they said, but I was able to guess before that.

"Hush, hush," said Jean, looking at his dark face and eyes. She put her fingers against his lips, kissed the back of her own quaking hand. I'm sure he felt her tremble. Matthew looked scared, surprised, but he didn't pull away. She turned in her seat, saw his terrified eyes, and then leaned an arm against the steering wheel.

"I can't," she said.

"What do you mean?" said Matthew. "You weren't going to do anything right in this car, were you?"

Jean smiled at his surprised, frightened face and said "No. No."

Her arm on the steering wheel seemed relaxed, but I knew the tendons there were as taut as banjo strings. Jean lit a cigarette and sat quietly while Matthew had a confused look on his face. He shook his head saying, "Were you going to do anything . . . ?"

"No," said Jean. "Let's get a Coke or something."

"These seats are lumpy," Matthew said. "How come you don't get a Buick? Your dad sells them."

Jean smiled and said, "Not to me."

Matthew watched her for a minute and said, "You won't go out with me or anything?"

"I can't," said Jean. "I just can't."

"I'll try to be quiet," said Matthew.

Jean looked at him and smiled with just the ends of her lips turning up, took Matthew's hand, and squeezed it, saying, "I know it."

Outside in the snow, Matthew ignored me. He seemed angry about having missed some unknown thing (although with each passing day his slow but ultimately rich imagination began to tell him what it might have been).

"Why? Why?" he said. "Why can't we?"

"Come on now," said Jean, pulling herself up, making her face into that expression (which, in theory, was not supposed to injure the skin), "Annie's here."

"So what?" said Matthew. "Annie knows everything anyway. No offense, Annie."

"Thanks," I said, walking a little bit behind them.

"All right, all right," said Matthew, in his anger and confusion, too. It was clear as water that it wasn't all right at all.

We were walking down the street now, toward the luncheonette which was also part grocery and stationer's (canned beans and ham, birthday cards and cheap guest books for funerals: the guest books might have been sold already signed, since the same people always attended the funerals, less one). There wasn't anyone out, not even young men or women from the theater shouting and throwing snowballs or making some other kind of trouble. I saw in the snow that most people had come out of the theater and gone down past the Elks and the library, and from there into a side street. The side streets were dark, filled with buildings made of stone which had been weathered to the color of ashes. The buildings served as warehouses for other businesses (the hardware store, the welder, the gas station that really specialized in repairing tractors, bailers, and rakes). If a building wasn't a warehouse it was empty.

"Shit," said Matthew.

Jean turned to me and said, "Where do you suppose everyone is?"

"I'll show you," said Matthew. "You want to see? I'll show you just fine."

"I'm sorry," said Jean. I saw her turning her face every now and then so that those small, sharp bits of snow touched her nose, cheeks, and forehead. She wasn't wearing a hat and the snow collected in her hair.

"I don't know if you are," said Matthew. "But I'll sure show you."

He turned and looked at her for a moment, and then we followed him down the street (where the majority of footprints led), although we should have had the sense not to, but we prided ourselves on knowing about everything that happened here, so we didn't have much sense about some things. Matthew walked ahead of us. I noticed that almost all of the prints in the snow were made by large boots, or boots that were worn by men, and that should have been a warning, but by the time we were halfway down the street it was dark, and we kept going, Jean walking in that alley or side street with that careful, upright carriage, enjoying the snow and thinking whatever she needed to (I would have taken Matthew in a minute, brains or not). She heard, as I did, those first distant sounds, a compendium or collection of voices and stomping feet in a large, empty space. Jean looked up with her brow wrinkled and then stopped, but Matthew said, "Don't you want to see? Don't you?" so sneering in his voice, so angry (because he was confused, hadn't had the time to think), that we just smiled and said, "Yes, why not?"

The snow had changed the acoustics in the street, and it was hard to identify what was in the center of that humming, buzzing noise, but it was certain that all sounds were coming from one building at the end of the street, where the town turns back into flatland again. It was an empty warehouse. There were large doors in the front and a small one next to it, and above them, across the front of the building, there were three windows with small panes in them, and through which there came some light and shadows. There wasn't much snow falling, so I saw that yellowish light and movement clearly. The noise was still there, and beneath it or beyond it there was a yowling, or muffled screech. We stood for a minute and listened, Matthew watching Jean, who looked at him and braced herself, but she still put her finger to her lips and ran it back and forth while we listened to the as yet undefined noise, Jean catching herself and putting her hand down, allowing me to see as she did so the mothlike flutter or tremble in it.

Matthew stood and listened, as though not certain about what to do, but still (and getting more so) angry: he was in the unenviable position of a man who has made a threat and is being called upon to go through with it, and this, of course, frightened him. Jean listened and leaned against the building, putting her head against the ash-colored stone, just to feel something solid.

"Let's go in," I said.

The sound seemed to come out of an eddy, out of some center of the warehouse, and it was widening: I thought of the pictures you see of spiral galaxies, their arms reaching into emptiness, and of the flat, black and white landscape beyond the town. It was the voices and echoes that made it impossible to resolve the sounds. There was only the dim yellow light from the windows above us, and by it I saw Jean's head turned up against the stone.

"Are you all right?" said Matthew.

"Yes," said Jean. "What's going on in there?"

"I'll show you all you'll want to see," said Matthew.

"Fine," said Jean. "Fine."

She started toward the door on the left side of the building, but

Matthew put his fingers on her hand, touching her briefly, just once. It was done delicately and with a certain amount of pain.

"No," said Matthew. "We better go around back."

That noise sounded now like a snarl or growl. I heard breaking glass, too, and a loud, awkward laugh, and then a shout, for someone "to prove it": there was that high, inflated, boisterous sound that men make when they are excited and drunk or drunk and afraid. We couldn't hear it so well as we walked in the alley between the warehouse and the next building, since there weren't any windows in that wall. When we came to the rear of the building Jean stopped Matthew for a moment and said, "Look. I'm sorry. I'm sorry."

He opened the door and we stepped into the noise, and the smell, which was of damp and dusty cement, the stench of tobacco and liquor. The light in the warehouse was nothing more than a bulb at the end of a cord which had been thrown over a beam. It looked like they were getting ready to lynch someone with whatever had been handy, in this case a cord that still had the light on it. Beneath the bulb and out of new sheets of plywood a pit or ring with eight sides had been made: you could smell the new wood, and on the two-by-fours which had been used to lace the pieces of plywood together I saw the bright beads of sap. They caught the light and made the ring looked jeweled, festive, and young. The pit was half-filled with dirt, and at each end of it there was a man who was holding a dog.

The dogs were muzzled, so that's why we hadn't been able to hear them clearly, and still couldn't. They were jumping toward one another, and you could tell by their necks how hard they were barking: the dogs were the most thick and stocky I had ever seen. There must have been thirty men around the ring, anyway, some drinking out of cups (which had snow inside instead of ice), others carrying tall, thin bottles of beer. Some men just stood back and watched. There weren't any women there aside from us. Most of the men who had businesses were there: the grocer, a short, jowly man with dark eyes and clothes that always seemed musty (even when he gave us, years ago, a free fireball or stick of Bazooka chewing gum); the vet (stocky, too, and not as kind as you'd suppose with animals, since he saw them more as machines than living things), Charley Pin (who ran the movie house and who was fat as a hog); his cousin Mickey, who was tall as any man I've ever seen but still just as fat as Charley and who ran the luncheonette and who still sent Jean a valentine every year (which was getting to be less of a joke with each passing February); the printer, with his small eyes and hands that were raw from the ink he used and to which he was allergic; the superintendent of the town road crew, Bowie, a tall man with a pot who stuttered and who was still nevertheless the most natural politician ever, always with his hand out and a smile that seemed friendly no matter what the circumstances, and cheerful, too (he's the only man I've ever seen who was able to do some politicking at those funerals where everyone signed the same book from the stationer's); the two morticians (one Republican, the other Democratic); the constable, with his .45 pistol under his coat, and his bald head clearly visible under that bright, makeshift light. The constable was in the warehouse in a double capacity, as sergeant at arms and spectator, and even as the house or casino bank, because a lot of money was being put up, and I imagine the constable (of fair-weather politics, a man of easy habits and no convictions) was not so inexperienced as to allow that kind of money around without picking up a few bills (although not too many) for his time, effort, and own amusement.

Jean stood at the back of the warehouse with me, and I saw by that light the melted snow in her hair, the drops of water. Jean was braced, back in a shadow a little, watching the men, especially those two who were opposite one another and who held the dogs, one of which must have had some Doberman to supply meanness (and some color, too, that brown and reddish white, a combination which by itself seemed to be the flag of wild viciousness) and for jaw size, the full extent of which I now saw as the handler took off

the muzzle: the dog was restrained by a choke chain with two
layers of links that had hinged spikes between them, but the dog
didn't notice them that much, as it threw its head from side to side
in the same manner as a kite in a wind that's too strong for it. Now
we heard that full, throaty howl and bark which seemed to come
from tundra and time far removed, especially so since it was in an
empty stone building, which magnified and made more resonant
that old sound, one that was terrifying to men long before anyone
planted a thing. The animal's jaws were large and were filled with
pointed and quite white teeth, which seemed more appropriate
to some unseen swimming thing, a crocodile or a shark, than a dog.
Jean stood against the wall now, half in shadow, half in light, the
melted snow forming small pendants in her hair and on her skin.
The men in the room were still shouting to one another, making
bets, their skin and eyes illuminated by the one bulb, so that there
were shadows cast by features, noses, brows, lips, ears, across skin
that was as pale as mushrooms. The shouting and bet-making went
on for a while more, men turning and speaking to one another or
across the pit, holding their heads to one side as though considering, sometimes in this attitude rolling their eyes so that the light
would catch them, and at these moments, against the ashy walls
I saw their round and half-shadowed cheeks, their grimaces of
disbelief or bluff below those points of light: the men were fixed
by their lighted eyes in a posture which seemed to be suggestive
of smugness and joviality that was barely, and just barely at that,
able to disguise a wild desire for release.

The other dog handler took the muzzle from his dog, which
must have had a little mastiff for endurance, and something else
(God knows what, wolf, or coyote) for meanness. The two dogs
growled and pushed the dirt back whenever they got a chance,
both of them pulling at the choker chains around their necks (the
second dog had one of the same restraints, with studs or spikes)
and howling or barking so loud that the sound seemed to originate
in one's own mind rather than in that empty and overheated

warehouse. Each dog still threw his head from side to side and occasionally one of them would be fixed, too, when his eyes were touched by a bright, lighted spot, which seemed so far above them, so remote, or just alien to anything the dogs were for. But when the light caught those eyes the warehouse seemed stilled for a moment, or so it seemed to me, and I was left with the sensation that the creatures before me would stay in their positions forever, as though painted or captured: the men with their round cheeks and glasses or bottles, straining at the presence of the dogs and at their own ill ease, the dogs themselves, caught in some snarl or open-mouthed attempt to snap, their teeth exposed, bodies thrown forward, muscles tense and solid. I saw Jean's face, and a drop of water that was running from her wet hair into the neck of her coat. She stood there, drawn to the dogs, her eyes fastened on them, her hands holding one another, or a cigarette, all this done now with the grace and luxurious casualness which we had learned at long hours of practice in the kitchen. Matthew still hung back and saw Jean's dark profile against the lighted pit, the men half in shadow, whitish, most of whom were dressed in old clothes or at least clothes which had been washed to the point of being pale remembrances of their original color. Jean lit a cigarette and exhaled, and Matthew must have seen a halo of snow-colored light around her. She turned to him and said, "I didn't hurt you. I never wanted to hurt you. So why did you bring us here?"

Jean stared at the dogs and occasionally put the back of her hand to her lips.

Matthew moved into the light. Bowie, the superintendent of roads, saw some movement and turned and said, "Who's that?"

Matthew stepped out a little more.

"Oh," said Bowie, "it's just the Hales kid."

But he saw the light as it fell across Jean's legs and shoes, the smoke from her cigarette.

"Who have you got with you, Matt?" said Bowie.

The dogs were snarling, barking, making the warehouse resonant with it. The men turned away from them for a moment and looked at us.

"Jean Cooper," said Matthew, "and Annie."

"Is Jean your girl now, Matt?" said Bowie, smiling.

All of the men watched Jean as she stood away from the wall and faced them.

"No," said Matt.

"He's just embarrassed," said the constable.

Jean stood with her hands at her sides and smiled just a bit, turning up the corner of her mouth, as though a gentle smile could somehow change what was going on in the center of the warehouse. It made things worse. The men seemed more awkward, and one angrily pushed another. The dogs strained at their chains, barking and growling. The hair on each back raised, and looked like wheat or long grass as it's blown one way by the wind.

"We've done enough betting," said the manager of the theater, pulling his pants up over his belly. "Let's see them."

He turned away from Jean.

"Good enough," said another man. "I'm ready to see one crack the other."

"Matthew," said Bowie, still watching him, and not yet intent on the animals. "You take Jean out of here. And Annie, too. This is no place for them and you know it."

"Get them out of here!" said a man with a cap pulled down so the bill was over his eyes.

Matthew opened the door and Jean and I turned and walked out. Then all of us stood in the alley, and Jean said to Matthew, "Thank you. That was real nice of you."

We started walking up the alley, and Matthew came up behind us and said, "Wait a minute. Just wait."

So we stood there, hearing the dogs which had been released and were snarling and biting, their cries (and it did sound like cries) being quickly muffled from time to time, and then louder as they were separated. The men were silent. It was as though the warehouse were empty, or had been invaded by two animals who both wanted possession alone, undisputed. The sound made my knees feel a little watery. There was a hard slap, a wooden drum-like noise when one of the dogs hit the plywood ring.

It had stopped snowing. Matthew stood before us in his jacket that just wouldn't fit. Jean looked at him and listened to the noise that was coming from the warehouse. Matthew flinched, and he looked for a moment as though he were drunk and on a fun house ride he just wanted to get away from. Jean took his hand and put it against her face and said, "All right. I know you didn't mean any harm, really."

"And nothing would have happened in your car tonight?" said Matthew.

"No," said Jean with a smile.

"Well," said Matthew, becoming angry again and confused and hearing those dogs still hitting that wooden barricade. They made an odd snorting sound, too, when their growls were muffled. "I'll go back in. That junkyard dog from Pennsylvania looks like a good one."

"Fine," said Jean, "you go ahead."

She turned and began to walk down the alley. I wanted to get away from that noise.

"I'll let you know which wins," said Matthew, as he stood at the warehouse door.

We walked back through the snow, seeing that it had cleared and that there were stars out, and they looked like glitter spread across black paper.

"I'm glad we got out of there," said Jean. "Contempt makes me feel like nothing at all. Then I want release, because after the contempt I'm so empty I can hardly tell you, and maybe being used would make me feel like I was real again, or that I had myself back. So I'm glad to get away. In a minute more I would have taken one of them or all of them and then I'd be here for the rest of my life."

There was a moon and it made everything look as though it were standing in a pile of black silk: trees, houses, telephone poles.

"How were the movies?" said my father when we came in.

"Fine," said Jean. "Just fine."

"That's good," said my father, "Glad you had a good time."

"Alan Ladd, wasn't it?" said my mother.

"Yes," said Jean, "it was Alan Ladd."

We went upstairs and got into our nightgowns and sat in bed. Jean was silent, the muscles in the arm behind her head taut and smooth in the light that came off the snow and through the window, her hair as shiny as a roll of new dimes spread over the sheet, her lips together, eyes open, fixed and touched by a bright spot in each one.

"What are you thinking about?" I said.

"That warehouse," said Jean.

In the morning, on Saturday, we went downstairs, and found my mother sitting at the table, drinking coffee and reading a new copy of *Harper's* magazine. There were some new fashion magazines on the table, and we sat down and had a cup of coffee and began to read the magazines from Paris, being careful not to wrinkle the pages because my mother didn't like them that way. "They feel like they've come out of a doctor's office after you girls have read them. If you can't keep them decent then don't read them until I'm finished."

My father was at the showroom, trying to sell someone a Buick.

"I heard you were at the amusement last night," said my mother, looking up and staring at Jean and then at me. My mother's hair had been silver blond and now was almost white. "Do you think young ladies should go to things like that?"

"No," I said.

"Jean?" said my mother

"No," said Jean.

And that was all. My mother let us know by the tilt of her head and her posture what she thought about us for having allowed ourselves to be seen in that warehouse.

"What do you think of the fashions," said my mother, "for the summer?"

We drank our coffee. Outside the snow was almost melted, because it was a warm, clear day, with warm winds, too. I knew that after we'd dressed we'd go out and walk up and down the road (it being too muddy to walk anyplace else), but we'd be glad for that.

"Mother," said Jean, holding her cup and taking a small sip, "I'd like to go away to school in the fall."

My mother didn't stop her reading, but said, "How can I let you go away when you behave as you did last night?"

"You can trust me," said Jean. "If you'd just trust me. . . ."

She was wearing a blue and brown bathrobe, and her hair was still a little messy, but she was sitting perfectly and staring across the table at my mother.

"Do you think so? Why did you go there last night?" said my mother.

"Matthew took me," said Jean.

My mother glanced up from her magazine, and took off the horn-rimmed glasses she wore.

"Now how can you ask to go away when you tell me things like that?" said my mother.

"He took me there because he was angry," said Jean, "and he was angry because I won't have anything to do with him." Jean put the coffee cup down and sat with her hands in her lap.

"Oh," said my mother, and went back to the new copy of *Harper's*.

We heard the slight clink of coffee cups against their saucers, my mother scratching a match along the rough paper on the box to light a cigarette. Jean turned the pages of the magazine and slowly moved her head from side to side, as though her eyes were a broom and she was slowly dusting everything on the page. When we were done with our coffee we began to go upstairs, and my mother said, "At least you were honest, and that counts for something. I can't promise anything, but I'll write this afternoon."

On Monday, though, the letter was still sitting on the icebox. "Shouldn't I mail that?" said Jean.

"Of course," said my mother. "I'm sorry. I must have forgotten."

Jean took the letter and walked out the door, with a light, bouncing gait, got into the Ford, drove to the post office, and bought a stamp from Mrs. Haley, a woman of remarkably smooth skin for her age, who looked at the envelope and said, "My, Vassar College. My, that's a long ways from here." Mrs. Haley then took Jean's dime, gave her her change, and watched as Jean smiled, shook the hair back from her head, and turned to look at the wanted posters (which Jean always did, enjoying, in particular, pictures of women, who, in addition to having scars in private places, were described as "armed and dangerous"). Jean flipped through the new ones, looked at the swirls of inked fingerprints, and read the new descriptions of scars.

Jean came back into the kitchen and poured herself a cup of coffee and started turning those pages filled with photographs of dresses of *crêpe de chine* and shoes that looked so light and delicate as to have been made from eggshells. She said to our mother, while keeping her eyes on those slick pages, "Thank you for writing, you just don't know what I've been—" when the telephone began to ring.

"Hello," said my mother, "why yes, hello . . . no . . . it wasn't meant to be a surprise. It's just a request for information . . . no . . ."

My mother came back and started her coffee again, while Jean looked up from the magazine and began again to say, "It's been difficult in ways—" when the telephone started to ring again: we had to wait, because the line was on a party, and it rang a different number of times for each house and ours was the last, so we had to wait for it to ring six times. My mother picked it up and said, "Why no, it's really nothing . . . just a request for some information . . . I know . . . Yes, yes . . . why of course I'd let you know. . . ."

Jean sat at the table, with her shoulders squared and one hand carefully turning the pages so they wouldn't be wrinkled or dirty, and drank her coffee, while my mother came back and looked out the window over the sink at that horizon and sky that came together like two pieces of metal, one blue and white, the other brown and green. The phone began to ring. I was outside the kitchen, in the hall, so I could see my mother at one end of the table and Jean at the other, neither doing anything but reading their magazines, more as though they were in a library where not a sound could be heard than in a kitchen where they had to wait for the telephone to ring six times before they didn't do anything at all. "Hello, Annie," said my mother as I went to join them and as the telephone started to ring. So I sat there, too, and counted and didn't do anything, either. After a while, when it seemed as though my mother and Jean were in some contest from which I had been excluded (and from which I wanted to be excluded), I said, "Maybe I should answer the phone."

"No," said Jean. "It's not necessary."

"It serves this town right," said my mother, "to worry about things for a while."

"Oh," I said.

Jean finished the fashion magazine and sat at the table. My mother watched her.

"I'm going to start looking for a job," said Jean.

"Doing what?" said my mother.

"It doesn't matter," said Jean, "does it? Just something to make a little folding money. I'll need that when I go."

"Oh," said our mother, obviously relieved, "I thought you meant something else, you know. I thought you were looking for a job because you were giving up. A permanent job. You won't give up, honey, will you, just because of a little prying? Because of that?"

Our mother gestured toward the ringing telephone.

Jean stood in the kitchen with that ramrod posture and that smile which was suggestive of Arctic wastes.

"No," said Jean.

"Good," said my mother.

"So," said Jean, "do you think it's a good idea to get a job?"

"Why, yes," said my mother, "I think that's a good idea."

In the morning Jean dressed, and combed her hair, and put on just a touch of makeup, although she looked better without it: it did, however, give her the aspect of meaning business. We used to call it putting on our war paint. Then she asked me if she could use the car and I said, "Of course, of course," and she went downstairs and said to my mother, "How do I look?" And my mother had to say, "Lovely, absolutely lovely," because she couldn't have gotten away with anything else. Jean had a piece of toast and then got into the Ford and started it, the rumbling of the engine filling the garage as Jean waited for it to warm up, and then backed out the driveway and drove to town, now passing the farms with the textured and dark fields open and ready for planting. She waved to the men on the machines, the farmers who were raking or who were disking or harrowing a field.

In town she parked, and went first to the theater, because although Jean was sincere, there was no sense in making herself miserable, and since she liked to watch the movies, she might as well get paid. There was Babs who sold the tickets now, and she was pregnant and about to give up her job, so Jean went to the theater and tapped on the glass door. Even though the place was closed, Mr. Pin had an office in the back where he went over his deposits, the money he owed the distributors, and where he saw the salesman who canvassed for M&M's, JuJubes, popcorn, and soda, and where he sat with a copy of *Variety* and a drink of some kind (and certainly a box of popcorn which he took right out of the machine as often as he liked) just to while the time away and to wait for anyone who might happen by to share a little gossip.

He heard Jean's knocking and came out and opened the heavy glass doors, blinking a little in the morning light, like the nocturnal and vaguely subterranean creature that a movie theater owner is.

"Well, well," he said. "Come in. Come in."

"I'd like to," said Jean.

"Then come in," said Mr. Pin. "I'm just doing a little book work."

They walked through the lobby which smelled of popcorn and chewing gum, Milk Duds, cigarettes, boredom and excitement.

"Would you like a candy bar?" said Mr. Pin. "Or a Coke? Popcorn?"

"No, thanks," said Jean.

"Think I'll just take a little popcorn," he said, "since it's on the house."

Jean smiled. Mr. Pin got his popcorn and they went back to his office. Jean sat with her legs crossed at the ankles in the oak chair with slats that was opposite him. Mr. Pin stared at her and ate popcorn.

"Well," he said, "what can I do for you?"

"I understand Babs is quitting," said Jean. "I'd like to ask for her job."

Jean sat opposite him with her hands in her lap and her face set in a friendly expression. She looked fresh and light, and made that dingy back office which had stale walls and old calendars, dust in the corners, and an ash tray that was emptied once every year (about the time of the Academy Awards) seem a little more cheerful, as though there had been a window in it (which there wasn't) which had been thrown open after a long, stuffy winter. Pin ate popcorn, shaking some from the box (which he used over and over again, so you could hardly tell what kind it had been originally) into his hand, and then throwing the popped kernels into his mouth four or five at a time, and finally, when the box was empty, putting back his head and emptying the box, saying, "The best ones are at the end, you know, the little salted ones that didn't pop." Pin went through this business of eating slowly, holding a few kernels and glancing at Jean, seeing the way her hips fit in the chair, the movement of her eyelashes, the slight rise of her chest as she breathed, the smile on her face.

"Well, yes," said Pin, "that's true. You know, that Barbara is a good girl and she's been out there selling those tickets for, well, it must be three years anyway, and she never made a mistake, not once. I'm sorry to see her going off and leaving me short-handed, especially, you know, when I'd gone and let myself get so used to her, and everything."

Pin went out and got some more popcorn and sat at his desk again, staring over the box.

"But, yes," said Pin, "that's right. Barbara is going off and leaving me to have a baby, which I guess is only natural, wouldn't you say? She's been married for a while now and her husband's a big strong fellow and I imagine they must have spent some nice times together. I remember them when they were courting right out there in the lobby and smooching in the back rows of the theater."

Pin ate some more popcorn and looked back at Jean.

"Don't you think that's only natural?" said Mr. Pin.

"Yes," said Jean, "I think it is."

Jean told me she was still smiling, watching Pin sip an extra-large Coke. His fingers picked at some of the papers on his desk, bills from distributors, announcements for candy bar promotion, junk that would have embarrassed anyone else, but which, in some strange way, made Pin feel as though he had just come off a back lot in Hollywood.

"That Matthew is a nice boy, isn't he?" said Pin.

"Yes, he is," said Jean.

"That's what I always thought," said Pin, getting down now to the end of the popcorn and beginning to tilt his head back to get what he called the best part of the box. Then they sat there for a while. Jean heard the fly-wing buzz of the fluorescent bulb. They just sat.

"Well," said Pin, "well."

Jean shifted a little in her chair, sat more on the edge of the seat, smoothed her skirt over her knees. Pin watched, rattled the ice in the bottom of the Coke.

"I came to ask about Barbara's job," said Jean.

"Yes," said Pin, "that's right, isn't it?"

"Yes," said Jean.

"Well," said Pin, "it's as I've been telling you, Jean. That girl went off and managed to get herself in that condition after I began to need her so much, if you understand me. A man tends to be very regular in his habits, you understand?"

"That's natural," said Jean.

"That's what I always thought. I'm going to miss the girl, so I don't think I could do that to myself again, you understand? She came in here and then she just walked out when it suited her. And from what I hear you wouldn't be wanting that job for very long, would you?"

Later, at night, when Jean was standing in the tub, toweling herself off and I was sitting on the seat watching her, she said, "You know it was private in there and dark with just that one buzzing light and all those bills and whatnot, and could you imagine the look on his face if I had just said, 'Well, all right,' and begun to take off some clothes, can you imagine those fingers with a little butter touching me here" (she touched herself along the side, under her breast) "or his mouth as he licked that butter and that salt?" Jean started to laugh a little.

"But you didn't," I said. "You wouldn't."

Jean looked at me after scrubbing her face with the towel and said, "No. But it was private. It was so private in there you could die."

So Jean sat on the other side of the desk as Pin allowed the last of the kernels to run from the gray and wrinkled box into his mouth, chewing them and looking at her.

"No," said Jean, "I had planned on five months. Until next September."

"That's what I heard," said Pin. "That school you're going to is a long way from here, isn't it?"

"I suppose so," said Jean.

That office seemed a little cramped, Jean told me, and I believe it, with that man who was over six five and heavy, sitting on one side of a small desk, his eyes touched with two bright spots from the lights overhead as he leaned back, still tilting that box, still waiting, even though he already seemed to have turned her down.

"Then you can't really expect me to give you that job, can you, Jean, if you're fixing to leave about the time I got used to you and began to depend upon you?"

Jean looked right back at him, at his jowled and perfectly shaved face, those eyes with the points from the fixture overhead. There were spots on the papers before him from the butter on the popcorn.

"I'd never make a mistake," said Jean.

"Is that right?" said Pin.

"Yes," said Jean.

"Well, I'm sorry to hear that," said Pin, "because that's exactly what I'm looking for, but I just can't expose myself to that kind of disruption, you understand? Now, if you weren't going off so soon, why maybe even a year and five months rather than just five, I might be able to work something out."

Jean shook her head.

"No hard feelings, now? This town is just too small for that."

"No, there aren't any hard feelings," said Jean, standing up now and looking at Pin, who was already holding the door of his office open.

They went back through that lobby with the large paisley pattern on the rug (or what had been a paisley pattern, and one, at that, which could only be seen when the sofa was moved, because the rest of the floor was covered with gum, cigarette burns, dark stains of one sort or another). Jean said the surface of the glass door felt good, and that Pin just took her arm for a moment as he guided her outside into the April air, which was so much different than the atmosphere of his office, the odor of condensed and old cigarette smoke, stale popcorn, the fresh, new invoices for candies.

"I'm sorry I can't help you," said Pin, politely seeing her through the door (they were always polite, at least in the beginning, anyway).

Jean stood in that morning sunshine and said, "That's all right. Don't worry about it."

"I'm glad to hear that," said Pin. "When you see Matthew, you give him my hello."

So Jean walked for a little way, downhill, and I can see her figure moving along that early forenoon street, the sun bright and making everything seem as though it were being presented through a lens: that's how clear it was that day. It was as though someone had cut a cucumber in half and held it up to your nose.

Of course she went on looking, each morning getting up and dressing and going downstairs and eating that piece of toast and getting into the Ford (if I didn't have classes, or driving me to school and then taking the Ford for herself if I did) and driving into town, each day returning from the box factory or the small plant that made bases for cosmetics, the library, the insurance office, the local Sears (which was just a small room with a book in it), each day returning with that expression learned through hours of discipline, a smooth and pretty and thoroughly charming face that didn't give the least hint of exasperation or anger.

"Well, well," said my father one evening when we all sat down to dinner, "well, well. How did the job-hunting go?"

"Bad," said Jean.

She ate her food regularly, without any hesitation or much obvious enjoyment. She just ate, because she knew she had to.

"Maybe there'll be something tomorrow."

"I'm beginning to doubt it," said Jean, "because I'm running out of places to look."

"Hmmmm," said my father.

My mother sat there and looked at Jean with approval, if only because Jean absolutely refused to allow the town to have its way, and because Jean also refused to give the town even the satisfaction of knowing that Jean was in any way hurt or mystified: my mother could have watched Jean doing that for twenty years, or a hundred, or forever. Now, whenever she spoke to Jean it was in French.

"What about at the showroom?" said Jean.

"What?" said my father.

"Is there anything I could do for you?" said Jean. "Anything. Sweeping out. Answering mail, typing, washing cars?"

"No," said my father, "I don't think anything like that would be suitable."

Jean finished her dinner without saying anything more, except for correcting my mother's use of the subjunctive.

"It's Saturday, though," said my father. "Aren't you and Annie going to the movies?"

Jean sat with her hands in her lap.

"Yes," I said. "Sure we are. We always do, don't we?"

Jean nodded and then we went upstairs to dress.

"Are you all right?" I said. "Are you tired?"

"I'm just fine," said Jean, as she pulled a sweater over her head. "Just fine."

It was the next day that Jean managed a job. She told us at the dinner table.

"Well I'll be damned," said my father. "Where did you get a job?"

"From Michel DeCroix," said Jean.

"Well, I'll be damned again," said my father, rising from the table and looking at Jean. "He would give you a job, wouldn't he? Doing what?"

"I don't know yet," said Jean.

"What the hell kind of job could he offer a decent girl?" said my father. "I think I'll go down to see him."

"No," said Jean, shaking her head. "No. It's all I was able to get and I want it."

"That man needs a good talking to," said my father.

"No," said Jean, sitting now in the perfect posture and turning toward my father, not raising her voice, but nevertheless firm as those lessons learned between those black lines on the floor. My father sat in his shirt sleeves and suspenders and his bow tie, with his fingers which were splattered with blue ink (he'd sold a Roadmaster that day).

"Well," he said, "if I find out it's not appropriate I'll talk to him."

"I don't think you'll have to worry," said my mother. "Jean knows better than that."

The light hit the chrome fixture in the sink and the drops that were forming at the end of it. We sat and listened to that dripping sound, and no one ate aside from Jean.

There was something else in Jean's tone, too, which suggested a number of men someplace, a barn or a shed, perhaps in the morning or evening but more likely at night, their faces grim and taut, none being able to look at another but all waiting around that place, whatever it might be, some not completely dressed, and none looking in (except perhaps for one who would see a bit of one long, slender and white thigh, a graceful and clenched hand, blue eyes absolutely crazed and wide open). When I tried to mention this to my mother she looked horrified, and said, "There's no need to worry. None. Jean knows how things are," which is to say, Jean understood that if she did anything that reflected badly on my mother, or in any way gave in to the town, then Jean would be denied the chance to escape.

After the dishes had been cleared my mother and father sat opposite one another. Each had a drink of Jim Beam.

"Have you heard from that college yet?" said my father.

"No," said my mother, "not yet."

"You know," said my father, "there isn't that much wrong with this town, or with me, either."

"Is that what you think?" said my mother, who then turned to me and began to speak French. My father followed the words every now and then, looking up and almost mouthing them. One day, later in the week, I dropped by his office and found in his desk, or actually on it, a French grammar, a dictionary, and a copy of *Paris-Match*, the margins of it filled with his large scrawl where he had translated an editorial as well as he could.

Michel DeCroix was short and in pain, and many people thought he was a Gypsy, but I don't think there is any truth to that. He lived out of town a little bit and had a truck, and usually he spent his days sitting in front of his shack, which was just below the road. DeCroix's house was decorated with hubcaps and had a yard filled with small windmills, all of them painted bright colors. They made a wonderful sound of fluttering when the breeze blew. There were some of these on the front of his house (built like a barn, just unpainted uprights, planks, on which there were nailed some pieces of wood that were supposed to pass for siding). DeCroix had a chrome kitchen chair in the front yard (along with a bunch of other junk which he picked up one place or another and saw some value in), and he'd go up to the store (which was just in walking distance), sometimes on his bike with balloon tires, sometimes on foot, and occasionally on a horse he had. He bought a quart of beer and came back to sit in his yard and listen to the sound the windmills made while he drank his beer. Sometimes he'd buy a large dill pickle, and he'd eat that with the beer. He usually wore some kind of dark overalls, cut from a black material and having two straps that went over his shoulders. He wore a white shirt. His legs seemed short and there was something humped under his shirt, something which was disguised by his clothes, but which nevertheless hurt him, because you could see that he had difficulty sitting still, and when he was drinking his beer and listening to the noise of the windmills he'd be rocking back and forth. His head seemed a touch too large for his legs and heavy chest, and his hair was dark and pretty, and his eyebrows were full. His lips were bright red, his eyes blue, and his teeth white, although his expression, his face, was stark, menacing, and ugly.

His business consisted mainly in attending auctions of the estates of people who had died, buying those things he thought were of some use, and selling them in turn to the buyers from Chicago or Toledo or Detroit. He also had that horse, which occasionally he rented to a girl or boy who wanted to ride and whose parents had tractors or pickup trucks, not to mention cars (Buicks, even), but who were short a horse. Next to DeCroix's house there was a barn, which was the rust color you see on wood when the red paint is about gone, and on which there had been stuck twenty-five or thirty of those small bright and noisy windmills. There was also a handwritten sign on it, in letters at least twelve feet high, which said Horses For Hire. It seems to me that some time ago there had been another horse, and it had died of old age, but DeCroix kept the sign with the "s" on it, probably out of hope and the knowledge that came from his business: you never can tell what's going to turn up, Genesis written on an enameled chamberpot, mementos of Queen Victoria's coronation, or a horse. The barn was filled with acquisitions, too, although his house was spare, but not necessarily clean.

Usually I saw DeCroix sitting on the chrome chair in his front yard, drinking his beer, listening to the soothing flipped-cards sound of the windmills and rocking back and forth because of the pain. Everyone in town was curious about the cause of it, but we never found out. The hurt didn't seem to come from the hump under his shirt, or from the joints of his arms and legs, which didn't point the right way (not to mention seeming to be in the wrong place), but from some constitutional ailment that kept him in constant pain all over. He kept a large jar of aspirin on the ground next to his chair, and he'd eat them like peanuts, to go along with the beer. This usually meant that he was getting ready to make a drive in his truck, since the bouncing hurt him, and the beer and aspirin helped.

He drove great distances, too, to attend an auction, or (more recently) to take a look around the house of the newly bereaved widow or widower or orphan and make what offers he wanted before the auctioneer ever got his hands on the stuff, driving these distances in his truck that had a pillow in the driver's seat and blocks cut from two-by-fours on the pedals. The distances, however, were getting shorter, and DeCroix had developed some other troubles, too (these I had from Jean), and he must have been sitting in that spring sun, rocking back and forth, drinking beer, feeling the cold tang of pain, and wondering about those troubles when Jean stopped our Ford in front of his house and got out.

Jean told me it was the last place she'd try (since she had been to every other place in town, and more than once, as well), although when she drove out to see him she occasionally felt uncertain or uncomfortable. She was dressed in a blue skirt and a white blouse and she had a sweater, which she had taken off because of the heat, and she was wearing stockings and a pair of decent shoes. She passed houses with white clapboards, the store where DeCroix shopped, the firehouse, and those empty and flat fields, which no one tended because they belonged to DeCroix. It was warm in the car and Jean felt her blouse sticking to her back, and she stopped when she saw the house and barn, the turning windmills, the yard filled with brass bedsteads, bathtubs, mattresses and springs, a thousand Mason jars. At least she slowed down at first and then pulled over to the side of the road and sat there, listening to the quick click of the windmills and seeing DeCroix tilted back in his chair, his brown bottle turned up, and his hand filled with aspirin.

"I didn't just stop because I wanted the job," said Jean in the evening after she was hired, "it was because I didn't want to hurt his feelings, since I had tried everywhere else. But he didn't care about that. He didn't give one damn about that kind of pride or silliness."

Jean got out of the Ford and stood there in her skirt and stockings and those shoes and waited for a moment, being startled by the sound of the windmills. She went through a little bit of gate and stepped around or over the junk that was in the front yard and stood before DeCroix, who was still in his kitchen chair with the chrome legs (which bright pieces of metal must have reflected that blue sky and grubby patch of earth in front of his house), and who was still tilted back against the weathered siding, his head leaning against the splintered boards, the brown bottle in his lap and a half cup of white pills in his hand: Jean was convinced he was asleep, so when she got to a place right in front of him she just stopped and looked at him.

His face was tanned and his lips were red in any case and made more shiny from the beer, and Jean said that even in his resting moments there was in his expression something that seemed to snarl or to imply the desire for seeing something torn apart. It wasn't for nothing that among the bathtubs, chairs, dressers, and mirrors that he brought home, there was also information he gathered about various fighting dogs, which he'd watch in Pennsylvania and over the whole state of Ohio and occasionally into Tennessee and Kentucky as well, which information was passed on to people in town who would then organize a meeting like the one that Jean and I went to about three weeks before. Of course he wasn't sleeping, but watching through barely opened eyes, listening to those windmills turn and flap.

"I understand that you're looking for a job," he said, "and that no one will give you one."

"That's right," said Jean.

"Can you drive a truck like that?" said DeCroix, pointing with the brown bottle.

"Why," said Jean, smiling, but still holding that posture, "I've driven just about every kind of car and truck ever made. Because of my father, you know. The trade-ins."

DeCroix swung both feet on the ground and put some of those aspirin into his mouth and began to chew them, while looking at Jean.

"Sit down," said DeCroix, pushing a chair at Jean a little. "I won't bite, you know."

Jean took the chair, sat there in the sun beneath the sound of the handmade windmills. DeCroix's face was set with some strain.

"You came to ride my horse about fifteen years ago," said De-Croix. "I don't suppose you remember. Your father brought you and you wanted to ride. The horse is dead now. You're grown up now. Aren't you?"

"Yes," said Jean, without vanity or embarrassment, but just acknowledging a fact. She sat on that chair and let the sun hit her face and lips, felt the coolness of the breeze which blew into the hollow where DeCroix had his house.

"No one's around," said DeCroix. "You want some beer?"

"Yes," said Jean, "I would."

DeCroix had a porcelain cup sitting at the side of his chair and he rinsed it in a bucket there that was filled with rainwater. Jean took the beer and drank it off, glad for its coolness. DeCroix told Jean that he had no objection to the smell of tobacco so Jean lit a cigarette, and DeCroix watched the smoke as she exhaled, the way her fingers held the cigarette.

"Yes," said DeCroix, "all grown up. You've got nice clothes and you look nice the way you walk. You speak French, don't you?"

"I know a few words," said Jean.

"Can you draw or is that your sister?" said DeCroix.

"Annie can't draw," said Jean with a laugh (and I know she put it this way because I can't and Jean has laughed at me ten times if it was once, even if I have to make a map to tell someone how to make a right turn).

"So it's you?" said DeCroix, his extra large head with that thick black hair (even though he was over forty-five) and that heavy torso moving toward her a little.

"Yes," said Jean.

DeCroix's hand dropped for a moment next to a leg of that kitchen chair, and Jean thought that hand was reaching for more aspirin and didn't look, but then something about DeCroix's lips and eyes, the quick and arch movement of his head, made Jean's eyes follow his hand. It was near the bottle of aspirin (the inside of it covered with a white dust from the thousands of aspirin that had gone through the jar), although a little more to his side, not quite pointing, but indicating in a blunt gesture the objects next to the jar, things which had obviously been scavanged from some sloppy and wet place (the town dump, to be exact), and among which there were a pair of mismatched ballet shoes, a toaster, some small window screens, and a pile of magazines of fashion from England and from France, the pile held together with string, and the top number still having in it a manila folder which contained those drawings of Jean's.

DeCroix didn't say anything. They listened to the hum and flap of those windmills, DeCroix reaching once for a couple of aspirin, which he chewed while he stared at Jean, who turned into the breeze, not flinching or in any way acknowledging that she'd seen a thing. Later, she told me, "I'm glad he didn't say anything, more glad than I can say. We sat there and I felt the breeze, the clothes I wore, the dampness under my skirt, the texture of the cigarette paper. He did stare though, but it didn't bother me at all. I felt relieved because he kept his mouth shut."

"All right," said DeCroix.

"All right what?" said Jean.

"All right, I'll give you a job," said DeCroix. "Come back tomorrow in some clothes you can get a little dirty."

"You're not joking with me," said Jean, "are you?"

"No," said DeCroix, rocking with that pain which fitted him like a suit of good clothes, "I don't make jokes. Leastways, not one you'd recognize right off and laugh at. No, it's a job. Come here tomorrow."

"All right," said Jean, and then turned, and walked back up the little bit of path through DeCroix's possessions (or junk), and then out to the Ford, where she sat for a moment, watching DeCroix as he rocked and moved his head from side to side, although obviously being soothed to some extent by the flapping sounds of the windmills.

"Wait," said DeCroix, just before Jean had gotten into the Ford.

"What for?" said Jean.

"Aren't you going to ask what I'll pay you?"

"You'll pay me what's fair," said Jean.

"You think so, do you? You think that's what will happen?"

"Yes," said Jean.

"All right," said DeCroix. "You come tomorrow."

That night, after my father had threatened to talk to DeCroix and had been stopped from doing so, and after dinner, we went upstairs and got into bed, and Jean told me she was glad to have the job, which, the next night, she described, or tried to describe. The men with whom DeCroix did business in Chicago and Detroit or Toledo were becoming more sophisticated and weren't so much junk dealers (which they had once been) and now no longer even used furniture dealers. They had become, DeCroix told Jean, Antique Dealers now, and they had told him that he had no taste.

"Which isn't at all true," said Jean, "not true at all. He understands simple lines and good wood. What those men in Detroit were saying is that *they* had no taste, and I reckon I'll be able to fix them just fine, because if there's one thing I know something about it's what people from around here think is what would be considered a big deal in New York or Paris." Jean nodded downstairs toward the kitchen where our mother sat. "So I'll pick up some of that cute stuff that is so ugly it could harm your eyesight and those men in Detroit or Chicago will be driving down here and begging DeCroix's favor. Oh, sure," said Jean, "sure. I'll fix them just fine."

"But why did he hire you?" I said.

"Because he thought I had enough sense to know what *not* to send," said Jean, "and as far as that's concerned, he's right."

Later, when we were almost asleep, and I saw Jean's hands behind her head as she stared at the ceiling, I said, "But that's not what I meant. Why did he hire you knowing he'd have trouble with the town, because you know he will?"

"Yes," said Jean, staring at the ceiling, "I asked him about that today, not directly, but just by giving him the chance, and he looked at me with those eyes which are furious and in no way warm, and with his face in that snarled and angry expression he told me that maybe I didn't have the same memories as he did or the time to think about them, either, you know, like about the time a young girl came to ride a horse that is now dead."

Now Jean left the house in the morning wearing a pair of boots and denim pants and a white blouse and her hair was sometimes done up in a bandanna when the roads were dusty. She started driving DeCroix to some of those places which he had become too tired or hurt to go to, Jean sitting behind the wheel of that truck, with her feet working the pedals with the blocks, DeCroix sitting next to her, eating aspirin and drinking beer. They'd drive right through the town so everyone could see them, Pin and Cousin, the men and women in Woolworth's, Sears, the tractor-repair shop, the gas station, everyone who had denied Jean a chance when she had asked for it.

A week went by, and Jean brought home some pay, which was, according to Jean, fair and adequate. The dirty talk, of course, began the day after Jean started working and didn't reach me until a few days later, because it was low. It was said that Jean was doing more than just driving that truck, more than picking out the cute and ugly things to go into the houses of people who had just acquired a lot of money in Detroit or Chicago, that Jean was lazing around in that shack where DeCroix lived. Which all may have been true, although I doubted it.

At the end of the first week, when Jean and I were at the movies, we noticed that there weren't so many of the boys as usual in attendance, and we remarked on it. Or at least I did. Jean found out later that a number had gone to DeCroix's sometime after dark, after he had gone to bed with his head full of beer and aspirin, and the lingering sensation of bouncing over those roads in that truck with Jean at the wheel. She guided them over those back country roads, a little moisture on the sides of her nose, laughing about the things they had bought, and occasionally taking a drink of beer from the bottle. I imagine that the bounces in the road were worse in memory than they were in fact, because DeCroix was now alone, or at least he thought he was, as he lay there trying to sleep, turning from side to side with the oddly shaped and painful body, listening to the windmills and wondering if his purchases would put him in solid with the men from Detroit, Chicago, and Toledo.

The boys and men from town parked their cars in front of the house and stood around drinking for a while, not really having planned on anything aside from "paying a visit" to DeCroix, most of them, Pin and Cousin, Samson (the contractor), and others, Matthew included (although he later told me he was there with dread and shame), trusting that the liquor would find the right thing to do, if they gave the hooch a chance. Which they did, and it wasn't long before they started picking up things from the road and throwing them at the house, or (among the most daring) going into his yard and picking up one of those Mason jars and throwing it, too. DeCroix was half-asleep when this part began, uncomfortable, as always, and full of imaginings that usually plagued his rest, or at least hearing sounds which he presumed were part of those same imaginings which kept him half-awake. He probably tried to decide whether to have more beer and aspirin and wondered why the imaginings were so strong on this particular night. The fluttering, bird-wing noise of the windmills was constant, unlike those times when the imaginings came and went, displacing and leaving that flapping hum. A breaking window and the smash of a jar on the roof woke DeCroix and left him feeling foolish, since he had expected trouble, but not anywhere near so soon.

The boys and men outside played their headlights across the house and then turned them off for a while and went back to drinking, not stopping, however, those voices (or words), which DeCroix had heard many times behind his back, and in his half-waking imaginings, and in town, in the stores and on the street, but previously only in a hushed tone, whispers unlike the yelling which was now outside his house, those shouts which made fun of his body and face, the odd hump under his clothes.

DeCroix lay there for a while, feeling the pain, I imagine, which hadn't been treated for a couple of hours, and which usually made him jumpy. The boys and men went back to throwing things, and some were already talking fire when DeCroix rolled over and put his bare feet into those boots which were made especially for him in Chicago by a cobbler who had letters after his name and who had studied at universities in Europe, as well. DeCroix put them on and chewed some aspirin while he went to the door and opened it and stepped out on the porch, that small and raised platform or landing over which there was a roof. The windmills were still flipping, but as soon as he stood outside, they seemed to stop, or he was distracted by the lights that shone on him as soon as he opened the door. He was wearing his trousers, the boots, and his nightshirt, so the men from the town were cheated of a look at the shape of DeCroix's injuries. He stood on the porch, squinting into the lights, behind which there was the drunken chorus, chanting those same words, those same insults which had followed him wherever he had gone for the last forty-five years.

"Who's there?" said DeCroix.

They yelled at him, but gave no names, which was quite unnecessary anyway. DeCroix was trying to buy a little time, and to guess, as well, how many there were and about what their positions were.

"You know damn well," said Pin, the one who ran the theater, "and you know why we're here, too."

The shouting started again, as did the throwing of rocks and those pieces of junk from the front yard. DeCroix went back into the house when there was more talk about fire and began to wonder (still not fully convinced that these sounds of things smashing weren't more of his imaginings), where he had put the cartridges for a Mauser (8 mm) he had run across years ago and which he kept in perfect condition, every week or so taking it out of the closet where he stored it and giving the rifle (which still had a leather sling in good condition) a thorough cleaning. Every now and then he'd take a shot from the chrome kitchen chair in the front yard, so it's not as though he didn't know how to use it, either. While he was puzzling over the whereabouts of the cartridges (which he had to order from a man in Chicago who loaded the used ones by hand, crimping the shells onto the new bullets with a little press) he picked up the rifle and opened the bolt. The men outside were throwing more bottles and junk and shouting, too. DeCroix was now fully awake (and not the least puzzled over the whereabouts of the cartridges, since they were in a Chinese box which was on top of a closet, the Chinese box being lacquered and red and having one of the oddest brass locks you've ever seen) and now being aware as well, that the sounds outside were the men and boys from town who were in fact outside and getting ready to burn his house, and him, too, if they could get away with it. So he loaded the rifle, slowly and with care, pushing each shell into the magazine until it was engaged, being careful not to get the shell too far forward or too far to the back, not wanting the rifle to jam in case he had to shoot more than once.

Jean told me later that he hadn't exactly been praying, but his thinking, as nearly as he could describe it, had a certain devotional quality, in which or through which he was torn: wanting, in equal proportion, the chance to walk outside and drop one of those men in his tracks and pleading, too, for the chance that he wouldn't have to do a thing, that those men and boys would leave him alone, so he could go back to that quiet life of drinking beer, eating aspirin, and listening to the soothing sounds made by those windmills. I have always been glad that I have never seen DeCroix's face in half or dim light when he was angry, but I can well imagine it, those lips, which are as red as the label on a bottle of catsup, pulled into a pained and angry grimace, eyes pointed with light, brows as black as a dark snake, and bushy, too, although still slick, his large head held on one side, his face and skull being certainly misshapen but in a manner that is not quite identifiable, but nevertheless held in that way which is suggestive of thought, of pondering how he could hurt another the most.

Pin, Matthew, and the boys and men didn't stop the calling of those names or the throwing of stones, either, so DeCroix finished the loading of the rifle (which was about as long as he was tall) and quietly opened the back door and walked along the back of the house, hearing those words which had always plagued him in the same way that the pain did ("Gypsy gimp," "lophead freak"), and worked his way to the beginning of his side yard, where he stopped. He couldn't hear the windmills at all. Nothing aside from those men and boys calling and breaking the bottles they'd brought, one harsh voice above the rest, calling for a torch or gasoline or a match, but certainly for a fire. DeCroix had no desire to kill anyone, no desire to be tested by people standing in front of his house and getting ready to fire it, no desire even to see such an event as a test, although he would certainly have to admit failure if he stood by and allowed people to take his life's work and possessions away from him. That anger and fierceness of expression, I imagine, were more a personal matter between himself and the body he lived in, and although other people had to take some of the viciousness from that struggle, it wasn't as though they were the direct cause of his anger, excepting, of course, this particular night and the men and boys who were in front of his house.

By this time of course the hooch was doing its work: there was more than one voice calling for gasoline and a match. So DeCroix stretched out on the grass at the side of his house, put his left elbow through the Mauser's sling and his left hand on the forearm grip, and tightened the butt against his shoulder (which didn't fit right), and put his finger on the trigger, popping the safety off. The men were still out there, some still throwing things and calling for him to come out. His face, set over the sights, was squinted and screwed into that vision of rage, but certainly not blind, with one eye open, in which there was that point of light (from the head-lamps) and through which he saw that brightness, just over the end of the barrel's bead: there was an aura made by the automo-biles, that spreading glow which seemed to make the sky bleached and misty, the center of the glowing whiteness the headlights, to look at the center of which hurt, if you stared, because the natural impulse was to turn your head or to close your eyes. DeCroix started shooting.

He put out one headlight and then another, working the bolt and letting each used cartridge fly onto the grass, keeping his cheek snugly against the comb of the stock, his eye set behind the rear sights and still touched by a bright spot, which was becoming dimmer as his eye began to ache less, and quickly at that, as the number of headlights diminished and as the men and boys got into their cars and drove away from DeCroix's house, leaving him there alone, feeling the slight tickle of the grass on his forearms and the dampness of it, too, his sighting eye now completely dark and his ears filled with the sound of the windmills working in the lazy breeze of a spring evening.

When Jean showed up in the morning she found him inside the house and still dressed in his nightshirt, trousers, and boots. The telephone operator had told me about the shooting and the bro-ken headlamps, and she sounded tired from putting those plugs in, from listening to those tense and whispering voices, the denials, surprise, and insinuations about who was and who was not outside DeCroix's house the previous night. I told Jean. She got up without the least sign of being in a hurry (although she was moving about as fast as she could), dressed, got into the Ford, and drove to DeCroix's, where she knocked on the door, which was propped open, and looked inside. DeCroix's usual red-rose complexion was now a little grayish and yellow, since he hadn't slept a bit, know-ing that the next time the men and boys came back they wouldn't waste any time trying to let the liquor work, and they certainly wouldn't let DeCroix know what they were about.

"Can you go to the store," said DeCroix, "and get some bread and cheese and a couple bottles of beer and some aspirin?"

Jean stood there, dressed in her blue denim pants and her face still smelling of the plain soap with which she had washed, and said, "You can put that away," meaning the rifle, "no one would bother you during the day."

"Just run up to the store," said DeCroix.

DeCroix started rocking on his seat, and Jean went up to the store and DeCroix drank his beer, and ate the cheese and bread, and began the curing or easing of his discomfort. Jean sat in a corner and read old magazines until DeCroix fell asleep, and then she sat as quietly as possible, after having picked up and loaded that long Mauser, reading those old fashion magazines and listening to the omnipresent sound of the handmade windmills. DeCroix twitched in his sleep, and groaned, and rolled from side to side.

No one came around, and in the evening DeCroix woke.

"You still here?" he said.

His color was back to its normal red color and his eyes were clear.

"I'll be going in a minute," said Jean. "Do you want me to come back tomorrow?"

"Yes," said DeCroix, "pull that truck of mine close to the house."

She did so and then DeCroix took his white, open tool box with the dowel handle over the tray, and started working on the inside ceiling of the truck, cutting slowly through the tin and headliner, and then making a place on the floor with some wood, a small U-shaped thing. Finally, he went inside and unloaded the Mauser and then brought it out to the truck and put it through the hole he had made in the roof and locked the stock into that wooden cleat next to the gearshift.

"It won't fit otherwise," said DeCroix.

"What are we going to do when it rains?" said Jean.

"Get wet," said DeCroix, taking the Mauser out of the

truck again in case he'd need it during the night. "What else?"

So Jean wouldn't quit (or couldn't, because I don't think my mother would have let her, now that the town made an issue of her working), and DeCroix would be damned if he was going to fire her. And he needed her, too, now more than before since he was awake all night and needed to sleep in the truck while she drove. On Monday she showed up in the morning and DeCroix ate and they started, driving right through the center of town so that everyone could see the Mauser in the truck, and Jean at the wheel, working those pedals with the wooden blocks, passing those men and boys (or at least some of them) who had been in front of DeCroix's house the previous Saturday night. DeCroix went to sleep as soon as they were out of town, waking only to go into a house of the new mourners and sit while Jean made the purchases, DeCroix paying for them by taking his wallet out of his pocket and putting down the bills, although now hardly noticing how much Jean spent or what she spent it on.

When Jean came home in the evening there was a letter from Vassar College sitting by her plate at the dinner table.

"You can open it after we eat," said my mother. "Some people called, and I told them you'd open the letter, that we wouldn't know anything until tonight."

So we ate, Jean sitting in her chair, slowly and carefully cutting into the overdone roast beef, the broccoli, mashed potatoes and gravy, once or twice touching her lip with a napkin, never once glancing at the envelope until we were finished. My father sat in his shirt sleeves (although still wearing his red bow tie) and looked from Jean to my mother and then to the letter. My mother sat with her head back, watching what seemed to be absolutely nothing in the space before her, but nevertheless actually enjoying more than she could ever say the restraint with which Jean ate her dinner.

We had coffee. My father once began to speak, but there was a look from my mother which quieted him.

Jean sipped her coffee and spoke of the things she had bought that day from the widows she and DeCroix visited, a flower stand, some pewter, an ugly but nevertheless old table.

"I think you can open it now," said my mother.

The stationery was a light cream color, and it had a texture, too, although the paper wasn't heavy. Jean ripped the envelope neatly, withdrew the letter, and read, not flinching or in any way showing interest or disappointment or even joy. She put it down at the side of her coffee cup and said, "The class for this year has already been filled. They're sending an application and a catalogue separately."

"It won't hurt to wait another year," said my mother. "Will it, Jean?"

"No," said Jean.

"I'm sorry," said my father.

"I know you are," said Jean. "I know that."

"What about that job of yours?" said my father. "Maybe we can find something better."

"But why," said my mother, "after Jean looked so hard to find it?"

"I think I'll keep the job," said Jean. "I'm being paid well."

"Of course you are," said my mother.

"We'll see," said my father, and by his saying so we knew that the matter was settled.

We sat at the table, the cream-colored and beautiful piece of stationery sitting beside Jean's place, the paper folded in three places, creases sharp and neat. We didn't say much, although my mother said something in French.

The spring became more pronounced, and the weather warmed up. You could smell the fields as they turned green, and the trees as they flowered. The days were spent pretty much as usual. Jean got up in the morning and went to work and I went to the teacher's college and came back. We'd have dinner and Jean and I went upstairs to read and talk. Jean still drove DeCroix's truck around the country with DeCroix asleep on one side and the Mauser rifle between them. At night, when it was hot and we were unable to sleep, we opened the windows and lay in the half light that came from the lamps downstairs, Jean with just the sheet around a leg, one arm behind her head, her eyes closed. She smoked a cigarette and languidly flicked the ash, turning all the way over and straining to put the ashtray down, making the muscles in her stomach contract into even segments and making her ribs show a little, too. Jean was more quiet now, as she sat there with that slight breeze moving across her skin, occasionally mentioning only the size and shape of some particularly ugly thing she had bought to send to the squat, solid houses of Chicago or the newer ones of Detroit. Jean had stopped looking at the magazines from Paris, but I didn't and I'd say, "Would you like to feel *crêpe de chine* against your legs, or satin, or silk," and Jean looked out the window and said, "Yes. Yes. That would be nice. I'd like that."

Of course the whispering didn't stop behind us in the dark of the movie theater on Saturday night, but Jean just sat now, staring at Alan Ladd or William Bendix or Stewart Granger, not responding in a way that anyone could discover (aside from me, because I was sitting right next to her and felt the tremor as she put her legs together and against the seat in front, and I was with her at night, too, when she'd sit as quietly as could be, staring into the dark and smoking a cigarette). As a matter of fact the whispering became more predictable, and the voice more intense, describing now in some detail things that were offered, pleasures hinted at. Jean went to the movies and to the luncheonette, still not responding, now not having even the luxury of touching someone for a moment. After a while Matthew began to drink heavily, and usually, when the place next to Jean had been left vacant at the luncheonette, he'd sit in it and stare at his hands, being too drunk to say anything.

Every year, in the late spring, the town has a picnic, in honor of a historical character who came through Ohio in the middle of the last century, dealing in liquor, rifles, and fraud of every description, selling everybody what they thought they wanted, including of course other human beings, Irish women being, as I've heard, something of a specialty. The man became rich before being murdered on the floor of the state Senate, and his memory is looked after now as an excuse to have a picnic. He spent some time in this region (the descendants of some of his bastard off-spring are some of the nicest people in town), killing Indians and selling land, and had the gall to refer to what became this town as his "home." There's a big barbecue and the volunteer fire department sprays some water around, and there are some speeches and the kids show off their livestock. It's held on a Sunday, out of town and down by the river.

On the Saturday night before the picnic, after the movies and after we'd come upstairs (and Jean had had her drink of Jim Beam to put her to sleep), I said, "Are we going to go to the picnic?"

And Jean said, "Yes."

In the morning I woke and turned and saw Jean with her eyes already open and set on the window, the blue sky and clouds beyond, the clear light that made things seem sharp and to have hard edges.

"Maybe," she said, "I'll go for a swim."

"That creek is still cold," I said.

"Yes," said Jean, "I'll be able to feel it bite. You want to come, too?"

"Maybe," I said.

"I was just thinking about it," said Jean, "you know, going into the cold water and feeling it burn."

We dressed and had breakfast and then killed the morning by reading, Jean sitting with her knees drawn up with a book balanced on top of her thighs. She was reading about glaciers, their Arctic coolness, the way they scraped the earth. Then, when it was late enough, Jean stopped in the pantry where my father kept his liquor and took a bottle of Jim Beam, and then we got into the Ford and started to the piece of land where the picnic is held. She had a drink when we turned out of the road and put the bottle under the seat, leaned back, and closed her eyes. We stopped in front of DeCroix's because Jean wanted to, and I waited in the car while she went in and found that short and ugly man asleep. Jean touched his face and came outside. I was waiting, having a little of that Jim Beam myself, and looking at the house and barn and the weathered sign that said Horses For Hire.

We drove to the picnic, which was held in a large field owned by Bowie and which he had mowed for the purpose, so it looked like one large and rectangular golf course. The light was strong, and on the way I noticed that houses, trees, telephone poles and their wires all cast strong, definite shadows, so everything seemed to have some black ballast. When Jean and I arrived we saw people leaving their cars and making their way toward a line of aluminum stands, or bins on legs, in which there was charcoal and over which halves of chicken were being roasted. There was a tent where people sat down to eat their food and where they bought beer. The morning had turned quickly, leaving the memory of cool breeze and the smell of recently cut hay. Beyond those hot aluminum boxes there were some people and they seemed stretched and distended, swayed by the heat, as distorted as images in a fun house mirror, but I was able to see Pin, his cousin, Bowie (who was still talking and smiling, wiping his brow and politicking), the manager of the box factory, men who worked at the gas station, the welders, farmers who only came to town to buy something or when there was something special going on in a backstreet warehouse, the constable, the town supervisor, the two morticians (one Republican, the other Democratic), all of them moving and evaporating, folding into themselves the way a sheet does in a gentle wind. The car window hurt your arm when you touched it. "My," said Jean, "it's plenty hot." We both had some more Jim Beam, Jean sitting opposite me and watching the people, one hand resting on her leg at the point where the shorts stopped. We had another drink, and Jean said, "Well it's a good thing it never shows when we're drunk."

"Well, that's true up to a point with me," I said.

We had another drink and put the bottle away and I parked the car. We stepped into the heat, felt the light immediately strike our eyes with that jumping quality of a flashbulb. For a moment everything had a blue gray afterimage, or the points of sunlight that had been reflected on the chrome strips, or headlights, or door handles of cars, not to mention those shiny aluminum boxes that were filled with coals had an afterimage: I closed my eyes and against that reddish interior I could see the blue-bruise color of the outline of the landscape. But we walked through that heat, trying to get to the tent where there was a little shade at least and some cold beer.

"Are you hungry?" I said, and Jean laughed and said, "Are you kidding. In this heat?" So we pushed our way through the crowds, saying, Hello, hello, feeling ourselves shifting and stretching and becoming almost partly invisible in the rising heat. Jean smiled. Mrs. Pin, Mr. Pin, and his cousin, Mickey, said Hello, hello, all of them smiling and standing behind one of those aluminum boxes, from which there came clouds of whitish smoke and the smell of cooking birds.

"Hot enough for you, Jean?" said Mickey, sticking a fork into one of the halved pieces.

"Yes," said Jean. "Couldn't get much hotter."

"That's a fact," said Mickey, who was still smiling, now calling out to someone else. We could see the tent wavering in the heat now and the people before it all appeared as though I were looking at them through cellophane which was being turned or stretched. Jean's head was up and back a little, so she could feel the sun on her face. We kept walking, away from those places where the cooking was being done, but it didn't seem much cooler. We stood around the tent, smelling its grass and soil odor, but we couldn't get inside because it was already filled. People came up to Jean and said, "Well, I hear you're not going to leave for a while," and Jean smiled and said, "Yes, Yes," standing there in her shadow, occasionally turning her face up to breathe.

Matthew was there, too, and he was inside the tent, drinking beer: I caught a glimpse of his back in his new shirt (bought for the occasion), and then the crowd in the tent began to make way and close behind him, forcing him in our direction.

"Hello," he said, when he stepped into the sunlight, "Hello, Jean."

He wouldn't look at her though. He stared at me, as though I'd translate.

"It's hot," I said, feeling the perspiration under my breasts and along the insides of my thighs.

"Yes," said Matthew, as he took a quick glance at Jean, who tried to light a cigarette, but was having a little trouble because the matches were so wet. Matthew took a lighter from his pocket (a big Zippo) and made a bit of flame at the wick and tried to give it to Jean, but someone jostled him and the cold beer he carried in a cup fell across her leg.

"I'm sorry," said Matthew, "I'm sorry."

"Don't you worry," said Jean. "It feels good and cold."

Matthew stared at the ground as people came by to say hello. I saw a woman demolish a bird. There were tubs of potato salad. The wind shifted so that the smoke and heat from the aluminum boxes came our way and the people around us turned their backs into it, just as though it were a snowstorm.

"I'm sorry, Jean," said Matthew, looking at me, and then at the ground. "I'm getting sloppy."

"Don't you worry," said Jean. She smiled at him, and touched his hand (took it in the most definitely friendly way possible) and said, "I'm not mad at you. Not a bit. You've just been getting some bad advice." Matthew looked for one minute at her eyes and hair and then turned to me.

"I wouldn't call it advice," said Matthew, "unless you're ready to say that you advise a pheasant with a shotgun."

Jean's face was a little harder as she looked through the heat, the moving, silky quality of the air that made everything, the mown field, the automobiles, the children and their pens of livestock (covered with makeshift roofs of bright corrugated metal), everything, the people, too, seem to be rising, light and ready to blow away like so many fluffs of dandelion.

Jean put her head back and said, "I can hardly breathe here, Annie, it's so hot."

Jean stared through the moving air at the stream, which was already low, its water reflecting the light so as to make the water look white or platinum-colored. There were boulders in the riverbed and they looked as though they were made of plaster of Paris.

"Let's go for a swim, Annie," said Jean. "Let's go down to the stream."

"Can I come, too?" said Matthew, asking me, still acting as though I were a translator, as though Jean and I were speaking only French.

"I don't think so," I said.

Jean looked at him and shook her head (although by her movement I knew she wanted to say Yes, come along, I want to go down there with you and we'll take off our clothes and stand on that sandy bottom and in that cold water, our legs and thighs aching with it, you know, not to mention feeling the sand between our toes: we'd be just touching one another, maybe at the knee or hip, and you could begin to do some of those things you've been whispering about in that movie theater, with your mouth and fingers and the tip of your tongue, in that cold water that would burn), and then both of us started to walk, with Jean taking the lead and going to the Ford where she took the Jim Beam from under the seat and had a drink before offering it to me. The liquor burned and felt as warm inside as the heat did outside. Through that streaked-glass quality of the air I saw Mrs. Pin, and the bright clothes she wore. She watched as we drank.

"Well," said Jean. "It's a good thing no one can tell when we're drunk."

We put away the Jim Beam and began walking toward the river, Jean moving with that perfect carriage and faint, half-knowing smile, not showing to anyone at all what she felt or wanted, although her eyes were set on that distant and mercurylike water. At spring flood the river was wide, but now it was down, and its bed was filled with boulders and white stones, although occasionally there were broad stretches which were shallow and still, reflecting that silver sky, and others that were shallow and troubled, filled with gravel and stones that made the water turn white, and then there were a couple of narrow places that seemed to be still, but were deep, allowing the whole river to run into them without making much more than a ripple at the head of the pool.

There was one of these deep places about a half mile upstream, and we laughed and walked along, sometimes in the river when it was shallow, and sometimes on the boulders at the side when it was quick. Jean was ahead, stopping every now and then to feel the sun. I turned once, or half slipped, and looked downstream, and it was difficult to see, because of the shimmering air and the white boulders, not to mention the sun on the water, so I couldn't be sure, but it seemed to me that I saw some men down below, following us. They appeared as small, upright creatures walking on a silver plate.

"Look," I said. "Jean."

She turned and looked, but said, "I don't see anything," and then continued until we got to the pool, where she stood, slowly easing herself into the water, feeling its bite (the water was cold here, because there was a spring underneath the pool, and if you looked hard you saw the bubbles in the sand where the water came up), saying, with her head back and her eyes closed, "Ah."

I sat and dabbled my feet, but I felt tired and drowsy, although the water made me perk up and try to see what was down below, and now I was certain there were men in that shifting, almost silver air. Jean sat down for a moment and let the water rise to the tops of her thighs, saying, "Oh, Annie, that feels so good and it's so cold, too." She moved her head from side to side and opened her eyes, which startled me with their color, that blue and silver and ashy quality, too. Her hair was wet, and streaming back from her forehead. "Annie," she said, "Oh, Annie, why don't you come in? Come on." She splashed a little water at me and said, "It's sobering, though, I can promise you that."

I was still looking into that moving, mercury air and staring at the men who were coming quickly along the bank. Jean stood there, and heard them, now, as they came. The men didn't say much, although occasionally a word or two was heard when someone slipped, or when someone suggested going back. I guess this last was Matthew. There was a turn away from me in the stream before the pool, so that just before I really saw them, before they arrived, they were screened by green brush and trees which had just come into leaf. Jean came out of the water, still listening, standing on that sandy entrance to the pool, looking downstream when the men, Mr. Pin, the constable, Bowie, Mickey Pin, Matthew, and some of the farmers and men who worked in the town came around the brush and stopped. Matthew now came to the front of them. I heard the strained breathing, especially that of the Pins, both seeming nocturnal and retiring and not at all comfortable outside, and certainly not in that heat.

"Go on," said the constable to Matthew. "Go on. Go for a swim. We thought we'd join you in a swim."

The rest of the men stared at Jean as that little bit of water ran down her legs. It was quiet, too, so much so that I could hear that gentle lapping as the river entered the pool. Jean looked each one in the face, her own expression one now of a poker player who shows absolutely nothing.

"Well?" she said. "Well?"

"Go on, Matthew," said Mickey, "she's your girl. What do you do with your girl on a nice hot day when you're taking a little skinny dip? What do you do?"

Matthew looked at me and then at Jean and shook his head. The heat was so bad that I had trouble seeing or hearing, so I couldn't distinguish the features or the faces of the men who stood against that background of white boulders and water that had the sunlight coming off it.

"Maybe," said someone at the back of the group, "maybe Matthew needs some help?"

"No," said Bowie, "he doesn't need any help. At least I don't think he does."

Jean stood and looked at each man, caught each one's eyes, when she could, and appeared as she did when she was walking between those black lines on the kitchen floor.

"Matthew," said Mickey Pin, "you got to remember that she's yours and you can do what you like with her."

"And if you need any help," said that same voice from the back, out of the landscape almost, those hot and dry boulders and that stream of silver water, "don't be afraid to ask."

No one laughed, and Jean went on staring at them.

"She's yours, Matthew. Now what are you going to do about it? Don't you want to take a nice swim, Matthew?"

"Take a swim, Matthew," said Bowie, "go on. She wants you. You can see that, can't you? It's just as plain as can be."

Jean took a couple of steps, so that she now stood completely out of the water, her gait in walking just as careful as any creature who is just discovering the fact of its being hunted. Her eyes moved from one man to another, searching out each man's face, going over the features she had known all her life, but she didn't seem frightened or anything, really, although I knew there would be a time, sooner or later, when she got plain angry. You couldn't tell. One finger brushed the side of her face, pushing a strand of hair back, and then touched her lips once.

"Go on, Matthew, go on. What the hell's wrong with you? She isn't going to give you any trouble, are you, Jean? Are you?"

Jean didn't say anything, but stared at Bowie, and at whoever else spoke, her eyes as cool as you could want, or imagine.

"Annie," she said, "Annie, I think you better go away."

It was so hot, and the bourbon made me feel funny, so I said, "Where?"

Someone laughed and said, "We don't want her, too, do we?"

"Annie," said Bowie, "I don't think there's anyplace for you to go, so why don't you just go up the bank and sit in the bushes while Matthew and Jean amuse themselves?"

I went up the sandy bank and into the shade there, feeling the heat and seeing the glare of the river.

"So that's it?" said Jean, smiling at them. "Is that what's going on here?"

Someone shoved Matthew a little, and he shrugged the push off by moving his shoulder. I could hear the stream although I couldn't see as well as I would've liked and some of the men had their backs to me so I couldn't hear them, and even Jean was turned a little to one side, so it was hard to make out exactly what she was saying. She looked right up at them now, not smiling. Matthew wouldn't look at her, and the men were jostling him a little.

"Stop it," said Jean. "You don't have to do that at all. Not at all. I'll pick" (it seems she said: the sound was so funny and the light had the silvery quality) "and you can watch. Matthew can watch and then we'll get married. You can watch us every day. But I'll pick right here one and then another. Pin," she said, "Pin, have you still got that butter on your fingers, do you? Do you?"

Jean moved her finger from her lip and along her hip to the zippered fastener of those white shorts and began to take them off. All the men stood in that heat and silvered light, just watching as she began, and none moved or said a thing, until Matthew turned and started running, going splashily upstream, running harder than you would think a man could in that heat and in that water. Jean looked up and said, "Well? Well?" That finger still moving just along her hip, and her expression still as severe as a new knife. I still heard Matthew as he fell and then got up, splashing in the water (running, he told me, not because he was afraid to fight for Jean but because it was the only way to get them to go, not caring that the men would hate him for the rest of his life).

"Pin," said Jean, "what about those fingers?"

The men started slinking away through the trees, leaving Jean alone with Pin and Bowie.

"You've got it all wrong, Jean," said Pin. "We just came for a swim."

As they were going I heard Jean screaming, shouting, "Is that right? Is that right?"

I came down from the brush and said, "Let's get away from here."

"Don't you worry, Annie," said Jean, "don't you worry about that for a minute."

We walked back along the river, along those white and aching boulders, the grounds where there were beasts on display and cooking animals, people laughing and listening now to a band of local musicians who almost always played whenever there were more than eight or nine people gathered in one place, through the kids and their parents and the men who had been down by the river, now each one of them trying to appear as ignorant as the rest, right through that crowd of people in the tent, only stopping once there, while Jean had a large cold glass of beer drawn for her and which she drank in one draft, leaving a little of the foam on her lip. She took one look around, put down the glass, and we went out to the Ford.

I drove home and Jean went upstairs, took a suitcase and started packing, neatly and carefully folding some of her underwear and a few dresses and a coat. She had a little case she never used before which she'd ordered from England and which had bottles with ribbed sides that held creams and makeup. There were spaces for her hair brushes, too.

"What's all this?" said my father. "What's going on here?"

His face was startled above the bow tie, his hair perfectly

groomed, since he was getting ready to go to the picnic (where he might be able to interest a drunk in taking a look at a Buick).

"I want to ask you a favor," said Jean.

"Sure," said my father, "ask."

"I want the papers for that Ford," said Jean, "and when you replace it with something for Annie to drive, make it something that isn't such a piece of junk."

He put his hands on her and she kept packing.

"My darling," he said, "what's wrong?"

"Plenty," said Jean, "and I'm going on a little trip. That's why I want the papers for the car."

My father looked at her, and I saw that he was as far from arguing as he could be: as a matter of fact he looked more relieved than anything else. He kissed her and said, "You'll write with your address?"

"Of course," said Jean, still putting things in that old suitcase with the tartan covering that was about worn through. Jean filled a box, too, and then took my father's hand and kissed it and said, "Thanks."

"The papers are in the office," said my father. He left the keys to it on Jean's bureau, and Jean picked them up, went downstairs to get them, driving the Ford through the empty street, past those elk horns and heads, and parked in front of that tiny Buick showroom, and went inside, where she found the papers and the French grammar and an article my father was translating, the words written in the margin in his sloppy, windblown scrawl. She wrote a note for him, which said, "Father, I'm more sorry than I can tell you. I'm sorry, and if I were you I'd throw this goddamned grammar away. Love, Jean." Then she went out through the showroom which held one new Buick and got into the Ford, driving now to DeCroix's, where she found him sitting under those windmills, chewing aspirin and drinking beer, already reaching into his back pocket for his wallet, being able to tell by the speed of the car and the gait with which Jean walked away from it that she was close to, or actually already on her way, out of town.

"I'll pay it back," said Jean.

"I'm not worried," said DeCroix. "Do you want to take the Mauser?"

"No," said Jean.

"Good," said DeCroix, "now at least I'll be able to go back to sleeping regular hours."

Jean turned and started walking back to the car, and she heard that harsh, breaking voice say, "Jean, you write to me. You write to me when you can. I want to hear something from you."

Jean nodded, and got into the car, not crying yet, but waiting for that first hundred miles or so out of town when she would have the freedom to do just about whatever she wanted, and left De-Croix as he seemed to doze, his face still furious, under those windmills and against the sign that said Horses For Hire.

My mother came down when Jean was loading the car with her one suitcase and that one box done up with string.

"Where are you going?" said my mother.

"New York," said Jean, "for starters."

"No, you aren't," said my mother, staring right at Jean, my mother's face all slants and lines with the rage. "No, you aren't, young lady. You're not going anywhere until I say so, and what I say for you to do is to stay in this town and rub everyone's nose in it until I'm done."

Jean got in the car and started it.

"Jean," said my mother, "Jean, you mind."

"Annie," said Jean, "come here for a minute."

I went to the side of the Ford, and Jean took my head in both of her hands and gave me a kiss and said, "I'll write. Don't you worry." And then put the Ford in gear and pulled away, leaving my mother in her long dress, half running out to the front yard, trailing after the car, and saying, "Jean, Jean, you wait. You've got another year and then you can go," and then stopping as the Ford went along that road, slowly becoming one black speck between those two planes, one blue and white, the other brown and green.

My mother walked back to the porch and climbed it, hearing those loose boards squeak, and went into the kitchen, where my father was having a drink and pretending to read the baseball.

BOOK III

BOOK II

Wade Cannon

The Farm. Summer. 1950.

It had been a month since Chip had proposed to Carolyn and since then he had finished in Cambridge and come to the farm, where he sat on the porch in the evenings, drinking a mint julep and smoking a cigar. He was alone. At times I thought he was all right. We even went to the movies a couple of times and sat before the flickering images. They still hadn't fixed the hole in the screen.

For the last week Chip had been killing time, waiting a few days before joining Pop in the West to do some fishing. He was already late.

Mrs. Mackinnon put an ad in the New York papers that read, "Wanted: woman with clear hand to transcribe notebooks. One month. Room, board, and one hundred and fifty dollars." It also gave our P.O. box, and the name of the town. The next day I was sitting in my room and staring out the window and I saw some movement there beyond the pine grove, on the road. It was white and quick, and I thought nothing of it until I saw a young woman walking along the road and across the bridge that went over the ponds. She was wearing a white skirt and blouse and was carrying a little jacket. She had ashy hair.

I watched as she went along, past the garage and up to the porch where Chip was sitting, and then I went downstairs and came up to the porch, where I waited. Chip stood up. He was wearing light trousers and a jacket.

"Are you lost?" he said.

"No," said the girl, "I've come about the job."

The girl put her hand to her mouth and smiled, but it wasn't just friendly. She frowned, but then stopped that, too.

"Here," she said, and showed the paper.

"I'll get my mother," said Chip. "Miss . . . ?"

"Cooper," she said, "Jean Cooper."

Chip had been waiting for tea, and Charlotte put it on the table. Chip waited. The tea service had been polished recently enough to reflect the blue sky, the color of Jean's skin and hair, Chip's eyes, tanned face, and stone-colored jacket.

"Good," said Chip. "I'll . . ."

He took a step toward the door, but he didn't go upstairs.

"Would you like," said Chip ". . . a cup of tea?"

"Yes," she said, "I'm a little tired . . ."

She didn't walk like it though, as she came up the stairs to the porch, moving up each one, carefully putting one foot in front of another, although you wouldn't have noticed it without watching. I was thinking of my wife, of the years I'd spent in the movie theater, of that tear in the screen in town. Chip said it looked like a bat. I stood and watched. She scared me, because she could be so steady.

"Why don't you sit down?" said Chip.

He held out the chair for her and then sat down himself. Chip filled a white porcelain cup by running the hot tea through a strainer, and then gave the cup to Jean, who took it, each finger touching the saucer. It didn't rattle. When she sat back I saw her elongated reflection in the service.

"Oh," she said, as she touched the tea with her lips, but she did not seem to hurry away from it, didn't appear to need to avoid the sharp hurt. She spoke with surprise more than anything else. So she

continued touching with her lips that hot, almost scalding tea, needing, I thought, to have something definite to set herself against.

"It's dusty," she said. "I had to walk. My car broke down."

She pointed up the road. Chip noticed her shoes, which were
new and inexpensive, but pretty and almost worn out on the
bottom.

"I'll see what I can do about getting it started . . . maybe towed,"
said Chip.

Chip asked Charlotte to get Mrs. Mackinnon, told her that someone had come about the job. They heard the heavy sounds of
Charlotte climbing the stairs, but nothing more: on the porch
there was silent waiting, without the least noise of discomfort or
extra movement. They sat opposite one another. I wanted to sit
down. I saw her close her eyes once, but that was all.

"I think it's gone . . ." said Jean, "the car I mean. It wasn't much."
Chip nodded.

"Of course," he said, "but I'll take a look."

"Don't," she said, "it's all right."

"There's no trouble," said Chip.

"Please," she said.

He nodded. There was something wrong with his hands so he
kept them under the table. Jean sat with the cup in her hands,
watching him, her eyes set on his face. He nodded, and then they
sat there in the cool breeze of the day.

Mrs. Mackinnon came onto the porch carrying a leather-bound
book, which was one that she had kept over the years. Her hair was
gray now, but her skin was still smooth and her eyes were still
questioning. Chip stood up, and Jean did, too. Mrs. Mackinnon sat
down, and looked at Chip and then at Jean.

"Is that what you'd like to have copied?" said Jean.

"Yes," said Mrs. Mackinnon. "Just some notes . . . "

"I'd like to make a sample," said Jean, "if you'd give me paper
and a pen."

Mrs. Mackinnon picked up her writing box, in which there were some pens, blotter, and ink. The box was made of walnut and had brass hinges and a brass clasp. Mrs. Mackinnon put the ink on the table with nothing under it. The bottle was dark blue and about two feet away from Jean. Mrs. Mackinnon clipped a piece of cream-colored paper to her writing board and gave it to Jean, along with a point holder and a nib of medium width. Jean took these and the book that was bound with leather. Some of the pages were a little yellowed, but they had been opened and closed over the years carefully, so the edges weren't frayed or dog-eared.

"I've kept notes . . ." said Mrs. Mackinnon.

Jean opened the leather-bound book and bent over it, moving one hand to the side of her head to push her hair away from her face. Chip waited, and his mother watched him for a moment, trying to understand, wanting to ask. Jean read for a while and Chip held the cup of tea in his hand, the surface of it trembling as he breathed. With Jean's head bent over the book and with her hair falling along the sides of her face she seemed intent and remote, but every now and then she looked directly at Chip. He tried to hold the cup without moving it.

"I can read it easily," said Jean. "Shall I use this ink?"

"Yes," said Mrs. Mackinnon, who sat with her hands folded together and with her eyes moving slowly from Jean's face and hands to Chip.

Jean's fingers picked up the pen with the cork collar and held it for a moment as she opened the ink bottle and put the top of it in a saucer. The ink was at some distance, and Jean didn't pull it toward her. She thought about it, but looked at Chip, began to move the bottle and then stopped: she bent at the waist and reached with both hands, one putting the top into that saucer and the other dipping the pen into the blue liquid. The table was covered with linen, and Jean had to move the pen over that and over her skirt, which was made of white silk. Jean's brow was furrowed as she glanced from the pen to the leather-bound book. Then she stopped frowning.

Behind them they heard the ticking of that empty house, the sound of Charlotte as she slapped something down in the kitchen. There was the running engine sound of the breeze in the tree tops, and the sound of a gate that was unlatched and banging against a post. Jean held the pen in one hand, just over the bottle. Her fingers were long and she had slender wrists which were covered with a slight, almost invisible down. Jean dipped the pen into the ink, glanced from the book to Chip and back, and began to move the pen over that space of linen and silk, and heard Mrs. Mackinnon say, "I've wanted these notes to explain . . . things." Jean looked up, holding the pen over the linen, the nib of which had hanging from it one bright blue drop. It was trembling. Jean held the pen over the cloth and glanced at the blue and delicate and trembling bit of moisture, which was held together by the surface tension. Jean saw that Chip and Mrs. Mackinnon were staring at it. She fixed her eyes on Chip's, her expression stark and horrified and determined, too. While her eyes were set on Chip, who had leaned forward and was straining as well, she stopped the trembling, willed it to go away. Jean then tapped the nib on the mouth of the bottle. It made a light click. Jean started writing. There was something wrong with Chip's hands and he kept them together under the table.

"Ah," said Mrs. Mackinnon, when she saw the tendons in Jean's hand stiffening and as Jean wrote out in a large, clear and feminine hand three or four lines of Mrs. Mackinnon's notes.

Jean wrote a while longer, and we all heard the scratch of the pen on the heavy paper. Jean touched the tip of the pen to the ink again and pulled it away and over the linen and silk, but her hand did not shake. When she was done she unclipped the paper and held it to dry. All of us heard the bond's slight, distant thunder as Jean's hand had, again, the shaking of age or Saint Vitus's dance.

"You'll stay for dinner, won't you?" said Mrs. Mackinnon.

Jean looked again at Chip with that same expression of horror and determination and said "Yes."

Mrs. Mackinnon held the paper in her hand, and I saw the color of her skin, the aging-brown that had nothing to do with sun. The writing was easy to read. They sat there for a while, no one saying a thing. Chip put down his tea and looked directly at Jean.

"Perhaps you should have written," said Mrs. Mackinnon. "It would have been a long drive for nothing if the job had already been filled."

"No," said Jean, "I had to get . . . away."

"Have you been in New York long?" said Mrs. Mackinnon.

"No," said Jean, with her face smooth again. "Two weeks. It was hard. I just couldn't breathe. I bought a dress, this skirt."

Her hands were carefully folded in her lap, and she smiled and then blushed.

"The job's yours, of course," said Mrs. Mackinnon, "if you want it."

"Yes," said Jean, "I do."

"That's good," said Chip. "I'll get your luggage from the car," and then the two of us went out to the Buick, the long dark one, and we drove up the road until we came to a Ford that had been built before the war. It was rusting and a window was cracked and in the glass there was an odd, bubblelike pattern where water had gotten between the two panes. It had Ohio license plates. The bags were one squarish suitcase with tin metal guards on the corners and one cardboard box wrapped with string. We put them in the car and drove back to the house, Chip sitting in the front seat on my right, staring at the landscape, but not seeing a thing. There was a trembling in his shoulders and head, and then he turned to me and stared for a minute, as though trying to remember my name. I parked in front of the house and we carried the bags upstairs.

Jean's room was at the end of the hall, on the left. It was painted white, had two windows, through which there were woods to look at, and a bureau, a bed, a desk, and a chair. Chip knocked at the door and she opened it.

228

"I didn't have the key to the trunk," said Chip. "I hope this is
. . . everything."

Jean stood at the door with one hand on it. There was an overhead light in the room and it fell on Chip's face. She watched his
eyes, and I saw a trembling of her own.

"Yes," she said.

I put the bags down and waited for Chip. Jean's fingers gripped
the door, and she frowned, and then stopped that and stared at
him.

"Thank you," she said.

"You know," said Chip, "I . . . could look after the car . . ." but
he stopped and stood in the doorway, still trembling but letting
her see a little more of it. She waited, with the woods at her back,
not thoroughly sure of anything it seemed, aside from his presence: I saw her slowly raise one eyebrow.

"Would you like to sit down?" she said.

"Yes," said Chip, moving into the room and touching her hand
as she gestured to the chair. They both stopped, moved their
hands away from one another quickly, and then Jean raised that
brow and looked closely again.

"Oh," she said, as though hurt, but then stopped herself. She was
straining now, as though she had trouble breathing. They didn't
notice as I turned to go and began walking down the hall. I
thought of my wife, and the years longing for her, and then of Chip
and the girl alone in that room with the unpacked suitcase and the
box tied up in string.

"What . . . ?" said the girl. "What . . . ?" I heard the bed creak
as she sat down. "Who are you? Who . . . ?"

I waited a minute more, smelled tobacco smoke as the girl lit a
cigarette, and then heard her say, softly, or with a certain hush in
her voice, "Maybe I won't unpack those bags . . ." and then I
walked away. I climbed the stairs to my room slowly and stretched
out on my bed, not wanting to do anything else. I stared at the
ceiling and smoked cigarettes and thought of the movies, and of

Chip's face since the war. After a while I got up and washed my hands and forehead, brushed my hair, but all I wanted to do was to stretch out, so I did.

I stayed there until it got dark, and then I looked at the windows of the house. The lights were on, but it didn't look cheerful. There was an elm in front of it, and I saw it in full leaf against the sky of late dusk. I still didn't go out, and after a while the house was dark, so I supposed everyone had gone to bed.

My room is in a strange position: it was built on what had been a loft before the barn was turned into a garage, and I have windows on the inside and out so I can look into the garage and at the house and orchard, too. I smoked cigarettes and stretched out on my cot again, and the only thing that kept me awake was fear of starting a fire. When I thought of Chip and Jean it made me feel tired in an odd way: I wanted to close my eyes but I couldn't sleep. I watched the reddish glow on my hands and heard the quick counting sounds of the mice in the wall. I must have slept for an hour or so after putting out my cigarette, and I woke with a start, finding before my eyes in the dark silky, purple, and undulant shapes. I was so throughly awake that I felt ill. I strained to hear what woke me.

There seemed to be nothing at all, and I strained with my hand at the side of my head as I sat up, listened until the silence began to hiss. I held my head and called out my wife's name, but not very hard, not loud enough to be heard. Then there were more sounds from below, shoes on hard, dusty earth, the bird squeak as the barn doors moved on the rusted track. There wasn't much light, but what there was spread over the Buick and Chip's car as the door opened.

They were quiet as they came into the garage. On the first trip Chip carried a bag for himself and his fishing things, and on the second he had a suitcase and a box tied with a string for Jean. They spoke as Chip loaded the car, and I heard in the still, dusty garage (or barn) Jean's breathy voice and in the dark I had the sensation of touching her lips, which seemed soft and textured. The only words I could distinguish were two, when Chip lifted that cardboard box of Jean's and as Jean said, with her face fully on him and in that soft, deep voice ". . . Oklahoma Gladstone . . ." After that they didn't speak, but I heard the sound of Chip's shoes on the packed earth of the floor, and what I imagined was the suggestion of loosely folded silk as Jean slid into the front seat. Chip drove out of the garage, letting the engine idle. I saw both of them in the front seat, neither saying a word as they faced early summer night, although I felt or imagined the tension in the front of the car, the chaotic excitement, and the terror, too. I went downstairs and closed the door and heard the diminishing hum of the car, and then I went back to my room and those drifting shapes in the dark. When I couldn't stand it anymore I put on the light and smoked cigarettes and held my head.

Two days passed, and I didn't leave my room and I wasn't called for, either. In the morning of the third day, I walked toward the porch, and found Mrs. Mackinnon there. She was wearing a brown suit and her hair was neat and she was reading her book, Johnson's *Termites,* which was large and had plates of insects in their brownish armor. Mrs. Mackinnon seemed fatigued but interested in the insects. She had found a note, and she held it out for me.

"Gone fishing," it read. "Best, Chip. Jean has come with me."

"At least he didn't bother to lie," said Mrs. Mackinnon. "I taught my son not to lie."

"He never lied to me," I said. "I don't think he'd start now."

The writing looked very steady, but a little larger than usual. I didn't know what to do so I stared at the paper. Mrs. Mackinnon had on the table before her the usual linen tablecloth, a silver coffeepot, a creamer, two cups, and some sugar.

"Would you like to sit down?" she said.

"No," I said. "It's not right. I'm your chauffeur."

Mrs. Mackinnon closed her book and said, "Does it have to be that way this morning?"

"No," I said, "I'll make an exception," and sat down, with my long legs rising almost to the height of the table. "Is that brandy you're putting in your coffee?"

"Yes," said Mrs. Mackinnon. "Here."

I poured some into the coffee she gave me and said, "That's not a shot. That's more what I'd call a slug."

She smiled for a minute and then put her hand to her face.

"How did you sleep?" she said.

I shook my head.

"I've been thinking," I said.

"Me, too," said Mrs. Mackinnon.

We looked at a plate which showed insects folding up a leaf.

"Do you think they're going to be all right?" she said.

I sipped the coffee and tasted the strong brandy, but I didn't say anything.

"It couldn't have been avoided," I said.

"I didn't think I'd bring her to this porch for him, though," said Mrs. Mackinnon. "I thought that could have been avoided."

I poured more brandy into my cup.

"Yes, ma'm," I said.

We looked at those red ants in another plate. They had lines that ran from the pointed ends of a leaf.

"He was waiting for her," I said.

"Yes, oh yes," said Mrs. Mackinnon, "but, Wade, I didn't know what to do. And she's just as disciplined. And that's where I have . . . questions."

I poured out more of Pop's brandy. He had a case in the cellar, and when he got back he was going to miss more than his brandy.

"Don't you have them, too?" said Mrs. Mackinnon, "Isn't that what you'd like to know about?"

"Yes, ma'm," I said.

We both sat for a while. I finished my coffee and said, "There's nothing to do but wait." I began to stand up, but I saw a truck turn at the beginning of the drive.

It was a blue flatbed and didn't have much in the way of a muffler. We heard the pounding. At the wheel was a man in his fifties, with a scar on his neck and who was wearing a shirt buttoned all the way up. He pulled as close as he could to the porch and stepped out. His eyes seemed hard and he walked with his legs out. One whitish eyebrow was raised as he saw us drinking coffee and I thought, Didn't they get any farther than a local hotel? Didn't they go farther than that? This man knows something's wrong.

"I was in the telegraph office. This came in," said the man, "I thought you'd want it. My name is Moore."

"Yes, of course . . . Mr. Moore," said Mrs. Mackinnon. "My husband has spoken . . . of you."

"I'm sure he has," said Mr. Moore, "and what he says is true. We understand one another."

Mr. Moore smiled, but it only made his scars seem whiter. He handed the telegram over, and Mrs. Mackinnon opened it.

"It's from Pop," she said. "He wants to know where Chip is." She held out the pasted script for me to see.

"I will take back an answer," said Moore.

"Wade?" said Mrs. Mackinnon.

"I wouldn't worry him," I said. "There's enough trouble coming his way."

"Will there be an answer?" said Moore, standing in the sunlight and watching us, trying to see if some sign were being passed. The orchard was in bloom, and the scars on his neck were about the same color. Swallows dipped in the air and cut the surface of the pond.

"Wade," said Mrs. Mackinnon, "you write it out."

We both had some more coffee and then I picked up Jean's writing board and pen and wrote out in my large, spluttered script, "Haven't the least idea Chip's whereabouts stop weather beautiful stop."

"Do you want to send love?" I said.

"Do you think he deserves it?" she said.

"That's something I wouldn't want to answer," I said.

Mrs. Mackinnon covered her face so that Moore couldn't see her frank crying. He watched carefully, almost as though squinting in light that was too strong. I wrote it and gave it to Moore unfolded, and he got into his truck after giving us one hard glance, and then he was certain there was something wrong and I thought, All right, you can wait, too, starting right now, as you turn your truck around and go out through the pines. We sat on the porch, not saying a word, hearing the distant and diminishing sound of the truck, the silent house behind us, and drinking Pop's brandy.

Mrs. Mackinnon's Book of Animals, Reptiles, Plants, Trees, Birds, Bugs, and Flowers.

Raccoons have a delicate sense of touch, and it is this quality which I find intriguing and haunting, too. Their grace is in their front paws. In other matters, such as walking or running, they seem clumsy. Nothing will compare with their paws, however. The raccoons are nocturnal, and although I have heard that many are active at dusk, I only see them after dark, and then by artificial light, so that the membranes of their eyes look like the silver reflectors of headlamps. A raccoon on this land is usually about two feet in length, counting the tail, has a coarse gray coat (or a coat comprised of gray hair and black), erect ears, dark, quite shiny eyes, a mask, and a tail which is banded with black over yellowish-white. They are omnivorous, and will adjust their diet according to the time of year, although it seems to me that in the summertime they catch frogs and enjoy them more than anything except, of course, green corn: I have heard them in a field, their movements being betrayed by the rustling of the silky leaves, and I am convinced I have heard a high, sharp bark of delight. But at other times they will take whatever they can put their hands on, garbage, lizards, snakes, carrion. In the springtime I have found the carcasses of deer, those from the winter kill, and they have been cleaned on the inside to the point where their rib cages make them look like primitive instruments, and I know this is the work of the coons. They will leave almost nothing of a turkey, just some feathers and a few bits. The coons are arboreal, and they climb well because of their hands, the sense of touch in them. Wood ducks and goldeneye ducks raise their young in trees, and many times at night, when the birds are sleeping, the coon will reach with a hand to take an egg or a nestling. I also like the coons because of their intelligence, which is of a special kind: they are curious and have the ability to investigate, but I have never found the coons to be cunning or malicious, although they do cause trouble. It is true, as well, that this benign curiosity is dangerous for the coon, since a trapper will hang the top of a tin can over a set, knowing the coon will touch it, just to see a reflection, a flash of light, or to feel the texture of ragged metal against a paw. I am heartened that even with the price a coon carries on his back, and after the trapping that is done for it, the coons, if anything, are on the rise. They are monogamous, and they usually mate in the late fall, and I have heard in the woods, near hollow trees or by streams the high, sharp cry of the female as she is receiving her mate. During gestation and after, the coons will inhabit a den, a dead and hollow tree being the favorite. Coons, as a rule, will not be found in pine and hemlock, since it is only the hardwoods, the oaks and maples which are resilient enough to provide a den. As many as eight coons will be found in one tree, and these will be members of a family. Other than this, the coons do not run together. The young will stay with the mother and the father (who helps rear the young, bringing food, for instance) through the first winter. In the first summer, if there is green corn available, a mother will lead the young to it as soon as they are large enough to leave the den. And a little later, perhaps, they will be seen in a melon patch, the taste for which is only surpassed by the coons' love of corn. By moonlight I have seen the coons fingering a cantaloupe to find the soft, ripe spots or touching the warty skin of a cranshaw. The sense of touch can also be seen when the coons spend time along a stream, turning over stones and catching crayfish and insects, and on occasion reaching into a stream and catching an idle trout. The coons are unrestrained, and they will go more than one night running to a hen house, where, if they can gain entrance (by using their hands to open a latch or to throw a bolt) they will kill much more than they could ever eat: a variety of madness, it seems, takes hold of them, but it comes from overzealousness or greed, rather than cruelty. Coons are usually killed as they approach a hen house on the second night. It is the sense of touch that beguiles, however. There are many nights when I lie in my bed, unable to sleep, and looking out the window, hearing the sounds of the coons as they caress the latches and the doorknobs, trying to gain entrance, cheerfully desiring to make their way into the cupboards where there are shiny tins. I will rest and be soothed by these sounds, or of others, as the hands are placed against the panes of a window, or over the hinges of the hen house door, or as fingers investigate the latch of the pump shed, and then I will sleep, and as I recline in my bed and my breath comes and goes so smoothly as for me to be aware of its texture on my lips, I feel the fingers of the coon upon my face, and I am able to distinguish each digit, each dark and padded tip: they feel as soft as the caress of a child who has learned to be gentle. Then I awake, and am left feeling harsh and alone, my hands seeming utilitarian and heavy with an intelligence which is so different from the coon's. Then I listen again and cannot hear the sounds outside that reassure me, although I remember the touch of those dark paws against my cheek and find myself wanting to feel them again. After I've had this dream in winter, I find my husband outside, with the door of our dark car open, my husband wearing his coonskin coat and holding a silver hip flask which, in its shininess, would have so fascinated the raccoons.

Pop Mackinnon

Yellowstone. 1950.

I was alone on the Henry's Fork. I gave the house to Chip, and then I thought I'd give him a fishing trip, too, since I had always wanted to fish the Madison, or the West Yellowstone, or the Snake. I took the train. Chip said he wanted to drive. I took the train from Grand Central Station and I saw plenty of landscape after we left that darkened space in New York, those sooty vaults of Grand Central which have the aspect of prehistory and Pleistocene gloom: they put me in mind of large birds with scales rather than feathers. After Chicago, or after the Mississippi, the land was flat, or rolling, and didn't make any sense, because even when you got to Wyoming you'd still have to own thirty thousand acres before it felt like anything.

The first sign I had was a telegram which read, UNABLE TO FISH WITH YOU STOP CHIP SOON ON HIS WAY STOP MORGAN. Robert Morgan was a friend Chip had invited, a man who was at law school with Chip and was a man who had no trouble getting a headwaiter's attention, since he looked like he could tell you exactly how a pair of riding boots should be made while at the same time slitting your throat. He was going through his meager inheritance fast and took advantage of things like free fishing trips to the Henry's Fork of the Snake. He'd backed out.

I had made arrangements with a guide. He kept the camp, cooked, and stayed out of the way. The telegram had been brought out by a man named Leo who was tall and thin and broad, too: he looked more like an open umbrella than a man. He had on a pair of muddy goggles and he was wearing boots that didn't match and that didn't have any soles. He also had a long green scarf. His motorcycle was covered with mud, but I think it was red. I sent a message back by him which read WHERE THE BLAZES CHIP STOP. The next day Leo came back and tapped me on the shoulder while I was wading and casting a fly to a rising fish. I wasn't far from the bank and Leo reached over the water and gave me another small yellow envelope which had an answer from my wife. HAVEN'T THE LEAST IDEA CHIPS WHEREABOUTS STOP WEATHER BEAUTIFUL STOP LOVE.

I sent Leo back without an answer.

"You know, Mackinnon," said the guide. "You're dropping your backcast. Use your left hand, pick up a little line speed."

I didn't say anything. I walked out of the water and sat at the camp where I could look at the river: it was flat and wide there, one long glide. On the far shore I saw tall firs and that hard, blue sky. There was a little moisture in the air. I sat with those two slips of paper. The guide gave me a drink.

In the evening I got back into my waders and went back to the river at the tail of a long glide. There were some fish working, rising, and I saw one jump, too, making one quick dash for an insect and coming completely out of the water, turning one half way around in the air and returning, nose down, just like a diver. The hatch wasn't what you'd call a Cahill, but something like a Grey Fox or Adams, so I tied on a little Adams fly (and had trouble doing it, too, with my thick and betraying fingers: they'd started hurting regularly now) and began to make casts of medium length, shooting the line a little and enjoying the appearance of the leader and fly as they stretched out on the water. I let the fly drift until it started to drag, and then retrieved it, lifted it off the water, just enjoying myself, casting over one rising fish (a trout that was on the bottom and coming up to take insects off the surface). It wasn't making the water bulge or tailing or finning: the trout came right up and took something to eat. I cast again, watched the fly float, and allowed myself the luxury or the relaxation of standing in the river in a pair of funny-looking boots while not thinking a god-damned thing. My face must have showed it, too: blank as a tin pan. Although not so smooth. The fly floated over a dimple in the water, and I came out of the mindless condition, the blurry lack of myself (which, certainly for me, is a wonderful gift) to find myself thinking, Where the hell is that son of mine?

The guide was quiet at night. For dinner I had a steak and a mushroom omelette. Then more bourbon. The guide and I sat opposite one another for thirteen days. We drank and talked a little, but we didn't learn a thing about one another.

In the tenth day I said, "Do you think my son's dead?"

"No," said the guide.

"Why's that?" I said.

"If he'd been killed, you would have heard," he said.

One night, before bed, I went for a walk, to be next to the river for a while, to watch the stars being reflected there. When I looked up I was reminded of the winter I spent at the farm with my wife, after we'd heard about John and when we knew that Chip was in some camp (likely to be shot): the house seemed empty and dark, and to get away from it we'd go outside, either during the day, into that blinding whiteness of the snow, or at night, to stand beneath that whiteness of the Milky Way and those stars, too, aside from some that had that bruised light color. The darkness was elimi-nated for a while by getting outside, but the silence stayed. My wife touched my hands at night, and the house became so empty, or seemed so empty it pressed us, pushed us together, and even though my wife is in her fifties there was still the chance of another child, but nothing came of it. At these times, when another month had passed and it was certain that the house would remain empty, my wife put her head in her hands and made a distinct and old sound, not quite part of human speech, but nevertheless certain in its meaning, which was to beg, or to plead not to be so thoroughly excluded. I took walks that winter, many times at night, with a chart of the heavens, learning the names of those bits of light, going as far, on some evenings, as Trout Cabin, which was covered with clear ice. I'd go, too, when the thermometer was below zero, and the snow then seemed to be dry and the only sound was the creaking of the trees. When I moved at night through those beds of snow, or along the ice of Trout Cabin I sensed some presence which would not allow itself even to be acknowledged, but was definite, far off, and absolutely indifferent. It left me standing in that snow, getting angrier by the second, since I had nothing to do, but to face the cold whiteness of my land and of the stars and heavenly bodies and the silence, too. I came back from one of these walks and found my wife sitting in her room with a book of plates in her hands, mosses and ferns or some such, and looking out the window at those bright, January constellations, Orion, Cygnus, although not seeing them: she was staring at nothing at all. I squeezed her hands and shoulders, standing before her with the ice on my brows and the moisture from my breath frozen to my cap and the back of my coat, and she said, Go away, just go away since there's nothing we can do. I went into my study and listened to the clock on the mantel ticking in that empty house, and thought, I've been defied enough, and then I went back outside to face the indifferent brilliance of that ashlike snow and the distant and white stars, the dust of the Milky Way.

On the morning of the thirteenth day I was pouring bourbon into my coffee and the guide was doing the same when I saw Chip walking through the trees above the camp. Leo was with him, and he was wearing his goggles, jacket, and that long green scarf. I sipped the coffee.

Chip was dressed in a jacket, a white shirt, and light trousers. The jacket was the color of fieldstone. He looked good, a little thinner, tired, but not fatigued. Remote.

"Where are your fishing things?" I said.

"In the hotel," said Chip.

Leo was still standing there, looking like some cheap pilot in those mud-splattered goggles.

"What are your waders and rod and vest doing in the hotel?" I said.

"I'll be staying in the hotel," said Chip. "I'll come out to fish mornings and evenings."

"Look," I said, "I didn't bring you across the continent for you to spend your time in any goddamned hotel. I brought you out here to sit with me on this goddamned river and no other place. I waited for you to be here and no other place. Is that clear?"

"I'll be in the hotel," said Chip.

He turned and after having taken a look at the river, went up the path, with Leo going after him.

"What's in the hotel?" I screamed at the fir, at those trees where Chip had disappeared. There wasn't any echo, or any sound at all aside from the hush of the river. The air was damp. I saw those bright Fourth of July sparklers, the spots.

The guide sat on a canvas chair, and took a leader from a box, and started tying it with a nail knot to the line.

"What's in the hotel?" I said.

"A woman," said the guide.

"How do you know?" I said.

"A woman is the only thing that would keep your son from fishing," the guide said. "Cards or liquor don't require a private bed, but a woman does."

"I had some plans," I said.

"I wouldn't know anything about that," said the guide.

I stood in the shade of the trees above the camp and I still saw those bright spots in the sunlight, those sparkler bits I last saw when chasing the ram from the Delaware to the farm. I sat down on a stool with three legs. A fish jumped in the river. I breathed easily for a while, hoping the lights would go away. They didn't, though, not for a long time, nor did the pain in the center of my chest, either, while I sat there, looking at the empty sky and those trees which only had stature because of their size, and thinking, Who is she? Who is she? And what am I going to do about her?

After a while the guide gave me a drink, but it didn't do anything. He stared at me from another camp chair. My brow was furrowed and I was toying with a leather fly book. There were some salmon flies inside which were as big and as gaudy as a pheasant.

"There's only one way to find out," said the guide, "if you're willing to let it get in the way of your fishing."

"What's that?" I said.

"Here," he said, and handed me the keys to his car. "It's got a full tank. There are two hotels in town, the Persian and the Oxford. They'll be at the Persian. The Oxford is filled with winos and crazy fishermen."

"What made them crazy?" I said. "Did they have sons?"

"Probably," said the guide, "but it's more likely they caught one fish too many or one fish too few. I'll trust you for the car."

He turned to the river and I started walking toward the Chevrolet station wagon that had wood on the sides. It was new, but inside it already smelled of varnish, bamboo, leather, dirt, and canvas. I drove along the river and thought, Now is the time for a cool-headed approach. I tried to calm down, even though I didn't feel like it, and after I did, I said, "He's gone Democratic on me," and felt that cold feeling in my stomach and chest.

I came into town and had no trouble locating the Persian Supreme, so named, I'm sure, because of the slave traders that were necessary to finish the railroad. All I had to do was to find Chip's red Buick, which was parked right in front and looked a little dusty and road weary. I pulled into a corner spot and waited just to see what I was dealing with, but they didn't come out, and after three or four hours I went to the Oxford and rented a room.

There was a man in the lobby who was wearing his bedroom slippers and reading a paper that was not fresh from the newsstand. Two other men were drunk and trying not to show it, and another young man was ragging them and asking them why they weren't out on the Snake. There were some potted plants which were dead, two sofas, far apart, and two ashtrays, which looked like large shotgun shells, set on end and filled with sand. Upstairs I stretched out on my bed. The springs were broken. In the next room someone was being sick, with the radio on. After a while I heard him sigh.

When it was getting dark I went into the bathroom and washed my face and hands and heard the man in the next room groan and roll over. The radio was still on. I walked back to the Persian Supreme, saw that Chip's car was still parked in front of it, and then sent a telegram through the hotel's clerk, which read WHAT THE HELL HAPPENED CHIP STOP SEND REPLY STOP LOVE POP. I sent the love so she'd know I was serious. Then I began to wait, again.

I sat at a table at the end of the bar from which I saw the stairs of the hotel and the desk, too. There weren't many women in the hotel, and the ones I saw were all over forty-five and frightened to let their men go so far to fish alone. I sat beneath a stuffed elk's head that had antlers which took up the spread of two umbrella frames, but as I sipped my drink, I was thinking, Don't they ever stop? Not even to eat?

After I had waited until ten o'clock, without seeing a thing, I had cold beer and some sardines and sliced onion on dark bread. A canvasser of some kind tried to tell me a dirty joke, but I stared at him until he went away.

At the desk I got the attention of the clerk, who was a tall man with a small mustache, perfectly combed but very thin hair, and gold spectacles. Looking at him reminded me of one of those boxes lined with velvet that hold chrome drafting compasses.

"My son is staying here," I said, looking at the clerk, "and I'd like to know what room he's in. Mackinnon."

"Mr. and Mrs.?" said the clerk.

"Yes," I said.

The clerk opened a little wooden box and took out a card, which he held with the tips of his fingers, and he let me read, in Chip's upright scrawl, "Mr. and Mrs. Chip Mackinnon," and the name of the town where I own some land. And where Chip owned some, too.

"That's right," I said. "Which room?"

"Upstairs, at the back," said the clerk. "Corner room. Two ten."

"Are they in, now," I said. "Mr. and Mrs., I mean?"

The clerk looked over his shoulder at the box marked 210 and said "No."

I nodded and stepped outside, thinking, So, when I went to lie down they came out and went for dinner. Then I turned into the alley at the side of the hotel. On my left, near the sidewalk there were some trash cans against the clapboard siding of the hotel, and behind me there was the neon light from the sign that said Persian Supreme. The light was red and dusty. The alley was clean, and I saw only a puddle of water and a newspaper that was twisting in the evening breeze. As I turned into the alley and strolled down it I saw at the back of the hotel a corner room, on the second floor, with the lights on. There was also a fire escape on the side of the building, the kind that has a long, tilted and counterbalanced staircase. I stood beneath it and jumped, but I couldn't reach it. I went back to the mouth of the alley for one of those trash cans to stand on and looked into the street and saw them, walking along the sidewalk, coming in my direction, her arm through his.

She had on a light skirt and blouse and she carried a sweater over her arm. It was dark, and I only saw them when they passed into the triangular and yellow sections of light that came from the hotel's front windows. I heard the click of her shoes as they walked slowly along, and I crouched down to stare at them before they went inside. There were was some dignity in her walk, and I saw her legs swing forward in those strides which were sharp and smooth. She was some kind of thin blondie, a little tight-assed bitch. I watched until they both went into the hotel.

I dragged the trash can behind me, and quickly, too, not caring about the noise, until I was beneath the fire escape. The evening was not very cool and there were a number of windows open, including one in that corner room with the light on. The shades were up, too. I adjusted the trash can and waited for a minute. The alley was only lit at the front and at the rear, and I felt myself become what I must have appeared to be from some distance: a vague, phantomlike figure. The fire escape creaked and then made a bang as it hit the asphalt of the alley. I climbed and put my nose outside the window, where I waited.

Of course I dismissed her. She was a hussy, a thin blondie, a woman of . . . bizarre motives. I wasn't troubled in the least as I sat on the fire escape and thought of the shape of her neck as she turned to look at Chip in that yellowish light before they turned into the hotel. There was an aura . . . which I denied. Without difficulty. I felt complete only where the light touched half my face and part of my shoulder. I thought I needed a better look, if only to know how to proceed. When the door opened I crouched a little more, so that my face was just above the brick sill. I smelled the bricks, their dry cementy odor, and it was these that made me later associate with her the smell of dry and porous stone.

The woman came into the room and closed the door. Chip wasn't with her, having stopped, I suppose, to take care of some problem downstairs. But I wasn't sure how long he'd be, although for one moment I turned quickly and looked into the alley below and flinched, feeling my skin crawl, when I saw something glint off a puddle of water there, but it wasn't Chip, so I put my nose almost into the open window and felt the white curtains as they blew against my face. The woman sat down and did nothing for a minute aside from staring at the wall next to the window where I was crouching. I saw fine features, smooth brow and cheeks, blue eyes and hair of a strange color. Of course I dismissed her. Just a ... Her carriage was remarkable, and she seemed ... strong. She took off her blouse and skirt and she was only wearing, after she had taken off her stockings, a small pair of pants. Look at that, I thought. White trash. Trash. Absolutely. But I wanted to stay, to find a procedure, an approach, so I waited, staring at her as she moved about the room. She came over to close the window and stopped before it, having caught a glimpse, I suppose, of my shoulder: she slowly began to lower her face, to bend at the waist, and push the curtains aside until she was able to put her fine, beautiful nose against mine. We stared into one another's eyes (with me thinking, Where did he find her? Where?) until she said, in a soft, breathy voice, "What the hell do you want?"

She had no shame, since she was almost nude and was still poking her slender nose at me. She didn't blink, and our noses were still less than two inches apart.

"Damn!" I said.

"You must be Pop," said the woman.

"That's right," I said, "in the flesh."

"Well, Pop," she said, "why don't you come off the fire escape? They'll arrest you if you don't."

I climbed through the window. Perhaps I am five pounds too heavy, but I am not an accurate judge in these matters. I was breathing hard and I'm not certain it was simply a matter of the climb. She stood before me wearing just that satin triangle, her hands on her hips and her eyes keen: she was trying to look into mine, being, for the moment, strangely unaware of herself.

"Thanks for the invitation," I said.

The woman went to her dresser and picked up a light, silvery robe and put it on. She lit a cigarette, and sat down in a stuffed chair and crossed her legs, and said, "I've been expecting you. You're not so old as I thought you'd be."

"That's kind of you," I said.

She raised an eyebrow for a brief moment and then let it lapse or pass away so quickly that it might not have happened. There was a floor lamp beyond her and I saw a white plume of smoke as she exhaled. I was still breathing hard and feeling unsure as to where I should put my hands. The room wasn't much to speak of: yellowish walls, some cheap curtains, a chair, a desk and bureau, large double bed, which had been made recently and turned back so that I smelled the sheets which had been washed in plain soap and dried in the air of the Rockies. The woman had a slight smile around her lips, and it hurt, since it made me feel old and unknowing. I saw plainly, though, that she was only concerned with the facts of the matter.

"Pop?" she said, still trying to catch my eyes with hers and still with that smile, which was not unkind in any manner. She made a gesture (it may have been a slight, impatient movement of a leg), and by it I was meant to begin, or to explain. She was not flirtatious: I am convinced of that, but yet . . . I stopped myself and felt my eyes getting wider as I stared.

"I'll be damned," I said.

The room seemed bright, even though it wasn't lighted very well, or the crests of the folds in clothes were lit and distinct next to the dark troughs.

"Where's Chip?" I said.

"He's in the hotel bar," she said, "having a drink."

"That's convenient," I said, "since it saves me the embarrassment of climbing into my son's hotel room when he is otherwise engaged."

She stopped smiling and had trouble with her cigarette since her hand and lips were not completely still. I had had no effect, nothing that I could count on. She put her head back and shook her hair a little and went back to waiting, to breathing slowly and seeing the creases the years have put in my face.

"How would you like a thousand dollars to leave town? Tonight, while Chip is downstairs having his drink?"

She looked at her hands and shook her head.

"Chip said when you offered it would be five hundred," she said.

"Ha," I said, "is that what he said? Well, I'll take that up with him separately."

She still looked at her lap, where the hand that held the cigarette was unsteady. The other hand rested on her thigh and moved a little and stopped, but she liked the texture there, the freedom it gave to movement. After a moment she stood and brought an ash-tray a little nearer and I saw that there was something in her movements that was gently rocking and at the same time controlled. I was reminded of a tray covered with full champagne glasses being carried slowly by a waiter. The color was the same, too. After a while she looked up and spoke with hesitation in that remote, breathy voice.

"I don't need or want to be insulted by you," she said.

"How about fifteen hundred?" I said. "I'll get the cash."

"No," she said.

"All right," I said, "two thousand and that's my last offer."

I had made the mistake of thinking she was naturally slow, and I now saw that she was being patient, and her way of doing that was to speak slowly, although there was something else, too, a strain against something which I became convinced was a kind of attraction. She strained hard. It made the room seem bright.

"That's my last offer," I said. "I came here in good faith and I should tell you that it is not a good idea to have me any angrier than I already am."

"I'm tired of being insulted," she said, and it came out as a sigh, softly at that, too. "Don't you understand?"

"What don't I understand?" I said.

"That I am not concerned about going away because of money," she said, "that I'm not doing anything for it. We need it to go on living, but not for itself. I want to spend time with him. If he has money it makes things easier but doesn't stop it. Do you under-stand?"

"I'm not an imbecile," I said.

She smiled and showed me something I hadn't expected, or at least not then: a delight, a joy in the soft bite, in the truthful hurt. "I never thought you were," she said.

"Are you in love with him?" I said, although I was not then willing to admit I was already jealous.

She looked at me and was silent: by this she meant I had asked something she thought was strictly private.

"You must," I said, making my eyes wide and blowing up my cheeks, "understand things. And have a sense of tragedy. Now, how much?"

"I never said I understood," she said, looking me full in the face.

The room had the atmosphere of outcasts and of desperation and of some peace, too. I knew I'd have to wait, and this didn't make me very comfortable.

"Chip has no job, has not passed the bar, and has no money aside from what I allow him," I said.

"We'll spend as much time together as we can," she said, looking at her hands.

"You understand as well that I own the land?" I said.

"What land?" she said.

"All right," I said, "there's a surprise waiting for you. Enjoy it."

I stood before her, almost yelling now, although she was still quiet and not quite as calm as she'd like to have been. But holding herself in a way I'd never seen.

"We'll find some other land," she said.

"That's where you're wrong," I said.

"I didn't claim to know everything," she said. "I never did that."

"And you won't take my offer?" I said.

"No," she said.

We stared at one another for a minute, and then I started for the window.

"My name's Jean Cooper," she said. "We haven't been introduced, so this will serve. You can use the door."

She stood with two fingers on my hand, and I swore I felt something there, some ebb and flow. Then I reached for the doorknob, one of those glass things with many facets, and stood in the hall, still seeing her as she first stood in nothing but that silver-colored triangle, and feeling, too, the lingering spots on my hand.

I went slowly down the stairs, still wondering, where? How did he find her? The lobby was empty and had that forlorn aspect of inexpensive hotels. The carpets were worn out, and the chairs were spotted, but the place was a step up from the Oxford and the crazy fishermen. I waited at the doorway of the bar so I could get a look at my son, too. He was the only one there and he stood at the bar, a drink in his hand, and his head bowed under the cone of light from the overhead fixture. There were no sounds. Chip looked up once and stared at himself in the mirror behind the bar. Chip had a cigar, too, and the smoke from it rose lazily in that cone of light. His eyes were in shadows and he didn't flinch at that mask of terror. My son seemed aware of the space in which he stood, the silence and the emptiness: he turned his head and looked in her direction, as though he could see through timbers, plaster, and furniture. I went away, without saying a word, leaving him to his cigar and drink, and the time that he could stand to be without her. It looked like a good cigar, probably one of mine he'd stolen.

I walked along the now almost deserted street, which was lighted by the occasional window and dim neon sign, but I smelled the mountains and the scent of fir and the asphalt, too, and as I walked I thought of Jean, with her legs tucked under her, waiting, straining after the sound of steps in the hall, her head bent over her lap.

In my room I stretched out on that flabby bed and stared at the ceiling. The room was dusty and the sheets seemed more sterilized (with a spray) than cleaned, but I lay there anyway, unconcerned for a moment about the everlasting stink of dust. The man next door still had his radio on (turned to the weather report and a station that gave the fishing reports, the day's catches) and he was still getting sick in the bathroom, over and over. After a while he stopped and I heard someone knock at his door. The man groaned as he got up to answer it and then he said, "Thank God, you've come, doctor. I've saved some of it for you."

I slept after that, not well and not deeply, still hearing occasionally the information on the radio about the trout. What sleep I got was filled with shapes in filmy or shiny and smooth garments, and when I woke in earnest the room seemed dark and all I was able to smell was the cloying odor of dust. I sat up and held my head and heard myself saying, even though I shook my head against it, "Jean, Oh, Jean, you . . . Oh." To the best of my ability I denied this. I sat with my feet still in their shoes on the floor and wondered about the two of them in the hotel across the town, but this didn't last long, and then I went back to thinking about the way she moved and feeling that outrageous confusion of age and beauty and that big hump of years on my back that was slowly getting heavier and giving me no peace. I couldn't sleep after this, so I stared out the window at the mountains.

I felt better in the morning, or at least more resolved. I went to a grocery store near the hotel that is open early and bought some beer. I brought a bucket from the guide's station wagon and filled it with ice so that by the time I reached the camp the beer was cold. When I came out of the trees I saw the river and the guide as he sat in a canvas chair before a small fire. I hadn't shaved and the stubble made me look as though my jowls were sticky and that they'd been pushed into white sand. The guide looked at me as I sat down in a chair opposite him. He opened a bottle of cold beer.

"Well," he said, "how are you now?"

"Just fine," I said.

The guide made light, fluffy scrambled eggs, kippers, pancakes, and sausage and gave me half a grapefruit. I thought of my land in winter, when you can see the tracks of wild turkeys and the marks made by the dewclaws of deer, and, of course, in the middle of it, I kept coming back to it, just as hard as though I'd fallen out of my chair onto concrete: her resilience and strength, that will which seemed to need no justification, that ash-colored hair and the smile which said, I can make you feel so good, so good.... I denied it some more: I strung up a bamboo rod, tied a new leader, arranged some flies, got out my waders, and sat with my unsteady fingers. The leader was easy: I had a box of monofilament, a number of spools of different sizes, so I started with a thick piece and added another, always tapering downward, the sections in the beginning and end being pretty long, those in the middle short, each piece being tied to the last with a blood knot. I sat in the canvas chair, working at the leader and enjoying the double-noose that appeared as I tightened each knot. I muttered angrily and the guide looked at me and I saw my breath in the early morning air. The guide made a movement with his head and I then saw Chip as he walked into camp. He was carrying his fly rod and waders.

"Are you ready?" I said.

"Of course," said Chip. "I said I'd come to fish. How's it been?"

I smiled like a hound and raised my eyes.

"Fair to good," I said. "Just let me finish this. Have you got a leader?"

Chip looked into his vest and found one.

"It's been good," said the guide.

The air was cool and crisp and it reminded me of those mornings when I was up early in New York and went to the open-air greengrocers, where I saw heads of Boston lettuce just after they'd been washed. Chip didn't put his things down, and I was under the impression that a slight scent, the faintest suggestion of a woman was in the air around him. I broke the last bit of leader and had to tie it again, and then we went down to the river.

We got into our waders and stood in the water. Chip's casting was good, better than mine, but then he'd had me as a teacher when I'd had none. We weren't so far apart as to be unable to speak. The air carried sound well.

"I've been wanting to talk to you about what's in the hotel," I said.

"It's none of your business," said Chip. "I'm not about to talk of her the way you speak of a woman in a bar or on a fishing trip."

His line sailed out after having formed a nice, tight loop.

"I want to talk to you," I said.

Chip stared at the fly on the water.

"I warn you, Chip," I said, "you better mind your manners and remember to whom you're speaking. I am not casual company. I am your father."

"It's none of your business," he said.

"There are certain things I want from you and by God . . ." I said, but he would not hear me. He shook his head.

A little white fly appeared on the surface and then another. A hatch had started. My hands were jumpy and I felt disoriented.

"You tried to see her," said Chip, turning his highly colored and (now) handsome face on me. I could see it full on. "Didn't you?"

"No," I said, "it wasn't—"

"You are lying to me," he said. "I thought I could trust my father not to lie to my face."

We stopped and stared at one another across ten yards of water.

"I'll be damned," I said.

"Didn't you?" said Chip. "You peeked through a keyhole or hung around in the halls or looked in a goddamned window or stopped her when she went for a walk. What was it?"

"I'll be damned," I said. "In a window."

"That's better," said Chip. "At least you aren't lying to my face."

"You remember that I warned you," I said. "You, Chip."

"What are you going to do?" he said, still facing me and showing a rage I never imagined possible. "She isn't interested in money."

"That's what she said. But it is only a matter of scale, that's all. And you need it to live, don't you? Don't you want me to look after your future?" I said. "That is, if you have one, and this point is seriously in doubt."

"What are you going to do?" said Chip.

"You're nothing but my son," I said. "You have no right . . ."

"It's none of your business," said Chip.

We stopped for a moment. I saw the mountains in the distance, the hard, silken clouds, which were gray on the bottom.

"Well," said Chip, "what are you going to do?"

"I'll take her myself," I said.

Chip saw my complexion was now red, high, menacing. I was blowing hard. We just stared at one another since for a moment we were both too angry to speak.

"Is that right?" said Chip.

"It's crossed my mind," I said. "Yes. That's right."

"She doesn't care about money," said Chip.

"We'll see. It's a matter of scale," I said. "And I have other charms."

Chip began to walk toward me, not wading or shuffling his feet, but stepping out the way one does on dry land. His face was marked white around the lips, eyes, and nostrils. After a few steps he stopped.

"Leave it at that," said Chip, "or I'll . . ."

He began walking again.

"You wouldn't dare," I said. "You wouldn't . . ."

Both of us had let our flies drag, but even so a fish rising to a nymph took mine. It was a fish of about twelve inches, a brown trout, and I played him for a minute. While I did so Chip reeled in and walked a little closer to me, so when the fish was completely played out my son was standing next to me. I pulled the fish in and picked him up, pulled him out of the water, and was able to see the dark spots surrounded by silver, the shape of the fish's body, the rays in the fins.

"There's nothing you can do about something as beautiful as that," I said.

Chip nodded and put his hand on mine, which were shaking.

"Pop," he said.

"Nothing," I said and killed the fish before dropping it into my creel. "You know you're on your own."

"Yes," said Chip, "I know that."

"I gave you many advantages," I said, "and don't you forget it."

"I'm sorry for your troubles," said Chip.

"Don't you dare apologize to me, boy," I said, "don't you dare. Maybe I feel wonderful."

I walked up to the camp, trailing water, and Chip came up a little later, although he didn't spend much time getting out of his waders and walking up to the place where his car was parked. He didn't say anything when he left, either.

I had another beer as the guide broke camp. We went back to town and I got the first train out. It moved slowly and I sat in it doing what can only be called a fair amount of brooding. I watched the flat land and thought, Where can he go? Aside from that one place I know he needs and loves? By Chicago I was answering myself, saying, No place. So I've only got to wait and then he'll be surrounded. And by the time we got to Grand Central Station and I was standing in the arched, imposing space, I was thinking, That's fine. Yes, sir. And what then?

Mrs. Mackinnon's Book of Animals, Reptiles, Plants, Trees, Birds, Bugs, and Flowers.

Brook trout are the most beautiful of fish. They are streamlined and quick moving, having tails that are the color of hickory bark and the texture of wet silk. There are delicate rays in the tails as well, ridges that are fine and symmetrical. It is the coloring, though, which distinguishes them. They are dark, either brown or a bluish-brown on the back, and they are almost impossible to see from above unless there are shadows. On their sides however, they are marked differently: the dark color of the back gives way to a silvery brown and then to a satinlike and dark silver which is spotted with circles of brown and light brown, which circles have the aspect of cut and polished hardwood, oak, chestnut oak, walnut, cherry, or very old woods of a lighter color which have been handled and waxed and rubbed into darkness: that of a dining room table, say, made before the revolution and used steadily. Below these dark spots there is a line of bright circles which are red or orange and bright, and they have the aspect of sequins, of a silver maple leaf in late fall. So when you hold one in your hand or when you look at a brook trout, at the speckled sides with that surprising line of red dots, it is as though you are staring not only at the side of a fish but at some mystery as well. The coloring seems to imply the enclosure or completeness of the streams, since the fish have that aspect or suggestion of the forests and stone through which and over which the water flows: there is the quality of surprise in the spots of orange that one finds when walking and putting up grouse in an otherwise bland landscape. When the brook trout are feeding or quietly finning in some deep current their presence is aloof and indifferent, but not unkind. Brook trout, or *Salvelinus fontinalis,* spend their lives in fresh water, the adults spawning in the fall, usually returning to the same place in a pool or stream where they themselves were spawned. The trout like gravelly beds at this time of the year, and this is so because eggs laid in gravel will be protected, washed clean, and less likely to be suffocated by silt. A female goes to a stretch of gravel and lays her eggs and the male follows, covering them with his milt. The eggs are heavier than water and will stay on the bottom. After fertilizing them the male will linger, gently fanning the eggs with his tail, washing the water over them, making sure that the eggs are clean and in no danger of being suffocated. The eggs hatch and the small-fry emerge, and they begin to feed on small bits, fresh-water crabs, midge nymphs, and, when they get larger, on the nymphs of mayflies, caddis flies, and stone flies, not to mention anything else that happens to fall into the stream. The fish grow and move into deep pools (where the current isn't so strong and where it takes less work to stay head upstream) and become larger, forming those spots on their sides. They are a sensitive fish, and I am convinced that they can feel in the water the vibration of men approaching (this is certainly correct when the water is low, in August or early September). I like to sit where I can watch their sides flashing when they feed on the bottom, and I take pleasure in them, in their presence, the gift they bring to ponds and streams, and I know at these times what dullness there would be to water without them. There are moments when I try to see them and can't and for one horrifying second I believe they have gone for good. Then I will hear the plop or see the dimple made by a rising fish. When I sit on the banks in the evenings of June or July I take faith in the brook trout's single-mindedness of purpose, one so profound as to lack (or need) anything like awareness. When my husband brings them home, three or four fish, each being about twelve inches, I have them cleaned quickly, dipped in a beaten egg and then in flour, and fried in butter. We eat them with Bass ale. The flesh is dark and delicious, clear and exciting, and at night, when I am in bed and looking out the window, I think of the dark waters, the brook trout in them fanning gently, slick and resilient: it is as though they almost long for those moments when they can quicken the stream with one silver, brown, and orange-spotted arc.

Jean Cooper

On the Road. 1950.

At night we took the bags, my old one, and my cardboard box with string, and Chip's leather one with his initials stamped onto it, and brought them inside. We unpacked them, only to find that in the morning we had to reverse the process, putting our things into the bags (and that box) and taking them back to the Buick. We thought we were moving from one place to another instead of going to the same place which was distinguished by being some distance from the last, and that was all that marked it. This began in Idaho, where that man insulted me. I didn't say anything aside from, "Let's put our things into the car. Let's go." I wanted the sense of movement, if only because it implied a destination that wouldn't hurt. Each night we stood at the back of the Buick and looked at our things.

We began by driving out of the Rockies and into the western grasslands of Wyoming, where there was a late snow. It was light and didn't stick and I remember seeing those sharp blades of grass poking through the white cover. I sat next to Chip, my head up, feeling the cold in the convertible, and I was thinking about putting my hand under his shirt and along the ridge of his chest or along his stomach, too, maybe holding him there, or on the side of his back (where there's a defined muscle), maybe even hurting a little and then waiting and putting my lips over the painful spot. I didn't. I watched the daggerlike and green blades of grass that came through the snow and minded my hands until evening, when we had come to another of the same places and had faced my bag and box and Chip's leather suitcase. Usually the buildings were of one story, covered with stucco, painted green or pink, having a few hired rooms, each furnished with a double bed, a bath with a shower and cement floor, empty wastebaskets, sterilized sheets, and the smell of disinfectant. I carried my box from the car and put it down and stared at it in the dim light of the room. I pushed it away with the toe of my shoe and I gave my bag a shove, too, and waited until . . . until I could breathe again. Then both of us stared at the green or pinkish ceiling, neither of us having spoken aside from my occasional and not intended word (or word intended, but not to be spoken): "sugar."

In the morning, Chip looked at the ceiling and then at me and said, "I'll take a shower," and I wanted, made him hesitate, said . . . sugar, and then I waited in the dim light while the shower ran. I stared at the box and the suitcase.

After I had my shower we still weren't ready. It was late.

"Well," said Chip.

"I'm not packed," I said and sat down.

"I'll help," he said.

"No," I said, "no, I'll do it."

I put the things in the suitcase and the box, my brush and toothbrush, robe, dirty clothes, and then stared at the closed luggage on the floor.

"Maybe we can get some Alka-Seltzer," I said.

"Of course," said Chip.

He took my hand.

"I'll carry the box and the suitcase," I said, and then we stood at the back of the car and put them in, two bags on the left side of the trunk, my box on the right, next to the spare tire and the jack, and then the fishing things went on top. We smelled the odor of canvas and rubber and pine-tar insect repellent, and then got into the front seat, relieved and feeling fresh, and hoping too that the next place would not have the same odor, or that the bedspread wouldn't have the same stains.

We ate at hard red counters without tablecloths. There were napkin holders, silverware that was as light as wood, a couple of booths in the back or at the side of the room, a jukebox, which sometimes was on when we wanted to have breakfast. We tried to sit for a while, but a woman, who wore nurse's shoes, came to the table and said to me, "Are you all done, honey?"

"Yes," I said, and smiled, and this helped, because not screaming was useful, since in the evening I felt my smile (and what it took to smile) running back into me, as I was able to feel running into me in the same way those hours when I sat in the car and watched the flat land (of Nebraska, say, any place in Nebraska) with my posture correct and my hands on the seat near him, but only touching him once and that was carefully awaited although it seemed casual. Of course, at night, the bedspread made the same scars on our faces when we slept against it, and the smell of disinfectant was the same. Once, when we were driving, I touched Chip before I should have (or when I said I wouldn't), and I said, too, One day you know I'm going to scream when I feel your beard along the inside of my . . . but then I stopped and went back to watching those lines approach us, which were reminders not of how far we were going but of how little headway we were making, as though the car were driving on a large wheel, fifty miles across, the rim of which was asphalt with lines that just went around and around. Both of us stood up to it, and at night I soothed Chip and watched his eyes as he said, quietly, "Ah. Ah."

I didn't understand the money. It helped each day, but did nothing, aside from scaring me, about the weeks and months that lay before us. I did not have money, and I pried, and then caught myself and stopped. When I discovered something it made the world seem farther away, but the inside of the car closer, so that even if I was losing his past to our differences, the immediate seemed harder, clearer. He had been to parties where women "came out," where a band played, and where the fog came up to a large house on the beach . . . was in the social register. ("How do you get in?" I said. "How?" "Five people write letters of recommendation.") Usually I was quiet when I felt the differences and waited for night.

"These things are of no consequence," said Chip.

I shook my head and stared at the road.

"That's the first lie you've told," I said.

I thought of the box and the suitcase which were waiting to be taken out of the trunk and into the next room.

"Come closer," he said.

"In a minute," I said. "I'll just wait."

I watched his hands though as they gripped the wheel: there was a vein which pulsed. I wanted to put the tip of my tongue to it, but I waited. . . .

"Do you have brothers?" I said.

"I had one," said Chip. "He's dead."

"What was he like?" I said.

"He played cards and was a snob," he said, keeping his face blank. "He was a good gambler and played polo. He rode beautifully and had that stylish sense of meanness one needs to win at polo."

"Did you care for him?" I said.

"I loved him," said Chip. "He understood discipline."

"I see," I said, "yes," and moved closer and put my hand against him.

"It doesn't go away," said Chip, "missing him. You'd think it would, but that's not so. It becomes worse with time, not better. Or more empty."

The land was flat, green with corn, but it did not change: we couldn't pierce it, couldn't make it pass.

"Did you play polo, too?" I said.

"Yes," he said. "I wasn't very good. Or I was adequate."

I watched the lines on the road and felt far away. The land went right to the horizon, cut it there, and I felt the heavy dome of the sky which had as its center the car in which I rode. Chip didn't have a watch and I didn't either, so I had to judge the time (which was important: the distance to the next place, the next stop) by the position of the sun. I knew what to do about the distance I felt between me and a polo field and a man who had ridden on one, knew how to change it into . . . I watched the sun. At night, after taking in my box and when Chip and I were lying in that waxy light that came from a bulb outside that did something to the insects I thought about the women Chip had spent time with. Tall and thin, or dark and dressed from Paris and wearing wonderful things next to their skin, and graceful, too, women who had gone skiing and riding and fox hunting in England from the beginning: women who had their hymens removed in a doctor's office, who spoke French, and who assumed their men were able to navigate a balloon, shoot grouse on the wing, survive in the desert, make a chocolate soufflé when the bombs were falling. These thoughts made me worry, so I turned away from them, or used them, let my hands move on the sheets to where he was sleeping. I imagined a woman in particular, beautiful enough to seemed masked by it, whose presence lit a room as though she carried her own lighting, an aura composed of infinitely fine and golden dust. I thought of her on a terrace, bored and haughty, standing in the reassuring breeze that only blows on the rich. Chip was next to me, and I put my tongue close to his mouth, tasted his breath, and then . . . let him sleep. I lit a cigarette and blew smoke into the air, and in the plume I saw the color of the dress of that particular woman's skirt and the movement of it, too.

In the morning, Chip said, "I'll carry the bags. I'll pack the car," but he didn't look at his bags or my box, either. We stood around the open trunk as Chip put the things in. I touched the box once, and then went back inside to wash my hands. The smell of disinfectant was there.

"What are you going to do about the woman you're supposed to marry?" I said.

"Nothing," he said.

"Do you think you can do that?" I said, watching him strain. "Is that really possible?"

"She'll understand," he said.

"But will she?"

"Let's not talk about it now," he said, and we sat side by side in the car, with me waiting and thinking, no, no, not now, you can't reach over . . . although if I tried I saw him clearly with no clothes on. At night he said, I couldn't stand looking at the stumps, at the wire, hearing the language, cooking with bits of paper, burying blood sausage, denying . . . the denial. I almost, almost, and then he blinked and stared at the ceiling before saying, After that I studied law. I remembered his face when he spoke of the desert as I gently bit him on his thigh, on the inside, not really hurting, but feeling him become tense. Sometimes we were dressed, lying next to one another, with just a bit of skin touching, a bit of my stomach, and he teased me, watched me, until I thought, but did not say (or maybe did), Please, please . . .

We lingered at those places where we ate and pretended we had someplace to go.

"Are you done, honey?" said the waitress.

The next morning when Chip came from the shower he found me standing in what was left of that cardboard box, the pieces ripped and thrown about, the string between my fingers as I sat at the side of the bed and looked at the brown shreds. I couldn't stop crying, and he said, "What's wrong?" and I said, "I've got no place to put my dirty underwear."

"I'll put them in my bag," he said, and started to clean up the mess.

"No, no," I said, "just leave them alone. Leave things as they are."

Chip went out and found in a drugstore another bag, and I packed it, but I wasn't able to look at it, either, as we went out to the Buick to put our things in. In the parking lots outside those restaurants and rooms I had the momentary terror and lack of direction I have in those dreams in which I don't know where I am or what I'm supposed to do.

"It will be all right," said Chip, "we just have to keep moving. That's all."

"That's not true," I said.

But we faced those white lines. Chip drove and watched them, his expression one of concentration as though it was important to find that one line was a little longer than another. Mile after mile I invented some scratch or movement, some prolonging, maddening device which at night would allow us to feel those fears and terrors flow out of us.

In the morning we came out of one of those rooms, and did not pack the car right away. The court had ten units, all together, and the Buick was the only car there, since the other people had already left. This was in Iowa, where the sky seems to have stolen everything from the land, but along the road there were some trees and understory, and we walked toward them. We had never walked a hundred yards together in a straight line before. There were posters on the trees which said No Trespassing, All Violators Will Be Prosecuted Under The Law. We walked on the shoulder, which was covered with bits of glass, broken beer and soda bottles, and these bits gave the soil a jeweled aspect.

"Let's get off the road," I said. "Let's walk in the woods."

I started to go down the bank.

"No," said Chip.

"Why not?" I said.

"It's posted," he said. "It's not ours."

"So what?" I said. "I'll take the signs down."

He shook his head.

"We've been in the car for weeks," I said. "Haven't we?"

I approached a sign.

"No," said Chip, "don't you dare touch it. No."

I stopped and turned and saw him at the top of the bank.

"Come on," he said, "we'll walk on the road."

"All right," I said.

"We'd just feel like strangers there," he said. "We don't belong there."

We started back toward that pinkish building with the flat roof and the small neon sign.

"I posted land every fall," he said.

He hadn't shaved and I ran my finger along his cheek, thinking, Someday I'm going to scream when I feel . . .

"I understand," I said, and we walked back along the road, not looking at the woods, and picked up the bags and put them into the car and started driving. Chip seemed relieved when he saw the lines. I was, too, because I was convinced by this time that Pop was following us.

We rented a house in Wisconsin for a week. It was two stories, faced a lake, and was surrounded by trees. There was a double bed upstairs with springs that creaked and a frame that was covered with cracked enamel. There were sheets in brown paper, and we made the bed, folded the corners so that they looked like the back of a white envelope, and then went to the grocery store and brought back bags which were filled with food and had the reassuring odor of waxed paper, fresh vegetables, and bars of soap. From the bedroom window and from the veranda downstairs we saw a small lake. The nights were cool, and sometimes we sat outside, having a drink and looking at the lake, which was black, an empty space which seemed covered with a shiny membrane.

We did not linger over meals when we had the chance. I listened for the sound of an approaching car, of Pop, since I was sure he would show up sooner or later. We ate little, barely slept, took one walk, but not far. I understood about trespassing, because doing so would have been a variety of imitation, and that it wasn't so much that Chip didn't want to walk on this land as needing to walk somewhere else, and the distant place was forbidden to him.

I was jealous, but there was nothing I was able to do: he missed something that was not a woman or any human thing at all.

We spent our time inside. Of course we were frightened, watching each other's eyes for a sign of less compulsion, for a weakening, for a fear of the perverse, but never finding it. At the end of a night, when we saw the lake turning gray, we would be able to breathe, to stare into one another's eyes with the absence of the ability to think at all, feeling only that we had once again chased or scared the world away. Chip had smooth and very white skin and it bruised easily, and I was thankful of this, glad in leaving my marks and for the salty taste of minor blood. At least, I thought, I can't be dismissed in a minute, in five minutes: he'll have to wait a week. Hush, I said, hush. It hurts if you move. Just lie still. Hush. Just strain. Later, when we were having a drink and watching the lake as it became the color of a nickel and as I felt muscles in my cheeks ache, I picked up Chip's trembling hand and saw his eyes as they took that metallic color: for a moment it seemed as though the lake and our eyes were filled with that same gray, frightening water. After three days I had my period, and he told me he liked it, that it made me seem fertile. I held his hand and pulled him against me and felt the tears rise as I said, "Do you think so?"

When I woke late the next morning, I found myself staring into Chip's eyes.

"Are you afraid?" I said, "of living without the . . . relief?" I made a circular motion with my hand that suggested us and those times when we were only bound by one another, when we were set free.

"Yes," said Chip, "I'm afraid of living without it."

"I know, I know," I said.

"Or more than afraid," said Chip.

"I know," I said, and then Chip got up to bathe.

At the end of the week I said, "I want to keep moving. I don't want to be caught."

We took the key back to the landlord and packed our bags. I thought I smelled the disinfectant. Chip loaded the car.

"I don't want to be abandoned," I said, "just left on the road. I don't want to have to go into one of those places where we eat to ask for a job until I have the money to take the bus."

"No," said Chip, shaking his head.

"That's why I don't want to be caught ʼn the road," I said.

"Pop wouldn't dare," said Chip. "And he's not that much of a fool. That's not what's happening to us. We're not going to be caught by *anyone*. Not by one person."

"But who then?" I said.

"Let's get in the car," said Chip, "let's go."

"Where?" I said. "What are we going to do when we run out of country. When we come to the Atlantic? What then?"

"I don't know," said Chip, as he started the car, but he only drove as far as a gas station where he stopped to use the telephone. I watched as he stood in the booth and dialed, smoothing back his hair after someone had answered on the other end. Chip nodded, but did not look at me. Cars went by and I felt the hard wind of them as it made the canvas top of the Buick luff. I watched each car that went by, tried to see who was driving. After a minute Chip came out and got into the Buick and said, "I don't know. But at least there's a place we can stop before we get there. Before we have to look at the ocean. It's in Pennsylvania."

"What's there?" I said.

"A hotel," said Chip. "I've made reservations."

"What hotel?" I said, but the map had stopped being so flat and spread out, and I could look in one direction, or a direction. The chrome in the car, the lines of the gas station, the telephone poles, the leaves at the side of the road didn't look, for a moment anyway, as though I were seeing them through an aquarium. They seemed clear and clean.

"Let's drive through," I said, "let's not stop in . . ."

"Yes," said Chip, "I know. No more rooms. We'll drive until we get there."

As we drove, though, the greenish light didn't stay away, and after dark I closed my eyes and saw the ocean, imagined that I tasted the salt, and felt the sand between my toes and on the soles of my feet. Chip's face was illuminated by the dashboard as he stared at the darkened road.

The hotel was a place where the Grant-Alstons went to be pampered. Grant-Alston's grandfather, of course (said Chip), was an oil man who had set up the milk trust in New Jersey. His sons and daughters haven't forgotten him or the milk trust and they try to make up for it with snobbery and public service, but they still draw the dividends (I wanted to ask here, How are dividends drawn?) and that while they're sure no one will cut them directly, they know that as soon as they've turned away someone says, "Say, do you know the one about Grant-Alston at the pearly gate?" (No, I thought, I don't). Chip wasn't impressed that Grant-Alston's grandchildren went there. He mentioned it to say that if you trusted money to make you comfortable, then you could trust the hotel. The flowers smelled like the ink on a new hundred dollar bill: fresh and suggestive of mysterious promise. Grant-Alston's sons and grandchildren got away with it (said Chip) because people *are* impressed by millions, and I looked at the passing diners and truck stops, saw my face in the darkened window of the Buick, and I had to agree, Yes, they are.

"It sounds proper," I said.

"Yes," said Chip, "it probably is."

"Do you think I'm a proper woman?" I said, still sitting straight up.

"Yes," said Chip.

"But that's not what you think," I said.

Stop, I thought, please stop. I felt my color rise, even though I pushed it down.

"Can you trust me to behave?" I said. "Will I be able to use the silver properly?"

"Jean, Jean," said Chip, "I'm not insulting you."

"Well," I said, thinking, not now, please, "tell me if I'm proper. . . ."

"All right," said Chip. "I don't want to think of you as proper or not proper. Those days are over. I don't want to think that way at all anymore."

I stared at the illuminated macadam and thought, It's supposed to be a treat, but he should know there aren't any treats, not where other people are concerned. I held my hands in my lap, wanting to touch him, to stop this, just to make everything stop for a minute. It had started to rain and Chip turned on the windshield wipers. I saw the glass and weeds at the side of the road slick with water.

"I have two silk dresses and a cotton skirt and a silk one," I said, "some blouses. Simple shoes. Will that be all right?"

"Yes," said Chip, "that will be fine."

I touched Chip's cheek with a fingernail, watched him deny it. We would be in the car two days, and I looked forward to the time. I began by touching him with a fingertip, and by that tip was able to push the world away, to balance it there. Occasionally I laid my fingers on him, or moved, shifted on the seat, came a little closer. It made the time interesting.

We arrived on the hotel's evening of the summer. It was not as formal as I would have imagined, but it was reassuring and bright and the atmosphere was buoyant and clean. At the center of the evening was a meal. There were silver platters on which there were bushels of oysters on a bed of crushed ice, roasts of beef (carved into thin slices, garnished with parsley and small moulds of horseradish sauce), turkeys, hams, platters of broiled lobsters, large dishes of caviar with chopped egg yolk and chopped egg white, glazed loafs filled with pâtés and Russian stuffings, silver trays of pheasant and grouse, decorated with the feathers from their wings and tails, and there were cold smoked salmon and trout, all of which surrounded a windmill carved from one block of ice. The windmill was five feet tall.

Two hundred people came to the dinner, which was served in a large room that looked over a lawn and the valley below. Our table was small and comfortable, near the window, and we were served by a man who seemed to care about us, although he was too polite to do more than suggest it. I was careful, but we drank champagne, and I touched Chip's hand once, and then stopped, sat up, smiled faintly. I remember seeing the gray pool of an oyster, the odd glitter in the room, the light that came from the ice windmill.

I still had the faint smile, when I said, "People are staring at us," but Chip refused them, ate his dinner, told me of the camp, the tunneling, the smell of dirt. I felt the room push in on us, but I did not give in. We had dessert and more champagne, and there were people who still stared, and then (after people had already started leaving) we went up to our room, which had a double bed and gray walls and a wing chair with a reading lamp and I remember the taste of his skin, the look in his eyes as both of us waited for the time in the car and the time at dinner to disappear: it finally did, and we lay in the room, smelling the flowers, the acrid and fresh odor of the ink of money.

I sat in the darkness and felt the hush of the hotel after two o'clock in the morning and knew why those people had stared: I was not known to them. They could tell by looking at me. I thought of putting my tongue against that ice windmill, of feeling the slippery texture of it. I wanted to wake Chip and make him tell me about my period, but I didn't. When I lit a cigarette in the dark, he said, "What's wrong?"

"You can do what you want with me," I said.

"Why?" said Chip.

"That's what I want," I said, and then saw, when I lay next to him, and by the light that came from the bathroom, the dark marks on his skin. "You won't be vain now, will you?" I said, gently touching with my lips those dark spots. "I couldn't stand that. You can do anything you want, only just don't be vain."

He tried to go back to sleep, and I sat next to him, my legs crossed Indian-style, and watched my hand against the ribs of his lower back. The hotel was quiet and the hush was reassuring, but sometimes I thought, I'm going to scream, I'm going to start screaming about us, the things we do, if only because I can't do anything else, can't stop.

Chip rolled over and saw me above him, my shoulders square against the light from the bathroom. His eyes were that gray color of nickel, and he said, "You should know that I am not in control of anything."

"Ah, sugar," I said, putting my hand to his face, "I know."

In the morning, after a hot, long shower we went for a walk, away from the hotel, through country that was rocky, but pretty, covered with scrubby birch and small oak. The rocks were marked by greenish, scaly lichen. Chip and I walked and smelled the air, and when we came back I said, "I'm hungry."

"Yes," said Chip, "let's eat."

In our room I managed a silk blouse and a white cotton skirt. I brushed my hair and put down my brush, although I wanted to say to it, You stay there, since objects seemed light and capable of flying around, leaving the places I had put them.

The dining room had been changed from the night before, and we sat nearer the center of the room. There was plenty of light now, daffodils in a small silver vase, and the linen was heavy, white as a sheet in sunlight, and comforting to touch. We sat for a moment, enjoying the atmosphere, the uncrowded and fresh-smelling room, but after a few minutes it began to fill up, although it did not get noisy. We ate an omelette and had a glass of wine. The omelette was light and very yellow, made from fresh eggs, and there was green and pungent parsley on the china plate. There were jeweled pats of butter and one small roll apiece, the crust of which was as thin as an eggshell. The wine was cool and I could taste it in my nose, feel it there. I watched the silver in Chip's hands, the shape of his lips . . . I tasted the scallions in the omelette and the mushrooms, too, and I imagined they had been gathered close by, the mushrooms growing to large sizes, black or light brown beneath spruce and pine, on beds of needles, fragrant, gilled. I was lulled by the taste and the sound.

"Don't make a fool of yourself," said Chip.

I looked at him over my glass, but he had turned his head and spoke to a man standing at some distance from the table. I hadn't heard him approach. He was dressed in a light gray suit, was about six feet tall, had silver hair and a red face. There was a scar near the ear. His eyes were blue, and his hair was neatly parted, brushed.

The other people in the room had stopped eating or making any sound at all. Some stared, but most of them listened. Chip looked into my eyes and continued eating. I tried to taste the mushrooms.

"How dare you?" said the man.

He stood with a hard, upright posture, and his face was set on the both of us.

"We're finishing our lunch," said Chip, looking at the man once.

"Who is he?" I said.

"My fiancée's father," said Chip. "Would you like some more wine?"

I shook my head. The muscles in the man's cheeks rolled and they gave an odd, quick movement to his face.

"I'll speak to you in a moment," said Chip. "Go away. Don't make a scene."

"Mackinnon," the man said, "I—"

"Jean Cooper," said Chip, catching my eyes, "Mr. Cooke. . . ."

Mr. Cooke turned his gaze on me, and in his eyes and face there was the color of old cotton, an uncertain gray, although there was nothing uncertain about his eyes. He stared at me, my hair, face, nose, hands, saw my dusty and not stylish shoes. I sat perfectly still, holding the glass of wine, seeing its color and shine, too, which reminded me of the sheen of new grapes, although hardened, polished.

The waiter removed my plate and put down a section of canta-loupe on a small, white piece of china.

"We haven't finished," said Chip.

But the man still stood there with the muscles in his face becom-ing taut and then relaxing as he swallowed. Chip watched me and

didn't seem, at first glance, to be concerned, but I noticed that at
the back of his head there had begun a trembling which was so
controlled and rapid as to seem vibrant. He looked at Mr. Cooke,
and said, "All right. Let's step into the hall."

I was left alone at the table in the center of the room. Chip's
gently folded napkin was sitting at the side of his plate. It was quiet
behind and around me, but I did not look down, and this meant
I had to see those pink and gray faces in the room. I ran the silver
spoon over the flesh of the cantaloupe, which had the color of
smoked salmon. My legs were crossed at the ankle, and I sat with
my shoulders against the chair. The people in the room did not
mind their manners, did not go back to eating. One rising, strident
voice was heard in the hall. The words ran together, but one was
stressed and clear. "Hussy . . ." said Mr. Cooke. I put the spoon into
the fruit and saw a slight bit of juice run along the eye-shape of
the silver. The melon was tasty and wonderful and I enjoyed it (or
would have enjoyed it: enjoyed in memory) and sat before the
faces which now began to turn away. Chip came back and sat
down, not smiling, but refusing to get up and walk out. I watched
his highly colored and handsome face and finished the wonderful-
tasting melon. Chip left the wine in his glass.

"Where can we go?" I said, still smiling for the people in the
room, but Chip shook his head, told me I had lovely hands, and
then looked over my shoulder at the valley beyond the window.
That tall man with the military carriage came back to the table,
but he just stood and looked at me as though trying to remember
well enough to describe me to the police, and although I went
back to eating the fruit, I wanted to say, I have no scars, no marks,
not one, and there are no wrinkles in my forehead. None. Nothing
that shows. He left, and later we saw his bags being carried by one
of the hotel's boys.

Chip and I stood up and looked at those angry pink and gray
faces and then went upstairs, where I said, in the smell of those
flowers and in the hush of the house, in the silence made by heavy

doors, I'm going to be vulgar now, I'm going to do some things, some things . . . ask for . . . but you'll understand, and we'll be all right after a while, you'll see, you'll see . . . and began to reach out for him, ripping the buttons off his shirt, feeling them pop against my face before they dropped to the floor. I think we should have screamed, I should have started screaming, but I didn't and Chip didn't either. In the early afternoon we woke and saw that aquarium light. In Chip's back the muscles slithered as he reached over the bed and picked up one of the buttons from his shirt and put it on the nightstand: I can still hear that isolated and delicate click. In the sound there is the reminder of that silent room where we left our evidence, or marks, and for all I know our blood, where we had found ourselves willing and light-headed, terrified of each other (if only because the other was as willing and as equal to our mutual demands), and where finally we were relieved long enough to pack: we just left, then, and watched those lines on the road as they approached us. At least there was a man to carry the bags.

We drove for about an hour, listening to the wind make the top flutter. We had not spoken for a long time, and I didn't know in what direction we were headed. East, I thought, to judge by the sun. We came to a long, slowly rising hill, and on both sides of the road there were pine and bright ferns.

"I can't go into . . . another one of those . . ." I said, "I can't."

Chip stopped the car and reached across me, opened the door.

"I'll get your bag," he said. "I'll leave you here."

"Yes," I said, "yes. Let's do that."

I stepped out. There was a breeze and it felt nice on my legs. At the top of the hill there was a gas station with a bright red Esso sign. I saw a two-story house there, too, covered with white clapboards. It wasn't that far.

"It's the only thing," said Chip, "the only thing that's correct."

The sun seemed very bright, and I saw the reflection on the chrome at the trunk's lock.

"Of course," I said, but when Chip put the key into the lock and opened the trunk, I saw the bag there and I said, "No. No." I put my hand on his and then I ‿at down on the bumper and felt the hot sun on my face. Chip sat next to me for a minute and then we went back to the doors (which had been left open) and got into the car.

"I'm not going anywhere," I said.

Chip started the engine.

"You better go up to the gas station," I said. "The tank's almost empty."

We parked next to those bright red pumps at the top of the hill. There was a large porch in front of the house, and beyond it, inside, there was the office of the gas station. I couldn't see past the screen door, and Chip and I just waited for a while, seeing the high, clear sky, and the movement of the trees. The white clapboard house and office were trimmed with green.

At one side of the porch there was a flatbed truck which had a sign on its stakes. The sign was made of plywood, hand painted, held to the stakes with wire, and it read "Boone and Horace, Snappers Unlimited." The paint was still wet, and a can of it (bright red, like nail polish) sat next to the truck with the brush still in it. Chip and I waited, but no one came out, so we went inside to get some help.

The office of the gas station was also a store. On the left side of the room there was a short rack, covered with glass, that held cheap shotguns and rifles, and on top of it there were hung some fishing poles, nets, vests, and some pieces of cardboard which had stapled to them clear envelopes of hooks. On the other side there was a small grocery section, a cooler that held a couple dozen eggs, some milk, luncheon meat and bread, mayonnaise. At the rear of the store there were a cash register and shelves that went from floor to ceiling and that held bottles (pints and quarts) of two kinds of liquor. Before the counter there were a couple of tables and chairs, and two men sitting there. Standing by the cash register there was a tall, heavy man of about fifty. He wore black jeans and a black shirt.

"I'd like some gas," said Chip. He stopped and looked at me and said, "And a quart of that liquor."

"Good," I said. "Thanks."

We sat down at a table which was a plank bolted to a metal stand. The bolts came through. The man in black gave us two glasses, and we put them on the table, too. Chip poured us each a good drink and we sat under the buzzing, insectlike sound of the fluorescent bulbs and smelled the gun oil and the dust on the fishing tackle.

"I just want to talk to somebody," I said.

"I'm not stopping you," said Chip, sipping that drink. "Go on."

"Are you two turtlers?" I said to the men who were at the next table.

"Was," said a man with red hair and a squint. His hands were scarred and he lacked the tip of his little finger. "We was turtlers. Our truck broke. We bought something at the gas station for it, but it didn't work and it cost a dollar."

The other man was tall and very thin and his hair was so blond as to be white. He was wearing a red shirt and had an ear pierced, although there wasn't anything in it.

"Do you mind?" said the man with the squint.

"No," said Chip. "Here."

Chip filled both their glasses. Thank God, I thought, we're not going to get into the car. Not just yet.

"I'm Horace," said the man with the squint. "That's Boone."

"Hello," I said, "I'm Jean. That's Mackinnon."

Boone, the blond man with the red shirt and the eyelashes that were so pale as to seem sickly or bizarre or bleached, glanced at us and then back to his glass and said to Horace, "Don't beg for liquor. We've got money for it."

"What's wrong with the truck?" I said.

"Are you his kin?" said Boone.

"No," I said.

"Then why are you asking all the questions?" said Boone. He didn't look up. Chip stirred, but didn't say anything, and I was grateful for that and for not being hurried. I sat in a hard oak chair and smelled the dusty, lonely odor of the room.

"Radiator leaks," said Horace, "it overheats and there's a hairline crack in the block."

"What have you done for it?" I said.

"He told you," said Boone. "We spent a dollar."

Boone looked angrily at his hands, and I noticed his eyes followed the man in black, the owner, as he came back in and as Chip paid him. Chip then stretched out his legs in the chair and took a cigar from his pocket and lighted it.

"My father sold Buicks," I said.

"You have an accent," said Boone.

"Yes," I said.

"Where are you from?" he said.

"Ohio," I said. "Southern part, down near Kentucky."

"I don't trust car dealers from Ohio," said Boone, as he looked at his hands: they were scarred a little, but nothing like Horace's. Boone had all his fingers. I wanted to touch Chip and say, Thank you. Thanks for just letting me talk. It's a relief. The air in the room was cool, and I smelled the tobacco.

"Miss?" said Horace. "Do you know of something?"

"How far do you want to go?" I said.

"New York," said Horace. "One way would be fine." His voice was soft and quiet. He must have been ten years older than Boone. "We'd leave the truck there."

"You'd be surprised how far a piece of junk will go," I said, "you'd be amazed."

"Yes, ma'm," said Horace, "I probably would, but New York would be far enough."

"Jean?" said Chip, looking at me and drawing on his cigar.

"Let's get a dozen eggs," I said, and then we stood up and went to the counter. The owner took them from the cooler and I asked him for a bucket, which he gave to me. Three of us went outside, but Boone sat with his pale eyes on his hands or on the owner.

Horace opened the hood and pointed to the leak in the radiator, pulled the dipstick and showed me where, in the oil, there were small spots of water.

"Boone is not to be wholly trusted, but then he's not completely dangerous," said Horace with his squint playing over my face and then Chip's. "He's been brooding. He was going to be married but he lacks the seventy-five dollars."

"What's the money for?" said Chip.

"Her father. That man inside. He's got her locked up and he wants the money before she can go. He says it's a debt, but it's just the money. You see where it's leaking?"

"Yes," I said.

Chip held the bucket and I broke eight eggs into it, putting the shells in the trash box which was on a post and had a place that held small squirt bottles of Windex. I beat the eggs with a forked stick until they were yellow and bubbles were rising out of them. Chip filled the radiator about halfway, and then stood with the cigar in his hand, staring at the road. I saw that same vibrant shaking at the back of his neck.

"You stay as long as you want," he said. "We need a little . . ." He stopped and held the cigar between his fingers. "Time," he said. "Before we go."

"Where's that?" I said, trying to look into his eyes.

"You take your time," he said.

"But where?" I said.

He smoked his cigar and looked up the road and at the Buick.

"Start it," I said to Horace, who was in the cab of the truck. "Let it run hot."

The truck started with a pop and a bang and then I couldn't ask again. The sun was out and some water had spilled on the macadam next to the truck and the light flashed off it, looked bright and cloudily silver. Chip stood before the smoking engine, holding the bucket and staring up the road. I stepped inside to get out of the sun and away from the sound and odor of the truck.

The man in black stood behind the counter and said, "How's it going?" I heard through the ceiling the sound of someone walking back and forth in the second story, from one wall to another: a woman's tread. The footsteps were loud in the cool and dusty room. There was a sign above the owner which spelled out in fading letters, "Hunting licenses sold here." "Just fine," I said, and left them, Boone staring at the woman's father and both of them hearing her patient tread.

The engine was hot and smelled like a tin roof in August.

"Pour it," I said to Chip.

The eggs slid into the radiator, and then we waited, with me thinking, At least we can stand here in the sunlight for a moment. I felt the breeze against my legs and was confused about which way was east, about where the ocean was. I kneeled next to the truck, still smelling that hot metal odor and the earthy scent of grease, and saw that the water, which had been dripping there, had stopped.

Chip drew on his cigar and kneeled next to me and looked, too.

"Stopped leaking," said Chip.

"Of course it stopped leaking," I said. "My father and I must have fixed five hundred trade-ins. Overnight. Then he'd drive them to Cincinnati to sell to a wholesaler. One time we fixed a Ford, sold it, and took it back the next week on a new Roadmaster. We didn't know it was the same car because it had been painted."

I pulled Chip against me, and said, "All right. We can go whenever you want."

"Take your time," said Chip with that gray-dawn look in his eyes. "Don't rush."

"Are you sick?" I said.

"No," said Chip, "let's have a drink."

We leaned against one another in the sunlight. The truck kept banging and that black smoke drifted past us. We were sitting on our heels, and that made everything seem large, gigantic, the red pumps for the gas, the house above us, the truck itself.

"But where are we going to go?" I said.

"Let's have a drink," said Chip.

Horace climbed out of the truck's cab, slammed the door, and walked to the open hood. I saw the raised welts on his hands, and the cleanly snipped little finger, and Horace's shiny red hair. He'd put something on it to make it stay the way he'd combed it.

"What about the truck?" he said softly.

"Take a look," I said.

Now there were no drips at all, not even one or two that might have fallen from the vibration of the engine. Chip filled the radiator to the top, and we waited for a long time, but we didn't see any water. Horace checked the oil stick, and there wasn't any more water in it, either.

"You'd be surprised how hard you can cook an egg if you don't burn it," I said. "It makes a gasket."

"Let's tell Boone," said Horace. "He'll ask you to see the turtles. Have you ever seen a snapper?"

Horace held up that little flipper.

"No," I said.

"Boone loves them, but it's just money to me," said Horace. "I don't mean to slander them, but . . . look at my hands." We began to close the hood of the truck, and Horace, with his squint moving between Chip and me, stopped us and said, "Sometimes Boone can be difficult." Horace reached into his pocket and pulled out a pair of metal knuckles, which were a gray aluminum color. "That's why I carry these. Don't get too close to him . . . not if he's behaving odd."

"Sure," said Chip. "All right."

"You don't have to worry about me," I said.

Horace put the metal knuckles into his pocket and went inside, leaving Chip and me in the bright sunlight. The Buick was sitting next to us, and Chip saw me looking at it.

"No," he said, "not yet. Let's breathe a little. That man's not dangerous."

"And if he was?" I said.

"We'd stay awhile," said Chip. "To see the snappers."

The room seemed dark after the sunlight and we heard that continual buzzing of the fluorescent light. Horace stood over Boone's table, had his hands on it, and his face close to Boone's.

"She fixed it," said Horace.

Boone had been holding his head in his hands, listening to the constant tread that came through the ceiling, but now he showed us his blue eyes and those lashes which seemed treated with peroxide.

"It doesn't leak?" he said.

"She did it with eggs," said Horace. "Says it will go to New York."

"All right," said Boone, "you come look at the turtles. Both of you."

"I'd love to," I said, hearing the steps of the woman upstairs as she came to a wall and turned. The floor was built over thin beams, and they were springy. When the woman walked they made a creak with two tones, one when she stepped down, one when she took her foot away. *Whee-ee, whee-ee,* like the call of some large bird.

Boone bought two quarts of liquor from the girl's father, and we followed him out to the truck. As he went through the door, he turned and said to the man in a black shirt, "I'm going to get the money," but the man in black just shrugged and took a fly swatter and brought it down on the counter.

"Wait a minute," said Horace, who went back into the store and bought three flares. "Just in case," he said.

I bought some extra eggs and put them in the Buick. Horace

dropped the flares, which looked like sticks of dynamite and were covered with wax, into the back of the truck. We started following it down the hill.

There were four or five bathtubs on the back: the newer ones were short and narrow, but some of the others were old, long, wide, and had lion's feet. There was chicken wire over the tubs. The truck let out a little blue puff of exhaust every time Boone changed gears.

"Where?" I said.

"There's a house I own," said Chip.

"Why not there?" I said.

"It's in the middle of Pop's land," he said.

"Oh," I said. "No. What's the house like?"

"It's made of stone," said Chip. "There's forty acres, too."

"Forty acres," I said. "You can keep people off forty acres, can't you?"

"Yes," said Chip.

"Please," I said.

I put my hand on the seat next to his.

"Please," I said. "It'll give us time."

Chip stared at the bathtubs of differing sizes and said, "Let's go look at the snappers."

The truck went downhill about a mile and then pulled onto a wood road, and we followed it until it stopped.

Horace pulled a wheelbarrow from the bed of the truck and we followed to the pool in a river that wasn't far from the wood road. It had a beach of gray sand on one side and a sheer wall of fieldstone on the other. The pool was deep and took the water from the river without much disturbance. There were birch and sumac and rhododendron growing on the side that had the beach. There was a small rowboat, turned upside down near the pool, and Boone righted it, made it float, and beckoned.

Horace rowed. I sat at the back, next to Boone. My knees were up and I saw the whitened pressure of the kneecaps, and felt the moist air that came off the pool. I saw Horace's hands as he rowed, the twiny welts, the silken patches. Boone's breathing was deep and a little hurried.

The trap was made of gray wood, weathered planking that had come from a barn. It was rectangular, had a ramp that led into the middle. The inside of the rectangle was spiked with twenty-penny nails. A piece of wood with rotting sardines on it floated in the middle of the trap. The turtles came up the ramp and tried to get the fish: that's how they were caught. The sardines were in the sun, and had been for days.

The trap was almost filled and the surface of the water heaved, rose and fell as though there were a stream of water under high pressure coming from the bottom: the turtles were moving. There were more than I could count beneath the gray-green surface of the water, and they were swimming from side to side. The shells were dark, edged with a blond rim, and their legs stuck out of the shells, flapping, moving backward. The stroke was powerful. The turtles had uneven skin, and I saw the small pyramids on it, the heads that looked like a cast-iron spike. The turtles were colliding with one another and snapping when they had a chance, but they were all moving fast and they snapped at random, at anything that passed them. In the water they were agile and graceful swimmers. Their feet had four long tines at the end, as sharp and as strong as those of a pitchfork, but not nearly so long. We waited for the turtles to calm down. They swam in that dark water, bounced off one another with a subdued clicking, made the surface of the water roiled and webbed. The sides and bottom of the trap were made from chicken wire, and we heard its distant hum as we stared into the pool and became drowsy.

"They're beautiful," said Boone, "damn, but they're beautiful."

Horace pulled on the oars and we stopped drifting away from the trap. The dark shapes still flitted back and forth.

"You'll excuse me," said Boone, only turning once from the turtles to show me his eyes, which were pale and had the same disturbed quality as the water in the trap, "but that son of a bitch wants money for his daughter. Well, I'm going to give it to him. I'm going to give him plenty."

"Now, Boone," said Horace, slipping his hand into his pocket. "We're going to get the money—"

"Shut up," said Boone, as he reached into the water near the end of the trap and undid a snaffle there. "Row."

We started towing the turtles. Boone snapped the end of the line to the boat.

"Look," said Boone, "we're going to make more than we need. For the wedding. You follow us to New York and we'll have a party."

We drifted into the beach.

"We need a party," I said, hearing my voice echo in that stone-and-water place.

"It's settled," said Boone.

"Fine," said Chip.

Horace and Boone loaded the wheelbarrow. Usually they put a stick into the trap and when a turtle grabbed it they'd pull him out. After a little while the trap was light enough to turn up and drain, and then some of the turtles were grabbed by their tails. The wheelbarrow was covered with chicken wire for each trip from the beach to the truck.

"Careful," said Boone.

"I'm always careful," said Horace. "I'm afraid of turtles. I don't think they're pretty. Is that pretty?"

He led up his hand and then began to wheel a load of turtles. We followed Boone and Horace up the hill to the truck, where they began putting the turtles into the bathtubs. Horace picked up an ax that was on the bed and looked into the wheelbarrow. A snapper moved toward him and he raised the ax and said, "I'd like to. I'd love it. You sweet son of a bitch."

Boone grabbed a fourteen pound turtle by the tail and threw it into a tub.

"Put that thing away," he said.

Horace pushed the ax onto the bed of the truck, next to the flares, and said to me, "I'm sorry. You'll understand I've been having some pretty bad dreams."

The turtles snapped when they'd been grabbed by the tail, and after they'd been dropped into the tubs I heard them moving, that dry slither and squeak as they showed their anger. Chip and I climbed up to look at them. Their flippers moved against the white porcelain and their eyes were fixed on mine: I saw the yellow ring around the pupil. After the tubs were filled, Chip and I looked again. The turtles glided back and forth and we heard that light and distant sound as they knocked against one another.

"I sent a postcard to the turtle buyer," said Boone, "and if he won't pay, there's always the Chinese."

Boone got into the driver's seat and started the first quart, which he shared with Horace. We followed. At dusk the first empty bottle flew from the driver's window and after a little the water started to splash over the lips of the tubs and run through the boards of the bed onto the road, where it made a wet, dark, and gently curving line. Before we got to New York City the truck was leaking again from the radiator.

It was dark when the truck pulled to the side of the road in the marshlands. Chip and I parked behind it and went up to see what was wrong and then Chip went back to the Buick for the eggs. We needed water, so Horace and I climbed onto the bed. Every now and then a long, dark car went by, bent on the city, and going fast. The cloth of my skirt was pushed against me by the wind. We weren't that far from the city, and I saw its lights reflected in the water of the tubs, and the sky, too, the stars, and my own face as dark as oil. The turtles were silent. Horace had a bucket and a tin can and we were going to dip some water. We pulled back the wire and the smooth surface changed: the image of the city and the stars disappeared as the turtles started to move. I stayed next to them, becoming peaceful as I stared into the tub where there was water and the sound of the turtles.

"Careful, Miss," said Horace. "Those will kill you."

I had put my hand on the side of the tub, and Horace picked it up and held it with his crippled one as we stared at those dark creatures. Chip had come to stand at the end of the bed, his shirt white in the glow from the city as he stood against the waste of marshlands. I heard the turtles behind me in the tub. Then Horace dipped some water out and we fixed the radiator, and Chip and I got back into the Buick.

I couldn't stop crying, and we drove along anyway. I put my forehead against the cool glass of the window.

"Hush," said Chip.

After a while I stopped, but I was still thinking of those dark shapes as they glided back and forth, disrupting the image of the city lights.

We followed the truck across a bridge and then into the city. Soon we were parked in front of a warehouse, which was two stories high and boarded up. There was one street light and by it we saw a sign that said Chapman's Sea Food. Beneath it someone had scrawled "Gone Out of Business."

"Goddamn," said Boone.

I smelled the damp, salty air of the ocean.

"The Chinese like turtles," said Boone.

He leaned against the side of the Buick and held in one hand the last bottle, and there wasn't much in it.

"Where are the Chinese?" said Horace, who was now standing at the rear of the truck.

"How the hell would I know?" said Boone.

"Follow," said Chip, "just follow me. I know where they are."

I put my head back, and then I remembered being parked on a bright street. There was the smell of fresh vegetables, mushrooms, and ginseng in the air, and the odor of glazed pork. Chip was parked behind the truck, on the bed of which Boone now stood, gesticulating and speaking to people who walked by. They were Chinese, and they stood quietly for a moment, and then ignored the truck and the bathtubs filled with turtles. After a little Horace and Boone sat on the truck's running board, and we came out to join them. When they looked at us we saw their yellow eyes, the reflection of a tall, lighted pagoda that was in front of the truck.

"That son of a bitch wants money. . . ." said Boone. "And what am I going to do with these monsters?"

He gestured to the back of the truck.

"Let's give them to the Chinese," said Horace, "Let's just leave them here."

"They'll die," said Boone.

"Let them," said Horace. "They can stay right here."

"You son of a bitch!" said Boone, looking up with that yellow light in his eyes. Horace put his hand in his pocket.

"Show me a freshwater pond," said Horace, gesturing to the street. Some of the Chinese walked by, looked once at us, and continued. "Find me one. I don't *want* to leave the turtles here to rot."

"You son of a bitch," said Boone, beginning to stand now and raising a long, thin, but still mean-looking arm.

"Wait," said Chip, stepping up to Boone. "I'll show you one. Can you drive?"

"Yeah," said Boone, standing up now, "sure."

"Me, too," said Horace, but he still kept his hand in his pocket.

Boone got the truck started again and Horace climbed in and they followed us. Chip drove straight uptown (hearing the loud, odd noise the truck engine made in the city) and parked on the West Side, near an entrance to Central Park. It must have been three o'clock in the morning, and there weren't any cars to respond to the traffic lights. The apartments above the park, on both sides, were dark.

"We can let them loose in the pond," said Chip.

I stood near the back of the truck. Chip spoke to Boone and to Horace, and then they dragged the wheelbarrow to the ground.

The signal changed, and Boone, Horace, and Chip were green, then yellow, then red. Some of the water had spilled from the tubs, and I saw the crimson, glazed surface of the bed of the truck. Chip said, "See? That way. Along that path . . ." and pointed.

Boone wasn't listening though. The three men seemed trapped or stilled for a moment. Chip had moved to one side, to the curb, and was now looking up at Boone, who stood on the truck behind one of the tubs with lion's feet. Horace stood next to the wheelbarrow, had his hands open, as though beginning to plead a case. I moved back, toward the car, when I heard the empty liquor bottle break. Boone still stood at the back of the truck, leaning over the tub and staring at Horace.

"You got no woman, no family, no trouble," said Boone.

Horace reached into his pocket, came closer to the back of the truck, had his hand on the flares.

"Boone," said Horace.

"All you've ever had to worry about was eating and sleeping," said Boone. "You son of a bitch."

Boone strained, lifted the tub, and poured the water in it and the snappers, too, onto Horace. It looked as though there were billows of black silk flowing from the tub, and for a moment I thought they would stay that way forever, arced, rayed with current. Chip stepped back, and I did, too, to the open door of the Buick. Horace had been trying to climb onto the bed of the truck when the water hit him, and I saw him raise those metal knuckles: for a moment he seemed to be standing in the surf and that a wave was breaking over him. He struck through the water with the knuckles and said "Ah. Ah. Ah." Boone put his head back and may have been laughing, but I couldn't hear, and really couldn't see, either, at least not for a minute. Horace's hand had reached the flares as the water hit him, and he had grabbed one. He still made that noise, that "Ah. Ah. Ah," but he was able to rip the flare, to start it. The back of the truck, the water that ran from it, and ten or so snappers became clearly visible. Boone seemed to vanish, levitating away from that flare which was so bright as to hurt when I looked at it. The snappers cast large, dark shadows against the cab of the truck, and all of them continued crawling toward Horace and across that slick redness of the water. Horace didn't notice the two or three large turtles which were at his ankles, which moved in the gutter and watched the bright, almost fuzzy or foggy light above them. I heard the tines of the turtles drag, and the scraping slither of their shells. By the light I saw Chip's face, the horror and amazement there, as he began walking to the driver's side of the Buick. The lights of a number of those apartments had come on, and we heard the sound of a police siren. The turtles advanced on Horace, who stood before them, holding the flare: we saw their black, pig-iron heads, the pyramid texture of the skin, the jaws. Horace threw the flare into the truck and started running into the park.

We had backed up a hundred feet and were pulling away when the police arrived. One man in uniform got out of his car and looked behind the truck and then screamed. We heard his long, hard cry as we went up the avenue. When we were a half mile farther uptown, and still going along the park, we saw Boone, his pale hair, and his long, thin-legged gait. He was running, and when we pulled next to him, he turned into the park and was gone. We waited for a while, but he didn't come out.

A patrol car drove by and we moved along.

"Not one," said Chip, "got into the pond."

We went across the bridge and it wasn't long before the sun rose.

"All right," I said. "Where?"

Chip looked at me and put his hand on mine.

"I can't guarantee anything," he said, "not a thing."

"I never asked you to," I said. "I just wanted a little time."

Chip nodded and said, "Okay."

So we started driving to the farm, and I put my head back and my arm out to touch him every now and then, thinking, We'll be able to go someplace and close the door for more than a night. I watched the things at the side of the road emerge from the foggy dawn, telephone poles and billboards: I was tired, too. When I put my head back and closed my eyes I saw the turtles, snapping, their heads looking like the top of spiked iron fences, and I saw that reddish flare explode, and heard, too, the sound of the turtles as they pulled themselves along.

Mrs. Mackinnon's Book of Animals, Reptiles, Plants, Trees, Birds, Bugs, and Flowers.

Ruffed grouse are hardy and delicate, and I am most taken with them because they are able to change the unexpected and the surprising into beauty. They are described as chickenlike, but I find this inaccurate and pejorative. It is true that the bird has a certain plumpness, and that the ruffed grouse spend a lot of time on the ground, but the similarities end there. Grouse are colored so as to be almost impossible to see. They are brown and dark brown in strips that run from the back of the head to the tail, and their wings, when folded, seem to suggest this same combination. Some of the best grouse cover on this land is in spruce and pine, near a creek which is lined with bittersweet. When grouse are quiet on the floor between the spruce and pine (or when they are moving, for that matter), it is almost impossible to see them. The camouflage is so perfect that sometimes when I long to see grouse and can't find them, I will go to a place where the ground is covered with pine needles, and since the colors and the odor of a softwood stand are so much associated with the birds, it is almost as though I had seen one. Grouse are eighteen inches long and they have a wingspan of thirty. They are a large game bird (bigger, certainly, than bobwhite and woodcock), and when I walk by them, without seeing them, they flush, or begin to fly quickly. It is my experience that a bird will stay still while I am walking, but if I stop, or hesitate, the bird becomes frightened enough to break into the air. This is a surprise and bewildering, even when I have caught sight of the bird beforehand. The bird rises from the ground, beating its wings against its oddly plump body. Its wings are disproportionately large. The beating is so great that you not only hear the first, strong movements, but feel them as well. As the bird rises, the beating of its wings becomes faster, and the individual pops or beats merge into one reassuring and increasing purr. I say reassuring because until one hears that purr one is frightened or unclear as to precisely what is happening, or it's as though the mind knows but the body does not. I wait, tense and uneasy as the bird rises, and it is at this moment that the surprise or fright becomes beautiful: as the grouse moves away and begins that movement between the trees, one which almost looks as though the bird is hung on a string and is being swayed back and forth like a pendulum, the grouse displays its tail, puts down a fan of brown feathers, which is marked, near the end, with a black band. It is so precise as to have been drawn with a compass. The band is about a half inch wide, bordered by a white line, and stands out clearly on the tail. So I will stand and be surprised and then awed as the bird breaks away. The sound diminishes and softens as the bird flies, moving in such a manner as to put as quickly as it can as many trees as possible between me and it.

In the fall I am glad to hear the drumming of the males, as they stand on a fallen log or a stone wall or on the ground and beat their wings against their breasts. This drumming may be heard for hundreds of yards, and by it the females are alerted. The sound, from a distance, is soft and lovely. The males will display and strut for the females they have attracted, who respond in a coquettish way of their own and move closer to the male. Usually, after mating, the female will make a nest on the ground and will watch over the

eggs and the young herself, but I have been told that while the
male seems distant, he is not: he spends his time watching the nest,
and if anything happens to the female, the male of the species is
perfectly capable and will readily take charge of the young. In the
spring I have seen ruffed grouse followed by small ones (whose
coloring nearly resembles the adults) as they move through the
orchards looking for grasshoppers and later in the patches of
blueberries, blackberries, and raspberries. By fall the young are
close to being full grown, and they disperse to find an acre or two
of cover (aspen being a particular favorite) in which they can live.
There have been times when I flushed a female with chicks, and
the bird has risen to the height at which a man would have fired
his shotgun and then the grouse pulls in a wing and falls, appearing
hit. If you come closer, you will find that the bird has walked off,
unharmed, and that the chicks have dispersed as well, having been
given the time to get away. I have seen grouse in winter, too, and
by the tracks in the snow I have seen that the birds have grown
small sacks that act as snowshoes. But it is the suddenness, the
fright, and the reassurance that I think of when I am reminded of
grouse. There are many times when I have felt that sudden fear,
when opening an envelope, or hearing the phone ring at three
o'clock in the morning, or when, say, I am driving with my husband, and at these moments I almost can feel the shadow or the
airy presence of the grouse and am all the more frightened when
I realize that I am alone, my fingers holding a sheet of unwanted
paper, or my eyes staring at some approaching hazard, without
that precise band and the purr of the grouse's wings.

My husband shoots grouse in the fall, and when he brings them
home and suspects that a shot has pierced the cavity, he will clean
them and peel an onion, and then stick the onion into the grouse:
this eliminates any unsavory taste, or taste that is not of the bird.
The grouse are hung outside the kitchen. I have stood before the
beam where there is a row of nails, one bird tied to each, and have
seen the color of the pine needles, the gentle shadings of brown

and dark brown, the fan that is folded and no longer capable of soothing one's fears. The birds are roasted with butter and salt and pepper and served with wild rice and large mushrooms, black ones, that have been sautéed. We drink cold white wine, and for a moment I feel those fears and can see that fan opening to protect me. The flesh tastes of chestnuts and is mild and white.

Pop Mackinnon
The Arrival. The Farm.
Summer. 1950.

The first sign was the dust. I saw it hanging in the road one afternoon when I was on what I must admit was a patrol, the object of
which was my son, although I was keeping an eye out for trespass-
ers or poachers. The dust hung in the road as though it were smoke
left by a locomotive. I noticed that the dust came along the road
through the orchard, but did not continue the rest of the way to
the farm. It lingered in the air in front of the gravel pit and then
over the road which leads to that stone house. There was nothing
I could do about the gift: it was Chip's free and clear. I dropped
into a crouch so I could look through the leaves. I was on the stone
house side of the orchard.

I had considered a number of alternatives to the gift, or ways of
reclaiming it, although none was workable, if only because all of
them called for the legal strategy of declaring myself incompetent
at the time of the conveyance. There may have been times when
I thought this was the case, but I didn't want to expose myself for
a madman *and* a fool, not to mention putting myself at the mercy
of my heirs. No, the place was his and there wasn't much I could
do about it aside from taking myself to task, in private and at

extreme lengths. The law had failed me, and this came as an unpleasant surprise.

I was wearing an old felt hat that makes me feel genteelly decayed when I am probably just decayed, but it was made in London and it covers my shiny head. There wasn't anything on the road, and I waited, but nothing else came along. So, I thought, it's only one car. I went to the back of the orchard, through the dump, and into the woods that run parallel to the stone house road. There were some young maples with leaves as green as a frog, and I moved through them, crouched, listening, and becoming more suspicious with each step.

I stopped. A poacher comes after dark with a light he can plug into the cigarette lighter of his car: he'll jack a deer and shoot it with a .22 (so as not to make any noise), and then he'll come back in a couple of hours to pick it up. He waits the two hours so things will be quiet even if anyone had heard that light crack of the rifle. And he doesn't bother gutting the carcass, either. A poacher throws it into the back of his car and drives circumspectly away. No, a poacher doesn't show up in the broad daylight of a Saturday afternoon.

I stopped and sat on a stone for a while, thinking about my wife and her belief that sitting on a stone gives you diarrhea. I put my cheeks into my hands and thought, I must be the Lord's own favorite, and sniffed the air that still held a little dust. Then I went back to the farmhouse, and I didn't stop to kill a snake that was crossing the road near the swamp, even though it was a copperhead. I sat on the porch and had a drink and called for Wade.

"Yes, Mr. Mackinnon," he said, after climbing down from his small room in the garage and walking to the front of the house. The porch had a new screen up, and it was silver and fresh looking. Wade stood outside with the bugs.

"Wade," I said, "I went down to that stone house which belongs to Chip. Just to look after his property. Which I conveyed to him out of the goodness of my heart. I can't find my cigar case, and I think I left it down there. Would you take a look for it? You can drive if you want."

Wade frowned, since he'd been waiting, too, and he said, "Do you want me to go right away?"

"Now," I said, and Wade went across the lawn, slapping at the bugs, to get that black car out of the garage. Since returning from Idaho I had only said to Wade "City," "Farm," "Pass that dumb shit," and that was all. I held Wade responsible, if only because he had been present when that Cooper girl walked into my house and took whatever the hell she wanted. Wade didn't look so much surprised that I had spoken to him as worried.

I sat with my dusty boots up on a small footstool, hearing the insects buzzing against the screen, as they tried to get to me. My wife came onto the porch.

"It's a beautiful day," she said. She had taken to wearing dresses of a lighter color, and she looked comfortable and fresh from her bath. She smiled, too.

"A beautiful day just brings out the *picnickers*," I said. "There's picnickers or some crazy poacher at Chip's house, and I sent Wade to investigate."

"I heard you say you'd lost a cigar case," she said.

"Have you been eavesdropping?" I said. "Am I not given the gift of privacy in my own home?"

My wife opened a book and began to read. It was a large book, filled with pictures and the Latin of science, which is different from the Latin of law, since the language is more inhuman and hateful. Law is sociable and binding: science does not understand legacy, which is the only thing men have: history. My wife and I have discussed this point, and by my expression she was aware that I was ready to begin again. Usually she can't resist me and says to herself, Let's make the old alligator snap his jaws, but instead my wife began looking at me over the pages of the book while keeping her head down. In a younger woman I would have called it flirting.

"All right," I said, "I have a deep voice. It has been known to carry."

She kept reading. I saw her hair had been fixed, and her nails, too.

"I know a sign when I see one," I said. "There was dust on the road. It turned at the gravel pit. What do you think it means?"

I was leaning forward, toward her.

"Do I have to see a marching band?" I said.

"No," she said, still looking over the top of her book at me. "The dust was good enough. Wade will find out. . . ."

I took my watch from my vest and stared at the Roman numerals and the hands that looked like small, black spearheads. I had never timed the distance, but it seemed to me it wouldn't take more than three minutes to get from here to the stone house, six minutes round trip, even if you weren't hurrying. I thought I'd take the Buick and give it a try, just to see. It was clear that Wade was not in a hurry.

My wife caught my eyes and smiled.

"Where the hell is Wade?" I said. "And why are you smiling?"

I put down my drink and spilled it, but I took out one of my handkerchiefs (which are of a large size) and cleaned up the mess, saying, "See? I'm not as crazy as you think."

"I don't think you're crazy," said my wife. "Maybe Wade found some poachers."

"Poachers don't take time," I said. "Either they go quickly or not at all. In either case it doesn't take much time."

I heard my voice in the empty house behind us, the plank floorboards being resonant enough to give the house a slight hum.

"I can stop shouting," I said. "See?"

"Yes," said my wife, looking over the top of her book. "Thank you."

"Why are you smiling?" I said.

Charlotte brought in another drink to take the place of the one I'd spilled.

"I was thinking it was a beautiful day and that you're still a handsome man," my wife said and then went back to her book.

"My face is ugly," I said. "Why, you're trying to charm me!"

"Perhaps," she said. "Isn't it nice to be charmed?"

"Why?" I said.

She put one hand to the back of her head and went on with her reading. My wife was not unattractive: her skin was still smooth and lovely after fifty-five years, although her heavy hair was gray. After a little she looked up.

"Why?" I said.

She wasn't smiling now, and in her eyes I saw that look which had been there first after I came back from Idaho and spent the evenings not over my foolscap and law books, but before my gun cabinet, where I toyed with two 6.5 mm shells. I just stood there, rubbing the soft points against my jacket. Now, as then, my wife looked frightened, but in the sunlight of the porch she tried to smile, and said, "We can't have any more children . . . I don't think we can, anyway."

"I am aware that Chip is our only child," I said.

"Good," said my wife.

She didn't stop though and went along, being kind and coquettish and flattering, too, and in every smile, in each bit of concern, in her scent, I was reminded that we had already lost a child.

"What's keeping him?" I said, and then both of us stared up the road and didn't see anything but the whitish dust in the sunlight: it looked white as ash and made my eyes ache with the brightness.

My wife didn't say anything.

"You know, I can be sociable, too," I said.

I pulled up my lips into a fair imitation of a smile.

"I know that, Pop," she said.

"That's right," I said. "Why, for instance, did you notice that when Wade drove out the Buick looked a little shabby?"

My wife had wanted a new Buick for years, and I had gotten used to the one we had, even though it canted over to my side and the upholstery was getting frayed. I liked it because it fit me, and I didn't mind the odor, which, if I were honest, I'd say was that of old hounds and cigars and a slight reminder of Chip's difficulties as a boy (which difficulties I cured by steadfastly not yielding to sentiment). I also thought it a good thing to soothe my wife, in case she was considering (and not as a ruse, either) the beginning of incompetency hearings. No one would lock up a man who is buying a new Buick. And I had noticed, too, that recently when I said, "Wade, pass that dumb shit," the Buick was unable: we pulled into the oncoming lane and died there, not having the speed. Wade had become ashamed of it, too.

"It's beginning to look distinguished," said my wife.

"What the hell did it look like before that?" I said.

"Secondhand," said my wife.

"But you don't mind it now?" I said.

"No," she said and smiled.

"What about that dog odor?" I said, but then we were both left with that bright prospect of the road. It was quiet and there was no breeze.

"What the hell's keeping him?" I said.

I patted my vest and pushed myself up to go to my study where my cigar case was (a leather one that held three cigars and had a top with a leather hinge), but I was saved from smoking a cigar I didn't want. A cigar when you're angry is a travesty, because you always draw too hard and this makes the smoke hot and tasting of ash. I was saved from it because, as I stood with one hand on the front door, I saw Wade coming up the drive in the Buick.

"I couldn't find the cigar case, Mr. Mackinnon," said Wade.

He spoke this to my wife, though, as though she were interested in cigars. I held the case up, as a badge, to let him know I hadn't sent him down there to look for it. My wife closed her book.

"It should be obvious I sent you down there for other reasons," I said.

Wade nodded and said, "I saw her."

"And what about my son? Has he come home?" I said.

"I didn't see him," said Wade, "but that young lady—"

"Her name, Wade," I said.

"Cooper," said Wade, "Mrs. Mackinnon and I met her . . ."

"That's right," I said. "What did the Cooper . . . woman say about my son. Is he in the county?"

"Yes," said Wade. "He's here."

My wife made a small, hurt noise as she took a full breath and then sat with an openly curious expression on her face, although her brow was furrowed, and she seemed drawn around the eyes: she was scared, too. Wade was uneasy. I held a long Cuban cigar in my hand, but I wouldn't have tried to light it.

"And?" I said.

"The Cooper girl may be wrong," said Wade.

I still held the cigar, but this was only something to occupy my hands: I thought of the girl in that milky triangle as she stood with her nose against mine. I saw her sitting in the cool atmosphere of that stone house, stretched out on a white sofa there.

"About what, Wade?" I said. "Speak right out, man to man. If you dare."

"He's posting his land," said Wade.

My wife flinched and said "Oh" quietly, before shaking her head from side to side. Wade looked at the ground, tilted his long head forward, and it was clear that he was straining, almost wanting to find the words at his feet so he could pick them up. His hair was all gray now and there were lines in his face, from his nose to his lips and around his eyes. Over his shoulder I saw the Buick sagging on its springs.

"I'll go down again," said Wade. "I'll talk to . . ."

I took from my vest pocket a small guillotine slicer and nipped the end of the cigar, and then I put the cigar into my mouth. This gave character to the side of my face, although I had to keep the cigar from trembling.

"That won't be necessary, Wade," I said. "That's all."

"I'd go anytime," said Wade, but I shook my head and Wade

walked across the lawn to the garage. He stopped once and looked at the house. By this time I had the cigar going and was enjoying the cool, fragrant smoke.

My wife sat with her hands pressed together, tips and palms both.

"He's our only and last child," said my wife. "I want you to do nothing for a while. I want him to have a little time."

My wife turned a hand palm out to the orchard and rubbed the back of it, quickly and without relief.

"That's not too much to ask," she said.

I grunted and tried to keep the cigar steady.

"Why are you smiling?" said my wife.

"Chip's made his first mistake," I said, "and he's only been here a few hours, at the most. So I'll give him the right amount of time. Why do you suppose he's posting his lines? That is if the . . . Cooper girl can be trusted."

"I don't think she lies about much," said my wife.

I thought of the girl's sleepy joy in the truth, in its surprising bite. Yes, I thought. Hmm. Trust.

"Well?" I said. "Why is he doing it?"

"To keep people out," said my wife, who was still rubbing the back of her hand.

"Anyone in particular?" I said.

"I wouldn't want to say," said my wife, "since . . . you gave him the land."

"Speak plainly," I said, my voice rising. "Who in particular?"

"You," said my wife. "But you don't have to go . . . down there."

Two white butterflies fell around one another outside. They looked like large pieces of confetti. My wife's eyes strayed to them for a minute and then came back to me.

"Do you think he has the right to post his lines?" I said.

"Yes," said my wife, "of course. He owns it, doesn't he?"

The cigar dampened my laughter, and I thought, Well, well, at least I've got a start.

"Only the rights to land can be conveyed, not the land itself,"

I said. "I find this hard to believe, but a son of mine did not read his deed . . ."

"What deed?" said my wife.

"The deed to that house and forty acres," I said.

"Oh," said my wife, sitting back and holding her hand, but not rubbing it. "And what was in it?"

"A covenant," I said, enjoying the sound of the word in my mouth, "concerning certain rights I will discuss"— I raised my brow and smiled unpleasantly—"with Chip."

We were quiet for a while, and I went through the screen door with the new silver wire and down to the flower bed, where I rooted around in the mint growing there, picking the best and most crisp leaves, smelling them as I bent over: they had a dusty odor at that time of the year. When I was in my chair again, I thought of the texture of the girl's pursed lips, and said to my wife, "Do you really believe that God loved Job the most?"

"Yes," said my wife, as she gazed into the orchard, straining, it seemed, to see beyond the end of it. "Oh, yes. I'm sure of that. More than anything else."

I was feeling better, since I had begun to think again (rather than just grieving, which is a horror), and I wanted no disruption, or wanted the atmosphere in the house to have that clean and ordered quality which is reassuring (something like fresh linen), so I said, "All right, we'll get that new Buick."

My wife left me in peace.

"Well, well," I said, "so he wants to keep me out. Well, well."

I finished my cigar and struck toward the woods, but then my wife came out of the house and began to follow me. Her gray hair was down over her ears and forehead and her eyes were full of tears, but she stayed close to me and said, "What covenant? What have you done, you damned lawyer?" I continued walking, but I turned toward her and said, "The law binds."

I went directly from the farm to Chip's land and was wondering whether I'd find him on his lines or near the house, or if the girl would be alone. The undergrowth was thick and I pushed through it and then the swamp, which was almost dry and still the worst place in the world for copperheads. I walked through those brackish and vile pools that were still left, each only being a few inches deep and having a silty tugging bottom: it made a sound like *op, pop, op,* as I went right along, wanting to see with my own eyes those posters that said Warning: No Trespassing.

When I gave the place to Chip, the surveyor blazed the lines and left his red flags at the stone corner-monuments, so the lines were easy to find. The monuments were three feet square, made of fieldstone and mortar, unmovable. In the fall I like to sit on one and feel the land's cold tang. I came through the short spruce beyond the swamp, smelling in the air the need for rain, and hearing, too, the distant but nevertheless distinct sound of someone using a hammer.

The first poster was a white piece of cardboard which had been bought recently: it didn't even have Chip's name printed on it. I ripped it down and went up to the next, doing the same, always walking toward the muted banging.

I saw Chip clearly. The surveyor had cut some small spruce so he could use his instruments, and Chip walked in that narrow, domed path. He looked good, carrying a bunch of signs under his arm in much the same manner as a schoolboy with his books, and he was intent on (or possessed by) putting up those cheap pieces of paper. I stayed back and ripped them down and watched until I had a good look. His movements were fast, maybe even hurried, but he hit those nails hard, and the air around him seemed charged. He had lost weight and looked the better for it and there was in the movement of that old scrub of a hammer (with its rusty head and taped-together handle) a definite arc, a certainty. I went along for a while more, pulling down the posters, and then stopped and stared. In the arc of that hammer there was the belief in his correctness. I hadn't expected it, and it made me stand back and rub my face and consider: there was no shame. No shame yet,

I thought, and turned back into the woods, where I went over that fieldstone ridge which runs through the center of my land.

I came out at the farm, and when I opened the new screen door, I found Wade and my wife and heard Wade say, "His car was dusty . . . the girl seemed careful, but not frightened. She was able to smile and to say hello. . . . I'd say they've been lonely." You see? He was already on my porch, drinking tea, but when he stood up, I said, "Rest easy, Wade. We're just getting to know one another after all these years, aren't we?"

"Yes," said Wade, "I think we have the chance."

"That's good," I said. "Don't move. There's something I want you to do for me."

I went into my study and cleared the paperwork off my desk (those sheets and documents which had been the mainstay of my life for close to thirty-five years and which I hadn't touched once in the two weeks since my return) and took a piece of my stationery and a pen and wrote, "Read your deed. Welcome home, Pop." I folded it up and felt the heavy rag paper crease reassuringly beneath my thumb.

"Wade," I said, "I've thought your offer over. I want you to go back down there and drop this off at the stone house."

He was standing now, and he took the envelope and said, "I'd be glad to."

I walked with Wade to the garage, and when he got into the car, I said, "Wade, you'll wait for an answer, won't you?"

"If you want it," said Wade.

"Yes," I said. "Wait."

The Buick went down the road and I climbed the stairs to the porch and called for Charlotte to open two dozen oysters and to bring them to me with horseradish and a bottle of Bass ale. My wife sat quietly for a moment, finishing her tea, and then said, "Do you remember, years ago, when we first went to France? Do you remember the coast . . . ?"

She said this in a soft, considerate voice.

"All right," I said, "I saw him. He seems light and healthy."

"And?" she said.

"That's all I could tell from a distance," I said, and then we waited.

"Well?" I said, when Wade was standing before me again. The Buick had a door open and was idling in front of the house as though we were living in a row block somewhere. "What did he say? Did he seem worried?"

"No," said Wade, "he didn't seem in any way particular about it. He wrote this, though, and gave it to me."

I picked up that heavy envelope and saw that Chip had turned it over and written on the back, "Haven't got copy. Can you provide? Best, Chip."

"Damn. Damn," I said, "he is becoming disorganized and insane."

Wade stood in front of me, and my wife looked at the note as Charlotte brought in a large platter and my tankard (which has a stag etched on it and a top with a hinge) and put them down on a small folding table. I had a couple of oysters and some of that Bass ale and then went into the study and found in my bottom drawer a copy of the document. I wrote on another piece of paper, "Here. Pop."

I brought it out and gave it to Wade, and he drove off.

"Care for an oyster?" I said to my wife, but she shook her head and stared into the open book before her, not seeing a damned thing, though. I had some more oysters, tasted the ocean in them, and thought of the document bouncing along on the seat next to Wade, and of Chip when he came across in the deed (after the compass headings) a reservation of rights, which explained that I will ". . . maintain a lifetime interest in the rights to hunt these same and above described forty acres and the conveyee will, to insure ease of access and in no way to impede such rights, not post any line or in any way mark or delineate same."

I finished the oysters and put my nose in the tankard to smell the odor of hops. Wade returned in the Buick, which he left running again and which he had driven so quickly that there was hanging in the air a layer of smoky dust.

"He sent this," said Wade, returning my envelope (with the deed neatly folded inside). I opened it and found a short note on a piece of paper torn from a grocery bag and written in pencil with a steady hand. "All right," it said. "But this means we will not be bothered between the hours of dusk and dawn. It is illegal to jack deer, although I doubt you need to be told this. Chip."

"What about coons?" I wrote when I was back in my study. "We've got more than anyone could want. And you can hunt them at night. Here is some stationery. Use it. Pop. P. S. Do you understand now how that deed and the law read?"

I brought out my large envelope, and Wade took it to the stone house, where he waited for the reply, which read, "Yes. Chip."

"Ah," I said, finishing the last of the Bass ale and smelling the dust from the road and knowing, too, that both of us understood that the only way I had legal rights to the land was to walk on it carrying a shotgun or a rifle, which is to say that I could only go armed.

"That will be all, Wade," I said. "You come back tonight and we'll talk about the new Buick. Maybe there's an extra that you particularly want?"

"I'm going now," said Wade. "I don't think I want an extra."

"Fine," I said.

I showed to my wife that heavy piece of paper with the two words on it, "Yes. Chip," and said, "At least he used the stationery."

I lit another cigar and watched it get dark, but I wasn't at ease, even though I had bested my son without trying that hard (which was some consolation). I thought it would make me feel good, but, instead, every now and then I saw those two words, "Yes. Chip," or worse yet heard them in a tone I didn't like or didn't understand or didn't want to understand. I sat in the dark and drank and thought about the land I gave away, and the Cooper girl, too. There was something in the bright aura about her (and I made no mistake here: there was one and it suggested something beautiful and alive and terrible, too) that made me want glory or fame or to do anything that was required . . . more than anything else it made killing seem not so unnecessary or strange. This is too blunt, but it suggests the . . . effect. An odd thing was that this sensation (or desire) was fleeting, so much so that one never had a chance really to know or to examine what charged and horrified. That aura, or mystery, was part of the tone of those two words, but it alone didn't explain why I was troubled. I imagined the Cooper girl in the early morning as she turned under a thin blanket, revealing herself in this way to be light and squirmy. . . .

I went upstairs early and sat for a long time, trying to read the newspapers I had ignored for the last weeks, but they didn't help, and then I took out the piece of stationery and stared at those words, "Yes. Chip," not understanding, not wanting to, but still being frightened. I wasn't helped, either, when I came across advertisements in the back of the paper for some fraudulent sauce to make my hair grow back, but I put out the light and fell asleep as I heard the sounds of the house, its nautical creaking. I didn't sleep so much as I had dark worry and the definite sound of my heart, and after a while I woke, sat up, and said, "Ah, ah, that's it. . . . Damn them, damn the both of them," because I knew that the two words, "Yes. Chip," only had to do with facts and did not acknowledge more. There wasn't in them the least sense of defeat. I spent the rest of the night, sitting up, bent over my knees, and trying to imagine the protection of Jean's bright aura.

I did not exercise my rights immediately. Days passed and I stayed at the farm and conducted my business by telephone and by mail, and badly at that, but to all appearances I was like any other man who was trying to avoid the heat of New York City in July and August.

One morning, as I sat at the side of my bed, staring at my ugly feet, I said, "Goddamn," and then dressed quickly and started walking, without coffee or a word to anyone, to the garage, where I stood and said, "Wade, Wade, will you be kind enough to run this down to Chip? I mean in a hurry, too."

I held out one of my envelopes, in which there was a note which read, "Meet me in gravel pit. Pop."

Wade had just shaved and I saw the smooth, bluish cast to his face as he stuck his head out the window and said, "Right away. I'll be down in a minute." I saw his shoes as they came down the stairs: they were perfectly polished but the soles were worn and they showed newspaper print.

I waited in the root cellar atmosphere of the garage until Wade returned with a note that said, "Good. Ten minutes."

It was one of those July days when it gets to be a hundred degrees before nine thirty in the morning. It must have been ninety-five when I started walking along the road, hearing, when I passed the swamp, the dry slither of the copperheads there. The gravel pit was four hundred yards long, a hundred and fifty wide, and I entered it from the eastern rim, walked onto the sand and around yellow boulders that were as big as a truck. The sand was already hot, and I felt the heat on the palms of my hands and on my chin, too. I got there after Chip, so he saw me emerge from the sunlight which was already bright and as hard as a slap.

The top buttons of Chip's shirt were open, because of the heat, but that was his only acknowledgment. There was a hard, flat expression in his eyes that reminded me of bullet lead.

"I want a favor," I said.

"You can have anything I can manage," said Chip, "but don't be frivolous about Jean. I won't have it, will not allow you to speak of it."

"I'm not asking about her," I said. "I want a favor and I'm willing to pay."

"I don't need money," said Chip.

"How's that?" I said. "How?"

"I had some saved." said Chip, and his head turned toward the woods. He seemed hurt for a moment, but then put those hard, flat eyes on me again. It wasn't that he seemed remote so much as only half here, half someplace else. "I don't need it."

"You'll find that with money it is only a matter of scale," I said, "in deciding whether or not you need it."

"No," said Chip, "speak plainly."

"Put money aside then, for a moment," I said. "Let's talk of gratitude. You know that I could be doing one hell of a lot to make your life unpleasant, don't you? I have the right to that land, but I have stayed away. Does that count for something?"

"Yes," said Chip.

"What have you done about Carolyn?" I said.

"I'm writing to her now," said Chip, "this week."

Chip looked over my shoulder at the brightness of those large stones: the boulders and the sand appeared to be covered with sheets of white cloth. I was surprised to see how light Chip's skin was, and I was reminded by it of the interiors of buildings, shade, dusk. When he turned his head, I saw on his upper chest a bruise, a small one, the shape of a fingertip.

"But you haven't mailed anything?" I said. "Is that right?"

"Yes," said Chip. "It's something I'll do, but I won't enjoy it."

"Will you wait to tell Carolyn?" I said. "There's no need to ruin her trip, is there?"

"She may already know," said Chip, "her father saw us. . . ."

"I'll take care of him," I said.

Chip waited for a moment and said, "Is that all?"

"For now," I said.

"All right," he said. "I'll wait until the fall, when she comes back."

Then I was left in the heat and light, watching that white shirt on Chip's back as he made his way into the pines. He had gone before we'd spoken of the Cooper girl, before I'd had a chance to say, You'll see. One day she'll be vulnerable. Everyone is sooner or later. It's just a matter of time. Instead, I watched him go and remembered (was condemned to remember) that bruise on the top of Chip's chest.

At the house, after I bathed and changed, I went into my study, reached for the telephone, and got the operator to connect me with Carolyn's father. He was drunk, not showing it, clipping his sentences and making his voice sweet.

"Hello? Cooke? Is that you?" I said. "Mackinnon calling. I understand from . . . yes, I heard about it, and I've taken it up with him myself. Have you told Carolyn? That's good, yes, as a matter of fact I'd say it was diplomatic. Of course, I understand. You and I are men of the world and we understand such things, and I suppose I should tell you that the whole thing was arranged as a sort of wedding present from some of those boys at that law school up there in Cambridge. I understand, sorry you had to check out of the hotel . . . but I've been led to believe by my son that this was a passing . . . incident, and no more . . . Does that reassure you? Good, good, glad to hear it . . . I wouldn't bother Carolyn. Chip behaves a little odd every now and then, probably from being shot down and locked up, but at least he didn't get killed like my other boy. Oh, you didn't know about him? I know you're sorry to hear it . . . Say, we haven't really gotten together, so why don't you and your sons—you've got two don't you?—and their friends come over to hunt deer? How does that sound? Good, good, let's make it definite then . . . there's no need to alarm Carolyn . . . or to make a scandal . . . I tell you it was just a prank . . . don't mention it and I'm sorry for your trouble . . . well, it would have made me mad, too. See you in November. We'll kill some deer."

I put my finger on the plunger, held the cool instrument in my hand, and then reached over and dropped it onto the cradle. When I was stretched out on my leather sofa, I closed my eyes, and heard that man's voice, which sounded as though he had a reed in his nose. He was relieved, too, but still angry.

"Who was that on the phone?" said my wife, standing in the doorway.

"Hmmm?" I said, lazing back and closing my eyes. "I was just trying to take my mind off my troubles and to arrange for a nice hunt this year. Do you have any objections?"

My wife picked up my hand and shook her head. I could barely feel her fingers, since I was thinking, All arranged. We'll wait until the fall, when the leaves are down and the soil's frozen. Then we'll settle this matter.

"Maybe Chip will hunt with you," said my wife. "Maybe we'll all feel better."

"That's right," I said, crossing my arms on my chest. "Maybe Chip will hunt."

I made a good attempt at appearances, considering that I am, in the best of circumstances, not what anyone with sense would call a good waiter, but I went back to work in the beginning of September when the weather had cooled off and when those high, angry skies were there for everyone to see. In the city I sat in my Mexican garden and drank beer, but I was thinking about it, ticking off the days.

One afternoon, in the middle of September, my wife and I had lunch together at the farm, and when we had sat down and had begun, she said, "I wonder how long it will be until he runs out of money?"

"Damn," I said, biting my fork.

"What's wrong?" said my wife. "Is there something in that fish?"

"No," I said. "Do you realize that Chip has savings . . . ?"

"I didn't," said my wife. "How much?"

"It is one of my regrets that I can't tell you," I said, now gesturing with a fork, "but it should be enough to get him into deep snow, January or February."

"We wouldn't let them starve, would we?" she said, "Not when they're just a mile—"

"That's my money he's spending down there," I said, "mine or something worse. Do you know what it was supposed to go for?"

"No," said my wife, "expenses, I thought . . ."

"It was supposed to go to show Carolyn a good time and for no other purpose. That money was extorted from me outside on the lawn and in my study," I said, now holding my napkin taut across my knees. "Do you know that my origins were humble and that I wanted Chip to take the sting out of them? Do you understand?"

"Don't scream," said my wife, putting down her fork.

"Do you?" I said, already seeing those bright bits of light floating around the room.

"Yes," said my wife.

"There are intangibles as well," I said, thinking of that girl, of her effect.

We went back to eating. Poached sole in some kind of watery cream sauce. I hate sole.

"But we wouldn't let them starve," said my wife. "Would we?"

I smoothed out the napkin which I had been trying to tear.

"My father was a coarse, charming man," I said, "a country lawyer who was paid in hogs, game, cordwood, and certain other favors from country women, and I have never denied him and hold his memory precious, but he could still stand a little improvement, and Chip could soothe his memory. Not to mention mine, which is, I assure you, of some consequence around here."

My wife put down her fork, again.

"That's dreadful fish," I said, "isn't it?"

"Yes," said my wife.

"Charlotte! Charlotte," I said, knowing damn well that she was right behind the door, never wanting to miss a word of any raised voice. She waited a moment and then put her creased and round and heavy face into the dining room. "I will not be tortured with such fish. Is that clear?"

"Yes, Mr. Mackinnon," she said and removed it.

There was something wrong, though, and it took me a while to be sure of what it was. A bottle of my brandy disappeared, and then the wheel of cheese which I had brought myself from the city, a bag of oranges (which were shipped from Florida), a roast turkey, loaves of bread, and finally, when I was sitting before the fender in my study and enjoying the fire there, I reached into the wooden humidor for a cigar and found that it was empty. Then I thought, That's it. He didn't have much put away or he's running out.

At night I had trouble sleeping, and I sat up and rubbed my head, thinking of that dismal hotel room which the girl was able to brighten or to make dramatic, of the girl herself as she stood before me, her nose close to mine, as she said, "What do you want?" I got up and put on my terry cloth and old bathrobe and went downstairs, where I first went into my study for a clipboard, a piece of good bond, and a bit of carpenter's pencil. Then I went into the pantry, which was in the cellar.

It was a large room with whitewashed stone walls, a ceiling which was just the joists and floorboards of the first story. It was always cool there, and inside, behind an oak door, there were cases of sardines piled over my head, wheels of cheese (in black, yellow, and red wax), cans of strawberry preserves from Canada, a barrel of oysters, boxes of semisweet chocolate, crates of champagne. There was a bulb in a socket on one of the joists, but I didn't turn it on immediately, since the odor was increased by the darkness: I smelled the Pyrenees in the slats of the cases of champagne, the sugar in the rope from which the hams were hung. Finally, though, I pulled the switch, ruled my piece of paper, and began by counting the cans of sardines. I had come to "Smoked pheasants, in basket, three dozen," when I heard the floor of the kitchen, which was overhead, squeak. I turned out the light, unscrewed the bulb, and went to the rear of the pantry where I sat against a stone barrel, in which there was corned beef.

The cases above me had the aspect of a warehouse and I found them comforting as I sat there and listened to those footfalls on the stairs, which I knew as well as my own. It was hard to see my wife,

because there was a light behind her, but she made her way to the
pantry's light cord, pulled it, and then went back upstairs. As I
waited I heard the rats moving on the floor of the cellar, their
claws trying to grip the smooth flagstone and slipping. When my
wife came back she had a flashlight, one that held six batteries, and
the beam from it fell across a rat. Its shadow was three feet long
and wide, spread on the floor like a black cape. I saw its eyes for
a moment, too, not protuberant as in the funnies, but dark, alive,
touched with light, stoic. There was the definite sound of a rat
falling from the top of a wall and landing on the floor: it was like
a potato falling on concrete. There was the whispered movement,
too, of snakes. My wife came forward, stepped on a footstool, and
strained to lift a ham from a hook screwed into a joist.

I cleared my throat and said, "Where are you taking that?"

"Oh," said my wife. She held the ham by her hand now, but did
not put it down even though it was heavy.

"Where?" I said.

"To Chip," she said, "I think they—"

"Think?" I said, "haven't you seen him? Don't you know that
he's short?"

"No," she said. "I wanted to give something—"

"So it was you?" I said.

"I haven't taken that much," she said.

"What about brandy, cigars, cheese, turkey?" I said.

She still held the ham, and I knew she would not give it up. As
we stood in the dark we heard the floorboards of the kitchen
squeak again.

"I won't have lying," I said.

I reached to the bulb, screwed it in, and turned it on. My wife
looked at me, her eyes filled with terror that was for more than
getting caught with a ham: it made her seem brittle and despair-
ing, although not without the hope, I supposed, that I would feel
my chest explode or fall down in the road and let a car run over
me.

The floor squeaked again.

"I took the cigars," said Wade, as he put his head in at the top of the stairs, "and the brandy."

"Are you aware, Wade," I said, "that I could have you locked up? Again?"

"Yes," said Wade.

"And you took those cigars and brandy to Chip?" I said.

"Yes," said Wade.

"And what are you doing now?"

"I came for sardines," he said, and held a shopping bag he'd brought along, "and some Spanish onions."

We were quiet for a while and I heard that almost inaudible disturbance that sounded like a man covered in leaves and breathing softly: that snake. Wade and my wife stared at me, and it was clear they had no shame, either. My wife's arm began to quiver under the weight.

"All right. It's yours," I said to my wife.

"Wade," said my wife, "will you take this?"

He came downstairs, opened the bag with a loud pop, and slipped the ham inside. I gave him two cans of sardines and a couple of onions.

"More," said Wade, with a flat, hard tone. "I came for more than two cans. You can take it out of my pay."

"I'll be damned," I said, watching his silhouette against the light. "What makes you so interested?"

Wade reached into one of the open boxes and took six cans: they looked like a small stack of silver bullion when he picked them up with the long fingers of his hand.

"Chip and I went to the movies together," said Wade, "before the war."

"So what?" I said.

"I appreciated it," said Wade, "that's all."

He turned toward the light and I saw him in profile now, his long, bent nose, the brows that were getting bushy, his head set forward on a thin neck. And when he turned I saw one angry, definite eye.

"You're taking a hell of a chance because of some *movies*," I said.

"*I appreciated it,*" said Wade, and stared into the darkness of the pantry. He made his bag rattle as he folded the top together.

"Who's taking these things down there?" I said.

"Wade," said my wife, who was now standing on the stairs, keeping her distance.

"Tomorrow. In the evening," said Wade. "I don't see Chip. I see her . . ."

Her, I thought, *her,* just like that. Are they familiar?

". . . in the field above the stone house."

"That's good. That's just fine," I said, looking at both of them. "I'll tell you what, Wade. You come and see me tomorrow evening, and I'll give you a little something from my heart to take along."

Wade still had that hard, angry expression, but he said, "All right. I'll see you tomorrow, Mr. Mackinnon," and then climbed into the light which came from the kitchen door. My wife went ahead of him, but she waited for a moment at the top of the stairs and said, "I heard a snake in there," before closing the door and going up to bed. I sat there for a while, listening to the dry, almost inaudible sound of it, and when I couldn't stand it anymore, I climbed the stairs to my study, and waited for the gray morning light to give me a little peace.

I needed time to prepare my present. I sat in my leather chair and took from my locked box in my bottom drawer a list of enterprises in which I had put money, some of which were little better than "schemes," but I have a few odd acquaintances whom I humor every now and then by throwing away some money. At least it gives me an excuse never to speak to them again. I flipped the sheets back and looked at the entries, all in my neat, cramped hand in black ink. After a while I made some coffee and continued moving the sheets back and forth. At nine o'clock, I decided about a few of those stocks and bonds and securities which I had so carefully considered, bought, and enjoyed.

When it was late enough I called my broker and banker and made arrangements for twenty-five thousand dollars to be obtained from the sale of certain securities and to be deposited in Chip's account, there being no restriction on the money aside from one: that he agree to take it. I had my banker send Chip, in my care, a telegram explaining the transaction and emphasizing that one condition.

About three o'clock a taxi arrived with the telegram. The taxi was a Dodge and it had on its roof a bathroom fixture with hand lettering rather than an ordinary sign, and the bumpers had split tires on them so it looked like a tugboat. PeeWee Harris was the driver and a fine politician (in local matters), who was receiving death threats every hour, since the local elections were being held this year. It meant he was going to win.

I propped the telegram on my desk and wrote on a piece of stationery a note which read, "Here's something from me, as well, since everyone up here has gone crazy and is carrying every edible away in the middle of the night. Pop." And when Wade appeared in my study, at six in the evening, wearing his green sweater and brown pants, a white shirt, and a new tweed cap, I gave the telegram and the note to him and said, "Wade, give these to the . . . woman when you see her."

I sat in my study and imagined Wade on the road and in the field, where there's a large oak and some sumac, too, next to a creek. I'm sure he didn't just hand the bag over, but put his long nose into the top of it and pointed out the ham, sardines, and whatever else he was able to put his hands on. I imagined that after a moment or two of this, he reached into his pocket and handed over the note and then waited. The girl must have taken it down to the house.

After a while I went to sit on the porch and my wife joined me.

I didn't have a drink or a cigar. The lamp wasn't on and my wife didn't read. There was only the pinkish light of evening. Wade found us sitting there.

"My, Wade," said my wife, "you look nice."

"Thank you," said Wade. "I bought a new hat."

He held it up for my wife to see, but he wasn't looking at her. In his other hand he had an envelope which I had given Chip to use. I opened it and found a piece of my paper, which was folded neatly into thirds and fit the envelope perfectly. I pulled the sheet flat, and read in Chip's small, cramped scrawl, one word: "No."

"Son of a bitch," I said, and then went into my study and sat for a moment, before taking up another piece of paper and a pen and writing, "What about the girl? She can have it. She can take every cent. Don't speak for her. Pop." I sealed the envelope and took it back to Wade.

"Here," I said.

"It's late," said Wade.

"It doesn't matter," I said. "Take it down there and wait for an answer."

I was left in the silence of the porch again, trying to grasp what I had found out. The twenty-five thousand was of no consequence, since I wanted to see by it how far Chip was away from me, or how far he was from the world. If he had taken it, then I could have approached him in some way that resembled the rational, but for my efforts I had that perfectly folded and almost inhuman (which is to say wordless) note of his which had about it the same tone of separation and protection that had kept me awake after we had discussed the deed. Of course I had found that Chip lived outside of practical considerations, and where the hell did that leave me? Chip did not see me as anything but a dream, some remote phantom. I had tried by that money to seduce him again into the world where a car will run you down if you step off a curb, where people are bound together by law and negotiation, humdrum need, and property, where no passion will exceed an exterior. Such a world seems regular and dull, but if denied, it lives for vengeance.

I was still curious about the girl. She did not look as though she had ever had much money, and the offer of a good deal of it at one time should have been a shock to her, that is, if she were able to put one foot down in the world of compromise long enough to understand what the hell was going on.

Wade emerged from the darkness, hat in hand, holding another long, heavy envelope. The night was warm, and it felt to the skin like someone else's dirty blanket. I put my fingers out for the note and said, "Good night, Wade."

I tapped the envelope against my teeth, being reassured by the sound of it.

"I'll wait," said Wade. "Maybe there'll be an answer . . ."

It was almost dark now, but there was a little light from the house. Wade stepped down, so that my head and his were at the same height, even though I was sitting. That new silver screen was between us. My wife sat opposite me. I opened the envelope and found another piece of paper, as neatly folded as before, on which there were five words, written in a hand that was new to me. "No," it read. "Thanks for the ham."

"You're wasting your time, Wade," I said. "There isn't going to be any other answer. Not now."

Wade's face withdrew from the wire, and he went toward the garage, looking over his shoulder, stooped as always, but not having to strain his ears to hear me say, "Goddamn. Goddamn. Goddamn."

"Please . . ." said my wife, but I wasn't listening since I had stopped standing on that porch with the crumpled piece of stationery in my hand and was already in my study, where I walked directly to the gun case, now not afraid in any way of exercising my rights. After throwing that piece of paper that thanked me for the ham into a corner (and hearing a light mothlike tap as it landed), I took down a Mannlicher and reached for a handful of cartridges.

"Now wait," said my wife, "perhaps I can read to you. Just wait."

She stood on the porch. I went straight through the orchard and into the woods, knowing my way almost by instinct and not having any trouble with the underbrush. The night was filled with a mist that came from the river, and all but a few stars were absorbed by it. The rifle was slung over my shoulder, and I swung it around, thinking that it was a good idea to have it loaded, since all summer a bear and two cubs had been working the ridge I was on. While I walked I pushed the tarnished, handled cartridges into the magazine, and closed the bolt, leaving a shell in the chamber, but with the safety on.

I did not trip or stumble, and as I moved in the dark, occasionally feeling the light brush of leaves or needles against my face, I knew I would not be able to speak to Chip or the girl, since (as far as they were concerned) my needs had been reduced to a substance that had the consistency of fog. It was certain the girl would be denied me.

I came to the top of the ridge. It is all stone, ragged, and looks from the side as though it were the back of some gigantic and prehistoric lizard, but I picked my way across it, finding that I was graceful and quite fluid as I moved out of the rocks and down to the old logging path. It is grown over, sweet and grassy (a place my wife compared to a formal garden), and from it I saw the yellow glow. They were still awake.

I went straight up the path, toward the house, and as I climbed I saw it rise from the slight ridge that separated us. I saw the sashes in the window, dark lines that divided the yellowish light into six parts. The house seemed large, since the window in the loft was lighted, too, and I was looking at it from the logging road below. The mist was cut by the light into yellowish beams that appeared to support the house. There was about it a strange nautical quality, and I thought of harbors I had seen or been near in hot and still weather. It was too warm for crickets, and they were, like everything else given the good sense of land, biding their time. I unslung the rifle and fingered the safety and stood there, staring into the lighted place before the house. I waited until everything hissed with the silence.

Go right up and knock, or don't bother knocking, go right in there and take a good look, I thought as I waited in the tall grass, and then went uphill, feeling my chest and lungs ache with the strain of having climbed along that overgrown and formal logging road. There is a little creek at the bottom of it, and when I was down there I heard it move and smelled the bitter cress that grows in it. I went toward the light which by its tone or color (in the mist) seemed soft to the touch and to the eyes, and then found myself standing before the wall of the house, the stones which I had lifted myself and put into place. So I stopped, and waited, running my finger over the mortar between the stones, and then moved over, still carrying that rifle, and looked into the window.

They were illuminated by two kerosene lamps. Chip held his head in his hands and was looking at the table before him where there was spread a large book, something which had by its binding and size the unmistakable look of the law. He was not wearing a shirt and I saw the long muscles along the side of his torso, the delineated ribs, the segments of his stomach, and I was surprised at his youth. The light from the kerosene lantern fell over him, cast shadows on his sides and on the table ahead of him, but the shadows were not distinct. I smelled the odor of the burning kerosene and I felt the night's heat. The girl was with him at the table, in that same light, and she was not dressed where I could see her, not above the waist. There was a glass of red wine on the table before her, and occasionally she reached for it with her fingers and carefully picked it up, bringing the rim to her lips, but she always kept her eyes on him. The bones in her shoulders were narrow and symmetrical, prominent. She put her hand under the table, but Chip did not look up. I smelled the kerosene and thought again of those harbors where there had been the same yellow glow of kerosene lamps: it dimmed features, sharpened faces. I was reminded, too, of the odor of opium, that cloying, piercing stench. They were sitting side by side in the heat and the light, and the girl stared at the corner of his eyes while she slid her hand in his direction, dipping her shoulder, and I found myself perspiring and leaning against the wall of the house, feeling a little ill, but still wanting to step inside, to stand there and speak to Chip, or to strike him, just as hard as I was able, and then I would be left alone for a moment, in that shame and terror, to face the girl. She lit a cigarette and leaned back on one arm, and I still stood there, damning those years on my back and almost feeling the sky turn on it. She put the cigarette to her lips, leaned her head back, shook her hair, stared at the ceiling, slowly closed her eyes. I stood with my hand against the stones and felt the perspiration on my face, an odd, internal chill, the desire to be sick. I saw the shape of the wineglass in her hand, Chip's fingers as he pressed his hand against his head. She was not smiling and neither was he when he looked up. She drew on the cigarette and the smoke rose in a whitish veil to the lantern. They noticed, with pleasure, the effect they had on one another, in that heat and in the cloying, yellowish air. I put my hand against the window, pressed against the glass: there was no need to worry about being seen. I waited until the book was closed, the wine finished, and then found myself moving away from the house, the rifle slung over my shoulder, and having the memory of her as she moved along the hard, polished bench they shared.

I only went fifty yards, and sat down on pine needles, bringing the rifle around so as to cross my knees. I was tired, and I smelled the needles, the mist from the river, the bark of the tree I leaned against. I was drowsy after a while, but I stayed and watched: they did not turn off the light, and I was left with it to stare at. I may have slept, I suppose, although if I did, I dreamed of the house before me, of it emerging from the gray mist of dawn. I was awake in earnest, though, when I saw the door open.

· I suppose it was five o'clock: it still gets light early in September.

The mist from the Delaware had fallen, or been compressed, and lay on the ground. It was only a couple of feet thick. The girl wore a pair of white shorts, a sweater, and some boots. I saw her shiver as they came outside. Chip wore a pair of pants, boots, a pullover shirt, and he carried a shovel. The girl's arms were crossed, and in one hand she held a piece of paper that looked old and creased. It shook a little when she shivered. In her other hand she held a silver compass, one I had given to Chip years before. They stood in the mist, and the girl didn't seem to mind the wetness on her legs. In that quiet, damp air I heard Chip say, as he pointed, "Up there." I followed. They went up the road, crossed the property line, turned into the woods on my land.

They went a couple hundred yards in that mist, which rose around them at each step, and then they stopped. Beneath a ledge which is cracked into perfectly fitting bricks there is a spring: it bubbles out of the ground, and the white sand on the bottom of it can be seen trembling in the flow. They stood at the edge of the water and Chip took the paper and the compass. The girl pointed at the bottom of the pool, then leaned, kneeled, and tasted the water. She splashed some on her face and shivered. Her voice was quiet as she said something to Chip. A drop or two ran down her cheeks, fell into the spring. "That feels good," she said. Chip had already looked at the piece of paper, and while holding the compass walked away from the spring, obviously counting his steps. The shovel made a slick noise in the sand and it rang when Chip hit a stone. The hole wasn't very deep when he stopped and kneeled and brought up a coffee can, which had been dipped in wax. The girl approached him, walking slowly from the spring, and then kneeled next to him. "Is that it?" said the girl. "Yes," said Chip and broke the seal.

They moved to another place, where they took a reading and counted steps, dug again, and pulled more money out of the ground. I couldn't see how much, but I was thinking, who's been burying money on my land?

The girl slapped at a mosquito. The mist was disappearing as the sun rose. Chip took the map, and they moved on. I heard the girl say, "How many years has it been?" but I wasn't able to hear the answer, and was left asking, How many, how long? They went to a number of places, without speaking, the girl sitting quietly, her chin on her knees while Chip dug. She carried the money. After a while they seemed bored: it was as though they were picking cherries, or apples. Chip said, "That's the end," and shouldered the shovel. The girl had been sitting on a stone wall, shivering a little, legs drawn up as she tried to wrap herself in her sweater. Chip beckoned, and she stepped down from the wall. She had been holding the paper, and now she left it on the stones. She took Chip's arm as they started walking back to the house. I heard her say, "I want a hot shower, some breakfast. Then we'll sleep."

I was afraid they'd come back, so I waited for a while, until the mist was completely gone. The sky was bleached in the east, but the land was still dark and gray, moist, and the paper itself damp when I picked it up. There were compass headings and landmarks on it, points which were labeled with dates in '37 and '38, when each can had been buried. At the bottom, in Chip's hand, there was a legend which read, "Map of holdings received from John Mackinnon."

"Oh," I said, sitting down in the girl's place on the wall and holding my head, "Oh." I folded the map and put it in my pocket, and sat there, fingering the safety catch of the rifle, and then looked at the map again. "Oh," I said, and started walking. I came to the top of the hill, passed the swamp, and the damp, painful air there. I stopped when I saw the lights of my house: it wasn't full day yet, and the house was lit in every window. That air of heat and coldness came over me and the desire for the girl, too. I thought of the way she sat on the wall. In the orchard all I smelled was dust and dryness.

I have lost control, I thought, even my dead son is defying me.

And, as I stood before that fully lighted, empty house, I felt his loss again, or the despair of it. So I went inside and made a mint julep and sat on the porch and drank it, not wanting to turn off any of those lights which had been ablaze all night. Yes, I thought, now I'm ready for the hunt.

Mrs. Mackinnon's Book of Animals, Reptiles, Plants, Trees, Birds, Bugs, and Flowers.

I have seen the bears in our woods, but it is difficult to do so, and it requires both patience and luck. We have black bears, not the largest, but a species which nevertheless has in common with other bears many characteristics, including even those of the grizzly. The average weight for an adult, three-year-old black bear is three hundred pounds, although one was shot a few years ago not far from this land, and that bear was over five hundred pounds. They have five curved claws on each foot, poor eyesight, good hearing, and a fine sense of smell. Their fur is black and quite warm. Black bears do not hibernate so much as lapse into a heavy sleep when the weather becomes cold, a sleep from which they can be easily aroused. I have seen a bear's den, or discovered its whereabouts in January, when the snow was on the ground, by the white spouts of breath that came from a hole beneath a windfall oak. Mostly, though, in spring, summer, and fall, the bears are difficult to locate: they are solitary (unless a she bear with cubs), nocturnal, and they cover vast amounts of territory. They also seem to be aloof, but I think this is an illusion. The best time, I've found, to see a bear is in the early summer when the blueberries are ripe. If you know where there's a good patch, you can usually see a bear there in the forenoon, slowly moving along, eating the berries with a good appetite. I have seen a female at this time with two cubs, ushering them along: the bushes of the berries were about two feet high, so mostly I saw the female and she looked like a seal in a green ocean with two younger ones breaching every now and then in brown arcs. The bears mate in June and the cubs are born in January or February, small creatures who are looked after in the den until the mother feels they are grown enough to forage with her, and, of course, they are playful and wonderful to see, each knocking the other down, one chasing another until the mother is angry enough to separate them. The males, as is well known, fight with one another for territory, and they mark their trails, or the trees along them, by scratching the bark. They like birch for this, or any other wood which has thin bark and which carries scars for a long time. The marks on a bear's trail are easy to see, each having four or five scratches made by the bear's claw: these serve to warn other bears of a male's presence. I have seen a bear's hieroglyphic, year after year, and have been able to identify him by it.

It is the bear's solitariness, his inability to be social, the prison-like quality of his life that interests me. A bear has no muscles in his face, nothing in cheeks or forehead to show anger, fear, or the desire to be friendly. He is confined behind that brownish skin and fur, in that lipped and thick expression he carries. The males are only with the females for a few weeks in June, and the females are usually with their cubs, but only spend a year with each set. I have seen the males alone, walking their trails in the woods, trying to catch the scent of other creatures, if only to avoid them. Bears are good swimmers, too, and I have seen a solitary bear floating in a broad and deep glide in the river, on his back there with his mouth open and feeding on a large hatch of mayflies. The trout jumped and rose around him, but the bear seemed oblivious to them, being intent on the light, fragile texture of the wings of the mayfly.

There was no way, though, for the bear to show his pleasure at the cool water of the Delaware and the taste of the mayflies. So the bear's desire can only be seen in action, when one male fights another, when a male and female strike one another (quite playfully) before they mate, or when (in late spring) a bear becomes hungry for pork and steals a young pig from my husband's barn. The rest of the time a bear is isolated and all the more alone for his want of expression, being left with that almost grinning, heavily lipped, and dull-eyed face, which is the appearance of the stamp placed upon bears. It is an expression I know well. Years ago a friend of my husband's came to hunt, and while in the woods waiting for a deer, a bear rose up before him, and he killed it, and was proud of it. It was not a big bear, not over two hundred pounds, but it still had the same expression on its face while stretched out on the porch that it had in life, when I had seen it eating mushrooms (large, orange chicken-of-the-woods or small brown mushrooms), or blueberries in early summer, or when it faced a rival in June. The men posed with the bear, cozying up to it, or shaking its paw, and had their picture taken. One man lay down next to it and lifted its head so that their cheeks were together: this made the bear seem more lonely, more incapable, too, of showing how much it longed for the woods at dusk when the weather is just a little cool, when the bear is full of summer fruit and is able to move and to explore. I see that incapable and to me solitary expression in many things, and can feel the frustration behind it.

Lately I have begun to dream of bears: I see them in the winter, usually one at a time, a large bear of more than five hundred pounds. It has long legs and arms and seems to be in pain, or worried, straining as it walks through the snow-covered land, its breath as white as ghosts in the air. The bear comes toward the house where I am sleeping and tries, I think, to come in, to climb the side of the house, and I can hear the scratching of its claws on the clapboards. I can see that same expression, that inability to tell or to explain: it is as though the bear is mute, but still making that cold sound in winter with its claws against the side of the house. Then I wake, in that gray-blue light of dawn, and see the woods, which are quickened by the bears' presence but seeming just as restrained, as aloof, and remote (and concealing as much, too) as that faintly grinning, heavy-lipped expression of the bear that was killed here years ago. At these times, I dress and have a cup of tea, waiting until it is lighter, and then I go out alone on a bear's trail, looking for tracks, watching for those trees where the bear has left its scratched, scarred message. Then I run my fingers over the jeweled scratches and feel the bears' presence and the woods as they hold the restrained ache of them. Once I woke after having this dream and I went to my husband and said, I am cold, and he said, Get back into bed. I did, and then he came into the room and spread over my bed the bearskin rug from his study. There, he said, that should keep you warm.

Mr. Moore

The Hunt. 1950.

The difference between us is this: when they hunt, they are dressed in red. I wear green. If you use land but do not go through the formalities of paying taxes and working with that book in the county seat, that deed book, then you are not interested in being seen. It brings you closer to game as well, in a way that those men who wear brown trousers and red coats will never understand, since if they understood, you'd have no chance of poaching deer and turkey and bear from their land without being discovered. They hunt in groups. I hunt alone.

The soil froze. Later I saw those cars coming up the road to Mackinnon's house, those LaSalles, Packards, Chryslers, and even some I didn't recognize which nevertheless had the stamp of something foreign, not wop, but probably Irish-like. I watched the men, since I was interested in where they'd be on the first day: if fat and breathing hard, not far from Mackinnon's house. If young and in training, far away.

The men came up in those cars and stood out in their grayish coats and ties and pressed trousers, and the cars were parked in front of that garage. I saw that tall thin one pointing his finger and directing the traffic so that by the end of the day all the cars were arranged like gravestones.

Pop did not know some of the guests and he stood up and shook hands and moved in a way I had not seen in him before. Pop was that way especially before a tall man with hair like silver and a straight posture which made me put him immediately in that category of people I would leave alone or kill. Pop went on with his greeting, and then they disappeared inside, and I went into the woods.

There was good sign, rubs on trees, scrapes in the ground. In the mud where the deer had cut marks with the tines of antlers I saw water moving. I had been that close: the water was a trickle, slow in its movement and carrying a small amount of whiteness, a little scum from the land. There were acorns, too, and shelled hickory nuts. The deer were in rut and were not so alert: their necks were swollen. It was cold, and this kept the deer moving. At night I sat out and listened to the sound of them, those black, split hooves striking the frozen earth. There was a moon, as well, and the deer moved under it in the cold.

I sat on the far side of Trout Cabin and thought for a while: the silver one was the father of that girl to whom the Mackinnon boy had been pledged. I had kept an eye on him, in the stone building with that girl he called Coop. She was not one of ours and she was not one of theirs, either. I had watched them together and if she had been one of ours I would have had trouble, and I minded the difficulty of Pop and the man with the silver hair. Their trouble would be greater, since they didn't settle a grievance in steel and flesh. They preferred paper. We are different. We do not, for instance, take benefit of clergy.

I sat. The hunt would be a good one. I was not satisfied, though, about Pop and that man with the silver hair. Pop had looked like a fox and the man with the silver hair seemed stupid or unknowing or certainly blank. And I had the desire for whiskey with which Pop was generous with me once a year, on the eve of the hunt. I went straight through the woods and then crossed back, so as to appear that I was walking along the road.

The men were in that room, all right. I saw from the road that it was lit, and I could almost hear the silver in their hands, or the clink of those glasses as they were raised to drink a man's health, and I smelled the roast potatoes and the venison in the air: I was surprised the deer were able to tolerate it. I came up to the house and crossed in front of the dining room window, which I passed without a glance. I do not look into a man's house unless it is through the front door (or, on occasion and when I am unable to resist, through a back door and with a little help from a female member of the house but on these occasions I do not ask about the man's habits, the preparation of his food, or his concern for charms). But I heard them, and I knew each man touched a brandy glass and held a cigar which Pop claims was made by a blind man and I believe this to be true considering the things I have seen the blind make.

There was a scent of fear in the air that made me stop. It was a harsh smell, or perhaps a sound, or a cadence that is not right, something similar to the sound of a buck who has been shot and is wobbling, you know, in breath, *huh-huh-huh-huh,* not otherwise, which is *huh-huh huh-huh.* It is foreboding. I heard it, and stopped short and stood in front of Mackinnon's house, and saw, as I stood there, that the door was open, or partway open. I stood before the house without moving, but without trying to hide myself. I saw then that Pop and the man with the silver hair had come out to the porch. Pop had a bottle of whiskey in his hand and an empty glass in the other. They stood in the cold, and I saw their words turning white and drifting away, and beyond there was the uneven, up-and-down sound of that fear inside, and I was glad when Pop closed the door so I could hear the two old men. The man with the white hair stood straight up, without regard for the difference between his height and Pop's, which was large. The man was drunk. All of them were. Intoxicated would be a better word, since they were not unruly, or stumbling or having the least trouble with their talking.

I was not hiding. I was still, and standing for everyone to see in the front yard, watching, as I stood there, those floating, harsh puffs of words that came from Pop and that man who at least came from some place definite: you were able to hear that he had a voice of his own and a way of speaking that made him part of a number of people who were a long way from us.

"You mean to tell me, Mackinnon," said that man, speaking into the air above Pop's head, "that your son is still . . . ?"

I watched those words in the cold, how they drifted away. I had been in the woods for hours and I was cold: when I walked I felt the frozen earth all the way into the bones of my legs, in my knees, in my hip, the pounding of it, the hardness of it.

". . . Yes, yes, yes . . ." said Pop, still looking up and holding the glass, and appearing earnest, or something more: I had not seen Pop ever ask for anything. But he was asking now.

The man with the silver hair did not flinch, did not seem surprised, but he was silent for a time and Pop was, too, although at least Pop had the bottle in his hand, and was able to open it and make the sound of a glass clinking against the bottle. I felt that stony and cold earth and the hours I had spent watching as the stars revolved above me, over those scratchy shapes of oaks, and the time I had spent listening to the water freeze as it splashed out of the bed of Trout Cabin and onto the rocks along it. I wanted whiskey. I stood in front of the house and saw now in the artificial light their breath drifting away. Pop had not poured the drink, and the man with the silver hair began again.

". . . and how, do you think, could we stay," he said, "my sons and their friends, how could we stay to hunt knowing that down there . . . ?"

He gestured into the woods, and I knew he meant the stone house and that girl. I was thinking that it was at this season that Pop was generous, and that I had always been able, up until this moment, to trust him on the matter of whiskey. But perhaps he did not understand . . . since he had just been devouring one of the carcasses from last year and had plenty of company. I still waited, although I was able to be seen plainly. The two of them were not interested in their surroundings, though.

"Yes, yes, yes," said Pop, "of course. But can you leave, knowing about it, about them . . . ?"

The old man turned, but didn't see me, and then looked back to Pop, trying to make out his meaning. I felt the hurt in my fingers from the cold, from the hours spent in listening to the ice form and the deer move in the beginning of their suspicion.

". . . after all, after all," said Pop, "my boy could have written to Carolyn."

"Yes," said the man. His suit was a pleasure to see, and it showed up well in the light from the porch: it was squirrel gray and he wore a blue tie, and I must admit that he held himself in a pleasing manner, but I was suspicious of him, since he did not understand Pop, or what Pop was offering. I waited, already imagining the warmth of whiskey, which I saw as sunlight spreading into the gray bark and stony landscape. I did not shake, however, like that man in the gray suit.

". . . but he didn't write, didn't write," said Pop, still holding the bottle, "can you tell me that he sent a word . . . ?"

The man shook his head.

"I don't think we can stay," said the man, but not with so much conviction.

". . . now certainly there's been a wrong," said Pop, "you'll have to admit that . . ."

"Of course," said the man in the suit, "that's obvious to any . . ."

The silver-haired man bent to Pop, just a touch, and the two of them stood quietly, and I saw Pop's hands open and close on that whiskey bottle, not with fear, not with the tone I heard coming from the room filled with young men, but with a desire and anxiousness that made me stand uneasily and put one finger to the scars on my neck. The silver-haired man still did not understand, and now I was scornful. I watched the whiskey.

"There is a way . . ." said Pop, still holding the bottle now and almost beginning to pour. I put out my hand, or felt myself begin and then stopped. On the far side of Trout Cabin I had sat on a rock pile, the leavings of a quarry, and there, beneath me, the copperheads coiled, one on top of another in the cold.

". . . the hunting will be good," said Pop.

"What way?" said the man with the silver hair, with what in a dog would pass for breeding. "You yourself said he didn't write . . . didn't inform my daughter . . . and now I find that he's here . . . perpetuating the . . . outrage . . . you explain, tell me . . . how can we stay . . . ?"

Pop poured the drink and I saw the blood color of it and could smell it, that sweet odor of whiskey.

"Chip will hunt with us," said Pop, rolling the whiskey around in the glass. "He will come out of the house and take his place. . . ."

"All the more reason . . ." said the man with the dog-nervousness, that quality you see in a good pointer near something that is not quite understood in tall grass. But he was on to it now, finally on to it. "For me to go . . . can you suggest that we stay . . . it was bad enough knowing he was on the property."

"With us," said Pop, looking into the tall man's eyes, and pulling him down, it seemed, if only because Pop wanted him to acknowledge the difference between them, or to deny that Pop was always destined to be reaching up for things. I thought he was successful in the cold. The man bent a little more. "I can promise you he will hunt with us. . . ."

"Perhaps . . ." said the man, now leaning forward a little more. "Perhaps I was moving a little too fast . . . I have been wronged."

"I know," said Pop, "and that can't be left down there . . ."

Pop made a gesture with the glass, but he did not spill it. The gesture was short, as though gesticulating with a knife he knew was sharp. He turned his head, too, in the direction of that stone house. I had watched in the woods: she walked carefully and I had enjoyed seeing her turn her head toward the movement of ruffed grouse.

"To fester!" said Pop. "To fester because it needs something! Lancing. Poison."

"I'll speak to my sons," said the man.

"There's no need," said Pop, "not now. You and I decide things here. No one else."

I stood in the light for them to see me, but they did not. The drink was even poured. I refused to hide: I am not ashamed. But at least they had come to terms.

"Can you guarantee he'll hunt?" said the man with the silver hair.

"He's my son," said Pop, "I know him. There's something in the tone of his note, or a note he sent me . . . he'll hunt. . . ."

"We'll stay," said the tall one, "there's no need to leave a wrong—"

"To fester!" said Pop, "Of course not. No. You can't walk away from it. Not for a minute. It festers. I have been thinking about it constantly these weeks, wondering why he did not write to Carolyn, why he had not done what I required."

Pop's nose was now an inch or two from the tall man and they did not have to strain to see the light in each other's eyes: Pop's voice was full and had a bark to it.

"Chip will drive the deer through the woods?" said the man.

"Yes," said Pop, "I guarantee it."

"And my sons and their friends and I will take stands?" said the man.

They were very close together now, Pop still holding the bourbon, the two of them lighted from behind.

"Yes," said Pop, "but not so often as to be obvious."

"Of course, of course," said the man in the gray suit.

"You understand," said Pop, out of the silence of the house (which was still filled with those frightened lillies inside), "that this is persuasion. It is not certain that anything has to happen . . . a mistake. . . ."

"Yes," said the man, "Chip may change his mind . . . don't you think?"

"Yes, yes," said Pop, "that is what I want . . . what I am trying to force . . . so that we can have some peace."

"I understand," said the northern man.

"Do you?" said Pop. "Then I'm glad. But understand that I want only a scare . . . a horror, but not much. I want him to have the vision, a look at what he is courting. . . ."

"Yes," said the northern man, lingering over Pop's eyes.

"Although I'm angry enough . . ." said Pop, "as I know you are . . . and there is danger in that. . . ."

Beyond them there was the light, and the scent from the house, and that presence of frightened men. I did not move.

"Of course," said the northern man. "I understand now."

"Good, good," said Pop, straining as he looked into the northern man's eyes, "but you listen to me . . . things could get out of hand and I don't want that . . . just a look at the horror . . . that's all . . . you understand he is my last and only son."

"Things will not get out of hand," said the northern man.

"Of course not," said Pop, "never . . . even though, even though . . . we are angry, angry."

The northern man nodded slowly. Pop blew up his face and smiled and offered the drink to the man with the silver hair. He took it quickly.

"It will be a good hunt," said Pop. "Although it's cold."

He filled the glass a second time and turned to see me standing there, in the light of the dining room. He did not start, being convinced that my ears are not sharp: but they are. He should spend more time alone, should will to hear the beasts as they rustle in anticipation of our coming.

"I was saying the hunt will be good," said Pop. "What's your opinion, Moore?"

"I have seen signs," I said.

"What do they mean?" said the man with the silver hair. The voice was nasal.

I felt one eye closing a little when I looked at him, but I stopped it there and smiled and said, "Rubbings. Scrapes. Acorns. The change in the runs. There are deer. Plenty of them."

"Is that right?" said the man with the silver hair.

"There's nothing wrong with the cold," I said. "It makes the deer move. They don't lie up in swamps. They'll move."

I still smiled.

"Whiskey, Moore," said Pop. "I seem to remember that in the fall, when the evenings cool off you like it."

"Yes," I said, "whiskey. It's been cold."

Pop took the glass and filled it and handed it down to me. I drank and felt some of that cold move, just a little. Pop filled the glass again. The silver-haired man looked thirsty, so I said to Pop, "Mackinnon, you need another glass. Your guest is thirsty. I think he doesn't need to drink after me."

"Of course not," said the man with that foreign voice. I do not like men from that far away, since I want to know a man's scars, how he got them, which way he turns when he sees the moon, or white fog, or a snake near the house. "Of course not. It's a hunt. Fill the glass, and I'll have a drink."

Pop looked at him and I saw Pop nod, and take the glass from my fingers, pour, and pass to the man in the dark tie and squirrel-colored suit. We kept the glass moving, around and around, and I felt the cold slide from my arms at last, as though I had been holding it up, pushing against it. My belly stopped its moaning, that crying for food which it does when I am sitting in the woods and listening.

"Will you hunt with us, Mr . . . ?" said the silver man.

"Moore," I said. "No, sir. You have a full house."

"That's true," he said. And he seemed relieved.

"A certain amount of privacy is soothing," I said. "Isn't that right, Mackinnon?"

Pop smiled and said, "We always got along, didn't we, Moore?"

"When it suited," I said, returning the glass. "Thank you for the whiskey. I count on you for it, these beginnings of the cold nights." I started walking then, but stopped and turned to him with the skin of my face having the feeling of hard white oak, the gray bark, and said, "That was good whiskey. And you know, mostly, that it suited us both, didn't it?"

I went up the road and across the bridge over the ponds, noticing that the ice had already formed there. I left behind the two men and the porch, the golden light from the house. As I walked I lingered over the memory of the glass going around, of Pop keeping it filled, of our eyes catching the light from the dining room, each pair meeting and lingering on another, Pop and the northern man with his silver hair having struck a bargain, to which I was a witness, the one who watched it being sealed with that strong liquor. Our breath had seemed like smoke, and when it drifted across the light in front of the garage there was a silken haze, a whitish color which made me drink deeply and smile at the two of them. I did not mind being witness, and I approved of nothing. It was cold and I wanted whiskey. I kept walking.

I did not stay on the road long, but went up the hill above the farm and sat there, on pine needles and fieldstone, and waited. It was possible, too, after Pop's generosity to be able to sit there in the cold for hours now, although that red liquor has such a roar in it at times I find it hard to distinguish slight noises, nighttime scuffling of fox, coon, skunk, and bear, owl talons on the bark. I like the luxury of so much time, but in very cold weather it is dangerous. I was mindful of frostbite. There was something wrong, and I was glad to be able to sit in the woods and think. It was not that I was a witness, nor was it knowing that something will be settled in one's own way. I was not offended by the man's silver hair and beautiful suit, although I knew he was capable of great wrongs: asking, for instance, of what it was that killed one's wife. I was offended because he was a stupid man and I had to worry over him. They should not have been afraid of the stone house and what was happening there. So I knew as I sat there, watching those stars and the sky shattered by the oak, that I would be vigilant. They were without a judge, and this offended me. They were arranging, each trying to keep at a minimum one's own involvement, trying to obscure but yet encourage the harsh ruling on that son: they had no one to take responsibility. I am not afraid of judgment and my sense of fairness is sharp.

I was glad of my decision, and I waited until the stars were so bright as to be almost noisy, and then started back through the woods, feeling a little sad that the mushrooms were gone, missing the taste of the large red ones that look like layers of shells or like coral, and which taste meaty and are resistant when chewed. I went slowly, and then stopped, hearing the roar of liquor. It stopped after a while and I heard again the movement of a bit of gravel. I sat down so that there was the road between me and Pop's farm.

I waited, hearing another pebble move, and I knew that there was something else that offended me as well: there was no one to speak for the woman, the girl. At least, I thought, she should have a knife, one with a sharp edge and a stiff point. I heard that rattle again of those pebbles on the road and then I heard the footsteps and saw him walking. I said to myself, or found myself saying, against my will, "Look."

It was his movement, the sureness of each step that had made me speak. He walked against the lights of the house. I watched him and was glad that I would not have to face him myself. It occurred to me that the men in the house might not have the sense to be afraid, or not know what to do about being afraid. But I laughed again as Chip walked to the farmhouse and knocked on the door.

Pop and the northern man appeared, and I saw the white puffs of speech, heard the words bouncing off the frozen surface of the pond. Of course, Chip took the drink they offered him, but he stood outside.

I said, again out loud, in defiance of myself, "There is a practical matter as well. He needs that rifle. The German one with the two triggers." The words still floated away from the porch, and Pop went inside and brought it out, the rifle that Chip had come for. Chip held it and spoke and then Pop gave him a box of cartridges. I sat and watched as the men went back into the house, as quickly as they could: I didn't need to be there to know they spoke of the morning's stands, of the time (before light), of the direction of the wind. All this was fine, I imagine, as far as it went. They were not alone enough to suit me. They sat together in that house, waiting for the warm breakfast they always ate before the hunt. I was surprised a man could feel anything in that condition: warm. There is no sense of the land this way and you cannot feel the motion of things in the plane beneath your lungs. I was thinking of how cozy and in what numbers they were as Chip passed, his rifle slung up and the cartridges for it rattling in that cold clear air. I was still thinking, How can a man, with his insides filled with pancakes and molasses, smell what's on the wind?

"Mackinnon?" I said.

I stepped into the road and we faced one another. He was watchful, but not arrogant. I would not have wanted to task him. There is a season for vengeance, spring being the best, after a hard winter.

"Hello, Moore," said Chip. "It should be cold enough for you tonight. With the frost and the ice."

"Yes, it is," I said. "Mackinnon, check the breech of that rifle, the bolt, the pin. Carry a round in the chamber. Pick the rounds carefully. Get rid of any that have been tampered with. I think that's all."

"My father's a gentleman," said Chip, in a flat voice and with a smile.

"I wouldn't know about that," I said. "Check the bolt and pin. Carefully pick the rounds."

"All right," said Chip.

I felt the hard steel in the blade of my knife: my brother labored in Pittsburgh, where they turned earth into metal and he picked this hard piece for me. It held an edge and never broke when I cut the pelvic bone of a deer. I had a stone taken from the land and I used it to keep the blade sharp. I did this in the morning, and I liked to watch the new light come into the house while I heard the scrape, scrape of the metal on that gray stone.

Chip waited, and I saw his skin by starlight, the paleness of it, but he did not appear weakened. I stood opposite him, and both of us heard in the distance the voices from the house, the air itself doing something to the noise, transporting it in the cold, preserving the words. Chip's hand had begun to move, if only because he was looking directly into my eyes. The cold didn't bother him, either. His hand rose and I put the knife into it and said, "For the girl. To protect herself."

He waited for a minute. It was comforting to stand there and to feel so understood.

"All right," he said and slipped it into his pocket, and then started walking down the road, not offering for me to go along, since that would have made more walking for me and he knew it. And he knew, too, that the knife was the best, since if the girl is outraged, it will be done at close range, the closest one known to men and women. I went through the woods, although I felt my knife as it moved along that stone house road in his pocket: the handle had been worn into the shape of my fingers and thumb, and my hand was asleep, it seemed, in missing it. I had another piece of that metal and I would make a new knife, but it took time, since the metal was so hard.

So I walked in the direction of my truck, which was parked by the Delaware, thinking, Yes, yes, I'll have to watch, and if I come across a deer, I will restrain myself, since I will be working near all the men. I sat in the truck, watched that river, ate the two onions and the venison jerky I had in a breadbag. The venison jerky was hard and it took a long time to chew, but then I tasted the wood with which it had been smoked, apple, and for a moment I thought I smelled the flowers of early spring, and that I tasted those apples a deer enjoys so much.

And now I am more than a witness, I thought, eating a little onion with a piece of venison. They might find the northern man or Pop or one of those boys face down with my knife sticking out of him, and I would be left only with truth for a defense: everyone knows that I would not leave my knife behind.

All right, I will take responsibility for the knife. I made my manners to that boy and he knew it: I did not speak of the girl's flesh, did not say that the knife should not be worn near it, should not be warmed by it, but that the knife should be worn outside, handy. She should be able to smell the danger.

And how much more than a witness? I ate the last bit of jerky and put my head against the metal of the truck, felt the cold there, and waited for the moon to tell me it was time to go. How much of a judge? I was curious, and not content, although the jerky had been good and Pop had been generous with whiskey. I sat with my head against the metal and waited, feeling the cold sharpen all the senses and my hands empty without my knife. I have never minded responsibility. I welcomed the curiosity that went with it, and then loaded my son's rifle, that half-blued and engraved 30/30, noticed the names of the lovers on it, the lovers my sons and their women had been, and watched the moon and the stars, thinking, How much? How much of a judge?

I wore green and made a concession to a pair of gloves, although I like to put a bare hand against the earth: I am reassured at how much I can feel. I went first to the stands that Pop and the northern man and his sons and friends had taken. I knew where each one was, both below and above the farm where the deer runs were overlooked by high ground. These were obvious and suited the shivering men. I knew they had eaten well, and they were trying to watch, but without success. I saw many deer, some with polished antlers, but I did not shoot. The shivering men were waiting until the drives began that afternoon: it was clear to me that no one would shoot, not so early, since then they would be forced to drive later, having already had the opportunity to take a deer. The men were spared having to do this, since none saw a thing. The men had those large breakfasts and they were unable to sit still. Some craved tobacco and were uncomfortable without it: I smelled it on their clothes as they sat and waited, and as I moved among them. I watched the manner in which they held their arms, how each set up on the stand, saw which were dangerous and unsteady, which dangerous and steady, and which were just miserable because of the cold: this was most. There was a son of the northern man, and he looked drunk and stupid and to my amazement, self-righteous in his stupidity. He had pale eyes and pale hair and a face which spoke of pocked whores and contempt for desire. But I kept moving, watching each of them, finding Pop quite still and admirable, the cold not bothering him even in those hands of his which are slowly changing, before his outraged eyes, into gray talons. The northern man was able to stand it, too, in addition to his son, who was probably able to withstand it because of lack of will, of emptiness, rather than otherwise. Just looking at the son gave me that feeling of a rock in my shoe, but, I thought, I will watch him as well, maybe more than the others.

Chip was still. There did not seem even to be scent near him, nothing on the air but the pure odor of ice. I watched for a long time, until the cold started to cut with its edge into the joints of my elbows and knees, but I did not see him move. He was wearing green. I waited even longer, and still did not see him give a sign or acknowledge the edge of the frost, and this made me so curious as to want to say to him, Do you have a silver coin between your teeth, is that why you don't tremble? Is there a root, a concoction, a charm?

I passed by that stone house, but I did not look in windows or in back doors. The girl came outside and bent over the pile of wood for the stove: her skin was buffed, marked by sleep, but her silver eyes moved over the landscape, and the breeze moved that ashy hair. She wore a smooth robe and had nothing on her feet. I saw her breath on the breeze, and I did not come across the scent of fear. I didn't see the knife, either, and I wanted to say to her, You must keep it with you. Always. Do not think you'll be able to take a step or two: there won't be time. Or may not be time, and what time there is will be moving with that high, sickening screech. I left her, with one arm curling the piece of oak against her breast and one hand reaching for some more. The smoke from the stove covered all scent, and I turned back to my survey of the stands.

The drives began at noon, and of course Chip said he would be happy to walk through the woods to the standers, pushing the deer before him. Pop and the northern man and the northern man's son (with that face of illness) took stands, and the others, probably ten or so, went with Chip. It looked like a good drive, especially since Chip had the wind at his back and had arranged to walk with it.

I was near the farm road where the men stood and I heard Pop say, before each man left to take his position, "At least no one's been shot. That's something." He looked at Chip. The northern man breathed into the air, just cold mist, not saying a word. Pop waited for a while, not wanting, it seemed, to be alone. No one said anything aside from that boy with the skin that looked newborn, who said, "What about Carolyn? Why will no one talk about it? What's he got down in the woods?"

"Quiet," said the northern man.

I went with Chip, not close enough for him to hear me or to see me, either, and this meant at some distance: I felt him demand it. I knew as well that he wasn't wearing green because it was a good thing to be invisible (or almost) to the men, but because he was disgusted by those bright colors that the men had prepared for themselves. I think he knew that a deer sees these colors as white, the same color as the underside of their tails, and as such a warning to them. It is hateful to be so separate from the deer as to be seen as deathly white. I followed Chip, and he moved through the undergrowth.

He stopped at the place where he was to begin and he stood there, waiting until Pop and the others were able to get to their stands. I saw Chip turn toward the wind, which was blowing from behind him, and sniff the air, to smell on it that cold stone, oak, and ice. Every now and then I saw birds, small ones, but I could not make them out, and saw nothing as proud as a hawk. As he stood he gave no sign in his face, and I wanted to ask, What charm? What vision? What knowledge separates you from these men who wear red and hunt together? It was bitter cold. I found myself wanting to turn away from it, but Chip did not. I followed him from the top of the ridge and down toward the lower part of his father's land, near the river. Chip stopped and started, giving the deer a chance to move and stop as well, driving them as it should be done: the deer would come to the standers at a walk or looking over their shoulders, giving the stander a good shot. As we walked, I watched the set of his face and felt that certainty of his and knew what charm: that woman in the stone house. I was ashamed I hadn't known it before. I continued to follow him: we were going downhill now, over fieldstone that pushed up everywhere and reminded me of a graveyard that had been vandalized a long time ago. The oak was whitish and gray, leafless, and we pushed between it, always moving downhill. There were creepers, the vines of wild grape, that hung from the oak, and the strands were large enough to take two hands to hold. The standers were at the bottom of the hill and they would be watching closely, would have to, because of Chip's movement, the stopping and starting, and because of the clothes. I kept watching for a sign, the scratch of a bear on a piece of birch or a dark, face-shaped welt on an oak, anything that would help explain and give guidance. The sky was cold and the same color as hickory bark, a special, old gray.

It is best to have a round chambered, I thought, and best to walk without the safety.

Chip stopped when he heard the action run a hull into the chamber, and I stopped, too, smiling with pleasure at the quality of the ears. I thought, he does not want to frighten them, but he will. I saw his eyes as they moved over the stone, those pieces of it that pierced the gentle, giving part of the earth's surface and showed what lay beneath. How much of a judge? I thought, How willing to meddle? We kept walking, moving toward the men, toward Pop. I watched the birds, tried to smell the odor of a feather, felt time beginning to moan in the oaks, becoming impatient. I watched him move, and I still had the safety off. There was a glorious odor on the air, the Arctic scent of Canada brought with the geese. We drove the deer downhill, Chip still stopping and starting, and the deer came out of the woods and stopped in front of Pop.

I kneeled and brought up the 30/30 with those names of my sons and the women they had loved, or at least lusted after successfully, engraved on the cheap barrel. I saw Pop's chest over the bead. The deer stood. Pop stared into the hillside, the oak of his land and those patches of pine trying to make out Chip, in those green clothes which had the shapes of leaves on them. The deer moved closer to Pop, a good buck among them. Pop, Pop, I thought, we have been with one another in spirit whenever it suited. I felt the trigger curl gently under my finger. I understood Chip as he continued to walk, as my eyes picked him out, understood that though he was not defiant by design he was in fact, because he was no longer one of them, one of those people in red coats and long black cars. Not one of mine, either. Alone with that girl and trembling (that was a sign, at last) with the rightness of it, or the strength of it, which by itself frightened Pop. In that cold and as I kneeled on the stone and held the bead on Pop's chest, I saw that Chip would acknowledge the authority of no one. I waited, hoping that Pop would know, in the moment at least, what to do with the fear that comes from seeing a man so taken with something that he will let you shoot him for it. Chip stopped. The deer came out of the woods, turned sideways, looked backward, over their shoulders. A nice buck was among them. Pop was on the other side, having an easy shot, but not taking it, still looking with those old eyes of his, searching over his land for his son.

Chip waited a little more and then started moving again, in the same halting manner, pushing the deer a little closer to Pop. I watched the old man as he stood with his rifle. I saw the bead on the middle of his chest, so it was hard to look at his face, too, but I knew it well. Chip drove the deer so close that Pop could have touched them, but Pop didn't shoot, and he still didn't see Chip. I saw Pop over that bead and beyond the engraved names of lovers as he finally made out the shape of his son.

It was cold. It began to snow, quickly, as though there had been seeds of it in the air, and they had bloomed. The wind came up and the snow cut the woods into lined sections, gray and white. I have always liked a tracking snow, one that shows a good blood trail. The snow blew downhill, against Pop's red jacket and brown pants, covering him with a white scale. The deer walked past him, and I wondered again, How much a judge? Of Pop's fear? The bead did not tremble, held steadily on the center of Pop's chest. Chip walked out of the oak, becoming less visible in the snow which came so hard now as to put my teeth on edge.

I moved closer, but I still did not put the hammer forward into the notch of the safety. Pop stared as he approached his son. I waited with the bead.

"Why are you standing before us like this?" said Pop, "Don't you know . . . can't you tell that there are men here who would take pleasure . . . in . . ."

Pop held his own, old Mannlicher by the forearm grip and made a quick, explosive motion, a jerk upward.

". . . using a rifle for more than these goddamned deer?"

Chip's face was still set on his father's, but he did not acknowledge the question since he was looking at Pop as though Pop were under glass, at a distance, making a display that was alien and nonsensical.

"I'll hunt alone," said Chip, "after this morning."

"Yes," said Pop, "at least you're finally seeing. Those men down the way are serious . . . and angry . . . as I am."

Chip's face was not blank, so much as remote, concerned about other matters.

"You can have the run of the place . . . can go anywhere . . . but at least you see, don't you . . . the danger . . . or horror . . . hunt the whole place, but stay away . . . now that you know."

"Thanks," said Chip in a voice that was flat, hard as the landscape. "I'll see how it goes. Maybe I'll push these deer down to the others."

I slipped the safety on, and strained in the cold to hear, although that is something I admire about the snow: the sounds are clear in it and have a timbre that is kind to the human voice.

"What?" said Pop. "What?"

Chip made a gesture farther down the line, toward the northern man and his son. The snow came hard again, and then broke fast, like fog blown by wind. It was light and one could see a good ways. Chip made the same gesture. I saw the deer, still with that good buck, and they weren't even thirty feet away, having stood still in the snow. It was cold, and the snow was dry: it tickled on the skin, and I felt it on my hard smile as I watched Pop understand a little more.

"I'm your father," he said, "perhaps I am a lenient man. . . ."

"The others are waiting," said Chip.

"You don't think they will shoot you?" said Pop.

Chip stared at him and then started walking, leaving Pop alone. I watched for a moment, knowing that Pop had at least had the sense to wait in his ignorance, but that the ignorance would fester. I was glad I had left the knife, even though my hand buzzed now. I remembered what Pop had looked like over the end of the barrel. I left him there, his face as gray now as bark (but not from will, not from the ability to sit in the cold), and I started moving along the ridge above Chip, now having no doubts about the degree of judgment necessary and the degree to which I would be willing to accept responsibility.

"Chip, Chip," said Pop, "You wait. You wait here. . . ."

We went downhill. Chip circled to my left, and picked up the deer, and started again, pushing them slowly, gently, almost as with a caress, and the deer began to watch him over their shoulders, buck included. They were disturbed, alert, and distant. Their gift was this: I felt the hard joy of being alone. In the animals I saw the knowledge of the gray stone and the taste of oak buds in winter. Pop disappeared behind us, his face (at last sight) showing a horror of the discovery which was so real as to be almost physical, like the beak of a hawk.

The next stander was the man with the silver hair and when Chip approached, the man shouldered his rifle (which was custom-made with a high cheek piece and had a bolt and barrel of steel so hard as to make an eddy). Chip stood before him, in the little bit of blowing snow. The man swung his rifle across the landscape and then settled on a spot near Chip, a stone, or gray, rotting piece of oak that was next to Chip's knee. The man had not looked at Chip's face, or the way he stood. I saw the barrel move just a little, from the rock or whatever target he had picked to the center of Chip's stomach, where the rib cage forms a steep arch. I had been watching and forgetful: I kneeled quickly and brought my barrel up, picked a head shot, slipped the safety off. We waited. The northern man did not see me, and my finger seemed numb, cold. I can't wait, I thought, not for the sound, not the opening and closing of the shot. Chip stood with his rifle slung up and looked at the northern man, full in the face, let the man see that remote lack of concern, the belief there that the northern man did not apply. I held the stock against my shoulder, still trying to decide. I felt the hot, sudden moisture on my forehead and lip. The northern man let the muzzle drop and then swallowed in anticipation of whiskey.

"I'm not afraid," said the northern man, "don't you dare suggest it . . . do you hear me!"

We kept on in the snow. I hoped Chip would hunt on the way home, that we could track a deer. It was perfect weather for it, but of course there was the last stander, the son with the complexion of stillbirth, degeneration. There was a scent from Chip (like that of near-setting concrete) and it made me smile and nod in my judgment. I breathed deeply, smelled the arrogance of the deer, the cruelty on the wind, and felt the turmoil in the air caused by a hawk or merlin. I had almost forgotten about that boy with the face of depravity, but Chip went right ahead, pushing the deer to him as well. Before I had a chance to look over the engraved names of lovers, the pale boy and the aura of whores vanished: the son felt his own loneliness, his helplessness before Chip, and was by this wilted into what he imagined was civilization. He turned that pale, pocked face aside, and Chip went back into the woods.

I had the safety on, and we went over the ridge, smelling the scent of the pines on the snow and seeing the sky gray again and the trees cutting into it. I celebrated in signs, the shape of deadwood, the shadow of quickly moving birds, the honk of a late goose: it made a tearing sound that lingered as we climbed. I stopped above that stone house and watched Chip descend. She opened the door and I saw those silver eyes look at him, her hand pull along his sleeve, tug at it gently.

I sat, and thought, Now a judge. But I will have to wait in the cold. Because of the fester. That word Pop used. I do not mind the cold. I hoped, too, that she will smell the danger on the wind and not do without the knife. They have been forced toward her.

The days were gray and short. The snow began, and those men stayed in Pop's house, saying, I imagine, that the weather was no good, that it was too cold, but they were afraid to face Chip, afraid to face what ripped at them, at their safe lives. I waited above the farm. They had whiskey and I went without. They are civilized men. It was because of this that the charms worked.

So I looked down upon them as their cars were loaded and as they left, still drunk, but damned glad to be going. I saw their ties, their shirts which had been made over in the laundry, their polished hands. I smelled the reek of fear, barbershop cologne, the exhaust of engines. I was glad to see them go.

I took my buck, gutted him, and hung him, but I did not stop my vigilance, since there was still Pop. The days grew shorter and the snow was dry now, piling up. I felt when I walked the power of it and the bluntness of its decision: there was a time to stay in one place. The frost increased. From the chimneys the smoke now was the color of mother-of-pearl: all moisture froze. But I still made my way to the top of the ridge above the farm and waited, having more trouble with each day that the sun rose later and set earlier. Pop was festering, bothering himself for not having touched the trigger of his German gun, probably tasking himself with the love a father has in spite of himself. I watched him come from the house, carrying a shotgun and looking as though he were out after grouse, but I knew this not to be so. I watched, moved quietly, always keeping a respectful distance. Some days he went but a short distance from the house, and stopped, blowing those white plumes into the air, and turned his brownish shiny eyes to the woods and stopped, but not with relief, not with satisfaction, or anything that allows a man to do what he should at this time, after the days have become as short as they get: to doze in front of a fire and plot springtime revenge. I watched. But I acknowledged the cold and was waiting to speak for it. Pop's continued attempts were unnatural: I knew he wanted to get down to the stone house and watch, to catch that girl out. I followed him, each day, to his vantage point, but he saw nothing. One day he turned his face toward me, and I saw the lines in it, the hard set of disappointment, the clear evidence of the strain it took to walk through the deep snow. He did not shoot at grouse, not even when he had good flushes. The frost increased.

I followed Pop out, and he waited, and I saw him squirming against the cold and heard his voice, rising a little when he felt he could stand it no longer. I understand the cold and had been made needy by it: I had to wait while Pop was taking his rest and good whiskey. I ate venison jerky in the hard frost. Pop sat watching the stone house, and I stepped out, holding my rifle, letting him see the names there.

"Mackinnon," I said, "I've been watching."

He looked at me with that face which now had the grayness that comes not from age or exertion but from disease. I did not want him to die in the snow: I would have trouble leaving him behind, especially with my tracks leading from him to my house.

"It's damn cold," said Pop. He said this through his teeth. "Isn't it, Moore?"

I nodded, watching that gray face.

"You need whiskey," I said.

"Yes, yes," said Pop, stepping close to me and taking my arm, pulling my sleeve, "but you understand, don't you? Of course you do, otherwise you wouldn't be out in this weather. . . . But you know, if there was an insult of some kind, if it was bad enough . . . no matter what they felt . . . no matter what . . . if the insult were bad enough . . . don't you see . . . they could be separated if the insult . . . were bad enough."

"You'll never know," I said, "when I'm here to watch."

"Well, you . . ." said Pop, opening one eye. "This is my land and you have no right. No right."

We stood facing each other: the woods are the last place I would encourage an argument. I approved of Pop, and he knew it: I approve of any anger that becomes a thing that eats and needs to be fed, that consumes, that makes the complexion look like the skin on dead feet. I approved of the girl, too, and of Chip's sureness. I would make the decision. I would judge, and not shrink from it. I knew as well that the cold had to be addressed.

"As I understand it, Mackinnon," I said, "this land now belongs to your son. I needn't trouble him about it?"

I smiled, showed my hard, white teeth. The scars on my neck tightened: they look like ice.

"You need whiskey," I said.

"Son of a bitch," said Pop.

He was troubled by the deed: the paper had never concerned me. I spoke of it because it concerned him. I would watch when I thought necessary, with or without benefit of paper.

"Go home," I said.

"Moore! Moore!" said Pop, taking my sleeve, and showing me his face that was made now with one eye squinted and the other open. "You understand though, don't you? Don't you . . . an insult . . . perhaps you, too, you might come along?"

"Go home," I said. "There are times to settle things. Take care of this in the spring."

Pop still had one side of his face screwed up and the color began to come into it.

"By then I should be ready, don't you think?" he said, "with some months of thinking about it? Some months of sitting in my house and drinking? Do you think that will help?"

"There is a chance," I said. "Good day, Mackinnon."

He walked uphill, toward the farm. I waited in the cold for the next day and the one after, but he did not come out. I stood on the ridge above the farm, knowing that he was there, at least there when the black car was, and that he was inside, troubling himself before the fire and waiting for spring. Yes, I thought, as I made my way to the place where I sleep and sit in winter, he should be ready by spring.

Mrs. Mackinnon's Book of Animals, Reptiles, Plants, Trees, Birds, Bugs, and Flowers.

Bats are eaters of insects, and in summer I have seen them around an outside light, their dark shapes looking like the shadows of the moths they are pursuing. The bats are not cold-blooded, and their wings are leathery to the touch: the texture is so fine as to put me in the mind of shoes for a pampered, beautiful, Oriental whore of two hundred years ago. The bats are outcasts, it seems, and this is why I am drawn to them. They are mammals, and they fly, although they have no feathers. Their skins are covered with a light fur, which varies in color. The bats we have on this land are brownish. Their faces are animate, although the necks are fixed, and the expressions and shape of the features of the bats remind me of foxes: it is as though, in the evening, the air is filled with hundreds of small flying dogs. They rest during the day, in a barn or large garage, in the trunk of a rotten oak, in hollows in rocks, and while one can't say they sleep, their state is sleeplike and lethargic, as they hang by their feet. The knees of their rear legs bend in the opposite direction to that of most mammals: in a man, if he had the same joint, when he squatted, his knees would fold up behind him. The bones of the bat's mammalian hand are long, as delicate as thin pieces of bamboo, and these tines form the spokes of the wing.

It is their appearance of freakishness which gives me a sense of their isolation, and it is as though in acknowledgment of being a creature that flies while all its kindred, all mammals, walk, that the bats appear at twilight, when the colors are turning gray, when the barns and trees are turning into silhouettes. In the evening they are quick checks in the sky: when they emerge from their lethargy they are thirsty, and invariably their first task after awakening, or after flying into the open air, will be the search of water. Sometimes they will come to one of my husband's trout ponds, and there they will dive, come close to the surface, and as they fly over it, open their mouths for a drink. Other times they go straight down to the Delaware, but soon they return, looking for insects, which they devour in enormous numbers. The bats have a good appetite. The isolation of the bats works to their advantage, since by the way they perch during the day and because they hunt at night, few predators harm them, although I have seen an owl take one over the orchard. Most young bats are killed by accidents, falls, or midair collisions. Disease takes its toll. Sometimes I think the bats are haughty, living without contact, or hardly in the same world as other mammals, but then, in the evening, when I see them streaming and flapping in that darkening air, I sense their odd loneliness, and their despair at their condition. Their sense of touch is extremely pronounced, and, of course, their hearing is a wonder: it is the bouncing of their high cries that allows them to navigate. In the difference in the pitch of a chirp, a bat can distinguish the texture of a beam, the shape of a door or of a man's hand. The sense of touch is so refined that I think sometimes they can feel the landscape below. Bats are gregarious, and large colonies can be found, as many as ten thousand together, although I don't think there are more than twenty in the barns. There is also a restrained quality about the bats, as though they are husbanding great strength when they spend time in a state of lethargy. As a matter of fact, when large numbers congregate, they produce guano: in the nineteenth century it was highly valued for its nitrogen and potassium which were used in the making of munitions.

The bats are carefully synchronized. All mating and birthing in the colony takes place at the same time. The bats mate in the fall, but the fertilization does not take place until the spring: the female holds the male element, the germ, until the weather is warm. The female hibernates, holding this bit, hanging upside down in the cold. The infants are born in the spring, and before birth, the females gather in their own roost, excluding the males and any female who is not pregnant. At the end of labor, the female stretches the leather between the bones of her wings, and catches the newborn as it falls from her. The infants are carried on the mother as she flies for the first few weeks, and then they are left at the roost while the mother goes for insects and for water. But soon, the young are emerging at night, against the gray-silk sky, navigating by those enquiring shrieks. The bats have the ability to adjust to the length of the day, so as the days become longer, they don't emerge until the hour of dusk: this is not done by vision (which is not very good), but by natural restraint, since until the hour for emerging arrives, the bats are hanging and lethargic. I can feel this desire to avoid heat and light, those hours when the other beasts would turn away from them. I have heard that bats will get into a woman's hair, or that they will bring bedbugs into a house, but I have never believed these things. I have become used to the bats now, and I do not recoil from them: I wait for those evenings in July and then strain to hear them, as they move from the barn, searching for water, their thirst being so much in need of quenching after a long day in the heat. Of course I cannot hear those shrieks, although I imagine what the years took to make those cries delicate enough to be able to distinguish a single strand of thread. I stand in the orchard so I can see those black and explosive shapes, the flapping of that delicate leather of the wing, and hear the gentle echo of the footsteps of that kept, Oriental whore. When I stand below them I am convinced that when I move my fingers or blink an eye, they can feel it, in the·skin, or in the ears: it comes from me as a caress, and I give it gladly, since I know that in order to find their way on this land they shriek and cry out to it.

Wade Cannon
The Farm. Winter. 1951.

PeeWee Harris's taxi came up the road. It crossed the bridge and drove up to the garage where I was standing at my window. It was February and the snow was deep. The cold seeped out of every crack in my room. I kept the stove going all the time but I always felt the weight of those frigid drafts on my back. I cooked on the stove, too, or warmed up the contents of cans on it, since I didn't like going to the house to take my meals anymore. It was odd about the taxi: I expected it to go to the house.

A woman stepped out of it and stood below me, before the garage. She was wearing a greenish skirt and a purple sweater under a coat which was old and dark from use. Her hair was dyed a bright red, and it was matted, damp: she seemed to be perspiring, even in the cold. She had a scarf over her head, but it had fallen back, and she didn't bother with it. The woman stood for a moment, looking at the house, the orchard, the frozen ponds, the scratchy trees. A breeze came up and she turned to the garage. It took me a moment to recognize my sister, Sherry.

I went downstairs to open the door, the small one next to the sliding panels for the cars. She tried to smile and tripped on a pebble. I put out my arm and she took it with a hard, earnest grip, and gave me a hug as well, clung for a moment, and in the cold, in that frost, I felt the fever. I took one of her hands and it was hot, too.

"Come inside," I said, trying to see if there were any faces at the window of the large house. Sherry passed me at the door, and I picked up her bag, but PeeWee said, "Wade, she has no money. I need the fare."

I had some upstairs in my bureau. I got it and gave it to him.

"Thanks for driving her out," I said.

"She has strange eyes," said PeeWee. "She must have been pretty."

I carried her bag upstairs, banging it against the stairs that were two up from the one I was on. Sherry stood at the top landing. Before my room there were heavy, rough-cut beams and the brown siding of the garage: it has always reminded me of a mine, the timbers there. Sherry didn't smile now and she was shivering.

"It's all right, isn't it? To be here?" she said.

"Yes," I said, but I listened for the sound of footsteps in the frozen snow. "It's good to see you."

"No, it isn't. But I had no place to go," she said.

"You could have written," I said.

She shook her head and sat down. The hair on her forehead was damp, as though this were an afternoon in August. I went into the bathroom and got a clean washcloth, but she didn't want it.

"I'm nothing to look at, but I was," she said. "There were men who cared."

"You need some rest," I said. "Why don't you stretch out on my bed? Or get under the covers."

"Under, under," she said, pulling them back and pushing her feet under the heavy army surplus blankets. She wouldn't take off her coat. I pushed her hair back from her forehead and felt the heat, but I wanted to see her face: it had been a long time. I took two more blankets from a trunk and spread them over her.

"What's wrong?" I said.

"I didn't have any place to go," she said.

I nodded and said, "Are you hungry? I think you should eat. I'll make something."

"No," she said, but then she lay back on the pillow. It didn't have a case and the covering of it looked like the cloth a barber puts around your shoulders. I opened a can of Dinty Moore's beef stew, and when the opener made its squeaking sound I stopped, thinking it was someone's shoes outside. When the stew was warm I got Sherry to sit up, but she wouldn't eat, not even just the juice. I gave her tea with brown sugar (which she liked as a child), and she took some of that. I helped her to the bathroom and then back into bed. I sat with her until morning, holding her hand and pushing the hair back: after a while I was able to see in her face the girl I had known in Wyoming.

"They put my baby in a bottle," she said in the middle of the night. "Didn't they? Wade?"

"Yes," I said.

"And people paid to see it?"

"Yes," I said.

"Do you think they got their money's worth?" she said. Her eyes were open and the fever seemed high. Her skin was so hot as to be dry.

"I don't know," I said. "Why don't you try to sleep?"

"I knew you'd stick up for me," she said. "I knew you'd get it back. I was never smart. I shouldn't have gone to the carnival. Then I wouldn't have seen it and you wouldn't have gone to prison. Would that have been better?"

I shook my head.

"Yes," she said, "otherwise it still would be there. In the carnival."

"Try to sleep," I said.

"I used to see your wife in the movies, Wade," she said, "but not since the war. Did she ever get to say something in one?"

"I don't think so," I said.

"Do you think about her? Do you miss her? Tell me you miss her," she said.

"You're very hot," I said. "I'll get some aspirin."

"Tell me," she said. "Do you?"

"Things are different now," I said.

She put her hand on mine, kept her eyes wide open.

"Do you miss her?" she said.

"Yes," I said, and that seemed to make her feel better. I shook out two aspirin and she took them.

In the morning her fever seemed better, and she took some soup I had from a can and a piece of toast I made by holding it up to the open door of the stove. The coals looked silky inside with the heat.

"I need a couple of days," said Sherry. "I'll go after that, Wade."

I pulled the blankets up.

In the afternoon, Mrs. Mackinnon wanted to go out for a ride, and I brought the Buick around. It was the old one that squeaked and smelled like a dog and cigars, since Pop hadn't done anything about the new one he'd been promising. I saw Mrs. Mackinnon's face in the rearview. She raised a hand to it, rubbed the skin along the sides of her nose, her cheeks and forehead, as though she could remove the taut gray mask she wore. We went along the Delaware, which was frozen now, the ice being ten feet thick in places. We drove through those turns above the river where there are springs that run even when it is twenty-five below zero: they make pillars as big around as a tire. The Buick was the only thing that moved in the landscape. The clouds were pale and high and still. There was no wind. Mrs. Mackinnon stared at the pillars of ice and the quiet river and said, "Wade, I'm tired now."

"Yes, ma'm," I said.

"Have you seen them?" she said. "Are they all right?"

"I saw them last week," I said. "They were all right then."

We drove along the frozen river and turned up the farm road.

It was hard now, and gray, having been covered with gravel which froze and was then plowed to make it smooth. We saw no deer, birds, or any tracks. I pulled up in front of the house and waited for Mrs. Mackinnon as she went inside, but in a moment she came back and said, "I need your help. Will you come in?"

I went up the steps and noticed that there was ice on the windows of the house: the pattern looked like the shape of the leaves of mint that grew along the front of the house in summer. I went inside and saw my clothes steam in the heat.

Mrs. Mackinnon pointed to the first landing of the staircase. Pop sat there, leaning against the wall as though he had fallen. Mrs. Mackinnon stood against those frosted windows and in the cottony light, her black clothes seeming heavy, her face set: she was too terrified to move. I took a step toward Pop and felt in the house something of the nights I had been avoiding, the reason I took my meals out of a can. During those hours after dark Pop spent his time walking the halls of the house, looking into rooms, into Chip's and what had been John's, into the cellar, the kitchen, continually walking, saying only that he was waiting for "spring." He wore his dark blue suits, which were always pressed and clean even during the nights when he had stopped eating and shaving, just drinking and spending his time in the emptiness of the house. During these hours, which were only broken by Pop's short, restless sleep, Mrs. Mackinnon read her books of animals and listened to the squeaking of the ice around the house.

"Mr. Mackinnon?" I said.

The siding on the wall was oak, which had been cut from this land: the grain seemed streamlike, the lines in it arced by a current. Pop leaned against the wall, his face turned toward the light, which gave his skin a yellowish cast. His cheeks were full, marked by lines, and he hadn't shaved, so there was that sandy quality to his lower face. I picked up one of his hands, held the short, thick fingers, slapped them and his palm. He opened his eyes, which were as bright as polished marble.

"I'm all right," he said. "You can keep your hands off me."

I dropped his hand.

"That's better," said Pop. He put a hand to his shiny head, but he kept those bright, strangely clear eyes on me. "You whoremonger. You panderer. You've been down there, haven't you? You've been visiting them, whenever the hell you wanted."

"Yes," I said, backing down the stairs.

"I knew it," said Pop, as he stood up. There was no unsteadiness in him, but his forehead and upper lip were bright with perspiration and he was breathing hard. "You have no loyalty."

"Yes, sir," I said.

"And you admit it to my face!" he said.

"Yes, sir," I said, feeling something fluid and weakish in my knees.

"And who's that out there in your room?" said Pop, his voice rising, and his neck trembling, too.

"My sister," I said. "She's sick."

Pop now stood on the top step, but the heels of his shoes stuck out from it so he was balancing on the balls of his feet. He looked down at me, over his shoulder. I saw the shadows on his face, the long, dark marks that looked like soot or ink. He tottered back and forth, but his bright stare didn't move away from me.

"Isn't she the one who had some monster somewhere?" he said.

Mrs. Mackinnon moved, made a rustling noise, and I heard a short, pained taking of breath. I stood at the bottom of the stairs, watching him rock back and forth.

"Yes," I said.

He stood there for a moment more, staring at me and then at his wife. We saw him sway, but he stopped that and said, "Not yet. Not yet. I'm not falling yet," and then began his walking along the upstairs hall, enjoying, it seemed, the sound those brown shoes made against the boards that were held down by pegs. Mrs. Mackinnon turned her face away from me and went into the dining room and sat down before the polished, empty table. I went outside and breathed the cold air and saw the ice on the glass, the pattern of mint leaves there.

In the garage I sat on the steps that led to my room, putting my chin on my knees and hearing the building creak in the cold. Then I went upstairs to see how Sherry was.

"You seem hot," I said.

"I don't know," said Sherry. "I just don't know."

"Will you have some tea? I've got a couple of shortbreads," I said.

"I don't think so," said Sherry, looking at me from the side, as though she had trouble seeing.

"I think you need a doctor," I said.

"No," said Sherry, "I need a little rest. That's all. The blankets aren't comfortable, I guess. I can't sleep."

"You need a doctor," I said.

She shook her head and stared at me from the side again. I put more wood in the stove, and pulled the covers up to her chin, and touched her cheek. "I'm going to get one," I said.

She shook her head and said, "No. I don't want anyone like that. They look down on me. I don't want a doctor. I promise you I'll walk right out of here if you get one."

She sat up. I touched her forehead.

"You're hot," I said.

"I know," she said.

I helped her to the bathroom, where I left her alone, and then she called me and I brought her back to bed. My room is small, and it was awkward. There was an odd, sweetish smell in the bathroom.

"I'd like to talk to a woman," said Sherry.

"There's Mrs. Mackinnon," I said. "She'd come."

"You work for her, don't you?" she said.

"Yes," I said, "but. . . ."

"No," said Sherry, shaking her head. "That will get you into trouble and she'll look down on me."

"All right," I said, picking up my coat. "I'll bring someone. A woman."

Sherry sat with her arms underneath the blankets. Her eyes were not wide open, but I still saw those irises which seemed partly purple and which made her skin seem white. The wall behind her was the color of old newsprint and had gotten that way by the years of my Camels: her eyes made me remember the new, fresh paint which had covered the siding when I first started using the room.

"Are you warm enough?" I said.

"No," said Sherry, "just bring someone I can talk to, you know, without having to be ashamed."

In the garage the air was so dry I felt it pulling at my skin, taking the water from me. All the moisture in the air had frozen, turned into bits that were indistinguishable from the floor's dusty soil. I didn't ask for the car. I opened the garage doors and then sat in the Buick and waited for the engine to warm up. The steering wheel was so cold it hurt my hands.

I went down the stone house road, and it was easy going, since there had only been a light, dry snow since Chip had last had someone come in with a plow. That road always has a sense of isolation in winter: it was so strong as to make the Buick seem uncanny, bizarre. I felt my skin crawl and had the sense of being watched, since the land seemed to be in wait, just at the edge of the road, having old scores to settle. It was afternoon, but the shadows pointed north: that's how far into the southern sky the sun was. After a while, I came to the stone house clearing and saw from the chimney, which is as big around as a hand-dug well, a bit of rising smoke.

The sound of my knocking was slight, but they had heard the Buick and hadn't been taken by surprise. I heard some movement, the cold sound of the moving bolt, and then Chip stood in the doorway.

"Hello, Wade," he said.

"I've come to ask for a favor," I said.

"Come in," said Chip. "It's cold."

I stepped inside and was dizzy with the warmth. The girl was in the bedroom behind the chimney. The door was open and I saw her rolling onto one bare leg a heavy sock. I turned my back and sat down on a bench in the front room.

"Thank you for the cigars—" said Chip, but he stopped and looked at my face, my hands which were folded together. I didn't want to look at him.

"I'm sorry, Chip," I said.

"What is it?" said Chip.

"It's not you I want to ask of . . ." I said.

Chip called the girl. She came into the room with her head bent to one side so that she could brush her hair. They'd just been trimming it, and I saw some bright leavings on the floor. When Jean saw me, she put down the brush and squared her shoulders, walked carefully to where I was sitting. I stood up, and she kept her eyes on me, although she smiled a little, and put one finger on my hands which didn't seem to stay still.

"I want you to come to my room," I said, "my sister's there . . . sick."

"If you want me to," she said. "If you think it's necessary."

"She needs a woman to talk to . . ." I said, and no more, didn't want to say there was around her the odor of warm and unstaunched blood. I had seen some signs.

Chip turned his head away for a moment, and then looked at the girl, and finally sat down on the bench. "I can't come with you," he said. "It will cause more trouble."

The girl took her boots from next to the door, sat down next to me on the bench, and began to put them on. She was wearing a heavy, whitish sweater, and I smelled the lanolin in it. On her neck, as she bent over the laces, I saw a few clipped filaments, the short strands from the haircut. She seemed oddly sleepy or remote in her movements, as she pulled at the boots, and every now and then she stopped, dropped a lace, and took a quick look at Chip. He stared back, and his expression seemed masklike, rubbery. He looked away and the girl finished the boots. I felt her irregular, heaving breath, but that was all.

"I'm sorry," I said.

"Don't worry," said Jean, putting a hand on me. She stared out the window, and then looked at Chip, and said, "Maybe we'll be lucky."

"Take this," said Chip, as he walked to the window and picked up a mean-looking knife. The girl put on her coat and took the knife and put it into her pocket. She stood straight now and smiled.

"Wade will look after me," she said.

"Yes," said Chip. "I was just thanking him for the cigars and the brandy. . . ."

"Look," I said, "my sister seems sick. She needs a doctor, maybe she'd listen to Jean . . . that's the only reason I came."

They stood opposite one another, before the door, both standing quite straight.

"I'll have dinner ready for you," said Chip. "There's a piece of venison."

The girl nodded, took his hand, squeezed it a little and smiled, and said, "Sugar."

"I'll keep the venison warm," said Chip, "there's a bottle of wine."

The girl nodded and walked out the door and got into the Buick. Her hand was in the pocket of her coat. I climbed into the Buick, too, and started it. I saw that smoke from the chimney turning to white silk. Chip stood in the doorway in his shirt sleeves, and then he stepped into the cold, stood at the side of the Buick, and put his fingers against the window. Jean rolled it down.

"Go back inside," she said.

Chip stared at her, shook his head.

"I'm going," said Jean, "there's a sick woman."

Chip stood for a moment and then said, "All right. It's cold. I'll have the dinner ready," and went back inside. I put the Buick into gear and we started up the road. There's a steep part, just after the house, and the wheels turned there for a moment.

"I always thought it would be something small," said Jean, "a pebble in the wrong place, a branch, a flat tire . . ." she looked into the woods as we went up the road. The Buick swayed on its old springs when a wheel hit a stone. "But Wade, I've got to live in a world where you can change a tire, or look after a friend's sick sister . . . do you understand . . . do you?"

The tires of the Buick spun, made a jungly noise, a shriek.

"Sherry seems sick," I said. "I wouldn't have come otherwise."

"I know," said Jean. We drove for a while more, still along the stone house road. Jean stared into the woods, rolled down the window, and it smelled as though she had just opened a freezer door. "Wade," she said, "if you only knew how much I hate that land."

Jean rolled up the window, put her finger against the glass, and around each fingertip white frost appeared. When we came to the farm Jean stiffened, held the coat to her neck, and stared only at what was directly in front of her. I stopped in front of the garage.

"Here," I said to Sherry. "This is a friend. Jean Cooper."

"Friend?" said Sherry. "You're so young. How can you be a friend? You're not twenty-five, are you?"

Jean had her hand in the pocket of the coat, on the knife there, but she let it go.

"No," said Jean, "but Wade and I are friends. What's wrong? May I touch your forehead?"

Sherry nodded and seemed to anticipate Jean's strong, slender hand, strained to it, but she watched Jean's coat and said, "That's beautiful. What a beautiful coat."

"You need a doctor," said Jean. "That's all there is to it."

"No," said Sherry, "they'd turn up their noses. I can't stand that anymore. I don't want it."

Jean sat on the side of the bed and picked up one of Sherry's hands and said, "I'll stay with you while he's here."

Sherry touched Jean's face, looked at her eyes and hair, the way she sat, and said, "All right. I just don't know."

Jean got up and stood by the stove, lit a cigarette, and threw the match inside. The door clanked as she shut it, made the room seem small, close.

"Are you bleeding?" said Jean.

"Yes," said Sherry, "all the time. It won't stop . . . and now there's a fever. I don't know."

"All right," said Jean.

She warmed herself by the stove and finished her cigarette, holding it up, touching the end of it with her thumb. I followed her as she went downstairs and into the dry air of the garage. She walked slowly, letting her feet linger on each of the thin, light boards of the stairs, but after we'd gone through the outside door, into the blue cast of late afternoon, Jean picked up her pace, and went quickly, as though she was in a slight hurry. I saw her legs, in their tight denim, swing between the panels of that expensive coat.

The house was on her left. It seemed crisp in winter, the clapboards of two stories parallel and clean, the windows trimmed in black. I saw its shape, an odd room here and there, Mrs. Mackinnon's study protruding from the roof and having windows on three sides, the bay window of the dining room. The entire place was covered by a large elm which was leafless, spinelike, and rooty against the sky. Jean walked directly toward the house, her hands in her pockets, not slipping on (and not noticing) the ice, her eyes set in an expression which betrayed nothing. We stepped onto the porch and saw Pop's face behind the mint-frosted glass: he had been looking through the curtains and he let them swing together. He opened the door and Jean walked up to him and said, "Hello, Pop."

He was wearing a tweed coat, a clean shirt, and a tie, but he was perspiring in the cold. He smoked a cigar. His eyes started, were wide open, as though a door had been slammed on his hand. He managed a smile though and said, "So you've come. Miss Cooper, or can I call you . . . Jean?"

"Jean," she said. "I want a favor."

"I'm sure you do," said Pop, staring at her, unable to look at anything else. "Shut the door, Wade."

I closed it, and stood behind them. There were footsteps upstairs.

"I'm going to have brandy . . . Jean," said Pop. "It takes the chill off. Will you have some with me?"

He didn't seem unsteady, and some color had come into his face. We heard him laboring to breathe.

"I never say no to a glass of brandy," said Jean, pulling her coat around her neck.

"Fine," said Pop. "Come here."

She followed him into his study where he poured the brandy. Jean rolled it around in the glass, looked at the color of it, and drank it.

"At least you are civilized in some ways," said Pop. "You've come into this house to talk . . . you'll forgive me . . . turkey, isn't that right? You wanted to see me?"

Jean put down the glass and said, "No. I want to use the telephone."

"Telephone!" said Pop. There was a slight trembling at the back of his neck.

"Or I want you to use it and call a doctor," said Jean.

"Is he sick?" said Pop, the flush coming back into the manilalike color of his cheeks. "How sick?"

"It's not Chip," said Jean.

"There are falls, cliffs in Trout Cabin, and ice at this time," said Pop. "I know he walks."

Jean waited until he furrowed his brow, raised his eyebrows.

"It's Wade's sister. Will you call?" she said.

"You haven't got my son out there in your room, do you, Wade?" he said, without looking at me.

"No," I said, feeling the cold work its way into the soles of my shoes.

"Goddamn," said Pop, drinking from his glass. He was still unshaven and he moved his head from side to side, just a little when he spoke: it was as though he were being given shocks of electricity that made him jerk, and he tried to deny them. He strained. "I thought he might have fallen in the woods . . . that he'd left you . . ." He steadied himself for a moment with one hand on the desk. "But the telephone!"

He had more brandy.

"And what consideration do I get for the call?" he said, looking at Jean, at the mist that rose from her hair and the raccoon coat.

"You're a gentleman," said Jean. "I had been led to believe that."

They waited opposite one another, Jean staring into his eyes, Pop jerking a little and trying to sip his brandy but not looking away. He smiled after a minute and picked up the phone, called the doctor. We heard the odd, muffled click as Pop put the instrument away.

"Why don't you sit down?" said Pop. He pointed to the leather-covered fender next to the fireplace, which was sooty, empty. "I'd like to talk."

Jean shook her head.

"Thank you for the brandy," she said, "but there's a sick woman outside."

"Is that right?" said Pop.

He was not smiling at all, but his face was full, his lips set in a straight line. He had one eye more open than the other and he fixed it on Jean. Her hands cradled the brandy glass and made it warm. I could have used a little myself. And for Sherry, too.

"And what do you know of sickness!" said Pop, leaning forward on his desk and still fixed on her. Jean had let the coat open and I saw the white sweater underneath. She touched the back of her neck where there were the bright specks, the fine bits of hair, and then put her hand down, at her side. "Or desire!" said Pop, still jerking in those small jumps, feeling those stabbing jolts.

"Thank you for the brandy," said Jean, putting down her glass. "And the phone call."

She started for the front door, walking with her coat open and seeing the pattern on the window which looked so much like white mint.

"You tell me!" said Pop. "You tell me what you know about it!"

Mrs. Mackinnon had come downstairs and was on the first landing. Her eyes were closed as she stood there, hearing her husband's voice as it rose and filled the house. I caught up to Jean and stood next to her at the door. Pop's voice held us, and we waited, not wanting to leave the house as he shouted into the cold. Mrs. Mackinnon leaned her head against the hard, comforting surface of the wall. Pop's voice stopped abruptly. Jean looked over her shoulder and into Pop's study. We were standing with the door open and we felt the wind, the iron-hard quality of it, as we saw him. He picked up the glass Jean had used, and in the coldness from the open door he felt the lingering warmth of her fingers. He held the glass to his cheek, his eyes half closed and looking at the desk before him, the glass top, the blotter and pen set, a manila folder filled with his papers. Jean's face was set against the white mint, the ice on the window, as she kept her eyes on Pop. She raised one brow, just a bit, and her mouth came into the shape of a word, which pursed her lips and made her seem isolated and betrayed, as though she tried to kiss someone who had already left her: the word was "sugar." Beyond the open door there was that wilderness of trees and snow, the frozen ponds, and the sky that was just thin smoke. Pop squeezed the glass, held it close and broke it in his hand. "Goddamn," said Pop, in a voice that was hoarse and came from deep in his chest. He watched as the blood ran from the cut in the middle of his palm and dripped onto the desk and those papers in that manila folder. Pop dropped the glass, the pieces of it, and they shattered on the glass top, where the blood ran in a slight, human cadence.

"Or loneliness!" said Pop, again filling the house with his voice.

"Come on, come on," said Jean, and we walked outside, feeling the weight and size of the house behind us. Pop stood before his books and next to the empty fireplace, one slight bit of blood running along the edge of his glass top and into the oak of the desk.

"Go on back to that woman and her sickness," said Pop. "You know she had a monster! Monster!"

The door swung shut on him and his voice was muted, but not stopped.

"Oh," I said, shaking my head and confusing the hard slap of wind with the word "monster." I followed Jean's hair. She was tall and her head wasn't that much below mine. There was still some light and it brought out the gray-blond color, which was almost the same as the woods at that time of the year. I felt better following her and was glad to get to the steps of the garage. The odor of dried soil was just inside the door.

"That was close," said Jean, "too close. But I can go back . . . down there, can stay longer."

I sat on the steps.

"Wade?" she said.

"It's passed. I'm all right," I said. "The doctor's coming. At least that's something. Let's go up."

We climbed the stairs and opened the door. Sherry was asleep, but the room had the damp atmosphere of fever. I looked at my clothes hung along the wall, the dark jacket and pants I used for work, a green sweater I wear in spring and fall. My room was small, but it had a lot of windows and that helped. I could see the house and into the closed space of the garage. Jean sat down and said, "I'll wait for the doctor."

The fever made Sherry's sleep light and feathery. She turned and made a noise when I put more wood in the stove and closed the door.

"Tea?" I said to Jean as I put the kettle on. "I've got shortbreads and jam."

"Thanks, Wade," she said. "I'd like that."

I made the tea and we had it, sitting opposite one another and not speaking. Jean's lips were pursed and she sipped the tea even though it was hot. Her eyes were on mine and she must have wanted to know about the monster, but didn't ask. It would have been hard to describe. After a while the doctor came, and I stepped aside and turned my back so that he could look. He had short fingers, a dark suit, a small mustache, and he didn't waste any time: he had come a long way and it would be dark soon. He said he'd drive Sherry to the hospital. I helped him carry her downstairs. Jean brought down her bag, too, and put that into the car.

"She shouldn't have come up here in this cold," said the doctor.

"Yes," I said. "You're right."

Jean and I looked into the backseat, where Sherry seemed to be comfortable under the blankets.

"Will she be all right?" I said.

"Depends. Probably," said the doctor, "but you've got to stop her from wandering around in this kind of weather. Is that clear?"

"Yes. I'll do that," I said. I nodded.

The doctor got into the car and rolled down the window.

"Say," he said, "How's Pop? I've heard he's having some . . . well, difficulties."

"I wouldn't know anything about that," I said.

"I'm curious," said the doctor, "I've heard rumors . . . talk. I've driven twenty miles on these roads in winter. What do you know?"

I shook my head, shrugged.

"Shit," said the doctor as he started the car. He looked suspiciously at Jean, pulled away from the garage, went over the bridge, and disappeared.

"I'll get warm," said Jean, "and then I'll go."

We went upstairs and Jean stood by the stove. I made the bed, folded the extra blankets, and put them in the trunk. There was a noise downstairs, but I didn't think anything of it. I sat on the smoothed blankets of the bed and felt glad that Jean was there even though the room was smoky and filled with that warm, sick-blood smell. Jean sat on my white kitchen chair and faced the stove. Her head was tilted back and she moved it from side to side: her short hair brushed the fur of the raccoon. Her legs were crossed at the knee and the one on top came close to hanging straight down. Something moved in the garage but I didn't think about it. In winter there are always scratching sounds from those creatures that come into an old barn like this, hoping to make the cold a little easier, but only finding that gray, Arctic dust, and those beams, which are harder than ever.

"I'll go now," said Jean.

I picked up the keys to the Buick and reached for my coat.

"No," said Jean. "Thanks. But I want to walk."

"It's cold," I said.

"I'll be all right," said Jean. "A walk would do me good. Being insulted has always affected me. Do you understand?"

She seemed taut, and when she looked at me she raised a brow.

"Yes," I said. "But take this." There was a ski mask hanging by a peg next to the door and I picked it up, pushed it into her hands. The mask was blue but one eye was knitted with orange yarn, the other with red, and the mouth was marked by a yellow circle.

Jean smiled and took it and started walking down the stairs. I stood behind the door and heard her boots as they touched each thin, dry plank: the sound echoed in the garage. There was that scurrying noise as something moved on the hard earth where that Buick was parked. The heat of the room made me tired and I sat down on the kitchen chair so that I could look through a window and into the garage.

There wasn't much light aside from the bit that came under the sliding doors: a crack ran from one end to the other and the light from it had a dusty, white-silver quality. The Buick sat near the steps and on the other side of it there was the truck, the small pickup which was used at hunting season and to bring in wood. The silver line brightened the windshield of the Buick. I waited for Jean to get to the bottom of the stairs, and when she did, I saw her stop and turn toward that noise of something in the garage.

Pop was there. It was hard to see because the light was bad and it gave the garage that hard, gray-stone quality. Things there seemed half formed, emerging: the darkness rose above my head, hid the beams and the underside of the roof. I smelled the dry odor of the frozen earth. Pop stood next to the Buick and he was smoking a cigar. Jean turned toward him and then stopped, not moving, aside from putting one hand into the pocket of her coat. She held the ski mask in the other.

I couldn't hear Pop very well, since he faced away from me and I was trying to hear him through glass. One of his hands was wrapped with a piece of cotton, a handkerchief probably, and it was held in place with thick tape. It wasn't a neat job. There was a dark spot on the cloth and it looked blue in that harsh light from under the door. He spoke, though, and I saw Jean listen. She did not back up or open the door. In that darkness which was cavelike, dense, Pop beckoned. He drew on the cigar and I saw the tip brighten momentarily and fade: it seemed double, since it was reflected in the car's windshield. Jean took a step or two closer, one hand still in her pocket, her eyes set on him, her carriage having a slight sway or swagger to it, and for a moment there was on her lips the suggestion of a smile. The cherrylike tip of the cigar moved as Pop gestured. Jean approached, still with her hand in her pocket. Pop turned a little on his heels, and I saw him clearly, his face turned toward her, but being set back and taking some light from my room. He spoke and raised his hand with the spotted bandage, as though it were the evidence, the proof of his intensity. Jean watched him, and there was an expression on her face I had never seen before: it seemed like she was straining, turning her head from side to side. Pop continued to speak, but the words weren't clear and they formed a hoarse sound which I felt in the glass of my window. The tip of the cigar moved, described the action of Pop's hand. It seemed that Pop's voice said ". . . wanted . . . for months now . . . but have been denied . . . always denied . . . privacy." Jean stood opposite him. She dropped the ski mask, which fell into a flat, one-sided head on the

floor, eyes, nose, and gaudy mouth in an open grimace there. "Now
... though ... to give. ..." said Pop. His face was round and his lips
quite full as he spoke and gestured, moving that cigar "... now..."

Jean stood before him with that odd expression on her face, part
curiosity, part restraint, but resisting, watching, listening as Pop
made a perfect arc with the cigar, saying, as he did so "... slut
... slut. ..." He tried to push that hot point into her face. Jean
moved a little. Pop raised the cigar and drew on it, stared at her,
and then shook his head, trying for a moment to deny that anything had happened. He put his fingers to his head, tried to steady
himself, but went on staring at her. "What you deserve," he
seemed to say as he approached her again and tried to burn her
skin, to mark that complexion, but she turned aside, and the cigar
fell onto the dusty, dry floor. Jean stepped on it, ground it out, and
then came closer to Pop, still having that odd expression on her
face. He had raised that hand which looked like a whitish club and
I saw his head move forward in two quick movements, as though
he were spitting. Jean flinched, but did not step away. I saw her
hand move in the pocket of the coat, saw her tremble. Pop spoke
again, quickly now and harshly, as he put that whitish club, that
hand wrapped in a handkerchief on the breast of Jean's coat. He
tried to open it. Jean stared at him, but did not push him away, and
Pop pulled her. She shook her head. They had moved so that the
Buick was between them and me, and the movement of Pop's feet
had stirred up clouds of that dried dust and bits of ice. But I was
able to see Jean stand without moving as that clawlike, arthritic
hand and the one wrapped in a handkerchief pressed against her
coat. "Bitch," said Pop as he turned again and jerked her toward
him. Their faces were opposite one another, and Jean stared into
Pop's wide-eyed expression of hatred and desire. "Please ... please
... " he said, looking at her and tugging her shoulder before he
reached out with that strange, bandaged hand and struck her. He
seemed to spit when she stood back. "Please ... please," said Pop.
"Oh, my God. ..."

The inside of the doors were dark, and they rose into the space above Jean, isolating her, but next to her feet there lay that ski mask, its eyes, nose, and mouth pulled into an expression which seemed to match Jean's as she saw Pop slide to his knees and push his head against her. The mask was one of horror and excitement. Jean shook her head and waited while Pop slid all the way down and sat on the frozen soil of the garage. As his bandaged hand slowly fell toward him he caressed the front panels of the raccoon coat.

"Don't you want . . . " said Pop as he moved back and sat on his haunches. "Don't you . . . ?" He took from his front side pocket some folded bills and threw them at her, or gave them a hard toss in her direction: they broke apart and floated in the silverish light, formed there shapes that were mothlike and unsteady. She stood in the dust, smelling the odor of frozen earth, her eyes fixed on the mask and its tempting, beckoning expression. For a few moments neither moved, and then Jean slowly turned toward him. His legs were splayed straight out and he leaned forward. I saw her hand move in the pocket of her coat and rise from it as she brought up that mean-looking knife: she held it in her hand, in front of Pop. He saw the polished metal and the cruel shape of the blade as Jean dropped it on the floor.

"For the phone call," she said. The bills had settled and they looked ashlike on the dirt. "I'll probably need something to get away," she said and picked up two crisp twenty dollar bills before she went out of the garage and left Pop on the floor, in that money and with the knife for company. She went into the cold without the mask. It must have been ten below.

Pop gathered the bills, put them in his pocket and then brushed the dust from his clothes as he leaned against the fender of the Buick. Jean had left the small door open, and there was more light. Pop grimaced when he saw his tracks in the dust. I stood and looked down at him from my window.

"Well, Wade," he said, or shouted, making his voice so loud as to be felt in the glass panes. "You know what? She's going. That's right, Wade."

He swayed and steadied himself with a hand on the hood: his bald head leaned back as he shouted into the darkness, the rafters and beams.

"And it only cost me a lousy forty bucks!" he said and then turned and sat on the bumper and held his head in his hands. I heard a cry or sob, a harsh muffled sound. It didn't last long.

"And you know what, Wade, you know what else?" he said, standing again and facing my dark shape at the window. "You can get the hell out, too!"

He picked up the knife and put it in his pocket before stepping around the Buick and going outside. He pulled the door quietly shut and I heard the slight click of the latch: it seemed to fill that old space of the barn.

I packed one small bag and went outside and looked at the house. I wanted to say something to Mrs. Mackinnon, but the house seemed distant and closed, forbidding, so I went back to my room and found a pencil and a piece of paper and wrote a note. "Dear Mrs. Mackinnon. I enjoyed driving you to your destinations. Best wishes, Wade."

I went into the cold again, wanting to look at the house and the barns, the ponds, the trees in front of the house, the porch where Pop sat, the drive, the pine grove. I walked in the cold until my hands hurt a little and then I turned into one of the barns: there were three of them built on the hill, each one a little higher than the last, like steps, each building connected. Only one barn had anything inside, sheep, and I liked to hear their hard-footed rumbling as they moved in the dark. I stood in the sheep barn and looked through a window at the house and then I sat on an overturned pail. The metal of it felt cold, but at least I was out of the wind. I lit a cigarette and put the match in my pocket. I didn't feel like moving at all: more than anything I felt sleepy and had difficulty thinking about how I was going to get to the station. The sheep rattled in the barn as they moved around. I stared at the floor before me and found it hard to see because of the tears, but I shook them away, squeezed my eyes shut, dropped my cigarette. I sat that way for a while, just squeezing my head, and after some time I noticed the odor of the hay on the floor as it started to smoke and burn. I squeezed my head and looked at the circle of flames, which was bigger than a large frying pan. Monster, I thought he said: monster. So what does he know of regret! *I* still look for the flickering image of the woman who had been my wife (not to mention searching those . . . magazines). There was in the wall the counting scratch of a cold animal that now had begun to smell smoke. I squeezed my shoulders as I sat on the cold bucket. The sheep were turning uneasily, their hooves making the floor comfortingly resonant and cheerful. I opened the pens and the doors to the pasture, and the sheep moved into the snow, smelling smoke. The sheep had not been shorn and they looked as though they were covered with layers of dirty snow. I started walking back to my room to get my bag. In the beginning, the smell was pleasant, like oatmeal bread baking in the oven. Let it burn, I thought, let it burn. I didn't look over my shoulder. I just stepped into the cold. It must have been ten below.

Chip Mackinnon

The Fire. 1951.

Wade took Jean up to the farm. I listened as the Buick went up the road. It made a slow, receding noise which reminded me of a passing airplane. Then I was left with the sound of the cold outside: at twenty below there is a taut stillness. I sat down and thought about dinner, but the dishes from lunch hadn't been done and on the table there were two dirty plates, some silver, a napkin piled opposite me, two wineglasses. I stared at the mark Jean's lips had made on hers. After a while I pushed the dishes to one side and took down a bottle of whiskey and poured myself a good one, but then I had to get up and put wood in the stove. The door clanged shut, made the house sound empty. I took another drink and then got up and washed all the dishes, and dried them. They went into their stack of two, one on top of another. I washed away the mark of her lips on the wineglass and dried it. Everything was clean. I brought in more wood, although there was plenty for a couple of days, and then I took the broom to clean up the slivers and bits of bark. I stripped the bed and put on clean sheets, and smoothed back the counterpane, feeling the texture of the blankets and hearing that sound of the coldness outside. Finally I took down her suitcase.

It was a cloth one with a hard inside, and the cardboard of it was sticking through the corner. The cloth was a plaid, something like a Sinclair hunting tartan. In the bedroom there was a bureau and the top two drawers were hers. There were some brassieres and nylons, and some underwear, too, some very fine and lacy, other pairs that were made of cotton. I put those in, and then her blouses, two skirts, two silk dresses, three pairs of shoes. She had her boots on. There were two sweaters, and I got those in, after I folded them very carefully. In the bathroom she had a box in which there were some cosmetics, lipstick, and rouge, and powder, and a little something for her eyes. She didn't wear these things, but I was glad she had them, since it implied some hope for a time . . . away from here. There was a diaphragm and some tubes and other things, and I put them away, in the same suitcase, which I then closed and put in the living room, near the door. I sat down at the table and had another drink, but that was insulting, so I put the cap on the bottle, and put it away, too, and rinsed out the glass.

But what about the dirty clothes? Damn.

I went into the bathroom and looked in the hamper. There was a blouse and a shirt she wore and some underwear. The underwear were a little soiled, so I took them into the kitchen and filled the sink with hot water and gave them a good washing and then put them outside, where they froze in about a minute, and I sat down to think. I brought them in and hung them by the stove, and since they were small and made of a light material they dried quickly. I put them in, too, next to her nightgown and that flannel bathrobe she said belonged to her father and which she wore to read, her knees drawn up and only her toes showing. I smoothed everything down and closed the suitcase again.

I took the money out of my wallet and put it in an envelope and sat for a while, staring at the ceiling, and the cathedral loft behind the chimney. There were a few handles of polo mallets there, and I just stared at them.

A few weeks before Jean said, "What are those?"

"Polo mallets."

"Do they come in sizes?" she said. "Does everyone have to use the same length?"

We were sitting at the long table we used for dinner and breakfast. Ten people could sit there easily. We were at one end and we were drinking wine out of water tumblers.

"No," I said. "Those are of medium length and weight. They're forty-eight inches long. Some people like them longer, fifty-two, others shorter. Why are we talking about this?"

She stared at me and drank the wine. After a while she started taking the whiskey and I read the law opposite her, trying to leave her to herself. I turned the pages and she drank from the same water tumbler, but she did not act at all drunk.

"I don't like them," she said, and she made a gesture with her eyes over her shoulder, toward the polo mallets.

"All right," I said.

I went upstairs and broke one over my knee and then another and brought the first two down and shoved them in the stove. I smelled the leather tongs burning. There were still two left.

"That doesn't help," said Jean. "I have never seen polo. I do not draw dividends. I do not own land!"

By then she was screaming, but she did not raise her arms, did not gesture. I sat opposite her. We waited. After a little she took my hand and she pulled me into the bedroom where she said, "Now, now I want . . . I want . . . " I remember seeing the blue light of sunrise, and her still-angry eyes, although we were both tired.

"My father sells Buicks," she said.

I shook my head, sitting up with her leaning against me, shaking it in that dawn light, as though movement could deny these things. I just shook my head.

I held the envelope in my hand, knocking the pointed end of it against the suitcase, and then I ripped the paper and put the money into my pocket, and then sat and listened to the cold outside, felt it press against the house. I remembered the men at the hunt and my walking up to those rifle barrels. If they saw your face today, I thought, What would they do? Shoot, I thought, shoot, of course. I worried about Jean for the first time.

I picked up a piece of that heavy stationery, brought out a pen and bottle of ink, and sat there, waiting with the ugly black stick in my hand, its nib seeming insectlike and capable of stinging, of injury. I put it down, and put the paper away, too, feeling the need to get outside. I put the suitcase by the door where she could find it. I wanted to spare her having to look at me.

I did not ask, because I knew the answer, did not have to say, Do you want to look, to see really where we can go, of what we are capable, of where we end when we turn all adversity, all discipline into desire? Do you want to see what happens when you deny the world's existence? Do you want to see the manner of its return? I went outside. The snow was light and very dusty because of the cold and it stuck to my pants like dry plaster, but I went straight ahead, up to the ridge, where I flushed a grouse and then another: they sailed away, showing the dark band in the tail, their motion being a zigzag as they went between the trees. I was scared, too. Because I thought I knew the answer, but was not certain, not absolutely. I could ask and see her stand before me, her face still, her posture straight, her eyes set on mine, that silvery hair lovely and catching the light as she said, Yes . . . Yes. There is no other choice . . . I will face anything.

I went straight out in the snow. Of course she would not say that, never, never, because it is what I would say . . . if I had the chance. So I went straight out toward the Delaware, along the ridge. I walked in the snow, not thinking, only wanting to give her the time. I went along the ridge toward the Delaware. The river was covered with ice, there being only a small, gray place in the center that still ran, that was fluid. The pines creaked in the wind. It is a grating, unpleasant sound. I listened to it and watched the river.

I had left the keys for the Buick on her bag.

My coat was a good one: wool on the outside and lined with down. There were felt liners in my boots, although it was my feet that bothered me, or stopped bothering me, first. My toes felt hard, so I started walking then, since there had been plenty of time.

She had been there and gone. The suitcase was gone, but there was a note, which I picked up and read and then started along the stone house road, uphill, breathing hard and going fast in that sharp air, thinking, It's too cold, too cold, she didn't take the keys to the Buick, the car.

Her steps in the snow were easy to follow. I didn't think she was that many minutes ahead, since she must have waited a little, a half hour, to get warm. Her footprints were definite, one following another in a long succession, since she had not stopped, rested, or looked back. I kept on the road, putting my steps next to hers. It looked, for a moment anyway, that we had gone together.

I had come all the way from the river and I had to stop. A breeze came up and over my breathing I heard the pines again, but there was something else on the wind, and I strained after it. The fire whistle at the volunteer firehouse started to blow. On the wind there was the scent of ash and smoke and it blew from the farm.

I went into the woods, through the deep snow, hoping to come out ahead of her. The snow pulled at my thighs, resisted me. I made a wake as I went and I smelled the smoke, the cloying odor of creosote, and heard the fire whistle, which went on and on until the woods themselves seemed to be filled with the despair of human beings.

I stopped again, near the road, and saw her. She must have been fifty feet away, carrying her suitcase. She had a scarf around her head and ears and mouth, and she was wearing her raccoon coat and a pair of boots I wore when I was fifteen. I stood and watched, bent at the waist, my nose almost touching the snow. I could not call out. On the road there was the sound of a truck when the fire siren fell, and I thought it would be one of the volunteers. Jean stopped walking as it approached.

I saw it clearly, too, a blue flatbed which was a little rusted, but still in good condition, since it was running in that hard frost. The rusted places had been patched with gray compound and not sanded or painted, either. The air was clear, since it could sustain almost nothing, and the truck left a white, curled, almost smooth-looking trail of exhaust. Jean put down her bag and waited and both of us heard the insistence of that fire siren.

It was Moore's truck and he was alone. His face was set, curious, and I saw that the smell of fire was not unpleasant to him. He pulled up opposite Jean.

"It's cold to be walking," said Moore.

"Yes," said Jean.

"I heard the fire whistle," said Moore. "What's burning up there?"

"I don't know," said Jean. "I've got to leave."

"Did you start it?" said Moore.

"No," said Jean. "No, but I've got to leave."

The exhaust caught up with them and blew past Jean.

"I came to help," said Moore, "when I noticed the scent and when I heard the siren. It is an unhappy sound."

"I've got to leave," said Jean. "It's a long ways."

"Let's look at the fire," said Moore.

"No," said Jean, "I've got forty dollars."

She put her hand in a pocket and held out two twenty dollar bills. I watched from the snow.

"That looks crisp," said Moore. "It must be Pop's money."

"It is," said Jean.

"Where's the knife?" said Moore. "That was good steel."

"Up there . . . " said Jean. "I didn't bring it away."

"Is that correct?" said Moore. "Is Pop alive?"

"Yes," said Jean, staring into those whitish eyes. The wind made her tear.

"Did Pop take it?" said Moore, watching Jean closely.

"No," said Jean, "I left it there."

"Left!" said Moore, his eyes widening. "As a present! I'm sorry I was not there to hear Pop scream. Was it loud?"

"No," said Jean, "not to the ear."

"Ha!" said Moore, "You are not one of theirs, that is certain. Mine would not leave the knife, no matter what it would do to Pop. He doesn't need a present to know we kill. Get in. Do you want the station?"

"Yes," said Jean, opening the door with the hand that held those two twenty dollar bills. She lifted her bag, and Moore let in the clutch. The truck climbed the hill away from the farm, Moore and Jean in the front seat, sitting far apart and appearing proper, rigid.

I went back along the stone house road, smelling the fire, and still hearing the siren. The cold had gotten into my hands and feet, and I was worried about them. There was another set of prints in the road, but I wasn't concerned, not then. I kept thinking of that truck and of the way Jean lifted her bag and put it in and slammed the door, her hair and face still wrapped in that long scarf, and her voice, as it said to Moore, "Thank you. I've got to leave."

I stopped near the end of the road, a hundred yards from the stone house, and turned my head to the side, unable to do anything more, confusing things, believing, for a moment, that the pain that made me turn my head was a perfect reflection of the cold. It was not, nor was the sickness what I thought it to be: that I was freezing to death. The smell of the fire was strong now, and I liked the odor of it, and I stood in the snow, breathing it, my eyes wide now, as I realized that what I felt was not the cold, or anything like it: it was her absence.

I came up to the house. Wade was standing in the doorway. He had on a coat and gloves and a hat, too. He held a small bag, not much more than something for overnight. He kept his nose pointed to the ground.

"Come in, Wade," I said. "There's no reason to stand in the cold."

"Yes, Chip," said Wade, moving the bag in his hands, "there is. I started the fire. It was a mistake, but I could have stopped it. I wanted you to know that I meant nothing against you. Nothing. We were friends, you know?"

"Yes," I said, "always."

"Even when you were growing up," said Wade.

I nodded and said, "Come in."

"No," said Wade, "there isn't time."

He gestured with his bag toward the darkness beyond the house, the road that went up to the gravel pit and from there to the closest town. Perhaps, I thought, he'll make the same train as Jean. Or he'd make it if he didn't walk. The smoke had a different odor now, being a little sweeter or more pungent, as though from paper rather than wood.

"They're after me," said Wade.

He turned and started walking, but I stopped him and said, "Wade, Wade. Wait. Here."

I took the keys to my Buick and put them into his hands, and then went into the glove box and took the papers for it and signed on the line to convey, using the same pen that Jean had used for her note.

"Go on," I said, "go on. At least they won't be able to say you stole this, too."

Wade held the keys for a moment and sniffed the air, and then got inside and started it. When he tried to back up the tires spun a little, sounding for a moment like a lion in a zoo. I went to the front and pushed, and rocked the Buick up and down, and it started moving backward. Wade turned around and looked at me through the windshield which was misting over, icing up, blinding him. He disappeared behind it, seemed to dissolve into cold mist.

"Spit on it," I said.

"What?" said Wade.

"So you can see," I said.

"All right," he said, and then cleared a place in the ice. We didn't wave or say good-bye. I smelled the odor of the fire and Wade did, too. We waited for a moment in it. I needed to sit down and put my head against something hard. Wade put the Buick into gear and began going uphill, in the odor of the fire, shaking his head in disbelief, not knowing whether to vomit or cry, but staring through that window, pushing the car up the hill, his face suggesting that he had looked into some dark place which all decent men would like to avoid. I stood outside until the Buick went up the first grade and around the bend and then was out of sight.

I sat down at the table and took her note out of my pocket. I spread it on the table before me, and then felt its surface on my forehead as I slowly bent toward it, just wanting to rest. I warmed up a little and didn't think I was freezing to death anymore, but the sickness was still there. I pushed my head against the table, since I had the odd sensation that the house was made of glass and that any movement would make it fall. The fire whistle continued, and I thought I heard a siren on the road by the gravel pit. After a while I sat up, and then went to the whiskey bottle and found a glass tumbler. I sat again and looked at the note which said, "Thanks for packing and for doing the wash . . . sugar."

When I looked up my father stood in the door of the house. He hadn't bothered to knock. His clothes were burned at the cuffs and were darkened. He smelled of smoke. One hand was bandaged and the adhesive tape and cloth of it were singed. There was the odor of burned hair and his pants were covered with the snow that looked like plaster dust. He didn't have a mask or a scarf and there were the sick yellow spots of frostbite on his cheek and nose.

"Hello, Pop," I said, looking up from the note and feeling the snow that had melted on my clothes. "I'm glad to see you. It's time we came to terms. Here's whiskey."

Mrs. Mackinnon's Book of Animals, Reptiles, Plants, Trees, Birds, Bugs, and Flowers.

The crows will not be frightened by their own dead. I have hung the carcasses around my garden, but the crows persist. I hate them because they do not have the possibility of being defeated. They are entirely black, and their feathers have a glossy shine to them which is like that of a phonograph record. I have seen them on the fence where their brothers hung, not caring at all, not being concerned about anything aside from where they will do their damage. They are capable of eating seeds, corn, insects, grasshoppers and grubs, weevils, ladybugs, and carrion. I have seen the crows picking at a dead deer, their shiny and faintly curved and pointed bills having that same gloss you see on the charred bits of wood left from a fire. The crows will also take a young chicken or turkey for food, and they will take the eggs of other birds, such as the nuthatches, grouse, bobwhite, phoebes. They will make their nest of almost anything they can find, twigs, string, cotton from the stuffing of a tractor seat, lint, leaves: I have seen them fluttering around Charlotte's clotheslines, the birds looking like their own shadows against the white and gently moving sheets. They make their nest in late winter or early spring, the nest being in a tree.

The eggs are green and spotted and they look like the back of a frog. The mother incubates and broods the eggs and chicks. The incubation time is short and the brooding time is short, too. The chicks grow very quickly, and this puts a demand on the parents to provide large quantities of food. All members of the same species will be ready to mate at the same time, and in the early spring, when the gardens and fields have been planted you will see the birds foraging for their young. They will not be stopped. Scarecrows seem to attract them, and tin cans, noisemakers, and reflectors are of no consequence. They are stopped from taking seeds in the spring by the leavings of fire: if the seeds are dipped in creosote, the birds will not touch them. They do not like the odor and I do not think they like the color, either, probably seeing in those treated seeds the image of themselves. There are now more birds than before the discovery of the New World. The crows come along with man, being almost always in his presence, since his landscape makes the crow comfortable. Their sense of distance is maddening. They may live near man, but rarely do they get close enough to allow him a shot. And for this I dislike them, too. They will be always close enough to do damage, but are never vulnerable to those who look after the fields. At a hundred yards they have seen me approach, and they fly with their long and lazily moving wings, making their cawing noise as they leave. The caw seems nasal and is grating, a sound that seems petty when given the cruelty of the woods and this land. I have heard their cry in the day, in winter, and have seen the birds flying from a branch of a tree, their bodies and their color seeming rank and startling in the snow. They do not like the great horned owl, and they will harass it, pecking at the bird on its perch during the day: these fights can be quite large, the crows coming long distances at the cry of distress. I have been told that some crows migrate, but the ones on this land do not, since there always seems to be something for them, even in the coldest of winters. They will not be defeated, and they delight in attacking the work one has done, and

this reduces them. It is true that when a crow is taken from the
nest at a young age and raised by a man the crow will be a good
pet, being able to perform many tricks. The birds are capable of
learning from us, and their survival is proof of their cleverness and
rapacity.

I do not like them because they are reminders. I have stood
outside in winter and seen the birds in flocks, turning against the
sky: it is then that I can sense their plumage, the dark color of it
that has the shine of the black silk of mourning. Their caw is
vibrant and hollow: the sound itself seems to be the emptiness a
man leaves behind.

Pop Mackinnon
The Fire. 1951.

I was sitting on my bed, my bandaged hand on a knee covered with dust from the garage floor, and thinking, Yes, yes, I am God's own favorite, a modern Job, when I smelled the smoke. At first I thought it was a cigar I'd left in the bedclothes or dropped on the floor, but the odor was not definite and did not seem to come from one place the way it does when it's a cigar. I walked around the room, but I didn't have the heart to look for long. I stopped and touched the thing in my pocket, the homemade knife. It did not make me feel stabbed, but as though someone had taken the knife and touched me on the neck with such a light hand as to make a minute, itchy cut. The smell of the smoke became so strong that I went into the hall and sniffed the air, thinking that something was wrong in the kitchen, or that a spark had jumped the fender in my wife's study, but the odor was weaker there than in my room. The hall was dark, and I saw the light coming from the crack under my wife's door. I rubbed my neck where it now actually did itch, and went back to my room. After a while I looked out the window and saw the delicate curl that was in the air above the barn. The curl was gray:

it appeared to be something cut by a plane from old wood.

I went down the hall and into my wife's room.

"What's that smell?" she said.

"Look out the window," I said. "That's Wade. I knew it. I knew it. Call the fire department."

My wife dialed the phone, pointed her finger at each number as though she were accusing it.

"There's no time," said my wife. "The woods, the buildings have never been drier."

I threw on my coat and started for the barn, still rubbing that spot on my neck. The smoke was coming from the corner of the middle of three stock barns that ran uphill. I opened the nearest door, which was on the end, and sniffed the air: there wasn't much smoke and it smelled only of manure and hay. I stepped back into the cold and looked for Wade, for any movement along the road or near the garage, but I saw nothing. And what if he sets another? I thought, What then? So I went back inside, up to the next section, and there I saw the flames.

The fire whistle began to blow as I found some empty feed bags and took them into the room where the flames were. The fire broke a window and then the smoke had an odd movement, as though it were being expelled in breaths rather than rising into the air according to natural law. I struck at the flames in the hay and manure, added dust to the smoke, and found that I couldn't control the empty feed bags. They were light and dry and they began to burn themselves. The wall started now, and the paint bubbled, turned brown, and peeled in the flames.

There was a faucet in that section of the barn and I went to it, turned it, but nothing came out: it must have been frozen. Get the stock, I thought, let them into the field, get the lambs into the field. They were in the next section, the next barn, which was connected by three steps to the one that was burning. I hadn't heard them milling around, pounding the wooden floor with their hooves, demanding and bleating, becoming hysterical in the smoke. This surprised me. When I passed the flames I saw they were brighter, yellower at the bottom. I went up the three steps to the next platform and found it was empty. I looked out the open door and saw the sheep standing in the snow-filled field, not thirty feet from the barn, their black faces set on me, and not with any kindness, either. I picked up a stick and threw it since I wanted the sheep further away from the building, and I noticed that as the stick flew away from me it made a high, trailing arc, marked in smoke.

In the middle barn the flames were now moving from floor to ceiling and touching the wall on their way: they curled and had the shape I have seen in the center of huge, breaking waves. The funnel was yellow and bright and gave way to smoke only in the very center. The heat was surprising and I felt the back of my hands blister as I heard the unceasing siren of the town's volunteer fire department. The flames made a noise, too: it was like driving a car fast with the window down.

I felt the itch on my neck and thought of the girl as she stood above me in the garage, just handing me the knife and leaving me there. My neck itched. I picked up the burning feed bags and went to the faucet, pushed them against the pipe and felt the flames' light and then compelling pain. I had hoped the heat would thaw the pipe, but I couldn't stand it for long and dropped the bag. Behind me the heat became stronger, more pronounced, and I saw when I looked into the lower barn that the fire had moved into it, too, and was now burning in the storeroom there. The flames had that same wave-breaking quality and were red, yellow, and bearded with smoke. I stepped back, onto the threshold where I could feel the coolness of the snow, and heard the water as it began to run from the faucet. At first it came in gurgling spurts and then it turned to steam, so there was a large plume of it, like the white feather of a fan dancer, sticking into those turning, rising flames.

I threw some buckets from the storeroom into the snow, and jumped out myself, seeing, when I landed, that my hands were burned and that the handkerchief I had wrapped around my palm was on fire. I put it out by rubbing it in the snow.

My wife was standing about twenty-five feet away.

"Pop, Pop," she said, "come away from there."

I was in the middle of the buckets I had thrown and there were bits of smoke rising, with the same curled and delicate shape, from my clothes.

"Water," I said. "Can't do anything without it."

The whistle sounded, but I didn't see any of the town's volunteers and heard no sirens on the road. As I stood in the buckets the center section of the roof of the barn began to smoke and look unsteady, hot, almost fluid. In the sound of the flames and the creaking of the roof there was the hoarse venting of the pipe inside the barn, its raspy hissing.

"It's just the barn," I said. "That's all."

"Yes," said my wife, "come away."

I stepped back into the storeroom and pulled out a sledgehammer and an ax that were kept there. The handles were warm and I kept dropping them, but finally the ax and hammer hissed in the snow next to the buckets. I heard their watery sigh as I faced the barn and waited: I had not expected the heat, the gale force of it. I rubbed my face with snow. Soot and small bits had began to fall and they were plainly visible on the white contours of the fields and the orchard. The cold shock on my face helped and I was able to say, "We need help."

"Derek's cutting wood," said my wife.

"Where?" I said. "At what distance? Can we follow the tractor's marks in the snow? Where is he?"

"I don't know," said my wife as the roof of the barn lifted for a moment, the shingles breaking apart and turning into flying bits, embers that rose in graceful, floating designs. The roof, in the center anyway, fell in. It made a crunching that was mixed with the noise of the fire: together the sound was of wind and ungainly movement.

"We need help," I said.

My wife was plainly visible even though it was almost dark: she stood with her dark shawl on her shoulders, in the bright, moving light of the fire. I had not expected the speed, either. The heat made both of us squint, recoil.

"He'll help," said my wife.

"I swear I'll kill him if he doesn't," I said, to the fire more than my wife, as if I could take a pledge to the flames and the smoke more binding than to any human being, "especially if I have to beg him first."

"There isn't time to talk," said my wife. "It's dry. The wind . . ."

"Yes, yes," I said, pushing through the snow. I pulled at my legs as I went down to the garage, where I thought, rubbing that spot on my neck, What if she's not gone? What if I have to beg in front of her, too? Or beg her? She can carry a bucket as well as anyone else. I turned and saw those flames rising from the center of the barn: they went straight up and seemed released, almost festive, although the smoke was dark and folded into itself.

When I opened the large door the ski mask was there to greet me with its expression of broad-mouthed horror. I kicked it out of the way when I saw the marks I had made as I kneeled in the dust before her, wanting her and needing to insult her into leaving. But before she went into the snow, perhaps . . . in the Buick . . . in that silver light. I smelled the burned cloth of my bandage and my burned hair, not to mention that singed wool odor which was almost enough to make me sick, and then I opened the Buick's door and started the engine, pleased with the easy way it turned over and caught.

When I pulled away from the garage the tires spun and made a howling noise I did not like. The Buick turned almost completely around on the ice and then I managed to get it going over the bridge and toward the gravel pit. I kept the accelerator down except for the turns, where I had trouble: my hands were burned, and I didn't like to grab the wheel hard, although its coolness was soothing. On the road I felt the winter's liquor, its grit, the fuzziness that comes from sleepless nights. I wanted to stop and use more snow on my face. I heard the siren and felt it in my chest, while I strained against being trapped in the rank odor of my burned hands and clothes. I need his help, I thought, and I will have it. It is a matter of will. Nothing more. It does not matter to me how, but what: and he will come with me to face those flames, even if he is crazy, even if I have to drag him up there and show him his . . . effect, before throwing him in and being done with him. I will face the courts.

On the stone house road the Buick slithered in the snow, bumped from side to side, became pitched at odd angles to the turns: I went fast enough to make even the stone walls seem undulant, floating. The siren still called the volunteers who must have been drunk or lazy or indifferent, since they had not yet arrived to help save the farm: the farm, I thought, Yes, it could be that, not just the barns. The wood is dry. I have never seen it so. I pushed the accelerator down.

I saw Chip's Buick, the red one, coming toward me, uphill from the stone house and at some considerable rate. There wasn't enough room for two cars to pass. On the right side of the road there was a stand of young spruce. I preferred it to the left side, where there were oaks, the smallest of which was the size of a barrel. None of the pine was bigger than two inches, and I pulled into them, seeing that oddly animate greenery quacking before the windshield. The trees broke off as I passed over them. I sat there and waited, knowing or thinking anyway that there were three possibilities. Chip was either running away, or running after that woman, or he was coming to help.

I rolled down the window. He was coming toward me and when he passed he'd be directly opposite, close enough to touch. I put my burned hand out of the car and moved it up and down, meaning by this gesture, Go slow, go slow. I want to talk. I knew the fire was spreading, and I thought of it as that car with the cream top began to go faster. The windshield of it was misty and white, except for one spot in front of the driver.

"There was one other possibility," I said as I saw Wade behind the wheel of that red Buick, his hand almost touching the top, his eyes set on the road before him. I heard the siren and smelled the smoke. Wade drove along.

"Thief!" I screamed.

Wade did not stop and did not look at me, but as he passed he held the registration against the window, and I was able to see that it had been signed in the appropriate place and in my son's hand. The Buick went by and I was left with the memory of Wade's face and that green official slip of paper. He was crying though and had not taken his revenge, had not gloated. He did not deny arson, though, not for a minute, and I thought, Fine, there'll be a moment when I take care of that tall fish.

The young pine scraped under the Buick as I got back onto the road. In the rearview I saw some of them spring up and wave back and forth, but most stayed down. It looked like a small twister had touched there: a disorder of limbs, white wood showing through the bark.

I stopped the car and went up to the house and saw through the window that Chip was sitting at the table with his head in his hands over a piece of paper. I opened the door and let him feel the cold air and waited for him to look at me, my face full and angry, hands burned, clothes in disarray and reeking of smoke.

He did not seem so young anymore, but there was something in his eyes I did not like. I would have expected otherwise. So I was surprised as I stood in the doorway, feeling that cold wind and the blisters on my hands. Chip seemed to study me for a moment.

"Hello, Pop," he said, "I'm glad to see you. It's time we came to terms. Here's whiskey."

I stared at him. We both heard the siren. Chip extended a water glass that was filled with reddish liquor.

"I need help," I said.

"Close the door. Come in," said Chip. "Here."

I drank it off.

"Is she gone?" I said.

"Yes," said Chip, as he folded that piece of paper and put it into his pocket.

I hadn't switched off the ignition of the car and we heard it idling, waiting for us.

"What you know is of no consequence," I said. "I need help."

Chip continued studying my face.

"Don't you hear that siren?" I said. "Have you lost your hearing? I need help. We've got to call the police, too. It was Wade."

"No," said Chip, standing now and coming closer.

I felt that hard, homemade knife in my pocket: its blade was pointed like some Arabian thing.

"Explain yourself," I said. "Wade set the fire and one barn is almost gone. Do I have to lose more? What do you want me to do?"

We faced one another and I still held that knife in my pocket and felt myself winding, slowly coiling in the horror of that whistle. Chip must have taken a deer in the fall: I smelled the sweetish odor of venison. The stone walls seemed fragile to me, shimmering.

"All right," I said. "What terms?"

"Wade always wanted a limousine service in New York," said Chip.

"And?" I said.

"Ten thousand should do it," said Chip.

"You're worse than before," I said, standing back, seeing the walls brighten, "worse than when that girl was here. Do you mean to tell me I've got to pay the man who set fire to my barns?"

The door was still open and Chip put on his coat so he could stand outside and sniff the air. The siren wouldn't stop and we saw over the tops of the trees the sparks and glow, the throbbing color of it, the movement of the smoke. The wind was stronger.

"And more than that," said Chip. "If we don't get up there and start wetting the roofs."

I thought of my wife in the snow, standing before the barns, her shawl over her shoulders, looking as though she was dressed in smoke.

"All right," I said. "Let's go. Come on. Come on."

But he stood there and looked at me. My hands seemed to have a life of their own, since the pain came now in a wave. I tried to lift my hands out of it, brought them from my pockets, showed that heavy, stiff-pointed knife.

"How are you going to find Wade?" said Chip.

"Goddamn lawyer," I screamed now, "I know you. It's entanglements and snares you're looking for."

"How?" said Chip.

"All right," I said. "I will call the police and give them your license number. When they catch him, on suspicion of arson, I will inform them I was mistaken, and then I will give the poor fish a check. Right then."

"And who takes responsibility?" said Chip, picking up a pair of heavy, leather gloves.

"I will, I will," I said. "Since I will have to call the police. I'd like to put it off on. . . ." I said.

"No," said Chip, "not on the girl."

"All right," I said. "I'll tell them it was a cigar, and a damned good one at that."

"I'll drive," said Chip. "How bad is the fire?"

"Everything's dry," I said. "Because of the cold. Can't carry water."

We went out and Chip turned the Buick around, working the wheel with the palm of his hand, and then let the car spring forward. We gained speed as we went along that gray ice- and snow-covered road toward the turbulence above the trees: it was red and pulsing, turning inward, hiding its center, which judging by the color, must have been inhuman and hellish. The trees were defined against it, each needle of the pines looking like a black pin on a red plate.

"She took forty dollars from me," I said.

He didn't flinch at the mention of her. I held the knife in my pocket, fingered the point as Chip drove through the snow which reflected the light: the floor of the woods had that cooked-lobster color. I touched the point. There was another matter that needed attention.

We came around the last turn and as Chip slowed down to cross the bridge over the pond we saw that the fire had spread. All of the middle barn had gone and it was burning so brightly I saw Chip as though by a red signal lantern, his eyes widening in awe as he faced the flames.

"Isn't there something we haven't discussed?" I said.

I gripped the knife. Chip stepped outside. The smoke was not illuminated as high as it went, so there was a fuzzy, cloudy glow over the barn. We went closer and both of us felt the heat. I noticed that the snow had melted near the barns, and that the water was running from them. The elm in front of the house was between us and the flames, and we saw each branch, twig, and bud.

"Let's attend to the fire," said Chip. "Let's see what we can do. I don't like that wind."

He stopped, though, and turned his face toward me.

"Call about Wade," he said. "Now."

I used the telephone in my study, and then we went to the barns.

My wife was standing in the snow, in her shawl, and she was not startled to see Chip, although she did look relieved. She put out her hand to touch him as we passed. The roofs of the two barns on either side of the one that had already gone looked unsteady. They were burning high up, in the rafters, and I didn't want to go in and neither did Chip. There was one other faucet inside and it had started to gurgle and hiss, too. We picked up the buckets and sledgehammer and went down to the pond. My wife came after us.

The ice was thick. Chip swung the hammer circus-style, in one continuing arc, smashing the ice, splintering it: the bits flew into the air like shattering crystal from thrown glasses. I saw him in profile, his jacket off now, swinging the twelve-pound hammer as often and as hard as he could. He grunted when it hit. The ice slivers splattered over my face and hands and felt good. The pond was covered with a foot and it took time for Chip to break through, but then he cleared a hole and started to dip the buckets and I started carrying them to the first barn. The hole in the ice looked like it was filled with the juice of crushed raspberries. I threw a bucketful and went back for another, my hands hurting. The water had turned to steam and drifted away.

"Let it go, let it go," said Chip. "The wind."

He stood at the edge of the pond, his eyes filled with bright light, his clothes looking as though he were dressed in red. Ice was forming on the sleeve of his shirt. Sparks rose from the sheep barns with an insectlike snap and floated toward the garage.

Chip went in through the sliding doors on the side of the garage away from the fire. He ran now and didn't say anything to me. Derek stood next to me, his one eye wide and filled with that same slick and hateful color, his hat (with the knitted visor) screwed onto his head.

"Som'bitch," said Derek. "Big flames."

Chip brought out an extension ladder we use to prune the apple trees and put it against the side of the garage. Derek was there to help him. My wife stood next to the pond, her shawl becoming stiff with ice as she filled up the buckets, not knowing, I didn't think, where they were going to be used (since I wasn't sure myself anymore), but insisting anyway that one filled buckets in a fire. I helped her.

Chip went up the ladder, and I saw him there, standing on the pitch of the roof, dark against the reddish glow, rigid, staring at the flames. Derek came to us and picked up two buckets, carried them back to the garage and tied an end of a rope Chip held to each of the handles. Chip pulled up one bucket and then another and splashed water onto the roof. They went up and down like counterweights. Derek kept them filled. My wife and I worked at the pond and the ice formed on our clothes. After a little I moved closer to what was left of the barns to keep my clothes from freezing. My wife came with me.

The fire engines arrived. Chip threw another bucketful on the roof, the water spreading out in a long, clear sail, edged with beads. The pumper stopped at the pond and the volunteers came off its back, one or two of them not steady by any means.

"We made it in record time, Mackinnon," said PeeWee Harris, as he stepped out of the cab of the engine. "Roads are bad."

The volunteers put the hose of the pumper into the pond and they went to work on the barns. Derek, my wife, Charlotte, and I kept along with the buckets, washing down the sides of the garage, without much effect. The pumper made a throbbing old sound, and I was surprised at the pressure: long spouts of water, having the quality of red blown glass, settled onto the burning barns. The garage seemed all right. Chip stood there, pulling up the buckets, still washing down the roof, but after a while, when the volunteers were working on the barns, he said, holding out his arm, which was covered now with beads of ice, or shouted (since his voice even then had that long quality of echoing down a corridor in a nightmare), "Look. The wind. The house."

The roof on the side away from us was plainly burning, and not with any chance of being put out easily. The fire was above my bedroom and my wife's study.

"Oh, Pop, Oh, Pop," said my wife as she squeezed my burned hands.

The volunteers pulled away from the barns and ran to the house and began spraying water. It went quite fast, or the first part, the roof and siding, did. Afterward the house resembled a large trunk with the top gone. The ashy contents floated away, drifted above us, or became a shower of black grit. There was the smell of burning paint and paper, wool, oak, mattresses. My wife stood in her thawed, wet shawl and stared at her study, which had flames rising out of it.

The firemen with the hose were intent on the house. My wife and I went down to the pond with the others and formed a line to pass buckets. Chip stood at the hole in the ice and I went to the end, which was at the porch. I opened the front door, and as the flames came along the staircase and into the dining room and out of my study, I splashed water on them. The pumper had been working for a while and the pond had been covered with a foot of ice that froze in a dry season, so there was only a little water now: I noticed, after the first twenty buckets, that there was something in them, and I stood and watched as the brook trout twisted and jumped in the air and then in the flames: they tried to swim while they were cooking. I looked into a bucket and saw them staring at me, trying to breathe, their snouts at the surface, their gill fins working. There was in those slightly protuberant eyes an expression of loss accepted, cruelty withstood, and the insistence that they would continue, even in the flames. So I stood there, feeling the heat on my already burned face and hands, holding the bucket, hearing the men behind me, each one of whom held a bucket filled with fish. I remembered the look of the brookies as they twisted in the flames, as their skin pulled away, as the flesh cooked and then burned. There was a moment when the orange spots on their sides were exactly the same color as the flames that were killing them.

"What's wrong, Mackinnon?" said PeeWee. "Throw the water!"

I turned around and said, "Stop. Now."

There must have been fifteen men behind me, all carrying buckets, and all of them looked into the containers they held, at the water lighted by the flames. We went back and poured the fish through the hole in the ice. It looked like there would be enough water for the trout, at least until the pond filled again.

By this time the garage had started as well and perhaps because the timbers there were the most dry, or because there was so much space inside, the flames were the brightest, the hottest, and the most tall: they formed gigantic, triangular pennants of red and yellow that were undulant in the breeze. At the end, after the roof had gone I saw that same circular pattern as in the beginning, the flames turning over on themselves, like the pictures I had seen of waves in the Pacific.

After a while the firemen went home. My wife, Chip, Derek, and Charlotte watched until the end, when the foundation of the house looked like the tip of a cigar glowing beneath an ash. I heard the sound of champagne bottles exploding, and I thought I smelled one of the hams baking.

The volunteers had left each of us a good blanket and we waited until dawn. After the light came, my wife, Charlotte, and Derek got into the Buick to keep warm. Chip and I stood before the pit of the house and stared at the few burned and segmented timbers that were left. In the breeze the ashes became agitated and flew around us like flies. A piece of paper drifted by and on it there was the photograph of a woman, nude except for a white garter belt and a small brassiere: the edges of the paper were burned and part of her face was obscured, but she seemed to be both inviting and laughing at the same time. It had been a page in one of those magazines which Wade usually carried in that overnight case of his. Chip watched the photograph drift by, too, and then went back to staring at nothing, at the absence of the house and barns. The wet ashes began to freeze.

I put my hand under the blanket and on the knife in my pocket. Chip's face was burned, but on him it looked good, at least for now. He seemed more tanned than anything else. I fingered the knife.

"I want to speak to you. Now. While we have the privacy," I said.

"I can hear," said Chip. "There's no need to stand so close."

"Wasn't there some other matter?" I said. "Something we neglected to take up since we were so occupied with other things?"

I gestured from under the blanket to the dark pits where the house and outbuildings had been. They looked inhuman and filthy, and the air was filled with the stench of the recently burned. The pits looked like the openings of dark mines.

"Yes," said Chip. "There was something else. We better settle that, too."

"Well?" I said.

We stood close together, each with a blanket over his head, and spoke, although we kept our eyes on those blackened pits. The blankets made us look like two monks, one tall, one short. Afterward, I said, "That's fine. I guess you better keep this. As a token of my good will."

I handed over the mean, homemade knife and Chip put it in his pocket. Then we walked to the Buick. My wife was in the backseat and Derek and Charlotte were in front. Chip got behind the wheel. Everyone's shoulders were covered by a green army blanket, and we sat there while the engine warmed up.

"Where are we going?" said my wife.

"Home," said Chip.

We drove along the Delaware, through those turns above it, and over a landscape that was covered with snow and ice, but we couldn't get away from that everlasting stink of burned wood. Chip drove carefully, but no one could stand the heater, so we went along in the cold. I wanted to stop for a drink, but the roadhouses weren't open, and I had the others to consider. We huddled under the blankets as we went through the marshlands.

"I want everyone to know," I said, sighing and picking up my wife's hand, "that Chip is going to get married. Just like he said he would."

Chip stared at the road and gripped the wheel. Only Derek spoke and he said, "I dunno. I dunno."

Mrs. Mackinnon's Book of Animals, Reptiles, Plants, Trees, Birds, Bugs, and Flowers.

I have seen the monsters, birds with no wings, the fox with no eyes, white bats, snakes that look like dowsing rods, coons dragging an extra hand, the albino deer. These creatures are shunned by their kind, pecked at and sometimes killed outright. There are rooted, immovable monsters, too, trees in spiny, chaotic growth, the witches'-brooms, flowers which cannot be penetrated, branches twisted into a thick spiral. I have seen an albino buck moving across the hard, fall landscape, shunned by the does: he will run separately and will not mate. The albino is not evil, but one creature of a color that is capable of reflecting our sins, our secret perversions and tortured natures: it is not from him that we shrink, but from ourselves. The bound legs, the lack of ears, the horrifying color, the feature only half-emerged from its own flesh and other such deformities touch me and I know why. All monstrosities are a perversion of birth and it is for this that I am sickened. When I carried my sons I felt possessed, and sometimes I did not know what it was I nourished. The monsters make me aware again of the nightmares I had at pregnancy, their atmosphere of panic. When I see the witches'-broom, or a blind bear, a seal limb on a deer, the paw bound into a stump, I am reminded of the most piercing privacy: the knowledge that I would love my monster just the same. Then I am frightened, because I am left asking, Where does such love come from? It makes me feel like a prisoner, although, through the terror, I have some awful peace. One year the potatoes had a leaf of a strange color, and then I noticed the fruit, the white bulbs, began to grow above the ground and looked small and had in them the suggestion of horror. I sat in the garden and stared, and my husband came to me and said, Is something wrong? and I said, Yes, just look, and then I bit my tongue to keep from crying.

Carolyn Cooke
Washington. Spring. 1951.

I returned from Florence to find something that amused and hurt me: I was cut from lists, and even my close friends avoided me. One day my younger brother, whose face is pale and ill-looking, drank too much and took delight in saying, "He's down there, in that stone place of his with some . . . slut." I laughed at him, and went upstairs, and read, and waited. No one called. I went in the afternoons for a walk in the snow, stopped at a liquor store and bought some (of Pop's) good bourbon, went to a flower shop, then came home, and put the flowers into a vase in my room, and sipped a drink: things brightened for a few hours, until it got dark. I would not have imagined anyone like me in a scandal. Sometimes I put my head back and laughed until the tears came. I read history and rank, obscene pornography. There were times when I envied him, since he had taken himself outside regularly conducted life, and I saw the hand of some nameless and faceless woman, moving along the muscles of his stomach. I was proud, and these visions gave me exquisite pleasure. Many times I was angry.

In the late winter my father came into my bedroom and said, "He's here."

"Who?" I said.

"Have you been drinking?" he said.

"Of course not," I said. "Who's here?"

"Mackinnon," he said. "I was going to turn him away, but then . . . after all."

"Yes," I said. "Of course." I started a laugh that went off into a giggle. "Considering everything."

"Yes," said my father. "Yes."

"I'll see him," I said. "I'll be down in a moment."

My father closed the door and went out, and I tried to brush my hair but found that my hand felt light and jumpy, and when I saw my face, I knew how much I had been . . . waiting. I washed my face and put on a little makeup, and went downstairs.

Chip was standing before a fireplace alone in a room that had a view of the street. He was wearing a gray suit and a green tie and his face and hands were peeling. He turned toward me, but he didn't smile. I did.

"How nice to see you," I said.

Chip nodded, looked at me, seemed to study my face. I was excited and didn't mind the glance.

"I didn't come to lie," said Chip.

"No," I said, "I don't think you did."

"I don't want to be gauche or vulgar," said Chip, "but if you want to know about anything, I'll tell you. With apologies in advance, but for the telling, not for what happened."

"You don't have to say anything," I said, "don't have to speak . . . I know all about it."

Chip looked upstairs, and I could see him searching for the whereabouts of my pale brother: even then I think Chip would have dragged that pale creature into the snow.

"Do you?" he said.

"Yes," I said. "You were in love."

Chip flinched, looked at me and said, "No. Different from that. Strong—"

"Let me call it what I like," I said. "You were in love. Don't worry. You will be again."

There was a fire set, birch logs, and they burned hot. Chip stepped away from them.

"Would you like a drink?" I said.

"No," said Chip. "Thank you."

"You could sit down," I said. "It might be more comfortable."

He sat down, and stared at me for a minute, and then said, "All right. I'll take that drink." So I went to the bar and got him one.

"Now," I said, "just for the pure . . . knowledge of it, how much has Pop offered? What cash do you have available? To . . . soothe?"

Chip began to laugh and reached for my hand. I didn't let him have it. Not then. I kept thinking of the waiting, of the longing, the time I stood up to being alone. I was excited.

"An awful lot," said Chip. "I didn't think he had that kind of money."

"Hmmm," I said, "but doesn't he know I'm damaged goods?"

"Those niceties escape Pop," said Chip, "and I don't care. Aside from what it costs you."

"I've been finding out who my friends are," I said. "You should try it sometime. It *is* a shock."

"All right," said Chip, "will you still . . . ?"

"Of course," I said, "yes. I may be in love with you myself. It's a good way to find out."

Chip blushed and rattled the ice in his glass, but we both laughed when I said, "Let's go tell my father. Get a good look at his face."

Then Chip started the long drive home.

Pop Mackinnon
The Wedding. 1951.

Carolyn came to look at the damage. I was living in my tent. I have never been able to get away long enough for a safari, but there may be a chance, and I thought this was a good time to get into training. I went to Abercrombie and let them sell me everything I needed. A good canvas tent with adjustable shades and netting, cots and feather beds, a dining room table that will seat ten: each of these things could be folded into a package not much larger than a case for binoculars. I bought a canvas ice box that was suitable for oysters, and it kept champagne at just the right temperature. I sat outside, under the large flap, with my wife, and we drank tea from a silver service and ate raspberries and cream and watched the fireflies blink through the netting. I bought a collapsible kayak in case things got boring. In the spring the Mongaup is high and swift. I had a telephone installed. And I also had a square metal cooker that would roast a wildebeest on a handful of grass.

I was sitting under the flap when Chip drove up in the automobile I had given him for passing the bar. It was a small green one, made in England. It had a wooden frame. Carolyn was along, and she looked out the window at the dreary ash heaps that had been the farm. She was wearing a white dress with small blue flowers, and when she approached the netting of the tent, her expression was just right: amazed by the destruction and impressed by it, as though we should be flattered by the black mess we'd made.

"Hello, Pop," she said.

"Hello," I said. "I'm thinking of going to Africa and this is a dry run. Leather and brass everywhere. Aluminum boxes for sandwiches. Champagne. Would you like a glass? I've got a kayak, you know."

"Yes," said Carolyn, "I'd like a glass of champagne."

I used the telephone to call Charlotte, who was living in a trailer behind the ash pit of the house. She came and served the wine, and I thought, At least we'll be able to indulge ourselves in ceremony, which is something no man should attempt to deny.

"I'm rebuilding. Everything the same. Barns, houses, trees. Same paint. Same mint growing in the flower beds. You won't know the difference." I sipped the cold champagne. "You two go for a walk. Enjoy yourselves. I've got a lying contractor on my hands and he wants a fortune for lumber. Well, I'm going to fix him. I'll cut some pine and have it taken to the mill myself."

The next evening Carolyn's father called. The ringing of the telephone never sounds right in a canvas room. He told me that he'd sold a piece of land he owned in Vermont, a farm that had been in the family for generations (he didn't say how many, though). I told him I was sorry to hear it, and what was he going to do with the, ah, proceeds, since I had a little something I did with my left hand, financing coffee growers. He thought that sounded fine. It should have been, since it was almost guaranteed and paid more than twenty percent. Carolyn's father said it was a crime he'd sold, and that if he'd known there was going to be a ceremony . . . why, he would have waited. He hadn't planned on my son's . . . troubles.

"We'll have the wedding here," I said. "Everything's new. Leave it to me."

"It's not quite . . ." he said.

"Don't you worry," I said, "meet me in New York next week and we'll make the arrangements for . . . the coffee."

"Yes, yes," said Carolyn's father. "All right."

So we came to terms. I put the instrument into its cradle and looked at my wife, who was staring at something through a magnifying glass.

"I'll need your help," I said.

"You'll have it on one condition," she said, still looking at whatever it was that had crawled into the tent, "and that is that you will say or do nothing to make anyone ashamed or embarrassed."

"Hmmm," I said, rubbing my chin.

"Well?" said my wife, now putting her dark eyes on me and tapping the glass against the palm of her hand.

"I know Carolyn's father is a man of great delicacy. He didn't come right out and ask for the goddamned money."

"That's what I mean," said my wife.

"You know I'm in a corner," I said.

"That's what it looks like to me," said my wife. She smiled. "Yes. In a corner."

"All right," I said. "Best behavior. Have it your way."

The contractor and the carpenters and I looked at the blueprints, which I'd spread over a sawhorse. I like to carry the roll around when I walk among the working men, in the smell of sweat, sawdust, and new nails, and when I see something wrong, I unroll the heavy, sharp-smelling paper and point out the mistake with my blunt finger.

"You haven't got time," said the contractor. He was a short man who wore a nail apron and had a tan the color of a cured ham skin. "Not for all of it."

"Don't talk to me of time," I said. "I've made promises."

"Look," said the contractor, pushing back his cap and rubbing his bald head, "we can frame everything in and put up siding on the front of each building. We'll put doors and windows in the siding and you can paint it. If you're standing in the right place you won't be able to see that it ain't but a quarter done."

"Fine," I said, "good."

I had the plumbing, gas, and electricity in, too. As soon as the frame was up for the rear of the house the large vans from New York arrived with the new ovens and ranges, ice boxes and freezers. As I sat in the tent, I saw Charlotte, between the studs of the open walls, putting away the groceries I'd ordered. She had on her face the same expression as when the ram was whacking her against the barbed wire.

The ram was gone. He had been seen, though, on the cliffs above the Delaware, his coat long and dirty white, his horns curled and broken. The animal had attacked cars.

The tent had a military atmosphere. We lived in it now and my wife spent hours on the phone to Carolyn's parents, arranging for invitations, caterers, and discussing style and matters of form. I decided on the menu. My wife went around with rubber bands on her forearms and a basketful of lists. Before I went to New York to buy new silver I dug around in the remains of the house looking for what was left of our first set. I found it, too. In the ashes, in which the snakes were resting because of the warmth, I picked up the odd, nuggetlike masses. In the evening the deer came out of the woods to stare at the tent and the half-finished house.

When the clapboard siding was up the painters made it white and the porch floor gray. There was a new screen around the porch and it was bright silver. A nursery in Pennsylvania sent flowers for the beds in front of the house. Some mint was planted, too. Large rolls of turf were put down in the orchard and around the house and barns.

I had also found, when I was digging through the ashes for the silver, the actions for my Mannlichers and the barrels for my L. C. Smith shotguns. They were rusted and looked like someone had sprinkled them with paprika. The actions worked, but the stocks were gone. I got in the new Buick, a '51, which was long, dark, and shiny, and drove down to New York and went to the Abercrombie gun room. The gunsmith was a clean, silver-haired Alsatian called Otto, and after pointing at one place and another with the tip of a mechanical pencil, he told me he'd fix things up: new stocks and bluing. A week later the mutton-leg cases arrived, and I took them into the house and with a piece of wood and a hammer and some nails I found, made a cleat for them where my study would be. The rifles and shotguns looked as good as new, and they'd be in their cases so the rain wouldn't bother them. I bought some ammunition and made a shelf for it with a scrap of wood.

The menu was set, too. Champagne, of course, and oysters, smoked trout, pheasant, racks of venison, beef, and vegetables (carrots, onions, peas that shone in butter). The bread was driven from New York, and the rolls and long loaves left a fragrance in the house, in the frame that still smelled of fresh wood. Charlotte worked in the kitchen and the heat made her glad for the open walls. I watched her in the evening before the stove, her large arms stirring pots, her hair in a white, lacy cap she had obtained from some restaurant.

The venison was a problem. I took Chip aside (when he came to visit) and said, "I am serious. We need meat. I want you to bring it home, and I don't care about certain niceties such as sex or anything. Bring home meat." It's easy to hunt deer in the springtime, since they browse through the fields every evening. My son was cooperative. At the end of the first weekend (one week before the wedding) six deer were hanging from a scorched tree behind the house. After they'd hung I had the butcher cut them into twelve crown roasts. Chip put the Mannlicher back into the case in the room that would become my study again.

My wife and I were up early on the day of the wedding.

The caterer arrived with his assistants, young and attractive and athletic men and women. They had dark uniforms. Charlotte was becoming hysterical, and I soothed her when I found her giggling over a saucepan. Derek, I noticed, was wearing a blue jacket which hung over his hands, and he was, for the day, wearing an artificial eye. My wife and I dressed in the tent. I always enjoyed tails, since they make me stand straight up, which is an advantage for a man of my stature. The linen had a fresh, soapy odor and it was smooth against my neck. My wife spent time at the mirror (which folded up like a chess set), and put on a blue dress, which was simple and quite flattering. It made her skin seem smooth and young and it gave an odd, appealing depth to her eyes. When she was ready she stood before me and said, "Pop, what do you think?" and I said that I thought she was lovely.

We waited for the guests to arrive: they came from New York, Connecticut, some from Vermont or Maine, others from Washington, Guatemala, and Europe. Before the first of the cars came up the road, however, the tent from Abercrombie was taken down. I had hired some men for the job, and they stood with the instructions in their hands and before the open cases of leather and brass. In a little while everything was folded, rolled, and put away, kayak included. The caterer put up, at angles to the house which made it impossible to see anything but those newly painted facades, a large tent with open sides. The wedding feast was to be there and the tables had been arranged.

There were rows of chairs before an altar.

Carolyn's mother and father and Carolyn had driven from New York. My wife took them in hand, behind the facade, where they had some privacy. Chip was on the other side of the house, in my half-formed study, having a drink with his best man. The cars stretched a half mile or more, all the way to the gravel pit. There must have been two hundred people, and they walked along the road, dressed in colors that were both festive and soothing. In the last few weeks, in the tent, I had begun to look through an edition of Paris *Vogue*. And I now saw, on that dusty road, the same silk dresses I had lingered over in the pages of the fashion magazine. The men wore dark, well-tailored suits, and their shirt collars were as white as sails. There was a brisk loveliness as the guests came toward the arrangement of chairs for the ceremony. The weather was fine, a high, blue sky with those reassuring puffs.

Two men had brought their organ from the county seat: it took one to pump and one to play. They began. I stood at the rear of the chairs and helped the ushers. The guests formed a loose procession as they came up the road and across the orchard, and at the end of it there was a man, isolated from the rest, moving slowly, and wearing a coat that was as green as lime sherbert.

He approached with a steady, sure gait, and I noticed, as he came closer, that he was wearing muddy boots and an orange tie. I smiled at the last of the guests as they took their seats, but I watched that coat and tie. The man had been to a barber recently and the sides of his head were white, his hair perfectly parted and made slick with pomade. He was carrying a cap, too, and it was the cap that made me recognize him at that distance, since there was already something familiar in the gait, although the clothes had been confusing.

"Hello, Mackinnon," said Moore, his whitish eyes set on mine and the scars on his neck looking milky in the sunlight. "I've come for my knife."

"Yes," I said, "yes. Sit down. We'll speak of it later."

There were two seats left in the last row. I pointed to one of them.

"You're having a wedding," said Moore. "I would not intrude."

"Sit down," I said. "Here." I pulled a chair a little closer. "You don't need an invitation."

"Not after this last winter, I suppose," said Moore, "and the deer I've taken from this land. We have no need of writing, do we, Mackinnon?"

"Sit down," I said. "I'll see about the knife."

"Will there be whiskey?" said Moore.

"Yes," I said.

Moore sat down, folded his hands, and ignored the sound of the organ and the minister, who now stood in his embroidered robes, facing the congregation, his back to the altar. He was a bald man with gold-rimmed spectacles. Moore's expression was stoic, hard: he did not stare or gawk at any of the guests. He had not moved when it was time for me to take my seat, and when I looked over my shoulder he raised his eyes to mine and nodded and gave what must have been approval, or at least understanding of ceremony.

When Chip was standing before the minister, and as I was moving toward my wife, I saw a taxi stop in the orchard. Sherry, Wade's sister, came toward us, her hair now gray blond near her head and crimson above. She was wearing a long black dress and high heeled shoes. There were spots of mold on the dress and the heels of her shoes sank into the grass. She was drunk.

"Where's Wade?" she said.

"In the city," I said. "Won't you sit down?"

I put her next to Moore, and when Sherry said in a loud, grating voice, "Well, I just love a wedding . . ." he put his hand on hers. She became quiet and stared at the ground.

I sat next to my wife at the front of the assembly. The minister's high, bald head shone in the sun, and he waited in those colorful and dark robes and in his severe gold spectacles. Chip and his best man stood on the minister's left hand. The organ played and Carolyn and her father came down the aisle between the rows of guests, who turned toward her. She wore a white, simple dress and no veil. Her father walked slowly, one step coming down in front of another. The minister spoke, and as he did so, I looked at the flower beds and newly painted house, barns, and garage, and felt the presence of the wedding guests behind me, and as I listened to the drone of words, I saw, at the top of the hill behind the house, that ram.

He stood with his side to us. His face was black and hard to see because of the long, gray, and ragged fleece: he had not been shorn since his escape and it made him look like a goat from the western mountains. His horns were long and swept back, although I don't think they were more than twenty inches from base to tip. They were grayish black and hard and one was a little broken, ragged. His head was lowered and he took the wind. After a few minutes he started drifting downhill, toward us, his shaggy, large coat bouncing with each step. He stopped when he was about fifty yards away from the assembly and stared at those men in white collars and dark suits, the women in bright dresses, the arrangement of chairs. The ram took the wind again, dropped his head, shivered, or twitched his fleece.

"Get on with it," I said to the minister.

My wife squeezed her hands, glanced over the bald shine, the harsh silvery light there, at the animal. The minister looked at both of us, and I stared back and made a hurrying motion with my hand. Charlotte was a few rows back, and I heard her say, "There he is. That's him."

The minister went on with his benediction, his words of love and grace and God. The ram was still, although his head twitched as he took the wind. Those people behind me, the guests in silk and wool, the polite men and women from Boston, Vermont, and Massachusetts, Chip's friends from Yale and law school, my associates and clients all maintained, for a moment, a gentle decorum. I stared at the shaggy monster's black face, the dark eyes which moved from one of us to another. Its gray fleece was so long in places as to form sloppily braided ropes, each ending in a mess of burrs and thorns.

Chip took Carolyn's hand, faced the minister, and turned slightly. He saw the ram. The minister went on with the ceremony, with the damned words. I motioned again, moved my hand around in a circle, but it did no good. My wife squeezed her hands. The faces before the minister must have suggested to him that there was an odd, or unknown, or dangerous thing just beyond his shoulder. The man was used to walls, to having something solid at his back, and did not look. The guests were silent. I hissed. The minister looked into Carolyn's eyes and then Chip's and hesitated before saying, "By the authority invested in me I—" and then broke off, startled by the moan that came from the congregation. The ram had begun his charge.

He came downhill, his strides long and reaching, but he turned from the guests and went to the tent, the champagne on ice, the tables set and waiting. Inside the light was pleasant, soft, and a little pink. One of the caterer's assistants, a young man in a black jacket and a small black bow tie, was arranging wine glasses when the ram struck him. He grunted and went down and the ram continued striking a large metal box which held ice and champagne. Two of the bottles broke and fizzed and the ram stopped before them and the bright, slick pile of ice.

"I never got rid of the pains in my legs . . . never . . . never," said Charlotte. Derek was sitting next to her, dressed in the blue coat which hung down to his knuckles, and he stood and tried to get to the outside, already looking for a piece of scrap, a bit of two-by-four to make a club. I don't know whether it was his movement, or Charlotte's voice, but the ram looked up from the champagne and ice, took the wind, and charged.

The ram hit Derek, and then Charlotte, and the guests heard her long cry of hurt and disbelief. The members of the congregation stood and looked over one another's shoulders as the ram continued, knocking the folding chairs out of the way. I saw the nylon stockings and white garter belt of a young woman who jumped from her row to the next. The animal went straight ahead, butting and hitting whenever he saw pin-striped trousers or long legs in stockings, or the thin legs of children, the flowered dresses of old women. The ram was not satisfied.

"There is no need for alarm," said the minister. The ram turned, slipped, and watched as the guests spread before him, knocking over chairs, leaving handbags and sweaters behind. There was an odor from the animal, part mildew, part musk, part rut. Some of the guests took chairs with them if only to have something between themselves and the ram. I heard Charlotte say, "Never stopped having that pain . . . mornings and . . . cold weather." The guests stood farther back and waited.

"There is no need—" said the minister.

Chip and Carolyn held hands and looked over their shoulders at the ram, who now stepped into the center of disorder and began to dwell on the man in the dark gray robes with the cheerful embroidery. The minister said, out loud, although not to the wedding guests or to anyone in particular, "We must not frighten the animal . . . that is all." Chip was wearing a high, white collar, a black and gray tie, a tailcoat, and striped trousers, and he let his outrage and disbelief show: there was a white, snowy color around his lips and nostrils. The minister stepped forward, and Chip said, after gently putting his hand on the minister's arm, "With your permission . . . don't. . . ." The minister continued. Carolyn stayed at the altar.

The ram swayed his head from side to side, as though he had trouble seeing, and, after springing forward, and dropping his nose, he drove into the gently approaching and well-meaning and softly speaking man. The minister was hit on the thighs, and I saw him sink into the chairs and the milling people as though into water. He grunted and I saw his head being struck by one of the ram's hooves.

"Mackinnon, Mackinnon," said Carolyn's father. "Can you hear me? There must be a reasonable way . . . we did not expect. . . ."

But then we were both moving fast, away from the ground between the ram and his object, which was not us, but the tent and those carefully laid tables, the venison, smoked trout, pheasant, bottles of wine, not to mention those men in black tie who held their glossy instruments while they waited to play Mozart. Behind us the guests shouted and moved into the orchard or onto the drive. I saw a man wading in the pond. The ram knocked down the tables: the silver streamed into the air like bits of ice blowing off the hood of a car. The waiters and caterers tried to strike with a chair, but this did no good, since the ram singled out anyone who molested him and charged, once, and then again, until there was a shriek, a grunt, and a voice that said, "Oh, please, please . . ."

The minister stood in the wreckage of chairs, one hand touching the blood that ran from the smooth crown of his head and from a deep cut above his eye. He tried to walk, put his fingers before him, and had the aspect of a blind man who has lost his cane. Carolyn tried to help him, but he shook her off, and made his way to the side of the barn where there was a little shade. Carolyn sat next to him.

The chief caterer stood in the mess of tablecloths, silver, broken plates, vases, and the splashes of wet, cut flowers and shouted at the ram. The man held a bottle of Dom Pérignon and smiled. The ram charged directly for him, driving hard, not caring when the bottle crashed over his head: the animal drove the caterer into one of the poles that held up the tent and a large section of it began to fall in an airy, rounded manner. It looked like a pink parachute.

Some of the men found themselves in the wreckage before the altar, and they spread into a straight line and approached, each carrying a chair above his head. There was movement under the tent, a pink hump that swayed from side to side. The men started swinging the chairs, striking hard, following through, and raising the pieces of wood again. The canvas made an odd noise, like a drum with a hole in it. There were shrieks, too, and the caterer rolled out of the tent, bleeding and holding his hand above his head. His nose was broken. The ram escaped, walked a few yards, and stared at us over his shoulder.

"Mackinnon," said Moore, "if you will give me that rifle with the funny triggers. If you will tell me where it is. . . ."

The members of the wedding were scattered over the orchard and down by the pond. One or two had climbed a tree, and a couple stood in the framework of the house. There were twenty-five or so men and women, some hurt, near the tent and the arrangement of chairs, and all of them were quiet, watching, but not relieved. The ram shook his head from side to side, took the wind, seemed intrigued by the people who had not been able to get away.

Chip held my Mannlicher as he stood on the porch of the house. His hair was combed back, away from his high forehead, and his clothes were neat, his flower still in his buttonhole, his jacket immaculate, his tie perfectly knotted, the shirt collar stiff with the triangular tips bent down. He held a few cartridges, too, and I saw his white lips and nostrils, his shaking hands, as he opened the bolt and pushed the brass hulls into the magazine. Chip left the safety off.

"Yes, yes," said Moore. "That's the one I meant."

We moved toward the new barns and pens, the garage, trying to get out of the line of fire. We stepped in the mint beds that the gardener had planted and I smelled the odor of it rising on the moist, early summer air. In the orchard the guests started running to the left and right and straight into the woods, but they were able to clear a large triangle which had as one of its points the porch of the house, where Chip stood with the rifle and waited.

The minister groaned and touched his face, but he did not faint. He bled freely and he was now leaning against the new white siding of the barn, although he let his head fall first one way and then another. Carolyn gave him a napkin, but it was quickly dark and wet. The ram was opposite him, nosing a piece of the tent, licking a bit of ice.

It was a difficult shot, since there were guests and caterers on the hill beyond the animal. A man threw a champagne bottle, but the ram only glanced at it and went back to licking the ice.

"Where is my knife, Mackinnon?" said Moore. "There are times when—"

The ram sampled the air and charged the side of the barn where the minister sat. Moore was next to me and he turned toward Chip. The minister seemed to be lucid for a moment as he saw that black-faced and shaggy and ugly animal bearing down on him. He groaned, and tried to scramble to one side. Carolyn was next to him, but she stood her ground, preferring to be hit by the animal than making a spectacle of herself as she ran in a white dress across that recently charred earth. The ram struck the building and the minister's arm. Everyone heard the thump.

The animal was stunned and he turned and ran back to the tent, this time crossing Chip's line of fire where there were no guests beyond. It was still an awkward shot: people continued to move in the orchard and along the drive. Chip had the rifle shouldered, and as the ram came directly opposite him, we all heard and felt the noise. It echoed across the orchard, over the ponds, against the ridge of the land.

I heard the tight-drum *thump* as the bullet struck the ram, but he only went down for a moment, and then was up again and running, although awkwardly, his feet rising first high and to the right and then to the left. It looked like he was jumping from one side of a low fence to the other.

"He runs like he's heart shot," said Moore.

I saw the red stains on the ram's side, the dripping wetness from the fleece. The animal continued into the tent and pushed through the scattered silver, broken china, glasses and vases, stepped over the tablecloths and stopped: the stain spread. We all heard him cough.

The ram wanted cover and jumped or bounded, ran with that deathly gait, and climbed under the corner of the tent which had collapsed. The animal worked under the pink canvas, crawled there, and was quiet. The stain spread on that pink cloth, and we all saw it. The animal still moved, and it did not look to me to be just the trembling of the end.

"No," said Moore, "he is not gone."

From the orchard there were shouts of inquiry, but the guests still kept their distance. I saw no one climbing down from a tree or coming out of the woods. No one laughed, aside from a woman who had become hysterical. A child was weeping, too.

Chip saw the movement under the tent and walked down from the porch and across the lawn, his carriage upright and definite, his clothes still immaculate, carnation still fresh and in place, although I saw him breathing deeply and keeping his mouth set in that tight, straight line. The stain on the canvas became larger. Chip lifted the tent and looked underneath. The ram jumped again, emerged from the pink cloth, and then we heard another explosion: the ram took two more steps and fell against the side of the house, in the mint of the new flower beds. Chip unloaded the rifle.

The minister leaned against the new siding, just beyond the outer circle of the smashed chairs, altar, and discarded clothes. The guests began to leave the orchard and the woods, and all of them seemed to be able to walk, although some were crying, and one or two had broken bones. Chip and Carolyn walked toward the minister. They both looked fresh and unhurt, Chip carrying the Mannlicher and Carolyn holding the bridal bouquet. Beyond them, in the sunlight, there were the fresh pieces of wood from the broken chairs, the torn-up turf, the splashes of the animal's blood, the half-collapsed tent. The animal quaked as it lay on its side and there were long waves of trembly muscular contraction that passed from its shoulders to its hindquarters. The minister turned away from the animal and looked at his fingers, felt the tickle of blood from his head wound. Chip and Carolyn stood before him. He tried to stand, but could not get beyond his knees. He waved away an arm offered by one of the wedding guests. The flies had begun to buzz in the early afternoon heat. The minister stayed on his knees, looked at Chip and Carolyn, and with his bloody hand gesturing toward them, he said, "All right...married...married..."

They did not kiss. Chip gave me the rifle as he and Carolyn started toward that small green car which had been parked at the edge of the orchard. No one said a thing, and it was not until they were halfway through the overturned chairs that someone reached into a small lace bag, withdrew a handful of rice, and threw it. The photographer took one picture of Chip and Carolyn, and it would only show their backs.

I pushed a round into the Mannlicher and fired into the air: the noise slapped like thunder. Both Chip and Carolyn looked away from that small green car and the photographer got a decent picture. Carolyn was highly colored and beautiful. Chip looked at Moore and nodded.

"The knife," I said to Chip.

"What?" said Chip.

"Moore wants his knife," I said.

The photographer worked, and Moore approached us in his green coat and orange tie, the scars on his neck seeming indistinct, smooth as fog. Chip reached into the glove box of that small British car and found the knife. He pushed it into Moore's hand.

Carolyn threw her bouquet to a girl of fifteen.

"Thank you, Mackinnon," said Moore. "I am glad to have it since it is a reminder of the hunt and winter and other things. Will I see you in the fall?"

"Yes," said Chip.

Moore nodded and said, "Good. Now I will drink whiskey to your health and the health of your wife and children. And to Pop, if he will have it and if the ram didn't get those bottles, too."

The photographer stopped and guests threw rice and Chip and Carolyn got into the green British car and went across the bridge and up the road. They disappeared between the rows of shiny, parked cars.

"I'm sorry for your trouble, Mackinnon," said Moore, putting the knife into his pocket. "You, Derek. I need a hand."

Derek approached and then they went to the ram and dragged it into the woods behind the house. It was bleeding from its nose, and the fleece of its sides was covered with a pinkish mud. The guests watched as it was carried away, and they seemed surprised at how small it really was.

My wife stood next to me, and I noticed that Carolyn's mother and father were only a few feet away. In the corner of the tent there was a table which had not been harmed. It was set for four. The silver was bright, comforting, the china substantial, and the cut flowers were fragrant.

"I think we should sit down," I said.

My wife took my arm. Carolyn's mother was tall and blond and her hair was streaked with gray. She had blue eyes and sharp features, skin that was beginning to freckle with age. She had a wonderful, square-shouldered gait and I thought she was going to be ill. She held her husband's arm. We sat down and as we heard the guests shouting and a car or two starting to take someone to the hospital, the caterer brought a bottle of cold champagne and poured each of us a glass.

"Open a bar for those . . . people," I said.

"Yes, sir," said the caterer. "It's being done."

He told me that he was able to give us smoked trout, a pheasant, a crown roast. We drank more champagne. Some people came to offer congratulations.

"I had no idea," said Carolyn's mother, "that there would be . . . well . . . so much of it . . . so much blood."

Her giggle had a bright, hysterical edge.

"I'm sure," said my wife, "they'll have better luck in southern France."

That's where they were going for a honeymoon.

When we finished the trout and were being served the pheasant, Carolyn's father said, "You know, Mackinnon, if you should happen to have some other . . . well . . . ideas . . . you understand, such as the coffee plantations."

My wife sipped her champagne and stared over the pine grove where a hawk was drifting on a thermal.

"This is a polite dinner table," I said.

"Of course," said Carolyn's father.

"Yes," said her mother, over whose beautiful, squared shoulders I saw the wreckage of the chairs and the blood on the new white siding of the house. "Of course."

"Then we will not talk of money," I said.

We began to eat the pheasant.

"You and I will do that later," I said to Carolyn's father, "afterward, as it should be done, in private, with brandy and good cigars. Mine come from Cuba."

"Be glad to try one," said Carolyn's father.

Her mother smiled.

In the evening my wife and I sat in our tent, which had been put back up. We were in our canvas chairs, drinking champagne and stout and watching the blinking of the fireflies in the orchard.

"At least," said my wife, "no one was killed."

"That's right," I said, although I had begun to feel those hard, quarter-moon shaped pains in my chest. It took some years for them to come to anything. "Yes," I said, "that's something."

Mrs. Mackinnon's Book of Animals, Reptiles, Plants, Trees, Birds, Bugs, and Flowers.

I hate vultures because they only frighten humans. The birds are large, having as an adult a wingspan in excess of six feet. Their coloring is primarily black, although some birds will have a stripe of gray at the trailing edge of their wings. Some birds have whitish flesh on their heads and above their claws, although most have reddish or purple-and-walnut textured skin from their crowns to the middle of the neck. They are grand soarers, and I have seen them with their wings set in a dihedral, turning lazily on thermals. The birds are always watchful. They have no taste for fresh meat and will not touch anything recently killed. The turkey vultures are enamored of carrion and when they find a large piece, they will eat so much that it is difficult or impossible for them to fly. They have no enemies and no animal is alarmed by them, since the vulture does no killing. If an animal or another vulture should approach one while feeding, the bird will snort through its nose, or hiss, or perhaps make a sound like a grunt. These are the only noises they ever make. If you approach closer yet, or come near them when they perch, they will vomit, and by this will turn into a weapon the remains of something that was once grand. A vulture prefers the use of filth over his claws or beak. In the evening, after they have soared and fed, they will find a perch, landing one bird at a time. They prefer dead wood, a standing tree without the cover of leaves. After the birds land on the perch they strut back and forth and get comfortable on the same dead limb. Often they will go on adding one bird until the dead limb breaks and leaves a pile of birds, a heap of blackness. They have a tropical laziness and exist only to be the final thing. I hate them because they are the opposite of history. In the springtime, after mating, they will not make a nest, but instead will find a swamp, or a stump, or any piece of ground and lay their eggs. They do not migrate, and they will try to stay warm during winter in whatever way they can. I remember hearing their grunt and retch in February, when there was snow on the ground. It was night and I sat in the house hearing that noise. I put on my coat and boots and went outside and saw in the moonlight the turkey vultures as they huddled around the top of the chimney for warmth. I went back inside and to my husband and said, Pop, Pop, I want you to load a gun and get rid of the vultures outside, but he was sleeping deeply and did not stir.

The Stone House
The Greenhouse
1979–1981